Text book written according to revised syllabus of F. Y. B. Com.
prescribed by University of Pune from 2013-2014.
Also useful for other universities in Maharashtra.

I0611869

Financial Accounting

Prof. Vaishali Apte

Chartered Accountant

Prof. Suresh Bhirud

Ex-Head, Department of Commerce,
Mahatma Phule College, Pimpri.

Prof. Bhaskar Naphade

Ex-Head, Department of Accountancy,
Bharatratna Dr. Babasaheb Ambedkar College, Aundh.

Diamond Publication

Financial Accounting

Prof. Vaishali Apte, Prof. Suresh Bhirud, Prof. Bhaskar Naphade

First Edition : June 2013

ISBN 978-81-8483-529-8

© Diamond Publications

Cover Page :
Sham Bhalekar

Published by :
Diamond Publications
264/3 Shaniwar Peth, 302 Anugrah Apartment
Near Omkareshwar Temple, Pune - 411 030
☎ 020-24452387, 24466642

info@diamondbookspune.com
www.diamondbookspune.com

Sale Distributor :
Diamond Book Depot
661 Narayan Peth
Appa Balwant Chowk
Pune 411 030
Tel. - 24480677, 66020282

University of Pune
(2013 - 14)
F.Y. B.Com.
Compulsory Paper
Subject Name -: Financial Accounting.

Objectives -:
1. To impart the knowledge of various accounting concepts
2. To instill the knowledge about accounting procedures, methods and techniques.
3. To acquaint them with practical approach to accounts writing by using software package.

Term I

Unit No.	Topic
1.	**Piecemeal Distribution of Cash** Meaning and Introduction, Surplus Capital Method and Maximum Loss Method
2.	**Amalgamation of Partnership Firms:-** Meaning and Introduction, Objectives, Methods of accounting
3.	**Conversion of a partnership firm into a limited company** Meaning and introduction, objectives, effects, methods of calculation of purchase consideration (Net Asset and Net Payment method), accounting procedure in the books of the firm and balance sheet of new company
4.	**Computerized Accounting Environment** Meaning and Introduction, application of accounting software package, Voucher entry through software package.

Term II

Unit No.	Topic
5.	**Introduction and Relevance of Accounting Standards** Overview of Accounting Standards in India-Concept, Need, Scope and Importance. Study of AS- 1, AS- 2, AS- 4 and AS- 9

6.	**Royalty Accounts [excluding sub-lease]:** Royalty, Minimum Rent, Short Workings, Recoupment of Short Working, Lapse of Short Working. Journal Entries and Ledger Accounts in the Books of Landlord and Lessee.
7.	**Hire Purchase and Installment System:** **[Excluding H. P. Trading]** Basic Concepts and Distinction, Calculation of Interest and Cash Price, Journal Entries And Ledger Accounts in The Books of Purchaser and Seller.
8.	**Departmental Accounts** Meaning and Introduction, Methods and Techniques, Allocation of expenses, Inter Departmental Transfers, Provision for unrealized profits

Contents

Part I

Chapter - 1   Piecemeal Distribution of Cash   1

Chapter - 2   Amalgamation of Partnership Firms   50

Chapter - 3   Conversion of a partnership firm   120
               into a limited company

Chapter - 4   Computerised Accounting Environment   164

Part - II

Chapter - 5   Introduction and Relevance of   183
               Accounting Standards

Chapter - 6   Royalty Accounts   208
               [Excluding sub-lease]

Chapter - 7   Hire Purchase and Installment System: 263
               [Excluding H. P. Trading]

Chapter - 8   Departmental Accounts   344

Chapter 1

Piecemeal Distribution of Cash

1.1	Introduction
1.2	Settlement of Accounts
1.3	Methods of Piecemeal Distribution
1.3.1	Surplus Capital Method
1.3.2	Illustrations
1.4	Maximum Loss Method
1.4.1	Illustration
1.5	Exercises

1.1 Introduction :

We have earlier studied the admission, retirement of a partner and dissolution of partnership firm. When the partnership firm comes to end due to death, retirement or insolvency of the partners, the partnership firm is to be dissolved. The dissolution of partnership firm means closing the business of the firm. A firm ceases to exist after the dissolution of the partnership. The partnership firm cannot remain in existence after the firm gets dissolved. In case of dissolution of the partnership firm, it is assumed that all the assets are to be realised on the date of dissolution and all liabilities are also to be paid on the same date. But in actual practice, it is not possible to realise all assets and make payments of all the liabilities on the date of dissolution. The above assumption is unrealistic. The realisation of assets takes a long time to fetch better price. In order to get better price, the assets are to be sold, when they have heavy demand in the market. In short, the assets are sold gradually to get better prices for them and the cash available is immediately paid to the rightful claimant or claimants.

Meaning of Piecemeal Distribution :

According to Partnership Act 1932 cash made available by gradual realisation should be distributed among the rightful claimants. It should not be retained with the firm till all the assets are sold or realised. So **"The process of distribution of cash in accordance with availability is called piecemeal distribution."**

In short, in piecemeal distribution assets are sold or realised in pieces, then only they fetch better price and liabilities like creditors, bills payable, partners' loan and capital of partners are also paid in pieces. Therefore, this method of distribution is called as 'Piecemeal Distribution.'

1.2 Settlement of Accounts and Order of Payment :

At the time of dissolution of the firm, we prepare Realisation Account and partners' capital account and assume that all assets are realised on the date of dissolution and payment of liabilities are also made on the same date. But this is not true. At the time of payment of liabilities, the question arises, "To whom the payment is to be made and what should be the order of payment?" This problem is solved by the Partnership Act 1932. The Partnership Act 1932 (Section 48) lays down the rules and regulations regarding the priority of payments. The liabilities are paid off in the following preferential order with the available cash.

1) Realisation Expense
2) Preferential Creditors
3) Secured Creditors
4) Unsecured Creditors
5) Partner's Loan
6) Partner's Capital

(1) Realisation Expenses/Dissolution Expenses :

Realisation Expenses are paid or become payable out of the cash available. These expenses include legal expenses, commission or brokerage to selling agent, repairs to assets etc. Out of the available cash, realisation expenses are paid first. If, in the initial stage, actual realisation expenses are not known, the provision for realisation can be deducted from available cash. When the amount of actual expenses is known, they are paid off and if the expenses incurred are less than provision, the remaining cash is added in the respective instalment of realisation and used for payment of liabilities. If the provision falls short than actual expenses, the remaining amount is paid from asset realised on that date.

(2)(a) Preferential Creditors :

After the payment of realisation expenses, preferential creditors are to be paid. Preferential Creditors are these creditors, who have preference in respect of payment of their dues over other creditors. Government or local body dues income tax, sales tax etc. are the examples of preferential creditors.

(b) Contingent Liability :

Contingent Liability means the liability which may or may not arise. For example Bill discounted with the bank. If the acceptor dishonours the bill on due date, the party discounts the bill has to pay the amount of bill to the bank. Hence, it becomes the liability and it is called contingent liability.

If there is contingent liability the amount for such liability is set aside before paying cash to any other party. If such liability arises, the amount set aside will be paid to claimant and if it does not arises the amount set aside is used for other claimant.

(3) Secured Creditors :

If any creditor is secured by the particular asset of the firm, the creditor is called as secured creditor. The secured creditor has a right to sell the asset and recover his dues. After the recovery of his dues, if there is any surplus it can be used for other secured creditors. On the other hand, if there is any deficit, the balance left unpaid will be treated as unsecured creditor and will be paid with other unsecured creditors.

(4) Unsecured Creditors/Third Party Liability :

After making the above payments, the available cash is paid to unsecured creditors/third party claimants. These creditors are not given any security, hence they are called unsecured creditors. They include sundry creditors, bills payable, bank overdraft, loans from outsiders etc. (Loan taken from the wife of the partner is also treated as third party liability). If the cash is sufficient to settle the claim of above unsecured creditors, then there is no problem. But if the cash is insufficient to settle the claim, the available cash will be distributed between/among partners to their proportion of dues. For example, suppose the third party liabilities (unsecured creditors) are sundry creditors, Rs.15,000, bills payable Rs.10,000 and bank overdraft Rs.5,000 and cash available is Rs.9,000. Then Rs.9,000 will be distributed among the creditors in their loan ratio of 15,000, 10,000, 5,000 i.e.3:2:1. So the available cash (Rs.9,000) will be distributed among creditors in the ratio of 3:2:1. Thus, the creditors would receive Rs.4,500, bills payable Rs.3,000 and bank Rs.1,500.

(5) Partner's Loan :

After the payment to third party liabilities, partners' loan rank for the repayment. If loans are advanced by two or more partners and the available cash is sufficient, it will be distributed among the partners. But if the cash available is insufficient, the loan will be repaid among the partners in proportion of loan. For example, if available cash is 3000 and loans from partners are A-Rs.4000 B- Rs.3000 and C-Rs.2000. Then cash will be distributed among partners in the ratio of 4:3:2.

(6) Partner's Capital :

Partners rank last for refund of their capitals. Once all other liabilities are paid, the partners shall start getting the payment. Sometimes, partners may not get full amount of capital contributed by them. In such a case, they have to forgo some portion of the capital. It is called as realisation loss.

While repaying the capitals, whether profit sharing ratio or capital ratio is used at the time of dissolution, the final unpaid balances (i.e. Realisation loss) may not be in profit sharing ratio. So, piecemeal distribution of cash is made in such a way that (i) no partner receives over payment or is put to heavy loss and (ii) the final unpaid balances on capital are in profit sharing ratio. To achieve this, the following methods of distribution of cash are applied.

1.3   (1) Surplus Capital Method
         (2) Maximum Loss Method

1.3.1 Surplus Capital Method :

This method is also called as Excess Capital Method/ Proportionate Capital Method or Highest Relative Capital Method. Under this method, the capitals of the partners are brought proportionate to their profit sharing ratio by paying surplus capital of a partner/partners. So, first of all, we have to find out the surplus captial of the partners.

For the calculation of surplus capital, 'A statement showing surplus capital or excess capital' is to be prepared. This statement is prepared as under -

1. Find out capital per unit of profit of each partner by dividing his capital by his share of profit.

2. The partner whose capital per unit of profit is lowest or minimum is taken as a base and it is multiplied by profit sharing ratio of each partner.

3. Thus, calculate expected captials of all partners. Such amount of capitals are known as 'proportionate capitals'.

4. Deduct the proportionate capital of respective partner from actual amount of capital.

5. Determine the excess figure which is known as surplus capital.

The same method is to be followed again and again to find out absolute surplus, if there are more than two partners or number of partners.

The above process will be clear from the following illustration.

Illustration :

A, B and C are the partners sharing profits and losses in the ratio of 3:2:1. Their capitals were Rs.30000, Rs.24000 and Rs.15000 respectively, when the firm was dissolved.

From the above, calculate surplus capital.

Statement showing surplus capital.

Particulars	Capital Accounts		
	'A' Rs.	'B' Rs.	'C' Rs.
Capital Balances as per B/S.	(i) 30,000	24,000	15,000
profit sharing ratio	3	2	1
Capital per unit of profit A' is having lowest capital per share of profit, hence taken as a base and it is multiplied by profit sharing ratio of each partner.	$\dfrac{30000}{3} = 10000$	$\dfrac{24000}{2} = 12000$	$\dfrac{15000}{1} = 15000$
	10000 x 3 =	10000 x 2 =	10000 x 1 =
	(ii) 30000	20000	10000

Particulars	Partner's Capital		
	'A' Rs.	'B' Rs.	'C' Rs.
Surplus or excess capital (i-ii)	(ii) (Nil)	4,000	5,000
Profit sharing ratio of remaining partners capital per unit of profit 'B' is having lowest capital per share of profit, hence taken as base and it is multiplied by p.s. ratio of remaining partners.		2 $\dfrac{4000}{2} = 2000$ $2000 \times 2 = 4000$	1 $\dfrac{5000}{1} = 5000$ $2000 \times 1 = 2000$
Absolute surplus capital.		(Nil)	3000

Payment of surplus capital to partner :

While making the payment of surplus capital to partners, the reverse order is to be followed. The absolute surplus capital is paid off first. Then the surplus capital is paid. Thereafter the remaining capital of all partners is paid in their profit sharing ratio.

In above example the priority of payment will be as under-

1. First of all the absolute surplus of 'c' i.e. Rs.3000 will be paid.

2. Secondly the surplus capital of B and C will be paid. At this stage, Rs.4000 and Rs.2000 (5000-3000) will be paid to B and C.

3. Remaining cash will be paid to all partners in their profit sharing ratio.

Note : If there is General Reserve or Credit Balance of Profit and Loss Account, it should be distributed among the partners in their profit sharing ratio and added to original capital balances. On the other hand, if there is debit balance in P & L A/c (loss) it is deducted from the capital balances at the beginning in profit sharing ratio at the time of preparing statement of surplus capital.

Distribution of cash

Suppose that the assets of the firm are realised gradually and cash received as follows- Ist instalment Rs.15,000 and IInd instalment Rs.24,000.

Statement showing Distribution of Cash

Date	Particulars	Cash Available Rs	'A' Rs.	'B' Rs.	'C' Rs.
				Capital Accounts	
	Capital Balance		30,000	24,000	15,000
	Ist Instalment 15000				3000
	Paid to 'C' -3000				
	(Absolute surplus)				
	Balance Due 12000		30,000	24,000	12,000
	Paid to 'B' and 'C'				
	(surplus capital) - 6000			4,000	2,000
	Balance Due 6000		30,000	20,000	10,000
	Paid the remaining balance i.e. Rs.6000 among partners in their profit sharing ratio (3:2:1)		3,000	2,000	1,000
	Balance Due		27,000	18,000	9,000
	IInd Instalment Rs. 24000 Paid to all partners in their profit sharing ratio. i.e.ratio i.e. 3:2:1		12,000	8,000	4,000
	Realisation loss.		15,000	10,000	5,000

Note :- Realisation loss generally comes in profit sharing ratio of the partners.

Illustration 1

A, B and c carried on business as a partners sharing profit and losses in the ratio of 2:2:1 respectively. Their balance sheet was as follows :

Balance sheet on 31st Dec 2012.

Liabilities	Rs.	Assets	Rs.
Sundry Creditors	15,000	Cash in Hand	6,000
Capital Accounts		Sundry Debtors	10,000
A 28000		Plant & Machinery	12,000
B 25000		Land & Building	50,000
C 10000	63,000		
	78,000		78,000

The partnership was dissolved and the amounts realised from the sale of assets were as follows :

First instalment	Rs. 8000
Second instalment	Rs.14000
Third instalment	Rs.16000
Realisation expenses were	Rs. 1000

Draw up detail statement showing distribution of cash.

Solution :

Statement showing surplus capital

Particulars	'A' Rs.	'B' Rs.	'C' Rs.
Capital Balances	28,000	25,000	10,000
Profit sharing Ratio	2	2	1
Capital per unit	28,000	25,000	10,000
	2	2	1
	14,000	12,500	10,000
C's capital is lowest	-20,000	-20,000	-10,000
hence taken as base and multiplied by			
profit sharing ratio			
Surplus	8,000	5,000	-
Profit sharing Ratio	2	2	
Capital per unit	4,000	2500	
Taking B's capital as base	-5000	-5000	
Surplus capital	3,000	-	

Repayment of capital
1) First Rs.3000 paid to A
2) Next 5000 + 5000 paid to A and b respectively
3) Remaining cash paid to all partners in their profit sharing ratio.

Illustration 2
Statement showing distribution of cash

Date	Particulars	Cash Available Rs	Creditors	A	B	C
	Balances		15,000	28,000	25,000	10,000
	Cash Balance	6000				
	- Realisation Expenses	-1000				
		5000				
	Paid to creditors	-5000	-5000			
	Balances	-	10,000	28,000	25,000	10,000
	Ist Instalment	8000				
	Paid to Creditors	-8000	-8000			
	Balances	-	2000	28,000	25,000	10,000
	IInd Instalment	14000				
	Paid to Creditors	-2000	-2000			
		12000	-	28,000	25,000	10,000
	Paid to Mr A	- 3000		-3000		
	Balances	9000		25,000	25,000	10,000
	Paid to Mr A & Mr B in					
	their P.S. Ratio	-9000		-4500	-4500	-
	(i.e. 2:2)					
	Balances	-		20,500	20,500	10,000
	III Instalment	16,000				
	Paid to Mr A and Mr B in					
	their P.S. Ratio	- 1000		-500	-500	-
	(i.e. 2:2)					
	Balances	15,000		20,000	20,000	10,000
	Paid to A,B and C in their P.S. Ratio	-15000		-6000	-6000	3000
	i.e. 2:2:1					
	Realisation Loss			14,000	14,000	7,000

P, Q and R were partners in a firm sharing profits and losses in the ratio equally. They decided to dissolve the firm on 31-6-2012. when their balance sheet was as follows -

Balance sheet as on 31-6-2012

Liabilities	Rs.	Assets	Rs.
Sundry Creditors	20,000	Fixed Assets	50,000
Income Tax	2,000	Current Assets	15,000
General Reserve	18,000	Cash at Bank	10,000
Capital Accounts			
P 20000			
Q 10000			
R 5000	35,000		
	75,000		75,000

As per discussion with the bank, it was decided to withdraw Rs.4000 immediately and the balance after 1st Sep.2012. The assets were realised as under -

Date	Fixed Assets (Rs.)	Current Assets
31st July 12	15,000	5,000
31st Aug. 12	25,000	7,000
30th Sept.12	11,000	600

The partners kept aside Rs.1000 to meet probable expenses of realisation but actually they amounted to Rs.600.

Prepare statement showing surplus capital and distribution of cash.

Solution :
Statement showing surplus capital.

Particulars	Capital Accounts		
	'P' Rs.	'Q' Rs.	'R' Rs.
Capital Balance	20,000	10,000	5,000
+ Reserve Fund			
equally distributed	6,000	6,000	6,000
Final capital Balance	26,000	16,000	11,000
Profit sharing Ratio	1	1	1
Per unit capital	26,000	16,000	11,000
R's. capital is lowest			
hence taken as base	-11000	-11000	-11,000
Surplus capital	15,000	5000	-
P.S. Ratio (equal)	1	1	
Per unit capital	15,000	5000	
Q's capital is lowest			
hence taken as base	-5000	-5000	
Surplus capital	10,000	-	

Repayment of capital
1) First Rs. 10000 paid to P
2) Next Rs. 5000 + 5000 paid to P and Q respectively.
3) Remaining cash paid to P, Q and R in their profit sharing ratio.

Statement showing distribution of cash

Date	Particulars	Cash Available Rs	Income Tax	Creditors	Capital Accounts		
					P	Q	R
	Final Balances		2,000	20,000	26,000	16,000	11,000
	Cash withdrawn	4000					
	- Realisation Exp.	- 1000					
		- 3000					
	Paid Income Tax	- 2000	-2000				
		1000	-	20,000	26,000	16,000	11,000
	Paid to Creditors	-1000		-1000			
	Balances			19,000	26,000	16,000	11,000

Piecemeal Distribution of Cash / 11

Statement showing distribution of cash (contd.)

Date	Particulars	Cash Available Rs	Income Tax	Creditors	A	B	C
	Ist Instalment			19,000	26,000	16,000	11,000
	Fixed Assets	15000					
	Current Assets	+ 5000					
		20,000					
	Paid to creditors -	19000	-2000	-19000			
	Balances	1000			26,000	16,000	11,000
	Paid to Mr. P.	1000			-1,000		
		-			25,000	16,000	11,000
	IInd Instalment						
	Fixed Assets	25000					
	Current Asset	+ 7000					
		32000					
	Paid to Mr. P.	-9000			-9,000		
		23000			16,000	16,000	11,000
	Paid to Mr. P & Q						
	equally	- 10000			-5000	-5000	-
		13000			11000	11,000	11,000
	Paid to P,Q,R	13000			-4333	-4333	-4334
	Balance	-			6667	6667	6666
	Cash withdrawn						
	from Bank	6000					
	Paid to P,Q,R						
	(equally)	- 6000			-2000	-2000	-2000
	Balances				4,667	4667	4666
	III Instalment						
	Fixed Assets	11000					
	Current Assets	+ 600					
		11600					
	Refund of						
	Realisation expenses	+ 400					
		12,000					
	Paid to P,Q and R (equally)						
		-12000			-4000	-4000	-4000
	Realisation Loss	-			667	667	666

Illustration 3

A, B and C were in partnership sharing profit and losses in the ratio of 2:1:1. They decided to dissolve the business on 31st Dec, 2012, on which date their Balance Sheet was as under-

Balance sheet

Liabilities		Rs.	Assets	Rs.
Capitals			Cash	10,000
A -	1,00,000		Debtors	90,000
B -	55,000		Stock	85,000
C -	25,000	1,80,000	Plant & Machinery	65,000
General Reserve		20,000	Land & Buildings	1,55,000
Income Tax		10,000		
Creditors		1,17,000		
Bills Payable		78,000		
		4,05,000		4,05,000

The assets were realised on piecemeal as follows.

on 1-1-2013   Rs.   15,000
on 31-1-2013   Rs. 2,11000
on 20-2-2013   Rs.   82,000
on 31-3-2013   Rs.   58,000

It was agreed that the cash should be distributed as and when realised. Dissolution expenses were originally provided for an estimated of Rs.5,000. The actual expenses amounted to Rs.4,000 spent on 31st March 2013.

Statement showing surplus capital

Particulars	'P' Rs.	'Q' Rs.	'R' Rs.
Capital Balances	1,00,000	55,000	25,000
+ General Reserve (2 : 1 : 1)	10,000	5000	5,000
Final capital Balances	1,10,000	60,000	30,000
Profit sharing Ratio	2	1	1
Per unit capital	55,000	60,000	30,000
C's capital is lowest hence it is taken as base and multiplied by P.S. ratio	-60,000	-30,000	-30,000
Surplus capital	50,000	30,000	
Profit sharing ratio	2	1	
Per unit capital	25,000	30,000	
as A's capital is lowest it is taken as base and multiplied by P.S. Ratio.	-50,000	-25,000	
Surplus capital	-	5,000	

Statement Showing Piecemeal Distribution of Cash

Date	Particulars	Cash Available Rs	Income Tax	Creditors Rs.	Bill Payable	A Rs.	B Rs.	C Rs
	Balances	10000	10,000	1,17,000	78,000	1,10,000	60,000	30,000
	- Provision for realisation							
	Expenses	5000	-5000					
		5000	5,000	1,17,000	78,000	1,10,000	60,000	30,000
	- Income Tax	-5000	-5000					
		-						
	Balances		5,000					
	Ist Realisation							
	Assets Realised	15000						
	- Income Tax	-5000	-5000					
		10000	-	1,17,000	78,000	1,10,000	60,000	30,000
	Paid to Crs. and B.P. in their Ratio 3:2 - -	10000		-6000	-4000			
		-		1,11,000	74,000	1,10,000	60,000	30,000
	IInd Realisation							
	Assets Realised	2,11,000						
	Paid to Crs. and B.P. (3:2)	1,85,000		-1,11,000	-74000			

Date	Particulars	Cash Available Rs	Income Tax	Creditors Rs.	Bill Payable	A Rs.	B Rs.	C Rs
	Balances	26000	-		-	1,10,000	60,000	30,000
	Paid to B	- 5000					-5000	
	(Surplus capital Balances)							
		21000				1,10,000	55,000	30,000
	Paid to A and B in the							
	ratio 2:1	21000				-14000	-7000	-
	Balances	-				96,000	48,000	30,000
	IIIrd Realisation							
	Assets Realised	82000						
	- Paid to A and B in their							
	P.S. Ratio 2:1	54000				-36000	-18000	-
	Balances	28,000				60,000	30,000	30,000
	Paid to A,B & C in P.S.							
	Ratio 2:1:1 -	28000				-14000	-7000	-7000
	Balances	–				46,000	23,000	23,000
	IVth realisation							
	Assets Realised	58000						
	+ Provision of realisation							
	Expenses	+1000						
		59000						
	Paid to A, B and C in P.S.							
	Ratio 2:1:1	59000				-29500	-14750	-14750
	Realisation Loss					16,500	8250	8,250

Illustration 4

Asha, Usha and Nisha were in partnership with a capital of Rs.60000 originally contributed in the proportion of 1/2, 1/3 and 1/4 respectively sharing profits and losses in the same proportion. The partnership was dissolved on 31st Dec 2012. The balance sheet on which date was as follows-

Balance sheet as on 31-12-2012

Liabilities		Rs.	Assets	Rs.
Capitals			Cash	8000
Asha -	40000		Debtors	84000
Usha -	20000		Stock	32000
Nisha -	4000	64,000		

Liabilities		Rs.	Assets	Rs.
Loans				
Asha	12000			
Usha	8000	20,000		
Bank Overdraft		40,000		
		1,24,000		1,24,000

It was agreed that net realisations should be distributed in their due order at the end of each calendar month. The realisations and expenses were-

Month	Debtors (Rs.)	Stock (Rs.)	Current Assets
January	16,000	8,000	2000
February	20,000	2,000	1000
March	18,000	16,000	2000
April	20,000	2,000	800
May	4,000	6,000	1000

The stock has been completely disposed off. It was agreed that Nisha should take over the remaining debtors at Rs.1200.

Prepare statement of surplus capital and statement of distribution of cash.

Solution

Statement Showing Surplus Capital

Particulars	Asha	Usha	Nisha
Capital Balances	40,000	20,000	4000
Profit sharing Ratio	3	2	1
Per unit capital	13333.33	10,000	4,000
As Nisha's capital is lowest, it is taken as base and multiplied by P.S. Ratio	-12,000	-8,000	-4000
Surplus Capital	28,000	12,000	-
Profit Sharing Ratio	3	2	
Per unit capital	9333.33	6000	
As Usha's capital is lowest it is taken as base and multiplied by P.S. ratio.	-18,000	-12,000	
Surplus Capital	10,000	-	

Statement Showing Distribution of Cash

Date	Particulars	Cash Available Rs	Bank O/D	Loan Asha Rs.	Loan Usha Rs.	Capital Asha	Capital Usha	Capital Nisha
	Balances	8000	40,000	12,000	8,000	40,000	20,000	4000
	Paid to Bank	-8000	-8000					
	(Bank overdraft)	-	32,000	12,000	8,000	40,000	20,000	4000
	Ist Instalment							
	Debtors	16000						
	Stock	+ 8000						
		24000						
	Expenses	- 2000						
		22,000						
	Paid to Bank	-22000	-22000					
	(Bank overdraft)							
	Balances		10,000	12000	8,000	40,000	20,000	4000
	IInd Instalment							
	Debtors	20000						
	Stock	+ 2000						
		22000						
	- Expenses	- 1000						
		21000						
	Paid to Bank	- 10000	-10000					
		11000	-	12000	8,000	40,000	20,000	4000
	Paid loan of Asha							
	and usha (3:2)	- 11000		-6600	-4400			
				5400	3600	40,000	20,000	4000
	IIIrd Instalment							
	Debtors	18000						
	Stock	+16000						
		34000						
	Expenses	-2000						
		32000						
	Paid loan of							
	Asha & Usha	-9000		-5400	-3600			
	Balances	23000		—	—	40,000	20,000	4,000
	Paid to Asha	-10000				-		
	Balances	13000				10000	20,000	4,000
	Paid to Asha &					30,000		
	Usha (3:2)	13000				-		
	Balances	-				-7800	5200	4000
						22200	14800	

Piecemeal Distribution of Cash / 17

Date	Particulars	Cash Available Rs	Bank O/D	Loan Asha Rs.	Loan Usha Rs.	Capital Accounts Asha	Usha	Nisha
	IVth Realisation			1,10,000	1,10,000			30,000
	Debtors	20000						
	+Stock	2000						
		22000						
	- Expenses	800						
		21200						
	Paid to Asha &	-17000				-10200	-6800	
	Usha (3:2 :1)							
	Balances	4200				12000	8000	4000
	Paid to Asha Usha & Nisha							
	(3:2:1)	-4200				-2100	-1400	-700
	Vth Realisation	—				9900	6600	3300
	Debtors	4000						
	Stock	+ 6000						
		10000						
	Expenses	-1000						
	+Debtors	9000						
	Collected	1200						
		10200						
	Paid to Asha							
	Usha & Nisha							
	(3 : 2 : 1)	-10200				-5100	-3400	-1700
	Realisation Loss					4800	3200	1600

Repayment of capital

Note : 1) First Rs.10000 paid to Asha.

2) Next Rs.18000+12000 paid to Asha and Usha.

3) Remaining cash paid to all partners in their profit sharing ratio.

4) It is assumed that amount paid to Nisha on 31st May 2013 includes Rs.1200 for Debtors and Rs.500 cash.

Illustraion 5

Anita, Sunita and Nita were in partnership sharing profits and losses in the ratio of 1/2, 1/4 and 1/4 respectively. The following was their Balance Sheet on 31-12-2012 on which day they decided to dissolve the firm.

Balance sheet as on 31-12-2012

Liabilities		Rs.	Assets	Rs.
Creditors		30,000	Cash	18,000
Income Tax		8,000	Stock	80,000
Loan from Bank		60,000	Debtors	1,20,000
(Secured by pledge of			Furniture	72,000
Stock)			Motor Car	50,000
Sunita's loan		13,200		
Nita's Loan		8,800		
Capitals				
Anita	80000			
Sunita	80000			
Nita	60000	2,20,000		
		3,40,000		3,40,000

Adjustments :

(1) Bank could realise only Rs.50000 on disposal of stock

(2) A sum of Rs.6000 was spent for repairs of furniture to get better price.

(3) Other assets were realised as follows :

Jan 2013	Rs.24000
Feb 2013	Rs.30000
March 2013	Rs.20000
April 2013	Rs.60000
May 2013	Rs.100000

Prepare a statement showing distribution of cash as per proportionate capital method.

Statement Showing Surplus Capital

Particulars	Anita	Sunita	Nita
Capital Balances	80,000	80,000	60,000
Profit sharing Ratio	2	1	1
Per unit capital	40,000	80,000	60,000
As Anita's capital is lowest it is taken as base and multiplied by P.S. Ratio	-80,000	-40000	-40000
Surplus Capital	-	40,000	20,000
Profit Sharing Ratio		1	1
Per unit capital		40,000	20,000
As Nita's capital is lowest it is taken as base and multiplied by P.S. ratio.		-20,000	-20000
Surplus Capital		20,000	-

Repayment of capital

Note (1) First Rs.20000 paid to Sunita.

(2) Next Rs.20000+20000 paid to Sunita and Nita.

(3) Remaining cash to all partners in their profit sharing ratio.

Statement Showing Distribution of Cash

Date	Particulars		Income Tax	Creditors		Partner's Loan		Capital Accounts		
		Cash Avail.Rs		Creditor	Bank od	Sunita	Nita	Anita	Sunita	Nita
	Balances		8000	30000	60000	13200	8800	80000	80000	60000
	Paid to Bank (Secured Loan) (Stock Realised)		8000	30000	-50000 10000	13200	8800	80000	80000	60000
	Cash Balance	18000								
	Paid for repairs of furniture	-6000								
		12000								
	Paid Income Tax	-8000	-8000							
	Balances	4000	-	30000	10000	13200	8800	80000	80000	60000
	Paid to Crs Bank Loan in the ratio of 3:1	4000		-3000	-1000					
	Balances			27000	9000	13200	8800	80000	80000	60000

(contd.)

Date	Particulars	Cash Avail.Rs	Income Tax	Creditor	Bank od	Sunita	Nita	Anita	Sunita	Nita
				Creditors		Partner's Loan		Capital Accounts		
	Ist Realisation	24000								
	Paid to Crs. & Bank									
	Loan (3:1)	-24000		-18000	-6000					
	Balances	-		9000	3000	13200	8800	80000	80000	60000
	IInd Realisation	30000								
	Paid to Crs. & Bank									
	loan (3:1)	-12000		-9000	-3000					
	Balances	18000		-	-	13200	8800	80000	80000	60000
	Paid loan of Sunita & Nita									
	(3:2)	18000				-10800	-7200			
		-								
	Balances					2400	1600	80000	80000	60000
	III Realisation	20000								
	Paid loan of Sunita & Nita									
	(3:2)	-4000				-2400	-1600			
	Balances	16000				-	-	80000	80000	60000
	Paid Sunita's capital								-	
		-16000							16000	
	(surplus capital)	-						80000	64000	60000
	IVth Realisation	60000								
	Paid Sunita's									
	surplus capital	4000							-4000	
		56000						80000	60000	600000
	Paid Sunita's & Nita's									
	Surplus capital	-40000								-
	Balances	16000						80000	20000	20000
	Paid Anita Sunita & Nita								40000	40000
	in P.S.Ratio (2:1:1)									
		-16000						-8000		
	Balances	-						72000	-4000	-4000
	Vth Realisation	100000							36000	36000
	Paid to Anita, Sunita &									
	Nita (2:1:1)	-100000						-	-	-
	Realisation Loss							50000	25000	25000
								22000	11000	11000

Notes : 1) Repairs to furniture as an expenses (preferential) deducted from cash balance.

2) Income tax being preferential creditors paid first

3) Bank recovers Rs.50000 from stock given as a security. The unsecured balance (60000-50000) Rs.10000 treated as unsecured and hence paid along with other creditors.

Illustration 6

X, Y and Z were in partnership, sharing profit and losses in the ratio of 2:2:1. They decided to dissolve the firm on 31st December 2012 when their Balance Sheet was as under -

Balance Sheet as on 31st Dec. 2012

Liabilities		Rs.	Assets	Rs.
Creditors		30,000	Fixed Assets	70,000
Loans : X	8000		Current Asset	32,000
Y	4000	12,000	Profit & Loss A/c	20,000
Reserve Fund		10,000	Cash at Bank	20,000
Capitals	X	20,000		
	Y	40,000		
	Z	30,000		
		1,42,000		1,42,000

As per agreement with the bank the partners were entitled to withdraw Rs.5000 immediately and Rs 15200 after 25th March 2013.

The Assets were realised gradually as follows :

Date	Gross Amount	Expenses Rs.
15th Jan. 2013	43,000	3,000
15th Feb. 2013	32,000	2,000
15th March 2013	24,000	4,000

Sundry creditors were settled at 5% discount show the distribution of each instalment as per surplus capital method.

Solution

Statement Showing Surplus Capital.

Particulars	X Rs	Y Rs	Z Rs
Capital Balances (original)	20,000	40,000	30,000
Add Reserve Fund (2:2:1)	4,000	4,000	2,000
	24,000	44,000	32,000
Less Profit & Loss A/c (Loss) (2:2:1)	8,000	8,000	4,000
Final capital balances	16,000	36,000	28,000
Profit sharing ratio	2	2	1
Per unit capital	8,000	18,000	14,000
as X's capital is lowest it is taken as base and multiplied by P.S. ratio.	-16,000	-16,000	-8000
Surplus capital	-	20,000	20,000
Profit sharing ratio.		2	1
Per unit capital		10,000	20,000
As Y's capital is lowest it is taken as base and multiplied by P.S. ratio.		-20,000	-10,000
Surplus capital		-	10,000

Statement Showing Distribution of Cash

Date	Particulars	Cash Avail.Rs	Credi-tors	Partner's Loan X Rs.	Y Rs.	Capital Accounts X Rs.	Y Rs.	Z Rs.
	Final Balance	Rs.	Rs.	8000	4000	16000	36000	28000
	- Discount on Creditors 5% on 30000		30,000					
	Balances		-1500	8000	4000	16000	36000	28000
	Withdrawn from Bank	5000	28500					
	Paid to Crs.	-5000						
	Balances	-	-5000 23500	8000	4000	16000	36000	28000

Contd.

(Distribution of Cash contd.)

Date	Particulars	Cash Available Rs.	Credi-tors Rs.	Partner's Loan X Rs.	Y Rs.	Capital Accounts X Rs.	Y Rs.	Z Rs.
	Ist Realisation Gross Assets	43000		8000	4000	16000	36000	28000
	Expenses	3000						
		40000				16000	36000	28000
	Paid to Crs.	-23500						
	Balances	16500	-23500	8000	4000	16000	36000	28000
	Paid loan of X & Y	-12000	-	-8000	-4000			
	Balances	4500		-	-	16000	36000	28000
	Paid Surplus capital of Z	-4500						-4500
	IInd Realisation Gross Assets	32000				16000	36000	23500
	- Expenses	2000						
		30000						
	Paid Surplus of 'Z' remaining	-5500						5,500
		24500				16000	36000	18,000
	Paid to Y & Z (Surplus capital) (2:1)	-24500					-16334	8166
	Balances	-				16000	19666	9834
	III Realisation Gross Asset	24000						
	- Expenses	4000						
		20000						
	Paid to Y & Z surplus capital (2:1)	5500					-3666	-1834
		14500				16000	16000	8000
	Paid to X,Y and Z in P.S. ratio (2:2:1)	-14500				-5800	-5800	-2900
		—				10200	10200	5100
	Withdrawn from Bank	15000						
	Paid to X, Y & Z in P.S. ratio (2:2:1)	15000				-6000	-6000	-3000
	Realisation Loss	-				4200	4200	2100

1.4 Maximum Loss Method

Maximum loss method is another method of piecemeal distribution. This is an alternative to surplus capital method. There is no difference between this method and surplus capital method in relation to the payments to preferential creditors secured creditors, contingent liability, third party liabilities and partners loan. This method differs from the first method only in respect of repayment of capitals.

In refunding the amount due to partners on piecemeal baris, great care has to be exercised that no partner will get more than for what he is entitled to.

If surplus capital method is adopted for repayment of capital, there is a risk that one or more of the partners may get overpaid, since the final amount due to each partner cannot be known until realisation is completed. Hence, if a partner who has received more than what would be due to him becomes insolvent, the excess payment may not be recovered and other partners may be put to a loss. To avoid this discrepancy the maximum loss method is adopted.

In this method, every realisation is treated as last realisation and it is presumed that remaining unrealised assets are worthless and no more cash will be realised thereafter and hence maximum possible loss is transferred to the capital accounts of the partners in their profit sharing ratio. In short, under maximum loss method the following procedure is adopted.

1) After the payment to third party liability and partners loan, maximum loss or notional loss is calculated. It is calculated as under.

Maximum loss = Total unpaid capital - cash available

2) Distribute the maximum loss or notional loss among the partners in their profit sharing ratio.

3) Find out the balance of partners capital Account.

4) If any partners' capital account shows debit balance, he is to be presumed as insolvent and his deficiency is transferred to capital accounts of the solvent partners in their profit sharing ratio (If Garner V/s Murray principle is not followed) or in proportion of capital balances (if Garner V/s Murray principle is followed.)

5) After the above step, if any other partner is capital account shows a debit balance, his deficiency is also transferred to solvent partner's capital account. If some amount is recovered from the private estate of insolvent partner, his deficiency should be reduced by the amount.

6) After completing the above step, the balance to the credit of partners capital account will be equal to the cash available for distribution.

7) Then pay the cash available to the partners equal to the balances.

8) After the payment of cash, balances on capitals are brought down and the same process is repeated upto last realisation. The loss at last is the real realisation loss.

Deficiency of Capital Account

After the distribution of maximum or notional loss among the partners, if the share of loss of a partner is more than his capital, the partner is treated as insolvent partner. The deficiency of a partner is distributed among the partners either by following two method.

1) Profit sharing ratio method.

2) Capital ratio method (Garner V/s Murray Rule)

1) Profit Sharing Ratio Method -

According to this method the deficiency of partners is distributed among the partners in their profit sharing ratio.

2) Capital Ratio Method -

According to this method, the deficiency of the partner is distributed among other partners in their capital ratio. capital ratio method is used in England because in the judgement of Garner V/s Murray case, the judge had given a decision that the deficiency of an insolvent partner should be distributed among the partners in the proportion of capital ratio of solvent partners. Hence, this method is also called as Garner V/s Murray rule or principle.

Note : - If nothing is mentioned in the problem the student can use any one of the above method, at the time of solving the problem on distribution of cash.

1.4.1 Illustrations -

Illustration 1

North, South and East sharing profits and losses in the ratio of 2:1:1 decided to dissolve their partnership as on 31st December 2012. Following is their balance sheet.

Balance Sheet

Liabilities		Rs.	Assets	Rs.
Capital Accounts			Cash in Hand	12,000
North	1,00,000		Investment	8,000
South	54,000	1,54,000	Plant & Machinery	1,63,000
Current Accounts			South's Current	
North		4,000	Account	2,000
East		2,000		
Sundry Liabilities		25,000		
		1,85,000		1,85,000

The Assets are realised as follow :

Jan 2013	Rs.52,000
Feb 2013	Rs.72,000
March 2013	Rs.17,600

Prepare the statement of distribution of cash as per maximum loss method.

Solution :

Statement Showing Distribution of Cash

Date	Particulars	Cash Available Rs.	Sundry Liabilities	North	South	East Rs.
	Balances	12000	Rs.	Rs.	Rs.	-
	Partners Current Accounts		25000	1,00,000	54000	+2000
	Final Balances	12000		+4000	-2000	2000
	Paid for Liabilities	12000	25000	1,04,000	52000	
			-12000			2000
	Ist Realisation	52000	13,000	1,04,000	52000	
	Paid for Liabilities	13000				
		39000	-13000			2000
	Maximum Loss = Total Capital - cash = 1,58,000-39,000 = 1,19,000 (Loss)		-	104000	52000	
	Loss shared by all partners in their profit sharing ratio 2:1:1					-29750
	Deficiency of East is shared by			-59500	-29750	-27750
	North and South in their profit			44500	22250	
	sharing ratio (2:1)			-18500	-9250	+27750
				26000	13000	2,000
	Cash paid to North and South	39000		26000	13000	
	Balance Due	-				
	IInd Realisation	72000		78000	39000	2000
	maximum loss = Total capital - cash = 119000-72,000 = 47000 (Loss shared by all partners in their profit sharing ratio (2:1:1)					
	Deficiency of East is shared by			-23500	-11750	-11750
	North and South in their profit			54500	27250	-9750
	sharing ratio (2:1)					
	Balance due			-6500	-3250	
	Paid cash to			48000	24000	-9250
	North and South	72000				
	Balance Due	-		-48000	-24000	-
				30000	15000	2000

(contd.)

Date	Particulars	Cash Available Rs.	Sundry Liabilities Rs.	North Rs.	South Rs.	East Rs.
	IIIrd Realisation 17600		Rs.			
	Maximum loss = total capital -cash					
	= 47000-17600 = 29400 (Loss)					
	Loss shared by all partners in their					
	profit sharing ratio (2:1:1)			-14700	-7350	-7350
	Balances			15300	7650	-5350
	Deficiency of East is shared by					
	North and South in their profit shar-			-3567	-1783	+5350
	ing ratio i.e. 2:1			11733	5867	-
	Paid to North and South 17600			-11733	-5867	
	Realisation Loss			18267	9133	2000

Note : - In this problem the deficiency of insolvent partners is divided in the profit sharing ratio of solvent partners as it is not specifically told to apply Garner V/s Murray principle.

Illustration 2

Sourabha, Sujeet and Sachin were in partnership sharing profits and losses in the ratio 1/2,1/3 and 1/6 respectively. The partnership was dissolved on 31st Dec.2012, when the position was as follows.

Balance Sheet

Liabilities	Rs.	Assets	Rs.
Creditors	38,000	Sundry Assets	1,44,000
Capital Accounts		Cash in Hand	6,000
Sourabha	67,000		
Sujeet	33,000		
Sachin	6,000		
Reserve Fund	6,000		
	1,50,000		1,50,000

Dissolution expenses amounted Rs.6000.

The assets were gradually realised and the distributions were made as and when cash become available. The realisations were as follows.

1st Instalment Rs.54,000
2nd Instalment Rs.45,000
3rd Instalment Rs.15,000
4th Instalment Rs.24,000

Prepare the statement showing the division of net proceeds among the partners so that the effect may be given to ruling in Garner V/s Murray at each distribution stage assuming that nothing further will be realised after that date.

Solution :

Statement Showing Distribution of Cash

Date	Particulars	Cash Available Rs.	Creditors Rs.	Capital Accounts		
				Sourbh	Sujeet	Sachin
	Balances	6000	38000	67000	33000	6000
	Add Reserve Fund (3:2:1) Rs.6000					
	Final Balances	6000	38000	3000	2000	1000
	Paid dissolution expenses - 6000					
	-		38000	70000	35000	7000
	Ist Instalment 54000					
	Paid to creditors - 38000		-38000	70000	35000	7000
	Balance Due 16000		-	70000	35000	7000
	Maximum loss = Total capital - cash = 112,000-16000 = 96000 (loss)					
	Loss shared by all partners in their P.S. ratio i.e. 3:2:1			-48000	-32000	-16000
	Deficiency of Sachin is shared by Sourabh and Sujeet in capital ratio (i.e.2:1)			22000	3000	-9000
				-6000	-3000	+9000
	Paid cash to Sourabh 16000			16000	-	-
	-			-16000		
	Balance Due			54000	35000	7000
	IInd Instalment 45000					
	Maximum loss = total capital -cash = 96000-45000= 51000 (Loss shared by all partners in their profit sharing ratio i.e. 3:2:1			-25500	-17000	-8500
	Deficiency of Sachin is allocated to Sourabh and Sujeet in their capital ratio i.e.2:1			28500	18000	-1500
				-1000	-500	+1500
	Paid cash to Sourabh and Sujeet			27500	17500	-
	-45000			-27500	-17500	
	Balance Due			26500	17500	7000

(Distribution of Cash contd.)

Date	Particulars	Cash Available Rs.	Creditors Rs.	Sourbh	Sujeet	Sachin
	IIIrd Instalment 15000					
	Maximum loss = total capital - cash					
	= 51000-15000 = 36000 (Loss)					
	Loss shared by all partners in their					
	profit sharing ratio (i.e.3:2:1)			-18000	-12000	-6000
	Balances			8500	5500	1000
	Cash paid to all partners 15000					
	-	-		-8500	-5500	-1000
	Balance Due			18,000	12000	6000
	IVth Instalment 24000					
	Maximum loss = total capital - cash					
	= 36000-24000 = 12000(Loss)					
	Loss sharing by all partners in their					
	profit sharing ratio					
	(i.e. 3:2:1)			-6000	-4000	-2000
				12000	8000	4000
	Paid cash to all partners 24000			12000	8000	4000
		-				
	Realisation Loss			6000	4000	2000

Illustration 3

Sudhakar, Madhukar and Subhash who shared profits and losses in the ratio of 3:2:1 dissolved their partnership on 30th April 2012. The Balance Sheet on that date was as follows.

Balance Sheet as on 30th April 2012

Liabilities	Rs.		Assets	Rs.
Creditors		20,000	Sundry Assets	1,40,000
Reserve Fund		6,000		
Capital A/c's				
Sudhakar	6,600			
Madhukar	35,800			
Subhash	71,600	1,14,000		
		1,40,000		1,40,000

The assets were realised piecemeal and the distribution was made as cash became available. The realisation after deducting expenses were as follows.

Date	Book value	Net Proceed
	Rs.	Rs.
May 2012	26000	20,000
June 2012	12000	9,000
July 2012	30000	33,000
Sept.2012	72000	54,000

Sudhakar was insolvent and only Rs.1800 could be recovered from his private estate on 30th Sept. 2012.

Prepare a statement showing distribution of cash giving effect to the ruling in Garner V/s Murray at every realisation.

Solution :

Statement Showing Distribution of Cash

Date	Particulars	Creditors Rs.	Capital Accounts		
			Sudhakar	Madhukar	Subhash
30th April 2012	Balances	20000	6600	35800	71600
	Add : Reserve Fund (3:2:1)		3000	2000	1000
	Final Balances	20000	9600	37800	72600
May 2012	Ist Instalment 20000				
	Paid to Creditors -20000	-20000			
	Balances Dues -	-	9600	37800	72600
June 2012	IInd Instalment 9000				
	Maximum loss = total capital - cash = 120000-9000 = 111000 (loss)				
	Loss shared by partner's in their P.S. ratio i.e. 3:2:1		-55500	-37000	-18500
	Balances		-45900	800	54100
	Sudhakar's deficiency is shared by Mudhakar and Subhash in the capital ratio. i.e. 1:2		+45900	-15300	-30600
	Sudhakar's deficiency is shared by Subhash.			-14500	23,500
				+14500	-14500
					9000
					-9000
	Cash paid to Subhash 9000				
	Balance Due -		9600	37800	63600
July 2012	III Instalment 33000				
	Maximum loss = total capital - cash = 111000-33000 = 78000 (loss)				
	Loss shared by all partners in their P.S. ratio (3:2:1)		-39000	-26000	-13000
	Balances		-29400	11800	50600
	Sudhakar's deficiency is shared by Madhukar and Subhash in their capital ratio i.e. 2:1		+29400	-9800	-19600

Date	Particulars	B's Loan Rs.	Sudhakar	Madhukar	Subhash
	Cash paid to Madhukar and Subhash. -33000		-	-2000	31000
	Balances Due -		9600	35800	32600
Sept 2012	**IVth Instalment** 54000 Maximum loss = total capital - cash = 78000 - 54000 = 24000 loss. Loss shared by all partners in their P.S. ratio i.e. 3:2:1		-12000	-8000	-4000
			-2400	27800	28600
	Amt. recovered from private estate of Sudhakar ___1800		1800		
	_____55800_		-600	27800	28600
	Sudhakar's deficiency is shared by Madhukar and Subhash in their capital ratio i.e. 1:2		$+600$	-200	-400
			-	27600	28200
	Paid to Madhukar and Subhash -55800			27600	28200
	-				
	Balance Due i.e. Realisation Loss		9600	8200	4400

Illustration 4

P,Q and R were partners in a firm sharing profits and losses in the ratio of 1:2:1. They decided to dissolve the firm on 31-12-2012, when their Balance Sheet was as follows.

Balance Sheet as on 31-12-2012

Liabilities		Rs.	Assets	Rs.
Capitals :	P	36,000	Cash in Hand	10,000
	Q	52,000	Stock in Trade	60,000
	R	16,000	Sundry Debtors	40,000
Reserve Fund		16,000	Furniture	30,000
Income Tax		5,000		
Sundry Creditors		15,000		
		1,40,000		1,40,000

On dissolution, the assets realised as follows

Jan. 2013	Rs.21000
Feb. 2013	Rs.8000
March 2013	Rs.6000

Dissolution expenses were originally provided for at an estimated amount of Rs.3000 but the actual amount spent in March was Rs.1000. 'C' became insolvent and could contribute only Rs.1000 from his private estate.

Prepare a statement showing piecemeal distribution of cash as and when realised as per maximum loss method.

Solution :

Statement Showing Distribution of Cash

Date	Particulars		Income Tax	Creditors Rs.	Partner's Capital		
					P Rs.	Q Rs.	R Rs
	Balances as per B/S		5000	15000	36000	52000	16000
	+ Reserve Fund (1:2:1)				4000	8000	4000
	Final Balances		5000	15000	40000	60000	20000
	Cash in hand	10000					
	- Provision for						
	Realisation	- 3000					
	Expenses	7000					
	Paid Income Tax	-5000	5000				
	Balances	2000		15000	40000	60000	20000
	Paid to creditors	-2000		-2000			
	Balance Due			13000	40000	60000	20000
	Ist Realisation	21000					
	Paid to Creditors	-13000		13000			
	Balance Due	8000		-	40000	60000	20000
	Maximum loss = total capital - cash = 120000-8000 = 112000 (loss)						
	Loss shared by all partners in P.S.Ratio (1:2:1)				-28000	-56000	-28000
					12000	4000	-8000
	R's deficiency borne by P & Q in capital ratio i.e. 2:3 (40000:60000)				-3200	-4800	+8000
					8800	-800	-

Date	Particulars	Income Tax	Creditors Rs.	P Rs.	Q Rs.	R Rs
	Q's deficiency is borne by P			-800	+800	
	Cash paid to A -8000			8000	-	
	Balance Due -			32000	60000	20000
	IInd Realisation 8000					
	Maximum loss - total capital - cash = 112000-8000 = 104000(Loss)					
	Loss allocated among P, Q, R in P.S.Ratio i.e.1:2:1			-26000	-52000	-26000
				6000	8000	-6000
	R's capital deficiency is borned by P & Q in capital ratio (2:3)			-2400	-3600	+6000
				3600	4400	-
	Paid Cash to P & Q 8000			3600	4400	
	-					
	Balance Due			28400	55600	20000
	IIIrd Realisation 6000					
	+ Excess Provision 2000					
	of realisation Expenses 8000					
	Maximum loss = total capital - cash = 104000-8000 = 96000 (Loss)					
	Loss allocated among all partners in P.S.ratio (1:2:1)			-24000	-48000	-24000
				4400	7600	-4000
	Cash Contributed by R from his private estate.					+1000
				4400	7600	-3000
	capital deficiency of R is			-1200	-1800	+3000
	borned by P & Q in capital			3200	5800	
	ratio (2:3)					-
	Cash paid to P & Q 8000			-3200	-5800	
	-					
	Realisation Loss			25200	49800	20000

Illustration 5

Amar, Akbar and Anthony were partners sharing profit and losses in the ratio 1:2:1 respectively. They decided to dissolve the firm on 1-4-2012. The Balance Sheet as on that date was as follows.

Balance Sheet as on 1-4-2012

Liabilities	Rs.	Assets	Rs.
Creditors	21500	Sundry Assets	1,31,500
Capital A/cs		Cash on Hand	10,000
Amar	36000		
Akbar	52000		
Anthony	16000		
Profit & Loss A/c	16000		
	1,41,500		1,41,500

The Assets were realised as follows.

Date	Rs.
1-5-2012	21,000
1-6-2012	8,000
1-9-2012	6,000

Estimated dissolution expenses were Rs. 3000 but actual expenses paid Rs.1000 at the time of last realisation. Sundry creditors were settled for Rs.20000 on 1-4-2012. Anthony became insolvent and he could contribute Rs.1000 only.

Prepare statement showing distribution of cash by applying rules as per Garner V/s Murray Case.

Solution :
Statement Showing Distribution of Cash

Date	Particulars		Creditors Rs.	Capital Accounts		
				Amar	Akbar	Anthony
1.4.12	Balances	10,000	21500	36000	52000	16000
	+ Profit & Loss Account			4000	8000	4000
	(Profit) (1:2:1)		21500	40000	60000	20000
	Less Discount from creditors		1500			
	Final Balances	10000	20000	40000	60000	20000
	Less					
	Provision for					
	Realisation Expenses	-3000				
		7000				
	Paid to Creditors	-7000	7000			
	Balances	-	13000	40000	60000	20000
1.5.12	Ist Realisation	21000				
	Paid to Creditors	- 13000	-13000			
		8000	-	40000	60000	20000
	Maximum loss = total capi-					
	tal - cash - 120000-8000 =					
	112000 (Loss) Loss shard by					
	all partners in their P.S. ra-					
	tio 1:2:1			-28000	-56000	-28000
	Balances			12000	4000	-8000
	Deficiency of Anthony is					
	shared by Amar and Akbar in					
	their capital ratio					
	(40:60 = 2:3)			-3200	-4800	+8000
				8800	-800	-
	Deficiency of Akbar is borne					
	by Amar			-800	+800	
				8000	-	-
	Paid cast to Amar	8000		-8000		
	Balance Due -			32000	60000	20000
1.6.12	IInd Realisation	8000				
	Maximum loss = total capi-					
	tal - cash 112000-8000 =					
	104000 (Loss) loss shared by					
	all partners in their profit					
	sharing ratio (1:2:1)			-26000	-52000	-26000
	Balances			6000	8000	-6000

Date	Particulars	Creditors Rs.	Amar	Akbar	Anthony
	Balances Deficiency of Anthony is shared by Amar & Akbar in their capital ratio. (i.e. = 2:3)		-2400	-3600	+6000
	Deficiency of Akbar is borned by Amar		3600	4400	-
	Paid cash to Amar & Akbar 8000		-3600	-4400	
	Balance Due -		28400	55600	20000
1.9.12	**IIIrd Realisation** 6,000 Add : Realisation Expenses (3000-1000) 2000 Cash available 8000 Maximum loss = total capital - cash = 104000-8000 = 96000 loss . Loss shared by all partners in their profit sharing ratio.		-24000	-48000	-24000
			4400	7600	-4000
	Cash Received from Anthony + 1000 9000				1000
			4400	7600	-3000
	Deficiency of Anthony is shared by Amar and Akbar in their capital ratio (2:3)		-1200	-1800	+3000
			3200	5800	-
	Cash paid to Amar and Akbar 9000		3200	5800	
	-				
	Realisation Loss		25200	49800	20000

1.5 Exercises

Objective Type

A. State whether the following statements are True of False.

1) When capitals of the partners are not in profit sharing ratio, distribution of cash can be made according to Maximum loss method or proportionate capital method.
2) Surplus capital method is also known as proportionate capital method.
3) In case of dissolution of firm it is assumed that all the assets are realised on the date of dissolution and all the liabilities are paid out on the date of dissolution.
4) On piecemeal distribution assets are sold and liabilities are paid in pieces.
5) Preferential creditors are treated as secured creditors unless otherwise stated.
6) Partner's loan if any are paid out before payment of outside liabilities.

Ans : - 1) True 2) True 3) True 4) True 5) False 6) False

B. Fill in the blanks :

1) Surplus capital method is also known as --------- capital method.
2) Maximum loss = ----------- minus cash available
3) Maximum loss should be distributed to partners capital accounts in their -----------
4) Before anything is paid to the partners all ----------- liabilities must be paid off.

5) In actual practice assets are realised -----------
6) The process of distribution of cash on availability of cash is known as ----------- distribution of cash.
7) First of all ----------- expenses are paid
8) Preferential creditors are creditors..... unless otherwise stated.

Ans : 1) Proportionate 2) Total Capital due 3) Profit Sharing Ratio 4) Outside/Third party 5) Gradually 6) Piecemeal 7) Realisation 8) Unsecured.

Exercises (Theory)

1. What do you understand by piecemeal distribution of cash? Explain the various methods of distribution of cash.
2. Explain the procedure how the proceeds be distributed among the partners if assets are realised gradually ?
3. What is the order of payment of various claims, if assets are realised gradually ?
4. Write short notes on.
(i) Proportionate capital method.
(ii) Maximum loss method.
(iii) Ruling of Garner V/s Murray.
(iv) Piecemeal distribution of cash.
5. How you will determine the excess capital of partners? Explain with suitable example.

Exercises (Practical)

1. Ghokale, Dhamale and Damale were partners sharing profits and losses in the ratio of 3:2:1. There balance sheet is as under.

Balance Sheet

Liabilities	Rs.	Assets	Rs.
Creditors	7500	Sundry Assets	25,500
Capitals			
Ghokale	9000		
Dhamale	5000		
Damale	4000		
	25,500		25,500

The assets realised gradually as follows.

Ist Realisation Rs.6,000

IInd Realisation Rs.4,000

IIIrd Realisation Rs.11,600

You are asked to show the distribution of cash among the partners on piecemeal distribution by using surplus capital method.

Ans : Realisation loss Ghokale 7050, Dhamale Rs.3700 Damale Rs.3050.

2. Ajay, Sanjay and Nitin are in partnership. The following Balance sheet as at 31st Dec.2012 on which date they dissolved the partnership. They share profits and losses in the ratio of 5:3:2.

Balance Sheet as on 31-12-2012

Liabilities	Rs.	Assets	Rs.
Creditors	42,000	Premises	40,000
Ajay's Loan	8,000	Plant	30,000
Capital Accounts		Stock	30,000
Ajay 50000		Debtors	60,000
Sanjay 15000			
Nitin 45000	1,10,000		
	1,60,000		1,60,000

It was agreed to repay the amount due to partners as and when the assets were realised.

Realisation was as under.

31st January 2013 Rs. 30000

26th February 2013 Rs. 73000

31st March 2013 Rs.47000

Prepare a statement showing how the distribution should be made by using proportionate capital method.

Ans : Realisation loss : Ajay Rs.5000 Sanjay Rs.3000 Nitin Rs.2000.

3. A,B and C trade in partnership sharing profits and losses in the ratio of 3:2:1. They decided to dissolve the firm with effect from 30th June 2012, when the firm's Balance Sheet stood as follows :

Balance Sheet as on 30th June 2012

Liabilities	Rs.	Assets	Rs.
A's Capital		Cash in Hand	28000
B's Capital	1,40,000	Sundry Debtors	2,94,000
C's Capital	70,000	Stock	1,12,000
Sundry Creditors	14,000		
	2,10,000		
	4,34,000		4,34,000

There was a bill for Rs.10000 due on 30th November under discount. It was agreed to distribute cash in their due order but as safely as possible.

The realisations and expenses were as under

Date	Realisation	Expenses
31-7-2012	84,000	7,000
31-8-2012	1,26,000	5,400
31-9-2012	70,000	4,900
31-10-2012	77,000	3,500
30-10-2012	35,500	3,500

The Stock was completely disposed off and amount due from debtors were realised, the balance being irrecoverable. The acceptor of the bill under discount met the bill on the due date.

Prepare statement showing distribution of cash.

Ans : Realisation Loss 'A' Rs.18,900 'B' Rs.12,600 'C' Rs.6,300

4. X, Y and Z were in partnership with a capital of Rs.30000 originally contributed in the proportion of 1/2, 1/3 and 1/6 respectively and share the profits and losses in the same proportions. The partnership was dissolved on March 31st the Balance Sheet on which date was as follows.

Balance Sheet

Liabilities		Rs.	Assets	Rs.
Capitals :	X	20,000	Cash	4,000
	Y	10,000	Debtors	42,000
	Z	2,000	Stock	16,000
Loan's	X	6,000		
	Y	4,000		
Creditors		20,000		
		62,000		62,000

It was agreed that the net realisation should be distributed in their due order at the end of each calender month. The realisation and expenses were : -

Month	Debtors (Rs.)	Stock (Rs.)	Expenses(Rs.)
April	8,000	4,000	1,000
May	10,000	1,000	500
June	9,000	8,000	1,000
July	10,000	1,000	400
August	2,000	3,000	500

The Stock having been completely disposed off, it was agreed that Z should take over the remaining debtors at Rs.600.

Show how the cash was distributed.

Ans : Realisation loss X Rs. 2400 Y Rs. 1600 and Z Rs.800.

5. A,B and C carried on business as partner sharing profits and losses in the ratio of 3:4:5. They decided to dissolve the partnership as on 1st July 2012 and agreed that the sales of the assets should not be forced but should be made gradually. As the realisation was not likely to be completed for over a year and the partners wished the receipts from the sale should be dealt with as and when received, you are asked to prepare a scheme for equitable distribution of such receipt.

Balance Sheet

Liabilities		Rs.	Assets	Rs.
Creditors		10,000	Sundry Assets	36,000
Loan from	B	2,000		
Capitals	A	12,000		
	B	8,000		
	C	4,000		
		36,000		36,000

The net amoutn realised from the gradual sales of assets were 1-10-2012 Rs.5000, 15-12-2012 Rs.10000, 2-12-2013 Rs.5100, 15-4-2013 Rs. 6300,30-6-2013 Rs. 5700.

You are required to draw up a detailed statement showing the distribution of each instalment.

Ans. Realisation loss : - A Rs.976, B.Rs.1300 & C.Rs.1625.

6. Anil, Sunil and Swapnil sharing profits and losses in the ratio of 2:2:1. They decided to dissolve their firm as from December 31st 2012, on which date their position was as under :

Balance Sheet

Liabilities	Rs.	Assets	Rs.
Bank Overdraft	7,000	Cash at Bank	5,000
Bills Payable	25,000	Stock	35,000
Sundry Creditors	25,000	Debtors	25,000
Partners Captials		Bills Receivable	15,000
Anil	10,000	Motor Car	20,000
Sunil	30,000		
Swpnil	3,000		
	1,00,000		1,00,000

They realised their assets gradually. The following were their realisation.

Date	Assets	Amount Realised
2013		
Jan.31	Bills Receivable	14,000
Feb.28	Motor Car	18,000
April 30	60% of the Stock	19,000
June 30	Balance of Stock	10,000
Aug.31	Debtors	14,000

Show the manner in which the piecemeal distribution among the partners will be determined assuming that Swpanil is insolvent and his estate will not be able to pay anything whatsoever.

Ans : Realisation Loss Rs.20,000

7. A, B and C Sharing profits and losses in the proportions of 2:3:5 respectively decided to dissolved their firm on 31-12-2012 when their Balance Sheet was as under -

Liabilities	Rs.	Assets	Rs.
Sundry Creditors	15,000	Sundry Assets	39,000
Capital Accounts			
A	12,000		
B	8,000		
C	4,000		
	39,000		39,000

The net amount realised on gradual sale of assets were :
Sale of assets were :

Month	Rs.
31st Jan.13	10,000
28th Feb.13	9,000
31st March 13	8,000
30th April 13	6,000

Prepare a statement of distribution of cash according to Maximum loss Method presuming at each realisation method presuming at each realisation that nothing further will be realised.

Ans : Realisation loss A - Rs. 1200, B-Rs.1800 and C Rs.3000.

8. A,B and C are partners sharing profits and losses in the ratio of 5:3:2. The following is their balance sheet as on 31st March 2013, on which date they dissolved the partnership.

Balance Sheet as on 31-12-2013

Liabilities		Rs.	Assets	Rs.
Sundry Creditors		20,000	Sundry Assets	1,57,000
Bills Payable		10,000		
A's Loan		17,000		
Capitals	A	50,000		
	B	15,000		
	C	45,000		
		1,57,000		1,57,000

It was agreed to repay the amounts due to partners as and when the assets were realised assets realised as follows.

First Realisation Rs.30,000
Second Realisation Rs.70,000
Third Realisation Rs.32,000

Prepare the statement showing piecemeal distribution of cash with the help of Garner V/s Murray principle.

Ans : Realisation loss A Rs.12500, B Rs.7500 C. Rs.5000.

9. Sita, Gita and Hema are partners sharing profits and losses in the ratio of 3:2:1. The partnership firm was dissolved on 1-4-2013. The position of the balance sheet was as follows.

Balance Sheet as on 1-4-2013

Liabilities	Rs.	Assets	Rs.
Capital Accounts		Stock in Trade	1,25,000
Sita	1,40,000	Other Assets	1,75,000
Gita	70,000		
Hema	14,000		
Sundry Creditors	76,000		
	3,00,000		3,00,000

The assets were realised as and when they get better prices and distribution of cash were made at each realisation.

The realisations were as follows.

Ist Instalment Rs. 1,08,000
IInd Instalment Rs. 90,000
IIIrd Instalment Rs, 30,000
IVth Instalment Rs. 48,000

Prepare the statement showing the distribution of cash by Maximum loss method applying Garner V/s Murray rule.

Ans : Realisation loss : Sita Rs.12000, Gita Rs.8000 Hema Rs.4000.

10. Desai, Mehta and Gandhi were the partners of Competition Engineers sharing profits and losses in the ratio of 3:2:1 respectively. Their Balance Sheet as on 31st March 2013 was as follows.

Balance Sheet as on 31 March 2013.

Liabilities		Rs.	Assets	Rs.
Sundry Creditors		30,000	Building	25,000
Desai's Loan		4,000	Machinery	18,000
Mehta's Loan		2,000	Stock	11,900
Capital Accounts			Sundry Debtors	9,000
Desai	20500		Cash	600
Mehta	15000		Profit & Loss A/c	9000
Gandhi	2000	37,500		
		73,500		73,500

The firm was dissolved on 1st April 2013 and the assets were realised in Instalment. Sundry creditors were paid at a discount of Rs.800.

The assets were realised as follows.

Instalment	Rs.
Ist	21,600
IInd	9,400
IIIrd	16,200
IVth	1,200

Gandhi became insolvent and only Rs.240 could be recovered from his private estate.

Prepare statement showing distribution of cash by Maximum loss method. Apply Garner V/s Murray principle.

Ans : Realisation loss : Desai Rs.8327, Mehta Rs.6733 Gandhi Rs.500.

11. Shankar, Deo and Mahesh were in partnership sharing profits and losses in the proportion of 1/2, 1/3 and 1/6 respectively. The partnership firm was dissolved on 31st March 2002 when the position was as under :

Balance Sheet as on 31-3-2012

Liabilities	Rs.	Assets	Rs.
Creditors	76,000	Cash in Hand	8,000
Capital Accounts		Sundry Assets	2,92,000
Shankar	1,31,000		
Deo	64,000		
Mahesh	11,000		
General Reserve	18,000		
	300,000		300,000

The realisation of assets and realisation expenses were as under:

Date	Amount Realised	Expenses
30-4-2012	1,03,500	3500
31-5-2012	91,500	1500
30-6-2012	32,000	2000
31-7-2012	49,000	1000

Prepare a statement of Piecemeal distribution of cash among the partners as per maximum loss method. Apply ruling in Garner V/s Murray case at each distribution.

Ans : - Realisation loss Shankar Rs.12000, Deo Rs.8000 & Mahesh Rs.4000

☐☐☐

Chapter 2

Amalgamation of Partnership Firms

2.1 Introduction
2.2 Meaning
2.3 Objectives of Amalgamation
2.4 Advantages
2.5 Accounting Methods and Procedure
2.5.1 Accounting Procedure in the books of Old Firms
2.5.2 Accounting Procedure in the books of New Firm
2.6 Illustrations
2.7 Exercise

2.1. Introduction :

When there is a cut-throat competition in an economy, it hampers the business as a whole. To remedy the above situation, businessmen adopt the process of business combination such a Pool, Corner, holding Company, Amalgamation etc. Normally businessman resort to the process of amalgamation with a view to increase managerial skill and efficiency and increase the funds of the business.

2.2 Meaning :

"When two or more partnership firms, engaged in the similar line of business decide to come together, combine together and thereby form a new partnership firm it is known as Amalgamation of Firms."

When two or more partnership firms of similar nature consolidate their business and form a new firm, the process is called as Amalgamation.

Amalgamation involves the formation of a new firm by the combination of old firms carrying on business of similar nature. The firms which decide to combine together their businesses are called as "Old Firms" and a firm which is newly brought into existence under a new name and style is called as "New Firm".

Example :

If A and B firms and C and D firms come together, and form a new fim called as A B C and D firm, it is called as Amalgamation. The following diagram will illustrate the idea.

Under process of amalgamation, a new firm comes into existence by taking over the business of each old firm as per the agreement (terms and conditions of amalgamation.)

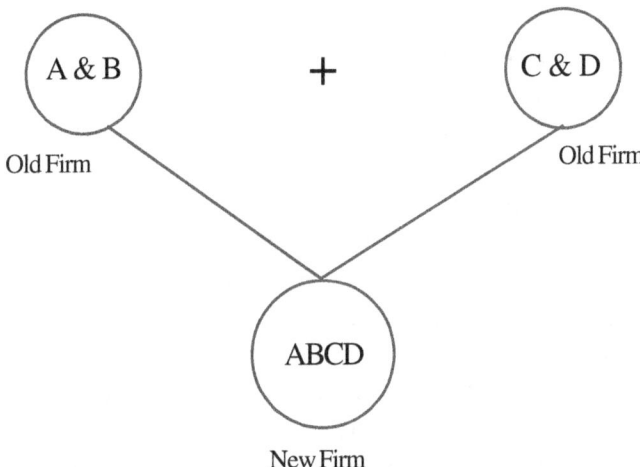

New Firm

2.3 Objectives of Amalgamation :

The objectives of amalgamation arises due to following factors.

(i) To avoid competition :

The intensity of competition in the business world is most important factor that leads to the development of amalgamation. When there exists cut-throat competition in economy, it affects small units. In order to avoid such competition the process of amalgamation is adopted.

(ii) Large scale operations :

It has been observed that large scale business organisation can effect considerable economy in production cost by bulk purchasing of materials and spreading of overheads over large quantities of output. Therefore, large scale operations are possible through the process of amalgamation.

(iii) Need of Funds :

When business expands it requires additional capital, management skill and efficiency. Under such circumstances it is convenient to the firms to amalgamate their business.

2.4 Advantages :

(i) Increase in Profit :

Due to amalgamation, cut-throat competition is avoided which results into increase in profit.

(ii) Reduction in managerial expenses :

The managerial expenses of number of concerns, such as office, administration, selling and distribution etc. are saved through complete consolidation.

(iii) Monopoly :

Business combination gives rise to monopoly so that benefits of monopoly may be utlised in a particular trade.

(iv) Large scale economies :

As the result of amalgamation the funds may be increased at sufficient level. The business is carried on a large scale, because of which large scale economies may be resulted.

(v) Increase in efficiency :

Amalgamation results into divisions of work. Due to division of work managerial efficiency might be increased which increases overall business efficiency.

2.5 Accounting Methods and Procedure :

In the case of amalgamation old firms loose their existence and a new firm comes into existence. It therefore becomes necessary to close the books of accounts of each old firm and to open the books of the new firm. Thus the amalgamation involves (a) accounting procedure in the books of the old firms (b) accounting procedure in the books of the new firm.

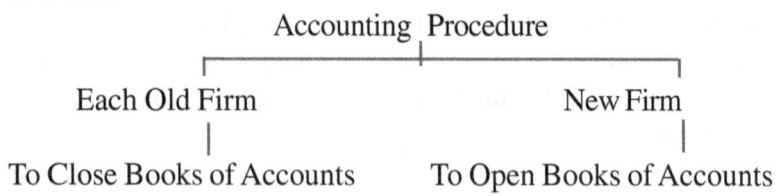

Accounting Procedure

Each Old Firm   New Firm

To Close Books of Accounts   To Open Books of Accounts

2.5.1 (A) Accounting procedure in the books of Old Firms :

The accounting procedure for closing the books of accounts involves the following steps :

(1) Revaluation of Assets and Liabilities.

(2) Valuation of Goodwill.

(3) Treatment of an asset or liability not taken over.

(4) Treatment of Reserves and Profit and Loss Account if any.

(5) Closing the books by transferring assets, liabilities (taken over at agreed value) and Partner's Capital Accounts balances.

(1) Revaluation of assets and liabilities taken over by the new firm :

Normally in case of amalgamation, it happens that new firm does not take over all the assets and liabilities at book value. The new firm assumes the assets and liabilities at revised value; so that any firm should not be benefited due to appreciation in the value of asset or any firm should not suffer loss due to depreciation of asset. Therefore, both the firms agree that all assets and liabilities must be transferred at proper values to the new firm.

For the purpose of revaluation of assets and liabilities an account is opened called Profit & Loss Account or Revaluation Account. Any decrease in the value of asset and increase in the value of liability will be debited to P and L Adjustment Account. On the other hand any increase in the value of asset and decrease in the value of liability will be credited to P and L Adjustment Account. The profit or loss on such revaluation will be transferred to Partner's capital account in their profit sharing ratio. In short, loss on account of revaluation will be debited and profit on account of revaluation will be credited to P & L Adjustment Account.

(2) Valuation of Goodwill :

Next step is to value the goodwill of each old firm engaged in the same line of business. This is because the standing of old firms in the same line of business may not be the same, on the date of amalgamation. Hence, each old firm has to value its own goodwill.

Goodwill is to be created in the books of each old firm at an agreed value. For this purpose, the Goodwill Account is to be debited and

Partner's Capital Accounts to be credited in their profit sharing ratio.

If the goodwill already appears in the balance sheet as an asset then it is to be debited or credited to the P & L Adjustment Account as it is the case of revaluation of asset.

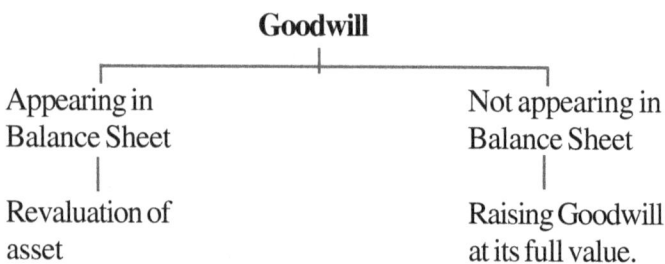

Goodwill

Appearing in Balance Sheet — Revaluation of asset

Not appearing in Balance Sheet — Raising Goodwill at its full value.

(3) Asset/Liability not taken over :

Some time it may happen that, a new firm may not a agree to take over a particular asset or a liability of the old firms. Therefore, an accounting treatment of such an item must also be considered.

(a) Treatment of Asset not taken over :

(i) Transferring to Partner's Capital Account; or

(ii) Selling if off and transferring Profit of Loss on sale of such an asset to P and L Adjustment Account.

(b) Treatment of Liability not taken over :

(i) Transferring to Partner's Capital Account; or

(ii) Paying it off and transferring profit or loss on settlement of such liability to P and L Adjustment Account.

(4) Reserves and Profit and Loss A/c, if any :

Transfer all reserves like General Reserve, Reserve Fund etc. to Partner's Capital accounts in their profit sharing ratio. Similarly transfer the P & L A/c Balance (Debit or Credit) appearing in the balance sheet to the partner's capital accounts in their profit sharing ratio.

(5) Closing the Books of Accounts :

After considering all above procedures the last step is to close the books of accounts of each old firm.

This involves :

(i) Transferring assets taken over to the new firm at agreed values.

(ii) Transferring liabilities taken over at agreed values to the new firm.

(iii) Transferring final capital balances of the partners to the new firm.

Journal entries in the books of old firm :
(1) Revaluation of Assets and Liabilities :
(i) When the value of asset decreased

    Profit and Loss Adjustment A/c................   Dr.

       To Asset A/c

(ii) When the value of asset increased

       To Asset A/c ....   Dr.

    To Profit and Loss Adjustment A/c

(iii) When the value of liability increased

    Profit and Loss Adjustment A/c...............Dr.

       To Liability A/c

(iv) When the value of liability decreased

    Liability A/c ....   Dr.

       To Profit and Loss Adjustment A/c

(v) If Profit on Revaluation

    Profit and Loss Adjustment A/c ....Dr.

       To Partner's Capital A/c

(vi) If Loss on Revaluation

    Partner's Capital A/c ....   Dr.

       To Profit and Loss A/c

(2) Valuation of Goodwill :
    Goodwill A/c ....   Dr.

       To Partner's Capital A/c

    (Being goodwill created in the books)

(3) Undistributed Profit and Reserve :
(i) P and L A/c (Credit Bal.) Reserve

    Profit & Loss A/c ....   Dr.

    Reserve A/c ....   Dr.

       To Partner's Capital A/c.

    (Being P and L A/c Credit Bal. and Reserve distributed among Partners in their Profit sharing ratio)

(ii) P and L A/c (Debit balance)

    Partner's Capital A/c ....   Dr.

       To P and L A/c

    (Being accumulated loss distributed among Partner's in their Profit sharing ratio)

(4) If any Asset and Liabilities not taken over by new firm :

    (i) If asset realised in cash

        Cash/Bank A/c ....   Dr.

           To Asset A/c

    (ii) If asset taken over by particular partner

        Partner's Capital A/c ....   Dr.

           To Asset A/c

    (iii) If liability paid in cash

        Liabilities A/c ....   Dr.

           To Cash/Bank

    (iv) If liability assumed by partner

        Liability A/c ....   Dr.

           To Partner's Capital A/c

Note : (1) If any asset or liability not realised or paid off or not taken over by any particular partner then it will be distributed among all partner's in their capital ratio unless otherwise stated.

    (ii) Loss or Profit on above will be transferred to P and L Adj. A/c

(5) Transfer of Assets and Liabilities to New Firm :

    New firm A/c .... Dr. (Difference between Assets and

                                   Liabilities taken over).

    Liabilities A/c .... Dr. (Agreed value)

      To Assets A/c   (Agreed value)

    (Being Assets and Liabilities transferred to new Firms)

(6) Transfer of Capitals to the New firm :

    Partner's capital A/c ....Dr.

      To New Firm A/c

    (Being Capitals transferred to New Firm)

    From the above journal entires generally the following three ledger accounts are to be opened to close the books of each old firm.

(1) Profit and Loss Adjustment A/c
(Revaluation - A/c)

Dr.   **Cr.**

Particulars	Rs.	Particulars	Rs.
To Assets (Decrease)	-	By Assets (Increase)	-
To Liabilities (Increase)	-	By Liabilities (Decrease)	-
To Profit Transferred	-	By Loss Transferred	-
to A -	-	to A -	-
B -	-	B -	-

(2) Partner's Capital Accounts

Particulars	A	B	Particulars	A	B
To P & L A/c	-	-	By Bal. b/d	-	-
(As per B/S)			(As per B/s)		
To Drawings	-	-	By Gen. Reserve	-	-
To Asset A/c	-	-	By P and L A/c	-	-
(Not taken over)			(As per B/s)		
To Bal. transferred		-	By Goodwill A/c	-	-
to New Firm.			(Created)		
			By Liability A/c		
			(Not taken over)		

(3) New Firm's Account

Particulars			Particulars		
To * Net Assets A/c	-	-	By A's Capital A/c	-	-
	-	-	By B's Capital A/c	-	-

* Net Assets :
    Total Agreed Values of
    Assets taken over by new firm.
    Less : Total agreed values of liabilities taken over.

    ----

* Net Asset's, Value - Debited to New Firm's A/c.

2.5.2 (B) Accounting Procedure in the books of New Firm :

The new firm comes into existence under the new name and style by taking over assets and liabilities from each old firm. Therefore it becomes necessary to incorporate such assets and liabilities which belong to the new firm. Sometimes, the goodwill account is to be written off in the books of the new firm. Sometimes, the partners' capital accounts are to be adjusted taking into account the capital requirement of the new firm. Therefore, the accounting procedure in the new firm involves the following steps :

(1) Recording of Assets and Liabilities taken over.

(2) Writing off Goodwill Account.

(3) Adjustment of Capital Accounts.

(4) Preparation of Opening Balance Sheet.

For these procedures the following journal entires are to be passed in the books of new firm.

(1) Recording Assets and Liabilities Taken Over :

Assets A/c...................... Dr.
    To Liabilities A/c
    To Partner's Capital A/c

(2) Treatment of Goodwill :

(i) In the books of new firm partner may decide that value of goodwill should be retained as it is like any other asset. In such a case no further entry is required.

(ii) If partner decides that the value of goodwill should be written off from the books of accounts, in such a case Partner's Capital Account will be debited with new profit sharing ratio and goodwill account will be credited with full value. The journal entry will be :

Partner's Capital A/c ....Dr.
    To Goodwill A/c
    (Being Goodwill written off)

(3) Adjustment of Capitals :

Usually total capital of the new firm will be decided by all partners. They also decide that capital accounts should be adjusted according to their profit sharing ratio. In such circumstances, if the original capital of a partner is less than the prescribed amount, he will bring necessary cash and the partner whose capital is more than the required amount, the excess amount may be paid in cash or transferred to his current account.

(i) If necessary cash brought in by the partner
    Cash A/c .... Dr.
    To Partner's Capital A/c
(ii) If necessary cash paid to partner
    Partner's Capital A/c ....Dr.
        To Cash

OR

(iii) If (necessary) excess capital transferred to current A/c
    Partner's Capital A/c .... Dr.
        To partner's Current A/c

4) From the above journal entries new firm will prepare its opening balance-sheet as follows :

Opening Balance - Sheet of New Firm As on................

Liabilities	Rs.	Assets	Rs.
Creditors		Machinery	
AB -	-	AB -	-
+ CD -		+ CD -	
------		------	
B.P.		Building	
AB	-	AB -	-
+ CD		+ CD -	
------		------	
Partner's Capital A/cs (if any)			

Liabilities	Rs.	Assets	Rs.
A -		Stock	
B -	-	AB -	-
C -		+ CD -	
D -		------	
Partner's current A/c		Debtors	
A -	-	AB -	-
B -		+ CD -	
C -		------	
D -		Cash	
		AB -	
		+ CD -	
		+ Brought in	
		by partners	-

2.6 Illustrations :

Illustration 1 : Two partnership firms, carrying on business under the styles of Black & Co., and White & Co. respectively, decide to amalgamate into Gray & Co. with effect from 1st April,1998. The respective Balance Sheets as on 31st March 2013 are :

Balance Sheet of Black & Co. as at 31st March 2013

Liabilities	Rs.	Assets	Rs.
Mr B's Capital Account	19,000	Plant and Machinery	10,000
Sundry Creditors	10,000	Stock in Trade	20,000
Bank Overdraft	15,000	Sundry Debtors	10,000
		Mr.A's Capital Account	4,000
	44,000		44,000

A and B share profits and losses in the proportion of 1:2.

Balance Sheet of White & Co. as at 31st March 2013

Liabilities	Rs.	Assets	Rs.
Mr X's Capital Account	10,000	Goodwill	10,000
Mr.Y's Capital Account	2,000	Stock in Trade	5,000
Sundry Creditors	28,000	Sundry Debtors	10,000
		Cash in Hand	6,000
		Cash at Bank	9,000
	40,000		40,000

X and Y share profits and losses equally. The following further information is given :

All fixed assets are to be devalued by 20%. All Stock in trade is to be appreciated by 50%. Black & Co., owns Rs.5000 to White & Co. as on 31st March 2013. This debt is settled at Rs.2000. Goodwill is to be ignored for the purpose of the amalgamation. The fixed capital accounts in the new firm are to be. Mr A Rs.2000 Mr B Rs.3000 Mr X Rs.1000 Mr. Y Rs.4000. Mr B takes over the bank overdraft of Black & Co. and gifts to Mr A the amount of money to be brought in by Mr. A to make up his capital contribution. Mr. X is paid off in cash from White & Co. and Mr. Y brings in sufficient cash to make up his required capital contribution. Pass the journal entries to close the books of both the firms as on 31st March 2013.

Solution :

Journal of Black & Co.

Particulars	Debit Rs	Credit (Rs.)
Revaluation A/c Dr. To Plant and Machinery (For Plant and Machinery devalued by 20%)	2,000	2,000
Stock in Trade A/c Dr. Sundry Creditors A/c Dr. To Revaluation A/c (For appreciation of stock in trade and debt owing to White & Co.settled for Rs.2,000 instead of Rs.5,000)	10,000 3,000	13,000
Bank Overdraft Dr. To A's Capital A/c To B's Capital A/c (For profit on revaluation transferred to capital accounts in the profit sharing ratio)	15,000	15,000

(Contd.)

Particulars	Debit Rs	Credit (Rs.)
Revaluation A/c Dr.	11,000	
To A's Capital A/c		3,667
To B's Capital A/c		7,333
(For profit on revaluation transferred to Capital accounts in the profit sharing ratio)		
Grey & Co. Dr.	41,000	
Sundry Creditors A/c Dr.	7,000	
To Plant & Machinery A/c		8,000
To Stock in Trade		30,000
To Sundry Debtors		10,000
(For assets and liabilities transferred to Grey & Co. for closing the books of the firm)		
A's Capital A/c Dr.	2,000	
B's Capital A/c Dr.	39,000	
To Grey & Co.		41,000
(Capital accounts of the partners closed by transfer to Grey & Co.)		

Note : The Accounting entries show that B's Capital Account has a credit balance of Rs.39,000 which is in excess by Rs.36000 of his required capital contribution. Since there are no liquid assets in Black & Co., from which B can be repaid, the excess amount will be taken in Grey & Co. as a loan from B.

Journal of White & Co.

Particulars	Debit Rs	Credit (Rs.)
Stock in Trade Dr.	2,500	
To Revaluation A/c		2,500
(For Stock in trade appreciated by 50%)		
Revaluation A/c Dr.	13,000	
To Sundry Debtors		3,000
To Goodwill		10,000
(For debt due from Black & Co. settled at a concession of Rs.3000; goodwill written off)		

Particulars		Debit Rs	Credit (Rs.)
X's Capital A/c	Dr.	5,250	
Y's Capital A/c	Dr.	5,250	
To Revaluation A/c			10,500
(For loss on Revaluation debited to partner's capital A/cs)			
Cash A/c	Dr.	7,250	
To Y's Capital A/c			7,250
(For cash introduced by Y to make up his capital to Rs.4000)			
X's Capital A/c	Dr.	3,750	
To Cash A/c			3,750
(For excess capital refunded to X to reduce his capital to Rs.1,000)			
Grey & Co.	Dr.	5,000	
Sundry Creditors	Dr.	28,000	
To Stock in trade			7,500
To Sundry Debtors			7,000
To Cash in Hand			9,500
To Cash at Bank			9,000
(For sundry assets and liabilities transferred to Grey & Co. to close the books)			
X's Capital A/c	Dr.	1,000	
Y's Capital A/c	Dr.	4,000	
To Grey & Co.			5,000
(for Capital accounts of partners closed by transfer to Grey Co.)			

Illustration 2 : X and Y are partners of X and Co., sharing profits and losses in the ratio of 3 : 1 and Y and Z are partners of Y & Co., sharing profits and losses in the ratio of 2 : 1. On 31st March, 2013 they decide to amalgamate and form a new firm M/s XYZ & Co., wherein X, Y and Z would be partners profits and losses in the ratio of 3 : 2 : 1. The Balance Sheets of two firms on the above date are as under.

Liabilities	X & Co Rs	Y & Co Rs	Assets	X & Co Rs	Y & Co Rs
Capitals :			Fixed Assets :		
X	4,80,000	-	Building	1,00,000	-
Y	3,20,000	4,00,000	Machinery	3,00,000	3,20,000
Z	-	2,00,000	Furniture	40,000	12,000
Reserve	1,00,000	3,00,000	Current Assets :		
Creditors	2,40,000	2,32,000	Stock	2,40,000	2,80,000
Due to X & Co.	-	2,00,000	Debtors	3,20,000	4,00,000
Bank Loan	1,60,000	-	Cash at Bank	60,000	1,80,000
			Cash in hand	40,000	20,000
			Due from Y & Co	2,00,000	-
			Advance	-	1,20,000
	13,00,000	13,32,000		13,00,000	13,32,000

The amalgamated firm took over the business on the following terms :

(a) Building of X & Co. was valued at Rs.2,00,000 b) Machinery of X & Co., was valued at Rs.4,50,000 and that of Y & Co. at Rs.4,00,000. c) Goodwill valued X and Co. Rs. 1,00,000 and Y & Co., Rs.82,000 but the same will not appear in the books of XYZ & Co., d) Partners of the new firm will bring the necessary cash to pay other partners to adjust their capitals according to the profit sharing ratio. Show journal entries in the books of M/S. XYZ & Co. and Prepare the Balance Sheet as on 31.3.2013.

Solution :

Journal of XYZ & Co.

Particulars		Debit Rs	Credit (Rs.)
Goodwill A/c	Dr.	1,00,000	
Building A/c	Dr.	2,00,000	
Machinery A/c	Dr.	4,50,000	
Furniture A/c	Dr.	40,000	
Stock A/c	Dr.	2,40,000	
Debtors A/c	Dr.	3,20,000	

Particulars		Debit Rs	Credit (Rs.)
Cash at Bank A/c	Dr.	60,000	
Cash in hand A/c	Dr.	40,000	
Due from Y & Co. A/c	Dr.	2,00,000	
To Creditors A/c			2,40,000
To Bank Loan A/c			1,60,000
To X's Capital A/c			8,17,500
To Y's Capital A/c			4,32,500
(Being the Assets and Liabilities of X. & Co. taken over)			
Goodwill A/c	Dr.	82,000	
Machinery A/c	Dr.	4,00,000	
Furniture A/c	Dr.	12,000	
Stock A/c	Dr.	2,80,000	
Debtors A/c	Dr.	4,00,000	
Cash at Bank A/c	Dr.	1,80,000	
Cash in hand A/c	Dr.	20,000	
Advances A/c	Dr.	1,20,000	
To Creditors A/c			2,32,000
To Due to X & Co. A/c			2,00,000
To Y's Capital A/c			7,08,000
To Z's Capital A/c			3,54,000
(Being the Assets and Liabilities of Y & Co. taken over)			
X's Capital A/c	Dr.	91,000	
Y's Capital A/c	Dr.	60,667	
Z's Capital A/c	Dr.	30,333	
To Goodwill A/c			1,82,000
(Being Goodwill written off)			
Bank A/c	Dr.	3,69,833	
To X's Capital A/c			3,38,500
To Z's Capital A/c			31,333
(Being the Cash brought in by X and Z to make capitals proportionate)			
Y's Capital A/c	Dr.	3,69,833	
To Bank A/c			3,69,833
(Being the excess capital withdrawn by Y)			
Due to X & Co. A/c	Dr.	2,00,000	
To Due from Y & Co., A/c			2,00,000
(Being the elimination of mutual indebtedness of the merged firms X & Co., and Y & Co.)			

Balance Sheet of M/s XYZ & Co. as on 31st March 2013

Liabilities		Rs.	Assets	Rs.
Capitals :			Building	2,00,000
	X	10,65,000	Machinery	8,50,000
	Y	7,10,000	Furniture	52,000
	Z	3,55,000	Stock	5,20,000
Creditors		4,72,000	Debtors	7,20,000
Bank Loan		1,60,000	Advances	1,20,000
			Cash at Bank	2,40,000
			Cash in hand	60,000
		27,62,000		27,62,000

Working Notes :

(i) Statements Showing the Computation of Purchase Consideration

	Particulars	X & Co.	Y & Co.
A	Assets:		
	Goodwill	1,00,000	82,000
	Building	2,00,000	-
	Machinery	4,50,000	4,00,000
	Furniture	40,000	12,000
	Stock	2,40,000	2,80,000
	Debtors	3,20,000	4,00,000
	Cash at Bank	60,000	1,80,000
	Cash in Hand	40,000	20,000
	Due from Y & Co.	2,00,000	-
	Advances	-	1,20,000
		16,50,000	14,94,000
B	Liabilities		
	Creditors	2,40,000	2,32,000
	Due to X & Co.	-	2,00,000
	Bank Loan	1,60,000	-
		4,00,000	4,32,000
C	Purchase Consideration (A-B)	12,50,000	10,62,000

(ii) Statements Showing the Computation of Proportionate Capital

	Particulars	Rs.
A	M/s XYZ & Co. (Rs.12,50,000+ Rs.10,62,000)	23,12,000
B	Less: Goodwill Adjustment	-1,82,000
C	Total Capital of new firm	21,30,000
D	X's Proportionate Capital (Rs.21,30,000*3/6)	10,65,000
E	Y's Proportionate Capital (Rs.21,30,000*2/6)	7,10,000
F	Z's Proportionate Capital (Rs.21,30,000*1/6)	3,55,000
		21,30,000

(iii) Statements Showing the Computation of Capital Adjustment.

Particulars	X	Y	Z	Total
	Rs.	Rs.	Rs.	Rs.
Balance transferred from X and Co.	8,17,500	4,32,500	-	12,50,000
Balance transferred from Y and Co.	-	7,08,000	3,54,000	10,62,000
	8,17,500	11,40,500	3,54,000	23,12,000
Less : Goodwill written off in				
ratio of (3:2:1)	91,000	60,667	30,333	1,82,000
(a) Existing Capital	7,26,500	10,79,833	3,23,667	21,30,000
(b) Proportionate Capital	10,65,000	7,10,000	3,55,000	21,30,000
(c) Amount to be brought in				
(paid off) [(a) - (b)]	3,38,500	(3,69,833)	31,333	-

Dr.   **Capital Accounts (In the Books of X & Co.)**   **Cr.**

Particulars	Total	Total	Particulars	Total	Total
	Rs.	Rs.		Rs.	Rs.
To Capital A/c-M/s	8,17,500	4,32,500	By Balance b/d	4,80,000	3,20,000
XYZ & Co. (Transfer)			By Reserve (3:1)	75,000	25,000
			By Goodwill (3:1)	75,000	25,000
			By Realisation A/c*		
			- Profit (3:1)	1,87,500	62,500
	8,17,500	4,32,500		8,17,500	4,32,500

* For Building Rs.1,00,000 and Machinery Rs.1,50,000.

Dr. **Capital Accounts (In the Books of Y & Co.)** **Cr.**

Particulars	Total Rs.	Total Rs.	Particulars	Total Rs.	Total Rs.
To Capital A/c-M/s XYZ & Co. (Transfer)	7,08,000	3,54,000	By Balance b/d	4,00,000	2,00,000
			By Reserve (2:1)	2,00,000	1,00,000
			By Goodwill (2:1)	54,667	27,333
			By Realisation A/c*		
			- Profit (2:1)	53,333	26,667
	7,08,000	3,54,000		7,08,000	3,54,000

* For Machinery Rs. 80,000.

Illustration 3 : Following were the Balance Sheets as on December 31, 2012 of two firms M/s A & B and M/s C & D.

Balance Sheet

Particulars	Total Rs.	Total Rs.	Particulars	Total Rs.	Total Rs.
Sundry Creditors	20,000	10,000	Cash at Bank	15,000	8,000
Bills payable	5,000	-	Investments at cost	10,000	8,000
Bank overdraft	2,000	10,000	Debtors 10000		
A's Loan	6,000	-	Less		
Capitals - A	35,000		Provision 1000	9,000	8,000
B	22,000		Furniture	12,000	6,000
C		36,000	Premises	30,000	
D		20,000	Land	-	50,000
General reserve	8,000	3,000	Machinery	15,000	-
Investment fluctuation			Goodwill	9,000	-
fund	2,000	1,000			
	1,00,000	80,000		1,00,000	80,000

The two firms decided to amalgamate their business on 1st January, 2013. For this purpose it was decided that the new firm shall not take furniture of both the firms and shall take over investment at 10% depreciation, land at Rs.80,000, premises at Rs.45,000, machinery at Rs.9000. New firm agreed to take over only trade liabilities of both the firms. They are to pay Rs.12000 to each firm for goodwill. Unrecorded typewriter with C and D, valued at Rs.800, was not taken over by the new firm. The capital of the new firm was agreed at Rs.160000 to be divided among partners equally. You are required to pass journal entries and prepare balance sheet of the new firm.

Books of M/s A and B
Journal Entries

Investment fluctuation fund account	Dr.	1,000	
To Investment account			1,000
(Fall in value on investment met out of fluctuation fund)			
Premises account	Dr.	15,000	
Goodwill account	Dr.	3,000	
To Revaluation account			18,000
(Being profit on revaluation)			
Revaluation account	Dr.	6,000	
To Machinery account			6,000
(Being loss on revaluation)			
Revaluation account	Dr.	12,000	
To A's Capital account			6,000
To B's Capital account			6,000
(Being profit on revaluation transferred to capital accounts)			
Investment fluctuation fund account	Dr.	1,000	
General reserve account	Dr.	8,000	
To A's Capital A/c			4,500
To B's Capital A/c			4,500
(Being accumulated profit distributed between partners in profit-sharing ratio)			
Bank overdraft account	Dr.	2,000	
A's Loan account	Dr.	6,000	
To Bank account			8,000
(Payment of liabilities not taken over)			

A's Capital A/c	Dr.	6,000	
B's Capital A/c	Dr.	6,000	
To Furniture account			12,000
(Assets not taken over transferred to capital accounts in the profit-sharing ratio)			
New firm account	Dr.	92,000	
To Bank account			7,000
To Investment account			9,000
To Debtors account			10,000
To Premises account			45,000
To Machinery account			9,000
To Goodwill account			12,000
(Being assets taken over at revised values transferred to new firm)			
Sundry creditors account	Dr.	20,000	
Bills payable account	Dr.	5,000	
Provision for doubtful debts account	Dr.	1,000	
To New firm account			26,000
(Being trade liabilities taken over transferred)			
A's Capital A/c	Dr.	39,500	
B's Capital A/c	Dr.	26,500	
To New firm account			66,000
(Being the elimination of capital accounts and new firm's account)			

Books of M/s C and D
Journal Entries

Typewriter account	Dr.	800	
Land account	Dr.	30,000	
Goodwill account	Dr.	12,000	
To Revaluation account			42,800
(Profit on revaluation of assets)			
Revaluation account	Dr.	42,800	
To C's Capital account			21,400
To D's Capital account			21,400
(Profit on revaluation transferred to capital accounts in profit-sharing ratio)			

Investment fluctuation fund account	Dr.	800	
To Investments account			800
(Loss on investments transferred to fund account)			
Investment fluctuation fund account	Dr.	200	
General reserve account	Dr.	3,000	
To C's Capital A/c			1,600
To D's Capital A/c			1,600
(Being accumulated profits transferred to capital accounts)			
Bank overdraft account	Dr.	10,000	
To C's capital account			5,000
To D's capital account			5,000
(Being non-trade liabilities not taken over tranferred to capital accounts in profit-sharing ratio)			
C's Capital A/c	Dr.	3,400	
D's Capital A/c	Dr.	3,400	
To Typewriter account			800
To Furniture account			6,000
(Being assets non taken over transferred to capital accounts in the profit-sharing ratio)			
New firm's account	Dr.	1,15,200	
To Bank account			8,000
To Investment account			7,200
To Debtors account			8,000
To Land account			80,000
To Goodwill account			12,000
(Being assets taken over transferred to new firm at agreed value)			
Sundry creditors account	Dr.	10,000	10,000
To New firm's account			
(Being liability taken over transferred to new firm)			
C's Capital A/c	Dr.	60,600	
D's Capital A/c	Dr.	44,600	1,05,200
To New firm's account			
(Being elimination of capital accounts and the account of the new firm's)			

Books of New Firm
Journal Entries

Bank account	Dr.	7,000		
Investment account	Dr.	9,000		
Debtors account	Dr.	10,000		
Premises account	Dr.	45,000		
Machinery account	Dr.	9,000		
Goodwill account	Dr.	12,000		
To Sundry creditors account			20,000	
To Bills payable account			5,000	
To Provision for doubtful debts account			1,000	
To A's Capital A/c			39,500	
To B's Capital A/c			26,500	
(Being assets and liabilities taken over at revised values credited to capitals of A and B)				
Bank account	Dr.	8,000		
Investment account	Dr.	7,200		
Debtors account	Dr.	8,000		
Land account	Dr.	80,000		
Goodwill account	Dr.	12,000		
To Sundry creditors account			10,000	
To C's Capital A/c			60,600	
To D's Capital A/c			44,600	
(Being assets and liabilities of the firm C & D taken over at revised values)				
A's Current A/c	Dr.	500		
B's Current A/c	Dr.	13,500		
To A'c Capital account			500	
To B'c Capital account			13,500	
(Being amount short of Rs.40000 debited to current accounts)				
C's Capital A/c	Dr.	20,600		
D's Capital A/c	Dr.	4,600		
To C's Current A/c			20,600	
To D's Current A/c			4,600	
(Being amount excess over Rs.40000 transferred to respective current accounts)				

New Firm
Balance Sheet
as on 1st January 2013

Liabilities	Rs.	Assets		Rs.
Sundry Creditors	30,000	Bank		15,000
Bills payable	5,000	Investments		16,200
Capitals :		Debtors	18000	
A	40,000	Less : Prov.	1000	17,000
B	40,000	Machinery		9,000
C	40,000	Premises		45,000
D	40,000	Land		80,000
Current accounts :		Goodwill		24,000
C	20,600	Current accounts :		
D	4,600	A	500	
		B	13500	14,000
	2,20,200			2,20,200

Notes :

1. Loss on investment is to be met out of investment fluctuation fund and remaining fund is treated as accumulated profit.

2. Since there is insufficient bank balance in the firm C & D. liabilities not taken over have been transferred to capital accounts.

3. Trade liabilities include liabilities on account of goods. Bank overdraft is a liability but not a trade liability. Similarly salary outstanding, loans are all liabilities but not trade liabilities.

Illustration 4 :

Ram and Shyam were partners sharing profits and losses in the ratio of 3:1 respectively. Their balance sheet as at 31st December 2012 was as under.

Balance Sheet as on 31-12-2012

Liabilities		Rs.	Assets		Rs.
Sundry Creditors		42,000	Cash at Bank		9,500
General Reserve		8,000	Bills receivable		6,000
Capitals		1,00,000	Debtors 20000		19,500
Ram	60000		- R.D.D. 500		
Shyam	40000				
			Stock		50,000
			Furniture		5,000
			Land & Building		60,000
		1,50,000			1,50,000

Following is the Balance Sheet of Anil and Sunil sharing profits and losses in the ratio of 3:2 respectively.

Balance Sheet as on 31-12-2012

Liabilities		Rs.	Assets		Rs.
Sundry Creditors		30,000	Cash at Bank		3,000
P & L A/c		15,000	Sundry		
Capitals		60,000	Debtors 30000		
Anil	40000		Less R.D.D. 500		29,500
Sunil	20000		Stock		10,000
			Machinery		26,000
			Buildings		36,500
		1,05,000			1,05,000

The two firms were amalgamated on that date and assets and liabilities were revalued as follows :

(i) Goodwill of Ram and Shyam was valued at Rs.20000 and that of Anil and Sunil was valued at Rs.30000 respectively.

(ii) Furniture was not taken over by the New firm which Ram agreed to take for Rs.4500.

(iii) Land and Building of Ram and Shyam was valued at Rs.64000 while that of Anil and Sunil at Rs.34500.

(iv) Reserve for doubtful debts was to be maintained at 5% on debtors of both the firms.

(v) Stock of Ram and Shyam was over valued by Rs.4000 and that of Anil and Sunil was under valued by Rs.5000.

Close the books of old firms and give opening entries and Balance Sheet after amalgamation in the books of New Firm.

Solution :

In the Books of Ram and Shyam
Profit and Loss Adjustment A/c

To Furniture (loss)	500	By Land & Building		4,000
To R.D.D.	500	By Capital A/c (loss)		
To Stock	4,000	Ram -	750	
		Shyam -	250	1,000
	5,000			5,000

Capital Account

Liabilities	Ram	Shyam	Assets	Ram	Shyam
Furniture	4,500	-	By Bal. b/d	60,000	40,000
P & L Adj.			By General		
A/c (loss)	750	250	Reserve	6,000	2,000
New Firm A/c			By Goodwill A/c	15,000	5,000
(transfer)	75,750	46,750			
	81,000	47,000		81,000	47,000

New Firm A/c

To Net Assets	1,22,500	By Ram Capital A/c	75,750
		By Shyam Capital A/c	46,750
	1,22,500		1,22,500

Goodwill A/c

To Ram Capital A/c	15,000	By Balance c/d	20,000
To Shyam Capital A/c	5,000	(transferred to New Firm)	
	20,000		20,000

Working Note :
(1) Calculation of Sundry Net Assets

Assets taken over (Agreed Value)	Rs.
Cash	9,500
Debtors	6,000
Stock	20,000
Machinery	46,000
Land and Building	64,000
Goodwill	20,000
	1,65,500
Less Liabilities taken over	
Creditors 42000	-
R.D.D. 1000	43,000
Net Assets Rs.	1,22,500

In the Books of Anil and Sunil
Profit and Loss Adjustment A/c

Liabilities	Rs.	Assets	Rs.
To Land & Building	2,000	By Stock	5,000
To R.D.D.	1,000		
To Capital A/c (Profit)			
Anil 1200			
Sunil 800	2,000		
	5,000		5,000

Capital Account

	Anil	Sunil		Anil	Sunil
To New Firm A/c	68,200	38,800	By Bal. b/d	40,000	20,000
(transfer)			By P & L A/c	9,000	6,000
			By Goodwill A/c	18,000	12,000
			By P & L Adji A/c		
			(Profit)	1,200	800
	68,200	38,800		68,200	38,800

New Firm Account

To Net Assets		1,07,000	By Anil Capital A/c	68,200
			By Sunil Capital A/c	38,800
		1,07,000		1,07,000

Goodwill A/c

To Anil Capital A/c	18,000	By Balance c/d	
To Sunil Capital A/c	12,000	(transferred to New Firm)	30,000
	30,000		30,000

Working Note :
(i) Calculation of Net Assets

Assets taken over (Agreed Value)		Rs.
Cash		3,000
Debtors		30,000
Stock		15,000
Machinery		26,000
Building		34,500
Goodwill		30,000
		1,38,500
Less Liabilities taken over		
Creditors	30000	
R.D.D.	1500	31,500
Net Assets Rs.		1,07,000

In the Books of New Firm (Ram, Shyam, Anil and Sunil)
Opening Journal Entries

(i) Incorporation of Assets and Liabilities of Ram and Shyam

Cash A/c .... Dr.	9,500
Bills Receivable A/c....................... Dr.	6,000
Debtor's A/c................................... Dr.	20,000
Stock A/c....................................... Dr.	46,000
Land & Building A/c .... Dr.	64,000
Goodwill A/c................................... Dr.	20,000

To Creditors A/c		42,000
To R.D.D. A/c		1,000
To Ram's Capital A/c		75,750
To Shyam's Capital A/c		46,750
(Being various Asses and Liabilities incorported)		

(ii) Incorporation of Assets and Liabilities of Anil and Sunil

Cash A/c	Dr.	3,000	
Debtors A/c	Dr.	30,000	
Stock A/c	Dr.	15,000	
Machinery A/c	Dr.	26,000	
Building A/c	Dr.	34,500	
Goodwill A/c	Dr.	30,000	
To Creditors A/c			30,000
To R.D.D.			1,500
To Anil's Capital A/c			68,200
To Sunil's Capital A/c			38,800

(Being various Assets and Liabilities incorporated)

Balance Sheet as on 1-1-2013

Liabilities	Rs.	Assets		Rs.
Capital Accounts		Goodwill		50,000
Ram	75,750	Land & Building		98,500
Shyam	46,750	Machinery		26,000
Anil	68,200	Stock		61,000
Sunil	38,800	Debtors	50000	
Sundry Creditors	72,000	- R.D.D.	2500	47,500
		Bills Receivable		6,000
		Cash		12,500
	3,01,500			3,01,500

Illustration 5 :

The following are the Balance Sheets of two firms M/s Slow and Fast and M/s Black and White as on 31st Dec.2012.

Balance Sheet as on 31-12-2012

Liabilities	Slow & Fast Rs.	Black & White Rs.	Assets	Slow & Fast Rs.	Black & White Rs.
Sundry Creditors	16,000	23,000	Land & Building	-	50,000
Reserve	10,000	-	Plant &		
Capital Accounts			Machinery	20,000	30,000
Slow	40,000		Patents	10,000	5,000
Fast	10,000		Stock	25,000	20,000
Black		50,000	Debtors	10,000	16,000
White		50,000	Investment	5,000	-
			Cash	6,000	2,000
	76,000	1,23,000		76,000	1,23,000

Slow and Fast sharing profits and losses in the ratio of 3:2 and Black and White sharing equally. The two decided to amalgamate their business on the following terms.

(i) Investment of Slow and Fast were not to be taken over by the new firm but were to be distributed among partner's in their profit sharing ratio.

(ii) Goodwill of Slow and Fast was valued of Rs.20000 and that of Black and White at Rs.40000. Goodwill was not to remain in the books of the New Firm.

(iii) Patents of Slow and Fast were valued at Rs.15000 and stock at Rs.30000. A provision of 8% was to be created on Debtors.

(iv) The Plant & Machinery of Black and White was to be written down to Rs.25000. Stock of Black and White was found over valued by Rs.2000. A Book debts of Rs.1000 was bad and had to be written off. Patents of Blanc and White were to be valued at Rs.8000.

(v) The new profit sharing ratio will be as under :
Slow - 2/10, Fast 2/10, Black 3/10 and White 3/10.

(vi) The total capital of the new firm was to be Rs.2,00,000 which is to be adjusted according to their new profit sharing ratio. Partners paying in or withdrawing cash as the case may be.

Give journal entries to close the books of the old firms and opening entries in the books of New Firm. Also prepare Balance Sheet after amalgamation.

Solution :

In the Books of Slow and Fast

Date	Particulars	L/F	Debit	Credit)
2012 31 Dec.	Reserve A/c Dr. To Slow Capital A/c To Fast Capital A/c (Being reserve transferred to their capital accounts)		10,000	6,000 4,000
	Slow Capital A/c Dr. Fast Capital A/c Dr. To Investment A/c (Being investment distributed among the partner)		3,000 2,000	5,000
	Goodwill A/c Dr. To Slow Capital A/c To Fast Capital A/c (Being Goodwill created in the books)		20,000	12,000 8,000
	Patent A/c Dr. Stock A/c Dr. To Revaluation A/c (Being increase in value of Assets)		5,000 5,000	10,000
	Revaluation A/c Dr. To R.D.D. A/c (Being Provision for Doubtful Debts created)		800	800
	Revaluation A/c Dr. To Slow Capital A/c To Fast Capital A/c (Being Profit on revaluation transferred to Capital A/c)		9,200	5,520 3,680

Date	Particulars	L/F	Anil	Sunil
2012 31 Dec.	New Firm A/c Dr. To Patent A/c To Plant & Machinery A/c To Stock A/c To Debtors A/c To Cash A/c To Goodwill A/c (Being assets transferred to New Firm at agreed values)		1,01,000	 15,000 20,000 30,000 10,000 6,000 20,000
	Sundry Creditors A/c Dr. R.D.D.A/c Dr. To New Firm A/c (Being Liabilities transferred to New Firm)		16,000 800	 16,800
	Slow Capital A/c Dr. Fast Capital A/c Dr. To New Firm (Being Capitals transferred to the New Firm)		60,520 23,680	 84,200

In the Books of Black & White

Date	Particulars	L/F	Debit	Credit
2012 31 Dec.	Goodwill A/c Dr. To Black Capital A/c To White Capital A/c (Being Goodwill Created in the books)		40,000	 20,000 20,000
	Revaluation A/c Dr. To Plant & Machinery A/c To Stock A/c To Debtors A/c (Being decrease in the value of Assets)		8,000	 5,000 2,000 1,000
	Patents A/c Dr. To Revaluation A/c (Being increase in the value of patent)		3,000	 3,000

Date	Particulars		L/F	Debit	Credit
2012 31 Dec.	Black Capital A/c	Dr.		2,500	
	White Capital A/c	Dr.		2,500	
	To Revaluation A/c				5,000
	(Being Loss on revaluation transferred to Capital Account)				
	New Firm A/c	Dr.		1,58,000	
	To Land & Building A/c				50,000
	To Plant & Machinery A/c				25,000
	To Patent A/c				8,000
	To Stock A/c				18,000
	To Debtors A/c				15,000
	To Cash A/c				2,000
	To Goodwill A/c				40,000
	(Being Assets transferred to the New Firm)				
	Sundry Creditors	Dr.		23,000	
	To New Firm A/c				23,000
	(Being Liabilities transferred to the New Firm)				
	Black Capital A/c	Dr.		67,500	
	White Capital A/c	Dr.		67,500	
	To New Firm A/c				1,35,000
	(Being Capital of the partners transferred to the New Firm)				

In the Books New Firm

Date	Particulars		L/F	Debit	Credit
2012 31 Dec.	Plant & Machinery A/c	Dr.		20,000	
	Patent A/c	Dr.		15,000	
	Stock A/c	Dr.		30,000	
	Debtors A/c	Dr.		10,000	
	Cash A/c	Dr.		6,000	
	Goodwill A/c	Dr.		20,000	

Date	Particulars	L/F	Debit	Credit
2012	To Creditors A/c			16,000
31 Dec.	To R.D.D. A/c			800
	To Slows Capital A/c			60,520
	To Fast Capital A/c			23,680
	(Being various Assets & Liabilities Incorporated)			
	Land & Building A/c Dr.		50,000	
	Plant & Machinery A/c Dr.		25,000	
	Patents A/c Dr.		8,000	
	Stock A/c Dr.		18,000	
	Debtors A/c Dr.		15,000	
	Cash A/c Dr.		2,000	
	Goodwill A/c Dr.		40,000	
	To Sundry Creditors			23,000
	To Black Capital A/c			67,500
	To White Capital A/c			67,500
	(Being various Assets & Liabilities incorporated)			
	Slow Capital A/c Dr.		12,000	
	Fast Capital A/c Dr.		12,000	
	Black Capital A/c Dr.		18,000	
	White Capital A/c Dr.		18,000	
	To Goodwill A/c			60,000
	(Being goodwill written of in new profit sharing ratio)			
	Slow Capital A/c Dr.		8,520	
	To Cash			8,520
	(Being excess cash than required capital refunded)			
	Cash A/c Dr.		49,320	
	To Fast Capital A/c			28,320
	To Black Capital A/c			10,500
	To White Capital A/c			10,500
	(Being required cash brought in by the partners)			

Balance Sheet of the New Firm 1-1-2013

Liabilities	Rs.	Assets		Rs.
Capital Accounts		Land & Building		50,000
Slow	40,000	Plant & Machinery		45,000
Fast	40,000	Patents		23,000
Black	60,000	Stock		48,000
White	60,000	Debtors	25000	
Sundry Creditors	39,000	Less R.D.D.	800	24,200
		Cash		48,800
	2,39,000			2,39,000

Working Notes :
(i) Calculation of Capital
Total Capital fixed in the New Firm Rs.2,00,000

Particulars	Slow	Fast	Black	White
Profit Sharing Ratio	2	2	3	3
Existing capital	60,520	23,680	67,500	67,500
(transferred from old firm)				
Less Goodwill written off	-12,000	-12,000	-18,000	-18,000
(Rs.60,000 in 2:2:3:3)	48,520	11,680	49,500	49,500
Required capital according to				
New Profit				
sharing ratio	40,000	40,000	60,000	60,000
(2,00,000/10 Rs.20,000 per share)				
	+8.520	-28,320	-10,500	-10,500
Cash Brought in by		28,320	10,500	10,500
Cash Paid to Slow	8,520	-		

(ii) Calculation of Cash Balances

Cash transferred from old firms	Rs.
Cash transferred from old firms	8,000
Add Cash Brought in by	49,320
Fast Rs. 28,320	
Black Rs. 10,500	

Cash transferred from old firms	Rs.
White Rs.10500	
	57,320
Less Cash Paid to slow	8,520
Shown in B/s	48,800

Illustration 6 :

Following were the Balance Sheet as at 31st December 2012 of two firms of M/s A and B and M/s C and D who were equal partners.

Balance Sheets

Liabilities	A & B Rs.	C & D Rs.	Assets	A & B Rs.	C & D Rs.
Creditors	40,000	50,000	Cash	11,200	13,400
Mrs. A's Loan	10,000	-	Stock	40,800	36,600
Capital A/c's			Debtors	30,000	40,000
A	80,000		Furniture	8,000	10,000
B	40,000		Premises	80,000	-
C	-	48,000	Investments	-	30,000
D	-	32,000			
	1,70,000	1,30,000		1,70,000	1,30,000

The two firms decided to amalgamate their business from 1st January 2013. For this purpose it was agreed that Mrs. A's Loan should be repaid and the investments of M/s C and D be not taken over by the new firm.

Goodwill of M/s A and B was fixed at Rs.16,000 and that of M/s C and D at Rs.20,000.

Premises were revalue at Rs.1,00,000 but the stock of M/s A and B was found overvalued by Rs.8,000 and the stock of C and D was undervalued by Rs.4,000. A Reserve of 5% on debtor's was necessary for bad debts of both firms.

The total capital of the new firm was to be Rs.1,60,000 and the capital of A,B,C and D was to be their profit sharing ratio which was to 3:2:3:2 respectively.

Prepare Profit and Loss Adjustment and Partners Capital Accounts in the books of each old firm and amalgamated Balance Sheet of the new firm.

Solution :

In the Books of A and B
Profit and Loss Adjustment A/c

To Stock	8,000	By Premises	20,000
To R.D.D.	1,500		
To Capital A/c (Profit)	10,500		
A- 5250			
B- 5250			
	20,000		20,000

Capital Accounts

	A	B		A	B
To New Firm A/c (transfer)	93,250	53,250	By Bal. b/d	80,000	40,000
			By Goodwill A/c	8,000	8,000
			By P & L A/c	5,250	5,250
	93,250	53,250		93,250	53,250

In the Books of C and D
Profit and Loss Adjustment A/c

To R.D.D.	2,000	By Stock	4,000
To Capital A/c (profit)			
C - 1000			
D - 1000	2,000		
	4,000		4,000

Capital Accounts

	C	D		C	D
To Investment	18,000	12,000	By Bal. b/d	48,000	32,000
To New firm A/c	41,000	31,000	By Goodwill A/c	10,000	10,000
(transfer)			By P & L Adj. A/c (Profit)	1,000	1,000
	59,000	43,000		59,000	43,000

Notes :

(i) Out of Cash Balance of Rs.11,200 of M/s A and B Mrs. A's Loan of Rs.10,000 will be paid and Balance of Rs.1,200 will be transferred to New Firm.

(ii) Investment of M/s C and D distributed among them according to their capital ratio, which is 3:2.

(iii) Calculation of Net Assets.

		M/s A&B		M/s C&D
Cash		1,200		13,400
Stock		32,800		40,600
Debtors		30,000		40,000
Furniture		8,000		10,000
Premises		1,00,000		-
Goodwill		16,000		20,000
		1,88,000		1,24,000
Less Liabilities				
Creditors	40,000		50,000	
R.D.D.	1,500	41,500	2,000	52,000
Net Assets Rs.		1,46,500		72,000

In the Books of M/s A, B, C and D
Balance - Sheet of the New firm as on 1.1.2013

Liabilities	Rs.	Assets	Rs.	Rs.
Capital Accounts		Goodwill		36,000
A	48,000	Premises		1,00,000
B	32,000	Furniture		18,000
C	48,000	Stock		73,400
D	32,000	Debtors	70,000	
Current Accounts		- R.D.D.	3,500	
A	45,250			66,500
B	21,250	Cash	14,600	
		+ Brought		
		by C.D.	8,000	22,600
Sundry Creditors	90,000			
	3,16,500			3,16,500

Working Note : (1) Adjustment of Capital
Total capital fixed in the New Firm was Rs.1,60,000

Particulars	A	B	C	D
New Profit Sharing Ratio	3	2	3	2
Existing Capital	93,250	53,250	41,000	31,000
(Transferred form old firm)				
Required capital according				
to New Profit				
Sharing Ratio	48,000	32,000	48,000	32,000
1,60,000/10 = Rs.16,000				
per share				
	+45,250	+21,250	-7000	-1,000
Cash brought in by			7000	1,000
Transferred to				
current A/c	45,250	21,250		
(Because cash is not available)				

Illustration 7 :

Ajit and Sujit are sharing profits and losses in the ratio of 3:2. Their position on 31st December 2012 was as under.

Balance Sheet as on 31st Dec.2012

Liabilities	Rs.	Assets	Rs.
Sundry Creditors	32,000	Machinery	60,000
Reserve	20,000	Stock	50,000
Capital A/c's		Debtors	20,000
Ajit	60,000	Investment	10,000
Sujit	40,000	Bank	12,000
	1,52,000		1,52,000

The decided to amalgamate their business with the competing firm of Salim and Nasim who share profits and losses equally. They have following Balance Sheet as on 31st December 2008.

Balance Sheet as on 31st Dec. 2012

Liabilities	Rs.	Assets	Rs.
Sundry Creditors	46,000	Premises	70,000
Capital A/c's		Machinery	50,000
Salim	75,000	Stock	40,000
Nasim	75,000	Debtors	32,000
		Bank	4,000
	1,96,000		1,96,000

The following were the terms and conditions of amalgamation :

(i) Goodwill of Ajit and Sujit was valued at Rs.30,000 and that of Salim and Nasim at Rs.20,000. But the New Firm will not show Goodwill A/c in its book.

(ii) The following revaluation were made in respect of assets of Ajit and Sujit :

(a) Bad debts were calculated at Rs.2,000.

(b) Stock was to be revalued at Rs.52,000

(c) Machinery was revalued at Rs.70,000

(iii) The following revaluations were to be made irrespective of assets of Salim and Nasim.

(a) Machinery was to be revalued at Rs.45000.

(b) Write off Rs.2000 for bad debts and also provide R.D.D. @ 5% on debtors.

(c) The value of premises increased by Rs.4000.

(d) The stock was overvalued by Rs.2500.

(iv) All the assets and liabilities were taken over by the New Firm except investment of Ajit and Sujit.

(v) The Capital of the New Firm fixed at Rs.3,00,000 which was to be in their new profit sharing ratio was as under :

Ajit -2/10, Sujit - 2/10, Salim -3/10, Nasim - 3/10.

You are required to prepare Revaluation A/c, Capital A/c in the books of old firm. Prepare Balance Sheet of the a New Firm.

Solution :

In the Books of Ajit And Sujit
Revaluation A/c

To Bad debts	2,000	By Stock	2,000
To Capital A/c (Profit)	10,000	By Machinery	10,000
Ajit - 6,000			
Sujit - 4,000			
	12,000		12,000

Capital A/c's

	Ajit	Sujit		Ajit	Sujit
Investment A/c	6,000	4,000	By Bal. b/d	60,000	40,000
New Firm A/c	90,000	60,000	By Reserve	12,000	8,000
(transfer)			By Goodwill A/c	18,000	12,000
			By P & L Adj. A/c (Profit)	6,000	4,000
	96,000	64,000		96,000	64,000

In the Books of Salim and Nasim
Revaluation A/c

	Rs.		Rs.
To Machinery	5,000	By Premises	4,000
To Bad debts	2,000	By Capital A/c (loss)	7,000
To R.D.D.	1,500	Salim 3500	
To Stock	2,500	Nasim 3500	
	11,000		11,000

Capital A/c

	Salim	Nasim		Ajit	Sujit
To P & L Adj. A/c (Loss)	3,500	3,500	By Bal. b/d	75,000	75,000
			By Goodwill A/c	10,000	10,000
To New Firm A/c (transfer)	81,500	81,500			
	85,000	85,000		85,000	85,000

In the Books of the New Firm
Balance Sheet as on 1-1-2013

Liabilities	Rs.	Assets	Rs.	Rs.
Capital A/c's		Premises		74,000
Ajit	60,000	Machinery		
Sujit	60,000	Ajit & Sujit	70,000	
Salim	90,000	Salim & Nasim	45,000	1,15,000
Nasim	90,000			
		Stock		
Sundry Creditors	78,000	Ajit & Sujit	52,000	
		Salim & Nasim	37,500	89,500
		Debtors		
		Ajit & Sujit	20,000	
		Salim & Nasim	32,000	
			52,000	
		Less Bad debts	4,000	48,000
			48,000	
		Less R.D.D.	1,500	46,500
		Bank		53,000
	3,78,000			3,78,000

Working Notes : (i) Adjustment of Capital

Total Capital fixed in the new firm was Rs.3,00,000

Particulars	Ajit	Sujit	Salim	Nasim
New Profit Sharing Ratio	2	2	3	3
Existing Capital	90,000	60,000	81,500	81,500
(Transferred from old firm)				
Less Goodwill written off	10,000	10,000	15,000	15,000
(Rs.50,000 in 2:2:3:3)				
	80,000	50,000	66,500	66,500
Required Capital	60,000	60,000	90,000	90,000
(according to New Profit sharing				
ratio)				
3,00,000/10 = Rs.30,000 per				
share	+20,000	-10,000	-23,500	-23,500
Cash Brought in by		10,000	23,500	23,500
Cash paid to	20,000			

(ii) Calculation of Bank Balance

Opening Bank Balance

Ajit & Sujit	12,000	
Salim & Nasim	4,000	
		16,000

Add Cash Brought in by

Sujit	10,000	
Salim	23,500	
Nasim	23,500	57,000
		73,000
Less Cash Paid to Ajit		20,000

Shown in Balance Sheet		53,000

Illustration 8

The Balance Sheet of M/s. Rahul and Atul and M/s. Sonu and Monu as on Dec.2012 was as follows, who share profits and losses equally.

Balance Sheet as on 31-12-2012

Liabilities	Rahul & Atul	Sonu & Monu	Assets	Rahul & Atul	Sonu & Monu
Capital			Land & Building	30,000	36,000
Rahul	30,000		Machinery	21,000	24,000
Atul	30,000		Furniture &		
Sonu		30,000	Fixture	9,000	10,500
Monu		30,000	Debtors	18,000	25,500
Creditors	45,000	30,000	Stock	24,000	30,000
Loan	-	30,000	Cash at Bank	9,000	3,000
Outstanding Exp.	6,000	9,000			
	1,11,000	1,29,000		1,11,000	1,29,000

The two firms decided to amalgamate with effect from 1st January 2013 Partners would share profits and losses equally between themselves. They agreed to the following revaluations of Assets and Liabilities.

	Rahul & Atul	Sonu & Monu
Land and Building	30,000	30,000
Machinery	21,000	24,000
Furniture & Fixture	7,500	7,500
Debtors	16,500	21,000
Stock	24,000	24,000
Outstanding Exp.	6,000	10,500

In addition to above it was decided.

(i) That the new firm would not take over the loan of Sonu and Monu which is taken over by the two partners equally.

(ii) The Goodwill of Rahul and Atul and Sonu and Monu was valued at Rs.30,000 and Rs.15,000 respectively. But for the prupose of the Balance Sheet of the new firm the combined goodwill be valued at Rs.36,000.

(iii) That the reconstructed capitals of partner should be Rs.42,000 each. Partners will introduce cash if necessary.

You are required to show Revaluation Account and Capital Accounts in the books of the old firm and Opening Balance Sheet of the new firm assuming that all arrangements have been duly carried out.

Solution :

In the Books of M/s. Rahul and Atul (Revaluation A/c)

To Furniture & Fixture	1,500	By Capital A/c (Loss)	3,000
To Bad debts	1,500	Rahul - 1,500	
		Atul - 1,500	
	3,000		3,000

Capital A/c

	Rahul	Atul		Rahul	Atul
To P & L Adj. A/c			By Bal. b/d	30,000	30,000
(Loss)	1,500	1,500	By Goodwill A/c	15,000	15,000
To New Firm					
A/c	43,500	43,500			
	45,000	45,000		45,000	45,000

In the Books of Sonu and Monu (Revaluation A/c)

To Land & Buildings	6,000	By Capital A/c (Loss)	21,000
To Furniture & Fixture	3,000	Sonu - 10,500	
To Bad debts	4,500	Monu - 10,500	
To Stock	6,000		
To Outstanding exp.	1,500		
	21,000		21,000

Capital A/c

	Sonu	Monu		Sonu	Monu
To P & L Adj. A/c			By Bal. b/d	30,000	50,000
(Loss)	10,500	10,500	By Loan A/c	15,000	15,000
To New Firm			By Goodwill A/c	7,500	7,500
A/c (transfer)	42,000	42,000			
	52,500	52,500		52,500	52,500

In the Books of New Firm
Opening Journal Entries

Date	Particulars		L/F	Debit	Credit
2012	Land & Building A/c	Dr.		30,000	
31st	Machinery A/c	Dr.		21,000	
Dec.	Furniture & Fixture A/c	Dr.		7,500	
	Debtors A/c	Dr.		16,500	
	Stock A/c	Dr.		24,000	
	Cash A/c	Dr.		9,000	
	Goodwill A/c	Dr.		30,000	
	To Creditors A/c				45,000
	To Outstanding expense A/c				6,000
	To Rahul Capital A/c				43,500
	To Atul Capital A/c				43,500
	(Being incorporation of various assets & liabilities taken over of M/s Rahul & Atul)				
	Land & Building A/c	Dr.		30,000	
	Machinery A/c	Dr.		24,000	
	Furniture & Fixture A/c	Dr.		7,500	
	Debtors A/c	Dr.		21,000	
	Stock A/c	Dr.		24,000	
	Cash A/c	Dr.		3,000	
	Goodwill A/c	Dr.		15,000	
	To Creditors A/c				30,000
	To Outstanding Exp. A/c				10,500
	To Sonu Capital A/c				42,000
	To Monu Capital A/c				42,000
	(Being incorporation of various Assets & Liabilities taken over of M/s Sonu & Monu)				
	Rahual Capital A/c	Dr.		2,250	
	Atul Capital A/c	Dr.		2,250	
	Sonu Capital A/c	Dr.		2,250	
	Monu Capital A/c	Dr.		2,250	

Date	Particulars	L/F	Debit	Credit
	To Goodwill A/c (Being excess goodwill of Rs.9000 written off among the Partner's)			9,000
	Cash A/c Dr.		6,000	
	To Rahul Capital A/c			750
	To Atul Capital A/c			750
	To Sonu Capital A/c			2,250
	To Monu Capital A/c			2,250
	(Being necessary cash brought in by each partner)			

Balance Sheet as on 1-1-2013

Liabilities	Rs.	Assets		Rs
Capital Accounts		Goodwill		36,000
Rahul	42,000	**Land & Building**		
Atul	42,000	Rahul & Atul	30,000	
Sonu	42,000	Sonu & Monu	30,000	60,000
Monu	42,000			
Sundry Creditors	75,000	**Machinery**		
Outstanding Exp.	16,500	Rahul & Atul	21,000	
		Sonu & Monu	24,000	45,000
		Furniture & Fixture		
		Rahul & Atul	7,500	
		Sonu & Monu	7,500	15,000
		Stock		
		Rahul & Atul	24,000	
		Sonu & Monu	24,000	48,000
		Sundry Debtors		
		Rahul & Atul	16,500	
		Sonu & Monu	21,000	37,500
		Cash in hand		18,000
	2,59,500			2,59,500

Working Notes :

(i) Goodwill transferred from the old firms amounted to Rs.45000. But the goodwill in the books of new firm valued at Rs.36,000. Therefore excess goodwill of Rs.9000 (45000-36000) written off among the Partners according to their profit sharing ratio.

(ii) Calculation of Cash Balance :

Cash transferred from old firms		12,000
Rahul and Atul - 9,000		
Sonu and Monu - 3,000		
Add Necessary Cash brought by Partner		6,000
Rahul -	Rs.750	
Atul -	Rs.750	
Sonu -	Rs.2,250	
Monu -	Rs.2,250	
Shown in B/s	Rs.	18,000

(ii) Adjustment of Capitals

Capital fixed Rs.42,000 for each partner.

Particulars	Rahul	Atul	Sonu	Monu
Profit Sharing Ratio	1	1	1	1
Capital transferred from old firm	43,500	43,500	42,000	42,000
Less Excess goodwill written off Rs.9,000 (45,000-36000)	-2,250	-2,250	-2,250	-2,250
	+41,250	+41,250	+39,750	+39,750
Required Capital in the New firm)	-42,000	-42,000	-42,000	-42,000
(Rs.42,000 each)	-750	-750	-2,250	-2,250
Cash Brought in by	750	750	2,250	2,250

Illustration 9 :

The following are the two Balance Sheet of Ajay and Amit and Suresh and Ramesh as on 31-12-2012

Balance - Sheet of Ajay and Amit

Liabilities	Rs.	Assets	Rs.
Capitals		Land & Building	45,000
Ajay	40,000	Plant & Machinery	58,000
Amit	38,000	Stock	16,000
General Reserve	6,000	Sundry Debtors	8,000
Sundry Creditors	35,000	Bills Receivable	1,000
Outstanding Wages	3,000	Cash in Hand	4,000
Bills Payable	10,000		
	1,32,000		1,32,000

Balance - Sheet of Suresh and Ramesh

Liabilities	Rs.	Assets	Rs.
Capitals		Furniture	10,000
Suresh	26,000	Stock	48,000
Ramesh	24,000	Sundry Debtors	25,000
General Reserve	9,000	Bills Receivable	10,000
Sundry Creditors	40,000	Investments	12,000
Mrs. Suresh's Loan	4,000	Cash in Hand	5,000
Bills Payable	7,000		
	1,10,000		1,10,000

Ajay and Amit shared profits and losses in the ratio of 3:2 where as Suresh and Ramesh shared profits and Losses in the ratio of 2 : 1.

The two firms decided to amalgamate their business from 1st January 2013 on the following terms and conditions.

(1) Plant and Machinery to be depreciated by 5%.

(2) Land and Building to be appreciated by 10%.

(3) Sundry Debtors to be taken after providing for Reserve for Bad and Doubtful debts at 5% of both the firms.

4) Provision for discount on creditors of both the firms was also to be made at 2%.

(5) Other assets were taken at book value.

(6) Outstanding wages are paid in full by the old firm. All other liabilities except Mrs. Suresh's Loan were taken over by the new firms.

(7) Mr's Suresh's loan was taken over by Suresh.

(8) Goodwill of Ajay and Amit was agreed at Rs.10,000 and that of Suresh and Ramesh at Rs.12000. It is further agreed that Goodwill shall not be retained in the books of the New Firm.

(9) The total capital of new firm was to be 1,60,000 and the capital of Ajay, Amit, Suresh and Ramesh was to be in their profit sharing ratio which was 3:2:3:2 respectively.

Prepare profit and loss adjustment account and partner's capital accounts in the books of old firm and the amalgamated Balance Sheet of the new firm.

Solution :

In the Books of Ajay and Amit
Profit of Loss Adjustment A/c

Liabilities	Rs.	Assets	Rs.
To Plant & Machinery	2,900	By Land & Building	4,500
To R.D.D.	400	By Reserve for Discount	
To Capital A/c (Profit)	1,900	on Creditors	700
Ajay 1,140			
Amit 760			
	5,200		5,200

Capital Accounts

	Ajay	Amit		Ajay	Amit
To New Firm A/c (transfer)	50,740	45,160	By Bal. b/d	40,000	38,000
			By General Reserve	3,600	2,400
			By Goodwill A/c	6,000	4,000
			By P & L Adj. A/c	1,140	760
	50,740	45,160		50,740	45,160

(1) Note :

Cash balance of Ajay & Amit transferred to the new firm will be	Rs.1,000
i.e. Opening cash balance	Rs.4,000
Less Outstanding wages paid	Rs.3,000
	Rs.1,000

(2) Calculation of Assets :

Land and Buildings	49,500
Plant and Machinery	55,100
Stock	16,000
Debtors	8,000
Bills Receivable	1,000
Cash	1,000
Goodwill	10,000
	1,40,600

Less Liabilities :

Creditors	35,000		44,700
Less Discount	700	34,300	
R.D.D.		400	
Bills Payable		10,000	
		Rs.	95,900

In the Books of Suresh and Ramesh
Profit of Loss Adjustment A/c

Liabilities	Rs.	Assets	Rs.
To R.D.D.	1,250	By Reserve for Discount on Creditors	800
		By Capital A/c (loss)	450
		Suresh- 300	
		Ramesh -150	
	1,250		1,250

Capital Accounts

	Suresh	Ramesh		Suresh	Ramesh
To P & L Adj. A/c (Loss)	300	150	By Bal. b/d	26,000	24,000
To New Firm A/c	43,700	30,850	By General Reserve	6,000	3,000
			By Mrs. Loan A/c	4,000	
			By Goodwill A/c	8,000	4,000
	44,000	31,000		44,000	31,000

Note : Calculation of Net Assets :

Furniture	10,000	
Stock	48,000	
Debtors	25,000	
Bills Receivable	10,000	
Investments	12,000	
Cash	5,000	
Goodwill	12,000	
		1,22,000
Less Liabilities		47,450
		39,200
Creditors	40,000	
Less Discount	800	
R.D.D.		1,250
Bills Payable		7,000 Rs.74,550

In the Books of Ajay, Amit, Suresh and Ramesh
Balance Sheet as on 1st January 2013

Liabilities	Rs.		Assets		Rs.
Capitals			Land & Building		49,500
Ajay	48,000		Plant & Machinery		55,100
Amit	32,000		Furniture		10,000
Suresh	48,000		Stock		
Ramesh	32,000		Ajay & Amit	16000	
Sundry Creditors			Suresh & Ramesh	48,000	64,000
Ajay & Amit	35000				

Liabilities		Rs.	Assets		Rs.
Suresh & Ramesh	40,000		Debtors		
	75,000		Ajay & Amit	8,000	
Less Reserve for			Suresh & Ramesh	25,000	
Discount	1,500	73,500		33,000	
Bills Payable			- R.D.D.	1,650	31,350
Ajay & Amit	10,000		Bills Receivable		
Suresh & Ramesh	7,000	17,000	Ajay & Amit	1,000	
			Suresh & Ramesh	10,000	11,000
			Investment		12,000
			Cash		17,550
		2,50,000			2,50,000

Working Note :
(1) Calculation of Cash Balance :

Cash transferred from old firm :		6,000
Ajay & Amit	Rs.1,000	
Suresh & Ramesh	Rs.5,000	
Add Cash Brought in by		20,310
Ajay	Rs. 3,860	
Suresh	Rs.10,900	
Ramesh	Rs.5,550	
		26,310
Less Cash Paid to Mr. Amit		8,760
Shown in Balance Sheet		17,550

(2) Adjustment of Capitals :
Total capital fixed in the firm Rs.1,60,000.

Particulars	Ajay	Amit	Suresh	Ramesh
Profit Sharing Ratio	3	2	3	2
Capital transferred from old firm	50,740	45,160	43,700	30,850
Less Goodwill written off	6,600	4,400	6,600	4,400
Rs.9,000 (45,000-36,000)	44,140	40,760	37,100	26,450
Required capital in the				

Particulars	Ajay	Amit	Suresh	Ramesh
New firm Rs.16,000 per share (1,60,000 x 1/10)	48,000	32,000	48,000	32,000
	-3,860	+8,760	-10,900	-5,550
Cash Brought in by Cash Paid to	3,860	- 8,760	10,900	5,550

Illustration 10 :

Following were the Balance Sheets as on December 31,2012 of the two firms M/s X and Y and M/s P and Q.

Balance Sheet as on 31-12-2012

Liabilities	X&Y Rs.	P&Q Rs.	Assets	X&Y Rs.	P&Q Rs.
Sundry Creditors	20,000	10,000	Cash at Bank	15,000	8,000
Bills Payable	5,000	-	Investment at		
Bank Overdraft	2,000	10,000	Cost	10,000	8,000
X's Loan A/c	6,000	-	Debtors 10,000	9,000	8,000
Capitals			Less		
X	35,000	-	Provision 1000		
Y	22,000	-	Furniture	12,000	6,000
P	-	36,000	Premises	30,000	-
Q	-	20,000	Land	-	50,000
General Reserve	8,000	3,000	Machinery	15,000	-
Investment Fluctua-			Goodwill	9,000	-
tion Fund	2,000	1,000			
	1,00,000	80,000		1,00,000	80,000

The two firms decided to amalgamate their business on 1st January 2013 under the name and style of Bharat Traders. For this purpose it was decided that the new firm shall not take over furniture of both the firms and shall take over investment at 10% Depreciation, Land Rs.80,000. Premises Rs.45,000 Machinery at Rs.9,000. The new firm agree to take over only trade liabilities of both the firms and pay Rs.12,000 to each firm for goodwill. The unrecorded typewriter of P and Q valued at Rs. 800 was not taken over by the new firm. The capital of the new firm was agreed at Rs.1,60,000 to be divided among partners equally.

Note : Furniture not taken over to be distributed in profit sharing ratio.

Show : (i) Ledger Accounts to close the books of the firm.

(ii) Opening Balance Sheet of the New Firm.

In the Books of X and Y
Profit and Loss Adjustment A/c

To Machinery	6,000	By Premises	15,000
To Capital (Profit)		By Goodwill	3,000
X - 6000			
Y - 6000	12,000		
	18,000		18,000

Capital Accounts

	X	Y		X	Y
To Furniture A/c	6,000	6,000	By Bal. b/d	35,000	22,000
To New Firm A/c	39,500	26,500	By General		
(transfer)			Reserve	4,000	4,000
			By Investment	500	500
			Fluctuation Fund A/c		
			By P & L Adj. A/c	6,000	6,000
	45,500	32,500		45,500	32,500

Bharat Traders A/c

To Net Assets	66,000	By X Capital A/c	39,500
		By Y Capital A/c	26,500
	66,000		66,000

Investment Fluctuation Fund A/c

To Investment	1,000	By Balance c/d		2,000
To Balance transferred to				
X 500				
Y 500	1,000			
	2,000			2,000

Working Notes :

(i) As there exists Investment Fluctuation Fund, the loss on investment i.e.(10% Depreciation) is adjusted against this fund and the balance on such fund transferred to capital A/c.

(ii) As the New firm has taken over only the trade liabilities, there is no question of transferring X's loan A/c to New firm. Therefore it is paid off by the firm itself. Therefore, the cash balance to be transferred to the New firm will be reduced to the extent of X loan A/c (Cash Rs.15,000 - X loan Rs.6000 = Rs.9000 transferred)

(iii) Net Assets

Assets taken over

Cash at Bank		9,000
Investment		9,000
Debtors		10,000
Premises		45,000
Machinery		9,000
Goodwill		12,000
Total Value of Assets taken over Rs.		94,000
Less Liabilities taken over		
Creditors	20,000	
Bills Payable	5,000	
Bank Overdraft	2,000	
R.D.D.	1,000	28,000
Value of Net Assets taken over		Rs.66,000

In the Books of P & Q
Profit and Loss Adjustment A/c

To Capital A/c (Profit)	30,800	By Land	30,000
P- 15,400		By Type Writer	800
Q- 15,400			
	30,800		30,800

Capital Account

	X	Y		X	Y
To Furniture A/c	3,000	3,000	By Bal. b/d	36,000	20,000
To Typewriter	400	400	By General		
To New Firm A/c	55,600	39,600	Reserve	1,500	1,500
			By Investment Fluctuation Fund A/c	100	100
			By Goodwill A/c	6,000	6,000
			By P & L Adj. A/c (Profit)	15,400	15,400
	59,000	43,000		59,000	43,000

Bharat Traders Account

To Net Assets A/c	95,200	By P's Capital A/c	55,600
		By Q's Capital A/c	39,600
	95,200		95,200

Investment Fluctuation Fund A/c

To Net Assets A/c	800	By Balance b/d	1,000
To Balance transferred to	200		
P - 100			
Q - 100			
	1,000		1,000

Working Note :
(i) Net Assets
    Assets taken over

Cash at Bank	8,000
Investment	7,200
Debtors	8,000
Land	80,000
Goodwill	12,000
Total Value of assets taken over	Rs. 1,15,200

Less Liabilities taken over

Creditors	10,000	
Bank Overdraft	10,000	20,000
Value of Net Asset taken over	Rs.	95,200

(ii) Unrecorded Typewriter :

The Typewriter which is an asset belonging to the firm which has not been recorded, therefore to record such an unrecorded asset Typewriter Account is debited and P & L Adjustment A/c is credited. After having recorded this asset has been transferred to Partners Capital Account in their profit sharing ratio.

In the Books of Bharat Traders
Opening Balance Sheet of Bharat Traders

Liabilities		Rs.	Assets		Rs.
Capitals			Goodwill		24,000
X	40,000		Land		80,000
Y	40,000		Premises		45,000
P	40,000		Machinery		9,000
Q	40,000	1,60,000	Investment		16,200
Current A/c			Debtors	18,000	
P		15,600	Less R.D.D.	1,000	17,000
Creditors		30,000	Cash		31,400
Bills Payable		5,000	(9000 + 8000 + 500 +		
Bank Overdraft		12,000	13500 + 400 = 31,400)		
		2,22,600			2,22,600

Working Note - Adjustment of Capitals

Particulars	X	Y	P	Q
Profit Sharing Ratio	1	1	1	1
Capital transferred from old firm	39,500	26,500	55,600	39,600
required capital				
(1,60,000 x 1/4)	40,000	40,000	40,000	40,000
	-500	-13,500	+15,600	-400
Cash brought in by	500	13,500		-400
Excess Balance transferred	-	-	15,600	
to current A/c				

2.7 Exercise (Theory)
Objective Type Questions
State whether the following statements are 'true' or 'false'

1.   Shares and debentures received from the purchasing company are distributed among the partners in the profit sharing ratio.
2.   All assets and liabilities not taken over by the new firm are transferred to the capital accounts of the partners.
3.   Any reserves standing in the books of the amalgamating firms will be transferred to the new firm's account.
4.   The new firm debits all the assets and credits all the liabilities at the values at which they appear in the amalgamating firm.
5.   When firms are amalgamated, realisation accounts are prepared to close the books of such firms.
6.   In the case of sale to a company the books of the firm are closed in the same way as in the case of dissolution.
7.   Amalgamation means combination of one firm.
8.   Any balance in the profit and loss account of the amalgamated firm will be transferred to new firm's account.
9.   Profit & Loss on revaluation is transferred to partners capital accounts when fixed capital method is adopted.

Ans : 1. True 2. True 3. False 4. False 5. False 6. True 7. True 8. False 9. False

Fill in the Blanks

1.   At the time of amalgamation any profit or loss on revaluation is transferred to .... accounts in the ....
2.   Assets and liabilities not taken over by the new firm are transferred to capital accounts of the partners in the .... ratio.
3.   The liabilities taken over by the new firm are............. to the new firm's account.
4.   The excess of net worth acquired by the company over the purchase price is .... to ....account.
5.   In Amalgamation of firm, assets & liabilities not taken over nor sold can be transferred to .... Account.
6.   Amalgamation means combination of .... firms.
7.   Any balance in the Profit & Loss account of the amalgamating firm will be transferred to .... accoung of the partner.

8. To ascertain profit/ loss on revaluation of all assets & liabilities .... account is opened.
9. All accumulated reserves/profits/loss to the capital account of partner in .... account is opened.
10. When Goodwill account is opened, partner's capital account are credited in .... ratio.

Answers : 1. partner's capital 2. Capital Profit Sharing ratio. 3. credited 4. credited : capital reserve.5. Partner's Capital Account 6.Two 7. Capital 8. Revaluation 9. Profit-sharing 10. Profit Sharing.

III. Indicate the correct answer :

1. In the case of sale to a company the profit or loss on sale is ascertained through.
(a) revaluation account
(b) memorandum realisation account
(c) realisation account.

2. Purchase consideration received in the form of shares and debentures is distributed among the partners in
(a) ratio of the final amounts due to partners.
(b) ratio of capitals
(c) profit sharing ratio.

3. Liabilities not taken over by the new firm (at the time of amalgamation) will be transferred to
(a) new firm's account
(b) revaluation account
(c) capital account

4. Any balance in the profit and loss account of the amalgamating firm will be transferred to
(a) capital accounts of the partners.
(b) revlauation account.
(c) new firm's account.

Ans : 1. (c) 2. (c) 3. (c) 4. (a).

Exercise (Practical)

1. Avinash and Bharat were carrying on business separately as sole traders in a competitive business. They decided to amalgamate and trade in partnership as from. 1st January 2012, when their position was as under :

Balance Sheet

	Avinash	Bharat		Avinash	Bharat
Sundry Creditors	15,000	12,500	Cash	1,500	2,000
Capitals	32,000	24,000	Land & Building	15,000	20,000
			Plant & Mach.	10,000	-
			Furniture	500	750
			Debtors	18,000	12,250
			Stock	2,000	1,500
	47,000	36,500		47,000	36,500

Assets were taken over by the new firm at the revalued figures as under :

(i) Land and building and plant and machinery were depreciated by 10%.

(ii) Stock was valued at 95% of their book value.

(iii) Goodwill of the two firms were valued at Rs.2500 and Rs.2000 respectively.

(iv) The profit sharing ratio was agreed 3:2. Pass the journal entries in the books of old firm and prepare balance sheet after amalgamation in the books of new firm.

[Ans. : Capital - Avinash Rs.31,900
        Bharat Rs. 23,925
Balance Sheet Total   Rs. 83,385]

2. X and Y are two sole traders. Their balance sheets on 1st January 2012 are following.

Balance Sheet's as on 1st Jan. 2012

Liabilities	X	Y	Assets	X	Y
Sundry Creditors	10,000	8,000	Plant &		
Loan from Bank	5,000	-	Machinery	7,500	10,000
Capital A/c	15,000	20,000	Stock in Trade	10,000	5,000
			Sundry Debtors	12,500	11,000
			Cash at Bank	-	2,000
	30,000	28,000		30,000	28,000

They amalgamate their business as on 1st January 2012. The details are given below :

(i) Plant and Machinery to be reduced by 10%.

(ii) Stock in trade were to be reduced in case of X by 20% and in case of Y 10%.

(iii) A provision of 2.1/2% is to be raised against sundry debtors.

(iv) Each partner is to be credited with goodwill of Rs.5,000.

(v) The Overdraft of X is to be paid by him.

You are required to close the books of X and Y. Give opening balance sheet in the books of new firm.

[Ans : B/s Total Rs.63,162.50]

3. Anil and Suresh together and Rajendra independently were carrying on separate business. Their balance sheets as on September 2012 were as follows :

Balance Sheet

Liabilities	Anil & Suresh	Rajendra	Assets	Anil & Suresh	Rajendra
Creditors	10,000	16,000	Cash	7,000	2,000
Bills Payable	12,000	-	Debtors	14,000	36,000
General Reserve	15,000	-	Stock	22,000	12,000
Bank Overdraft		13,000	Investments	-	12,000
Capital Accounts			Motor Car	-	9,000
Anil	30,000		Machinery	38,000	-
Suresh	40,000		Building	26,000	-
Rajendra		42,000			
	1,07,000	71,000		1,07,000	71,000

Anil and Suresh were sharing profits and losses in the proportion of 3:2. The firms were amalgamated on 1st October 2012 on the following terms :

(i) That the goodwill of Rajendra's business be valued at Rs.7,700.

(ii) That a provision at 5% be made on all debtors.

(iii) That stock of Anil and Suresh be depreciated by 7.1/2% and that of Rajendra's by 5%.

(iv) That the machinery and building be taken at Rs.42,000 and Rs.30,000 respectively.

(v) That Motor Car be retained by Rajendra.

(vi) Investment be taken at Rs.16,000.

(vii) That the new firm's capital should be Rs.1,40,000 out of which Rs.1,00,000 should be held by Anil and Suresh equally.

Close the books of old firms and Give opening balance sheet of the new firm.

[Ans. Profit of Anil & Suresh Rs.5,650.

Profit of Rajendra Rs.1,600

B/s Total 1,91,000]

(Poona University 1971]

4. A & B and C & D were trading in partnership separately. They decided to amalgamate in the name of ABCD from 1st January 2013. Their balance sheet as on 31st December 2012 were as under:

Balance Sheet as on 31-12-2012

Liabilities	A & B	C&D	Assets	A & B	C&D
Creditors	10,000	20,000	Cash	1,000	-
Bank Overdraft	-	10,000	Buildings	16,000	6,000
Reserve	20,000	-	Debtors	15,000	24,000
Capitals			Furniture	2,000	-
A	30,000		Machinery	21,000	-
B	20,000		Stock	25,000	25,000
C		15,000	Goodwill	-	5,000
D		15,000			
	80,000	60,000		80,000	60,000

The old firm's the partner's use to share profits in their respective capital ratio. They amalgamated according to the following conditions.

(i) Four partners of the new firm will share the profits in the ratio of their capitals after all adjustments have been made.

(ii) Building of M/s A & B is to be taken over by the new firm at Rs.20,000 and of M/s C & D at Rs.10,000.

(iii) Goodwill of M/s C & D was worthless.

(iv) All other assets were taken over by the new firm at book values.

(v) The new firm pays off the bank overdraft.

(vi) B, C and D each to bring Rs.5000 as additional capital after all adjustments have been made.

On the completion of the arrangements on 1st January 2013 record journal entries in the books of the new firm and prepare its opening balance sheet.

[Ans. B/S Total Rs.1,48,000]

5. M/s Manish and Nitin and M/s Ajay and Vijay are two partnership firms carrying on similar type of business, sharing profits in the ratio Manish and Nitin 8:7 and Ajay and Vijay 3:2 respectively. They agree to amalgamate their business as on 1st Jan.2013.

Balance Sheet as on 31-12-2012
M/s Manish and Nitin

Liabilities	Rs.	Assets	Rs.
Creditors	12,800	Free hold Land	15,000
Outstanding Exp.	1,400	Furniture	3,600
Current Accounts		Machinery	5,000
Manish	2,000	Stock	11,800
Nitin	1,200	Debtors	14,200
Capital Accounts		Investments	3,000
Manish	24,000	Cash	9,800
Nitin	21,000		
	62,400		62,400

M/s Ajay and Vijay

Liabilities	Rs.	Assets	Rs.
Creditors	11,200	Free hold Land	10,000
Bills Payable	1,000	Furniture	2,800
		Machinery	3,400
Capital Accounts		Stock	13,400
Ajay	22,000	Debtors	13,000
Vijay	15,600	Cash	7,200
	49,800		49,800

The terms of amalgamation are :
(1) Assets to be revalued as under :

	M/s Manish & Nitin Rs.	M/s Ajay & Vijay Rs.
Stock	11,400	12,400
Machinery	4,600	3,000
Furniture	4,000	5,000
Freehold Land	19,000	15,000

(2) Provision to be made for doubtful debts of M/s Manish and Nitin for Rs.800 and of M/s Ajay and Vijay Rs.1,000.

(3) The creditors of both the firms were to be taken by the new firm at a discount of 2.1/2% and other liabilities are paid in full by the respective firms.

(4) Manish to take over the investment at Rs.2,400.

(5) The Goodwill of M/s Manish and Nitin is to be taken at Rs.15,000 and that of M/s Ajay and Vijay at Rs.10,000.

(6) The capital of the new firm is to be Rs.1,00,000 and the capital of Manish, Nitin, Ajay and Vijay was to be in their profit sharing ratio which was to be 6/20, 5/20 and 4/20 respectively.

You are required to prepare revluation accounts and partner's capital accounts in the books of both the firms and balance sheet of the new firm.

[Ans : Profit of M/s Manish & Nitin Rs.2,520
Profit of M.s Ajay & Vijay Rs.5,080
B/S Total Rs.1,39,400]

6. M/s. Mani & Co. having Vairamani and Velumani as equal partners. decided to amalgamate with M/s. Swami & Co. having Radhaswami and Rangaswami as equal partners. The following were the balance sheets of both the firms on 31st December 2012.

Balance Sheet on 31-12-2012

Liabilities	Mani & Co.	Swami & Co.	Assets	Mani & Co.	Swami & Co.
Creditors	10,000	5,000	Cash at Bank	7,500	4,000
Bills Payable	2,500	-	Investments	5,000	4,000
Bank Overdraft	1,000	5,000	Debtors 5000		
Vairamani's Loan	3,000	-	- R.D.D. 500	4,500	4,000
General Reserve	4,000	1,500	Furniture	6,000	3,000
Investment Fluctua-			Premises	15,000	-
tion fund	1,000	500	Land	-	25,000
Capital Account			Machinery	7,500	
Vairamani	17,500		Goodwill	4,500	
Velumani	11,000				
Radhaswami		18,000			
Rangaswami		10,000			
	50,000	40,000		50,000	40,000

The terms and conditions of amalgamation were as under :

(i) The new firm named M/s Mani Swami & Co. to take over the investments at 10% depreciation; Land at Rs.40,000 premises at Rs.22,500, Machinery Rs.4,500 and to take over only trade liabilities of both the firms. The debtor is taken over at book value including reserve.

(ii) The new firm to pay Rs.6,000 to each firm for goodwill.

(iii) typewriters at the written off value of Rs.400 belong to Swami & Co. and not appearing in the balance sheet, were not taken over by the new firm.

(iv) It was also agreed that the furniture belonging to both the firms should not be taken over by the new firm.

(v) All the four partners in the new firm were to bring Rs.80,000 as capital in equal share.

You are required to give journal entries to close the books of both the firms and show the balance sheet of M/s Mani Swami & Co.

[**Ans.:** B/S Total Rs.97,500]

7.Two firms 'P & Q' and 'R & S' agreed to amalgamate their business. Their positions as on December 31 2012 were as follows :

Balance Sheet of 'P & Q'
As on December 31, 2012

Liabilities		Rs.	Assets	Rs.
Creditors		1,04,000	Cash at Bank	1,56,000
Capitals			Debtors	1,30,000
	P	1,82,000	Stock in Trade	42,000
	Q	1,30,000	Office Building	78,000
			Furniture	10,000
		4,16,000		4,16,000

Balance Sheet of 'R & S'
As on December 31, 2012

Liabilities		Rs.	Assets	Rs.
Creditors		52,000	Cash at Bank	65,000
Capitals			Debtors	1,04,000
	R	91,000	Stock in Trade	26,000
	S	65,000	Furniture	13,000
		2,08,000		2,08,000

Creditors and debtors were not taken over by the new firm PQRS Office building was retained by P and Q but new firm agreed to pay a monthly rent of Rs.400. The cash required for working of the new firm was estimated at Rs.1,30,000 to be provided by the partners in their new profit-sharing proportions as under : P 3/10; Q 3/10; R 2/10; S 2/10.

(1) Write the books of P & Q and R & S ;

(2) Give the opening balance sheet of PQRS. State your assumptions, if any clearly.

(Balance Sheet total of the firm PQRS Rs.2,21,000)

8. Behari, Waheed and Green carried on a manufacturing business in partnership sharing profits and losses: Behari two-fifths, Waheed two-fifths Green one-fifth. They agreed to amalgamate as on 31st December 2012 with Faquir who carried on a similar business.

The summarised balance sheets of the two firms as on 31st December 2012 were as follows :

Liabilities	Behari, Waheed & Green Rs	Faquir Rs.	Assets	Behari, Waheed & Green Rs	Faquir Rs.
Capital accounts :			Premises	6,000	-
Behari	8,000		Plant	3,600	2,400
Waheed	6,000		Stock	6,000	2,500
Green	4,000		Debtors 7000		
Faquir		3,000	Less Provision		
Trade creditors	9,000	2,000	400	7,000	3,600
Bank overdraft		3,500	Bank	4,400	-
	27,000	8,500		27,000	8,500

It was agreed :

(1) Behari was to be retired on 31st December 2012 and balance due to him being left on loan with the new firm.

(2) Profits were to be shared : Waheed one-half, Green one-quarter, Faquir one-quarter.

(3) The values of goodwill were agreed at Rs.10,000 for the firm of Behari, Waheed and Green and Rs.4,000 for Faquir.

(4) The new firm was to take over all the assets and discharge all the liabilities of the two businesses, but certain of the assets were to be revalued at follows :

	Behari, Waheed and Green Rs.	Faquir Rs.
Premises	8,000	-
Plant	3,200	2,900
Debtors	6,800	3,160

(5) The capital of the new firm was to be Rs.10,000 and was to be contributed by the partners in their profit sharing ratios, any surplus or deficiency being transferred to current accounts.

(6) No account for goodwill was to be maintained in the books, adjusting entries for transactions between the partners being made in the partner's capital accounts.

You are required to give : (a) journal entries in the books of the old firms and the new firm and (b) The opening balance sheet of the new firm.

[Behari's loan Rs.12,560 : Current accounts - Waheed Rs.1,440 (Dr.) Green Rs.280 (Cr.), Faquir Rs. 1,060 (Cr.); Balance sheet total Rs.34,900]

9. B and S are partners of S & Co. sharing profits and losses in the ratio of 3 :1:. S and T are partners of T & Co sharing profits and losses in the ratio of 2 :1.

On 31st October 2012 they decided to amalgamate and form a new firm M/s. BST & Co wherein B, S and T would be partners sharing profits and losses in the ratio of 3:2:1.

Their balacnes sheets on that date were as under :

Liabilities	S & Co.	T&Co.	Assets	S & Co.	T&Co.
Due to X & Co.	40,000	-	Cash in hand	10,000	5,000
Due to S & Co.	-	50,000	Cash at bank	15,000	20,000
Other credtiors	60,000	58,000	Due from T & Co	50,000	-
Reserves	25,000	50,000	Due from X & Co	-	30,000
Capitals			Other debtors	80,000	1,00,000
B	1,20,000	-	Stock	60,000	70,000
S	80,000	1,00,000	Furniture	10,000	3,000
T	-	50,000	Vehicles	-	80,000
			Machinery	75,000	-
			Building	25,000	-
	3,25,000	3,08,000		3,25,000	3,08,000

The amalgamated firm took over the business on the following terms :

(a) Goodwill of S & Co. was worth Rs.60,000 and that of T & Co. Rs.50,000. Goodwill account was not to be opened in the books of the new firm, the adjustments being recorded through capital accounts of the partners.

(b) Building, Machinery and vehicles were taken over Rs.50,000 Rs.90,000 and Rs.1,00,000 respectively.

(c) Provision for doubtful debts has to be carried forward at Rs.4,000 in respect of debtors of S & Co. and Rs.5,000 in respect of debtors of T & Co.

You are required to :

(i) Compute the adjustment necessary for goodwill.

(ii) Pass the journal entries in the books of BST & Co assuming that excess/deficit capitals (taking T's capital as base) with reference to share in the profits are to be transferred to current accounts.

(For goodwill B and T to be debited with Rs.10,000 and Rs.1,667 respectively and S credited with Rs.11,667; Amounts to be transferred to current account. B Rs. 54,250 (Dr.); S Rs. 1,10,250 (Cr.)]

Chapter 3

Conversion of a Partnership Firm into a Limited Company

3.1   Meaning and Introduction
3.2   Objectives of Conversion
3.3   Concept of Purchase Consideration & Methods of Calculation of Purchase Consideration.
3.4   Accounting Procedure
3.4.1 Accounting Procedure in the books of Firm
3.4.2 Accounting Procedure in the books of Company and Balance Sheet of New Company.
3.5   Illustrations
3.6   Exercises

3.1 Meaning and Introduction :

When partnership firm converts its business into a limited company, the process is called conversion of a partnership firm or when partnership firm sells off its business to a limited company the process is called sale of business to a limited company.

3.2 Objectives of Conversation :

When any business firm grows and expands the scale of its operations, it faces number of problems which makes it necessary to take another look at the existing form of organisation and consider change over to another form of ownership organisation. In the same manner when partnership firm expands its business. it faces number of problems which compel the firm to convert its business into a limited company. Generally, following are the main objectives because of which firm converts its business into a limited company.

(i) Increase in Financial Requirement :

Due to increase in the scale of operations, organisation requires huge amount of capital which can be easily facilitated by forming a limited company. It can collect the capital from the public which is required by a medium scale or large scale business.

(ii) Liability :

An existing business carried on by a firm may be converted

into a company with a view to limit the liability of members; because liability in case of partnership firm is unlimited. If the business is of speculative nature and demand for the product is erratic in such a case member prefers limited liability.

(iii) Control :

In case of private limited company the member can retain effective control over the business by appointing managing officials, which is rather difficult in case of partnership firm.

(iv) Management :

In a partnership firm every partner has a voice in the management of the business. If number of partners is large and if they do not have understanding amongst themselves, in such a case efficiency of management may suffer to a great extent. In case of limited company, the directors are responsible for management. Therefore, decisions can be taken more quickly to achieve effective management.

(v) Internal Reorganisation :

If partnership firm requires internal reorganisation such that of division of work, additions to departments, and effective supervision, it can be easily provided by converting the firm into a limited company.

(vi) Audit of Books of Accounts :

In case of limited company, it has to file its audited accounts with the registrar of a company, but audit requirements is not applicable to partnership firm.

In short, partnership firms are converted into a limited companies, particularly with a view to limit the personal liability of the partners or to raise large amount of capital required to finance business which may be rapidly expanding.

In case of conversion or sale to a limited company, the partnership firm looses its existence and it becomes dissolved. Therefore, the books of accounts of a firm selling its business must be closed. The accounting procedure under this case is similar to that of dissolution of the firm. The only difference between the 'sale to a limited company' and dissolution of the firm is that, in the former case the business is sold to the company, whereas in dissolution, the assets are sold in the market.

3.3 Concept of Purchase Consideration :

When partnership firm converts its business into a limited company or sells its business to a limited company, the purchase consideration is required to be fixed in the first instance.

"Purchase consideration means the amount at which the company agrees to purchase the partnership business. It is that price at which the firm agrees to sell off its business to a company." It is the value at which the company is to take over the partnership business. It is the price paid by the limited company to the firm for the purchase of assets and liabilities of the firm.

The conversion into or sale to a company involves the purchase and sale of partnership business. Therefore, there should be general agreement between both the parties as to the price at which the purchase and sale of business should take place. This price is known as purchase consideration or purchase price.

It is necessary to know the purchase price, without which the profit & loss on purchase and sale of business can not be ascertained. "Sometimes, the purchase price may be directly given in the problem. when it is not given, it becomes necessary to find out the purchase price."

The purchase price can be ascertained by the following methods.
(i) Net Asset Method.
(ii) Sum Total or Payment Method.

(i) Net Asset Method :

Under this method purchase consideration is calculated on the basis of agreed values of assets and liabilities taken over. It is the difference between the agreed values of assets taken over and agreed values of liabilities assumed. Therefore, the formula for calculating the purchase price under this method is as follows :

Purchase	Agreed Values		Agreed Values of
Consideration =	of Assets	-	Liabilities taken over

i.e. **P.C = A - L**

Values of Assets Taken Over .

Machinery	Rs............................
Buildings	Rs............................
Stock	Rs............................

| Debtors | Rs........................... |
| Goodwill | Rs........................... |

Total values of Asset taken over Rs..........................
Less : Values of Liabilities taken over
        Creditors   Rs...............
        Bills Payable   Rs...............
        Other Liabilities Rs...............

Total values of Liabilities taken over   Rs...............

Purchase - Price   Rs...............

(ii) Sum Total or Payment Method :

This is yet another method for calculating purchase consideration. Under this method the purchase price is calculated by taking into account the amounts to be paid by the company in cash, shares and debentures. The company agrees to pay the purchase price in the form of cash, shares and debentures. Therefore, the purchase price can also be ascertained by taking into account the amounts to be received in these forms. This method is followed only when how much amount to be received in cash, in shares and in debentures is specifically given in the problem.

The formula is :

Purchase Consideration = Cash + Shares + Debentures, to be received from the company :

    i.e. **P. C.**   **= C + S + D.**
                    Cash (C)   Rs. ....
                    + Shares (S)   Rs. ....
                    + Debentures (D) Rs. ....
                    Purchase Price   Rs. ....

Note :

Generally, the purchase price is to be calculated by the second method; if the amounts to be received in different forms are given in the problem. If the amount of any particular form is missing then the purchase price will be calculated by the first method.

For Example :

(1) 'X' Ltd. Co. agrees to take over the business of a firm for which it agrees to pay Rs.2,00,000 in cash Rs. 3,00,000 in 5% debentures and Rs.6,00,000 in shares of Rs.10/- each.

In this problem the purchase price will be calculated by the second method as the amounts to be received in each form is given.

Purchase Price = Cash + Shares + Debentures.

Rs. 11,00,000 = 2,00,000 + 6,00,000 + 3,00,000

(2) 'X' Co. Ltd. agrees to purchase the partnership business for which it pays Rs.6,00,000 in shares and Rs.4,00,000 in Debentures and balance in cash.

In this problem, the purchase price can not be calculated by the second method, because the amount to be received in cash is not given. Therefore, for calculating the purchase price, method No.1 is to be followed.

3.4 Accounting Procedure :

In the case of conversion into, or sale to a company, there is a purchases and sale business. Firm sells off its business. Company purchases the business. Partnership firm is partially dissolved. Therefore, one has to take into account the accounting procedures in the books of firm and in the books of a company.

(A) Accounting procedure in the Books of Firm.

(B) Accounting procedure in the Books of the Company.

3.4.1 (A) Accounting Procedure in the Books of Firm :

As the partnership firm is dissolved it becomes necessary to close the books of accounts of the firm. For this purpose the accounting procedure is exactly similar (with few exceptions) to that of in the case of Dissolution of the Firm. Following are the important steps involved in the accounting procedure to be followed to close the books of accounts of the firm.

(1) Ascertain Purchase Price, if it is not specifically given in the problem.

(2) Open Realisation Account and Transfer all assets, whether taken over or not, at their book-values to it. (including cash if taken or excluding cash if not taken over by the company)

(3) Transfer all Third-party Liabilities, whether assumed or not, at their book-values to Realisation A/c.

(4) Show that the Purchase Consideration, so arrived at, is due from the purchasing company by Debiting Company's A/c and Crediting Realisation A/c with the amount of p.c.

(5) Show that the Purchase Price is duly received from the Company.

(6) If any asset is not taken over by the company, then either transfer it to partner's capital A/c's or sell it off.

(7) If a liability is not taken over by a company, then pay it off or transfer it to the partner's capital accounts.

(8) Record Realisation / Dissolution Expenses, if any, met by the Firm itself. If the company agrees to meet the firm's expenses then ignore it.

(9) Close Realisation Account and Transfer the profit or Loss on Realisation Account to partner's capital accounts, in their profit-sharing ratio.

(10) Distribute the Shares and Debentures received from the company among the partners, either in "Specific Ratio" given or "Final Capital" - Balance - Ratio".

(11) Make the final settlement of capital accounts in cash.

For all these steps, following Journal Entries are to be passed in the books of the Firm.

Journal entries in the Books of the Firm.

The following Journal entries are passed in the books of the firm to close its books of accounts.

(1) Transfer of Assets (at Book Value) to Realisation Account.

    Realisation Account ....   Dr.

        To Assets A/c.

(2) Transfer of Liabilities (at Book Value) to Realisation Account.

    Liabilities A/c   ....   Dr.

        To Realisation A/c

(3) When purchase consideration is due

    Purchasing Company A/c ....   Dr.

        To Realisation A/c

(4) If Sale of Assets for Cash

    Cash/Bank A/c ....   Dr.

        To Realisation A/c

(5) If any Asset taken over by the Partner

       Partner's Capital A/c.................................   Dr.

           To Realisation A/c

(6) If any Liability paid by the firm.

       Realisation A/c...   Dr.

           To Cash/Bank A/c

(7) If any Liability taken over by the Partner

       Realisation A/c ....   Dr.

           To Partner's capital A/c

(8) For Realisation expenses :

       Realisation A/c ....   Dr.

           To Cash / Bank A/c

(9) If Profit on Realisation

       Realisation A/c ....   Dr.

           To Partner's Capital A/c

(10) If Loss on Realisation

       Partner's Capital A/c ....   Dr.

           To Realisation A/c

(11) On Receipt of Purchase Consideration

       Share A/c ....   Dr. (If any)

       Debentures A/c ....   Dr. (If any)

       Cash A/c ....   Dr.

           To Purchasing Company

(12) Distribution of Shares and Debentures among Partners

       Partner's Capital A/c ....   Dr.

           To Shares A/c

           To Debentures A/c

(13) For Final Payment of Cash :

       Partner's Capital A/c ....   Dr.

           To Cash A/c

From all these Journal Entries following Ledger Account will be opened in the books of the Firm.

Model For Ledger Accounts
(1) Realisation Account

Liabilities	Rs.	Assets	Rs.
To Sundry Assets		By Sundry Liabilities	
To Machinery -		Creditors -	
To Stock -		Bills Payable -	
To Debtors -		Mrs. 'X' loan -	
To Building -		----	-
------		By Company's A/c (p.c.)	-
To Cash (Exp.)	-	By Cash A/c (Sale of	
To Cash (Liability not		Asset not taken over)	-
taken paid-off)	-	By Loss transferred to	-
		A -	
Profit transferred to		B -	
A	-	----	
B	-		
	-------		-------
	-------		-------

(2) Company's Account

	Rs.		Rs.
To Realisation A/c	-	By Cash A/c	-
(p.c)	-	By Shares A/c	-
	-	By Debentures A/c	-
	------		------
	-		-
	------		------

(3) Shares Account

	Rs.		Rs.
To Company's A/c	-	By A's Cap. A/c	-
(Received)	-	By B's Cap. A/c	-
	-	(Distributed)	-
	------		------
	-		-
	------		------

(4) Cash Account

To Bal. b/d		By Realisation A/c	
(As per B/s, if not taken over)	-	(Exps.)	-
Realisation A/c		By Realisation A/c	
(Sale of Asset)	-	(liab.Paid)	-
		By A's Cap. A/c	
		(final payment)	-
		By B's Cap. A/c	
		(final payment)	-
	------		--------
	-		--
	------		--------

(5) Debentures Account

To Company's A/c	-	By A's Cap. A/c	-
(Received)		By B's A/c	-
		(Distributed)	
	------		------
	-		-
	------		------

(6) Partner's Capital Account

	A	B			
Realisation A/c			By Balance b/d	-	-
(Loss)	-	-	(As per b/s)		
To Shares A/c	-	-	By Reserve	-	-
To Debentures A/c	-	-	(if any, as per B/s)		
To Cash A/c			By P & L A/c	-	-
(final payment)	-	-	(As per B/s)		
			By Realisation A/c	-	-
			(Profit)		
	--------	--------		--------	--------
	--	--		--	--
	--------	--------		--------	--------

3.4.2 (B) Accounting Procedure in the Books of Company and Balance sheet of New Co. :

Journal Entries in the Books of a Limited Company :

(i) When purchase consideration due

Business Purchase A/c ....Dr.

To Vendors A/c (firm A/c)

(ii) For incorporation of Assets & Liabilities taken over

Assets A/c ....Dr.

To Liabilities A/c

To Business Purchase A/c

Note : If purchase consideration is given in lumsum there may be goodwill or capital reserve.

(i) If purchase price paid is more than the net assets of the business, the excess amount must be goodwill.

Goodwill = Purchase Price - Net Assets

(ii) If purchase price paid is less than the net assets of the business, the resulting figure is capital gain which is credited to capital reserve.

Capital reserve = Net Assets - Purchase Price.

Payment of purchase consideration

Vendor's A/c (firm A/c) ....Dr.

To Shares Capital A/c

To Debentures A/c

To Cash A/c

3.5 Illustrations :

Illustration 1 :

A and B were partners. On 31st March 2013 their Balance sheet was as follows.

Liabilities	Rs.	Assets		Rs.
A's Capital	75,000	Fixed Assets	140000	
B's Capital	35,000	Less : Provision for		
A's Loan	10,000	Depreciation	45000	95,000
Sundry Creditors	26,800	Joint Life Policy		6,300
		Stock		27,000
		Debtors		15,000
		Cash		3,500
	1,46,800			1,46,800

On that date, the partners dissolved the firm. Fixed assets were sold to Jupiter Co. Ltd., for Rs. 1,00,000 payable in the form of 10,000 shares of Rs.10 each. A took over joint life policy at an agreed valuation of Rs.5,000. Stock and debtors realised Rs.23,700. Expenses came to Rs.300. A and B agreed to distribute shares in Jupiter Co. Ltd. between themselves in the ratio of their final claims. Sundry creditors were paid at book value. show the necessary ledger accounts.

Solution :

Dr.		Realisation Account		Cr.
Particulars	Rs.	Particulars	Rs.
To Fixed Assets	1,40,000	By Provision for Depreciation	45,000
To Joint Life Policy	6,300	By Sundry Creditors	26,800
To Stock	27,000	By Jupiter Co. Ltd.	1,00,000
To Debtors	15,000	By A's Capital A/c (Joint Life	5,000
To Cash A/c (Payment of	26,800	Policy)	
creditors)		By Cash A/c (Stock and Debtors)	23,700
To Cash A/c (Expenses)	300	By Loss on Realisation transferred	
		to A's Capital A/c	7,450
		B's Capital A/c	7,450
	2,15,400		2,15,400

Dr.		Jupiter Co. Ltd.		Cr.
Particulars	Rs.	Particulars	Rs.
To Realisation A/c (Purchase Price)	1,00,000	By Shares in Jupiter Co. Ltd.	1,00,000
	1,00,000		1,00,000

Dr.		A's Loan Account		Cr.
Particulars	Rs.	Particulars	Rs.
To Cash A/c	100	By Balance b/d	10,000
To Shares in Jupiter Co. Ltd.	9,900		
	10,000		10,000

Dr.   **Partner's Capital A/c**   **Cr.**

Particulars	A Rs.	B Rs.	Particulars	A.Rs.	B. Rs.
To Realisation A/c (J.L.P.)	5,000	-	By Balance b/d	75,000	35,500
To Realisation A/c (Loss)	7,450	7,450			
To Shares in Jupiter Co. Ltd.	62,550	27,550			
	75,000	35,000		75,000	35,000

Dr.   **Cash Account**   **Cr.**

Particulars	Rs.	Particulars	Rs.
To Balance b/d	3,500	By Realisation A/c (Payment of Creditors)	26,800
To Realisation A/c (Sale of Current Assets)	23,700	By Realisation A/c (Expenses)	300
		By A's Loan A/c	100
	27,200		27,200

Dr.   **Shares In Jupiter Co.Ltd.**   **Cr.**

Particulars	Rs.	Particulars	Rs.
To Jupiter Co. Ltd.	1,00,000	By A's Loan A/c	9,900
		By A's Capital A/c	62,550
		By B's Capital A/c	27,550
	1,00,000		1,00,000

Notes :

(i) As enough cash is not available, for the balance of A's loan account, shares in Jupiter co. Ltd. are given.

(ii) There is no need to establish the ratio of final claim, as the only assets available for closing the capital accounts are 'Shares in the Jupiter Co. Ltd.'

Illustration 2 :

Anu and Sonu were in partnership sharing profit and losses in the ratio of 2:1. Their summarised Balance Sheet as on 31st March 2013 was as under.

Liabilities		Rs.	Assets	Rs.
Capital Accounts :			Fixed Assets	1,40,000
Anu	1,00,000		(including two motor cars for	
Sonu	80,000	1,80,000	Rs. 28,000)	
Current Accounts			Stock	70,000
Anu	40,000		Debtors	1,00,000
Less : Sonu	23,000	17,000	Bills Receivable	25,000
Loan from Sonu		63,000	Bank	20,000
Creditors for Goods		1,10,000	Advertisement Suspense	15,000
			Account	
		3,70,000		3,70,000

They decided to dissolve the business and accepted the offer of Nanak and Co. Ltd. to acquire stocks and fixed assets excluding two motor cars at a total price of Rs.3,35,000. The debtors realised Rs.97,000 and bills receivable, Rs,24,000. Creditors for goods allowed a discount of 5%. The purchase consideration was to be discharged by a cash payment of Rs.83,000. the allotment by the company to the partners of 8,000 preference shares of Rs.10 each (valued at Rs.9 each) and the balance by the allotment of 9,000 ordinary shares of the firm. The partners agreed that following should be the basis of distribution on dissolution of the firm.

(a) Anu to take over on Motor car at a value of Rs.25,000 and Sonu, the other car at Rs.15,000.

(b) Sonu to accept preference shares for her loan to the firm, the remainder to be taken over by Anu.

(c) The ordinary shares to be taken over by Anu and Sonu in proportion of their fixed capitals.

(d) The balance to be settled in cash.

Prepare the necessary accounts to close the books of the firm :

Solution :

Dr.   **Realisation Account**   **Cr.**

Particulars	Rs.	Particulars	Rs.
To Fixed Assets	1,40,000	By Creditors for goods	1,10,000
To Stock	70,000	By Nanak & Co.	3,35,000
To Debtors	1,00,000	By Bank (Debtors)	97,000
To Bills Receivable	25,000	By Bank (B/R)	24,000
To Bank (Creditors)	1,04,500	By Anu's Capital A/c	25,000
To Profit on Realisation		By Sonu's Capital A/c	15,000
transferred to :			
Anu's Capital A/c 1,11,000			
Sonu's Capital A/c 55,500	1,66,500		
	6,06,000		6,06,000

Dr.   **Partner's Capital Account**   **Cr.**

Particulars	Anu Rs.	Sonu Rs.	Particulars	Anu Rs.	Sonu Rs.
To Realisation A/c	25,000	15,000	By Balance b/d	1,00,000	80,000
To Equity Shares in			By Current A/c	1,41,000	27,500
Nanak & Co.	1,00,000	80,000			
To Pref. Shares in					
Nanak & Co.	-	9,000			
To Bank A/c	1,07,000	12,500			
	2,41,000	1,07,500		2,41,000	1,07,500

Dr.   **Partner's Current Account**   **Cr.**

Particulars	Anu Rs.	Sonu Rs.	Particulars	Anu Rs.	Sonu Rs.
To Balance b/d	-	23,000	By Balance b/d	40,000	-
To Advt. Suspense A/c	10,000	5,000	By Realisation A/c	1,11,000	55,500
To Capital A/c	1,41,000	27,500			
	1,51,000	55,500		1,51,000	55,500

Dr.   **Sonu's Loan Account**   **Cr.**

Particulars	Rs.	Particulars	Rs.
To Pref. Shares in Nanak & Co.	63,000	By Balance b/d	63,000
	63,000		63,000

Dr.   **Bank Account**   **Cr.**

Particulars	Rs.	Particulars	Rs.
To Balance b/d	20,000	By Realisation A/c	1,04,500
To Realisaton A/c	97,000	By Anu's Capital A/c	1,07,000
To Realisation A/c	24,000	By Sonu's Capital A/c	12,500
To Nanak & Co.	83,000		
	2,24,000		2,24,000

Dr.   **Nanak & Co.**   **Cr.**

Particulars	Rs.	Particulars	Rs.
To Realisation A/c	3,35,000	By Bank A/c	83,000
		By Pref. Shares in Nanak & Co.	72,000
		By Equity Shares in Nanak & Co.	1,80,000
	3,35,000		3,35,000

Dr.   **Pref. Shares in Nanak & Co.**   **Cr.**

Particulars	Rs.	Particulars	Rs.
To Nanak & Co.	72,000	By Sonu's Loan A/c	63,000
		By Anu's Capital A/c	9,000
	72,000		72,000

Dr.   **Equity Shares in Nanak & Co.**   **Cr.**

Particulars	Rs.	Particulars	Rs.
To Nanak & Co.	1,80,000	By Anu's Capital A/c	1,00,000
		By Sonu's Loan A/c	80,000
	1,80,000		1,80,000

Illustration 3 :

   Mr. M and Mr. D were carrying on business as equal partners. The firm's Balance Sheet as on 31st December 2012 was as follows :

Liabilities	Rs.	Assets	Rs.
Sundry Creditors	65,500	Stock	54,000
Bank Overdraft	30,000	Plant & Machinery	1,82,000
Bills Payable	12,500	Office Furniture	15,000
Capital Accounts :		Book Debts	73,000
M	1,50,000	Joint Life Policy	9,500
D	1,48,000	Leasehold Premises	34,500
		Profit and Loss A/c	26,000
		(Debit Balance)	
		Drawing Accounts :	
		M	9,000
		D	3,000
	4,06,000		4,06,000

   The business was carried on till 30th June, 2013. The partners withdrew, in equal amounts, half the amount of profits made during the period of six months (From January-June, 2013) after 10% P.A. had been written off leasehold premises, 10% P.A. Plant and Machinery and 5% p.a. off office furniture. Meanwhile sundry creditors were reduced by Rs.10,000. On 30th June, 2013, Stock was valued at Rs.63,400. Bills Payable were reduced by Rs.2300 and Bank Overdraft by Rs.15,000. Book Debts were valued at Rs.65,000, the Joint Life Policy was realised for Rs,9,500 and the amount was utilised to reduce the Bank Overdraft. Other items remained the same as on 31st December 2007.

   On 30th June, 2013 the firm sold the business to a Limited Company. The value of the goodwill was estimated at Rs,1,08,000 and the rest of the assets were valued on the basis of the balance as on 30th June, 2013. The Company paid the purchase consideration in fully paid equity shares of Rs.10 each, at par. Prepare a Realisation Account and Capital Accounts of the partners as on 30th June, 2013.

Solution

Dr.		Realisation Account	Cr.
Particulars	Rs.	Particulars	Rs.
To Leasehold Premises	32,775	By Sundry Creditors	55,500
To Plant and Machinery	1,72,900	By Bank Overdraft	5,500
To Office Furniture	14,625	By Bills Payable	10,200
To Stock	63,400	By .... Ltd, Co.	
To Book Debts	65,000	(Purchase Consideration)	3,85,500
To Profit on Realisation transferred to :			
M's Capital A/c	54,000		
D' Capital A/c	54,000		
	4,56,700		4,56,700

Dr.			Partner's Capital Account			Cr.
Particulars	M	D	Particulars	M	D	
	Rs.	Rs.		Rs.	Rs.	
To Profit & Loss A/c	13,000	13,000	By Balance b/d	1,50,000	1,48,000	
To Drawings	9,000	3,000	By Profit & Loss A/c	17,500	17,500	
To Drawings	8,750	8,750	By Realisation A/c	54,000	54,000	
To Shares in Co.	1,90,750	1,94,750				
	2,21,500	2,19,500		2,21,500	2,19,500	

Working Notes :

(i) Net Assets as on 30.6.13 = Leasehold Premises (After depreciation) + Plant and Machinery (after depreciation) + furniture (after depreciation) + Stock + Book Debts - Sundry Creditors - Overdraft - Bills Payable.

= (34,500 - 1,725) + (1,82,000 - 9,100) + (15,000 - 375) + 63,400 + 65,000 - 55,500 - (15,000 - 9,500) - 10,200 = Rs. 2,77,500.

(ii) Net Assets as on 1.1.13 = M's Capital + D's Capital - Profit and Loss A/c (Dr. Balance) - Drawings

= Rs.1,50,000+ Rs. 1,48,000- Rs. 26,000 - Rs. 2,000 = Rs. 2,60,000.

(iii) Profit earned and retained
(i.e. notwithdrawn) = Rs.2,77,500- Rs. 260000 = Rs. 17,500

(iv) Profit earned = Profit retained + Profit withdrawn

= Rs.17500 + Rs. 17500 = Rs. 35000.

(v) Purchase Consideration = Net Assets (excluding goodwill) +
Goodwill.
= 2,77,500 + Rs. 1,08,000 = Rs.3,85,500.

Illustration 4 :

Ajit, Ajay and Akashya were partners carrying on partnership business and sharing profits and losses in the ratio 1:2:3. On March 31,2013 their balance sheet was as under :

Balance Sheet
as on 31st March 2013

Liabilities		Rs.	Assets	Rs.
Partners capitals :			Building	20,000
Ajit	10000		Machinery	30,000
Ajay	20000		Motor Car	5,000
Akshaya	30000	60,000	Stock	15,000
Ajay's loan (carrying			Debtors	20,000
interest 8% p.a.)		20,000	Cash	9,000
Creditors		15,000	Investment	1,000
Bills payable		5,000		
		1,00,000		1,00,000

On the above date a private limited company was incorporated to take over the above business on the following terms and conditions :

1) All assets (except cash and investments) and all liabilities (except Ajay's loan) to be taken over by the company for which all assets are valued at per except building which is considered worth Rs.27,000 and stock as worth Rs.14,000. Further, goodwill is valued at Rs.30,000.

2) Ajay's loan to be partly liquidated by his taking over the firm's cash and investments at per. For the balance he is given 8% debentures received from the company in part discharge of purchase consideration.

3) The balance of the purchase consideration is received in the form of equity shares of the company which are to be appropriately distributed amongst the partners.

Show ledger accounts to close the books of the firm.

Realisation Account

Particulars	Rs.	Particulars	Rs.
To Building	20,000	By Creditors	15,000
To Machinery	30,000	By Bills Payable	5,000
To Motor Car	5,000	By Purchasing Co's	1,06,000
To Stock	15,000	account	
To Debtors	20,000		
To Partners Capital accounts -			
Profit on realisation :			
Ajit 6,000			
Ajay 12000			
Akshaya 18,000	36,000		
	1,26,000		1,26,000

Partner's Capital Account

Particulars	Ajit Rs.	Ajay Rs.	Akshaya Rs.	Particulars	Ajit Rs.	Ajay Rs.	Akshaya Rs.
To Equity shares in purchasing company	16,000	32,000	48,000	By Balance b/d	10,000	20,000	30,000
				By Realisation A/c	6,000	12,000	18,000
	16,000	32,000	48,000		16,000	32,000	48,000

Notes :-

Calculation of purchase consideration :

		Rs.
Assets taken over :		
Building	27,000	
Machinery	30,000	
Motor Car	5,000	
Stock	14,000	
Debtors	20,000	
Goodwill	30,000	
		1,26,000
Less : Liabilities taken over :		
Creditors	15,000	
Bills payable	5,000	20,000
Total purchase consideration	Rs.	1,06,000

Illustration 5 - Amit and Asit were in partnership sharing profit and losses : Amit two-thirds : Asit one-third. The summarised partnership balance sheet as on 31st March 2013 was as under:

Liabilities		Homi Rs.	Assets		Homi Rs.
Fixed capital accounts :			Fixed assets		70,000
Amit	50,000		Current assets :		
Asit	40,000	90,000	Stock	35,000	
Current accounts :			Debtors	65,000	
Amit	20,000		Balance at bank	15,000	1,15,000
Less : Asit	10,000	10,000			
Loan - Asit		30,000			
Creditors		55,000			
		1,85,000			1,85,000

The fixed assets included two motor-cars having book values of Rs.8000 and Rs.6000 respectively.

The partners desiring to retire from business, accepted the offer of Western India Limited to acquire stock and fixed assets, other than motor cars at an agreed purchase price of Rs.1,60,000.

The purchase consideration was to be satisfied by a cash payment of Rs.56,000, the allotment by the company to the partners of 400, 5% preference shares of Rs.100 each, and the balance by the allotment by the company to the partners of 900 equity shares of Rs.100 each.

The debors realised Rs.61,000 and the creditors settled for Rs.51,000.

The partners agreed that the following should be the basis of distribution on dissolution of the partnership :

(1) Amit to take over one car at a valuation of Rs.12,000 and Asit the other at Rs.8,000.

(2) Asit to be allotted preference shares to the value of his loss, the remainder to be allotted to Amit.

(3) The equity shares to be allotted in proportion of fixed capitals.

(4) Both the preference and equity shares to be valued at Rs.80 per share.

(5) The balances to be settled in cash.

You are required to prepare :
(a) The realisation account
(b) the bank account and
(c) the partners, capital accounts showing the final settlement between them.

Realisation Account

Liabilities	Homi Rs.	Assets	Homi Rs.
To Sundry Assets :		By Sundry Creditors	55,000
To Fixed Assets	70,000	By Western India Ltd.	
To Stock	35,000	purchase price	1,60,000
To Debtors	65,000	By Amit's Capital A/c car	12,000
To Bank Creditors	51,000	By Asit's Capital A/c - car	8,000
to Profit on realisation :		By Bank - debtors	61,000
Amit 50,000			
Asit 25,000	75,000		
	2,96,000		2,96,000

Bank Account

	Homi Rs.		Homi Rs.
To Balance b/d	15,000	By Realisation A/c- Creditors	51,000
to Realisation A/c - debtors	61,000	By Amit's Capital A/c	66,000
To Western India ltd.	56,000	By Asit's Capital A/c	15,000
	1,32,000		1,32,000

Partners Capital Account

	Amit Rs.	Asit Rs.		Amit Rs.	Asit Rs.
To Current Account -			By Balance b/d	40,000	40,000
transfer	-	10,000	By Current account -		
To Realisation Account			transfer	20,000	-
- cars	12,000	8,000	By Loan account		
To Preference Shares	2,000	30,000	- transfer	-	30,000
To Equity Shares (5:4)	40,000	32,000	By Realisation account		
To Bank	66,000	15,000	- profit	50,000	25,000
	1,20,000	95,000		1,20,000	95,000

Western India Ltd

	Homi Rs.		Homi Rs.
To Realisation Account	1,60,000	By Preference shares (400 @ Rs.80)	32,000
		By Equity shares (900 @ Rs.80)	72,000
		By Cash	56,000
	1,60,000		1,60,000

Illustration 6 :

Suresh and Vinod sharing profits and losses equally decided to convert their business into a limited company on 31st December 2012 when their balance sheet stood as follows :

Balance Sheet as on 31-12-2012

Liabilities	Rs.	Assets	Rs.
Sundry Creditors	48,000	Sundry Debtors	60,000
Loan Creditor	40,000	Bills Receivable	10,000
Bank Overdraft	16,000	Stock in Trade	36,000
Reserve	6,000	Patents	8,000
Capital Account		Plant & Machinery	16,000
Suresh 40,000		Land & Building	60,000
Vinod 40,000	80,000		
	1,90,000		1,90,000

(i) The goodwill of the firm was to be valued at two years purchase of the average profits of the previous three years.

(ii) The loan creditor had agreed to accept 7.5% redeemable preference shares in settlement of his claim.

(iii) Land & Buildings and Plant & Machinery were to be valued at Rs.1,00,000 and Rs.24,000 respectively.

(iv) The vendors to be allotted equity shares of the value of Rs.2,10,000.

(v) The past working results of the firm showed that they had made profits of Rs.30,000 in 2010, Rs.36,000 in 2011 and Rs.42,000 in 2012 after setting aside Rs.2,000 to the reserve fund each year.

You are required to show realisation account, capital accounts in the books of the firm.

Solution :

In the Books of the Firm
Realisation A/c

Liabilities		Rs.	Assets		Rs.
Sundry Assets			By Liabilities		
Debtors	60,000		Sundry		
Bills			Creditors	48,000	
Receivable	10,000		Loan Creditor	40,000	
Stock	36,000		Bank Overdraft	16,000	1,04,000
Patents	8,000		By Purchasing Company		
Plant & Mach.	16,000		A/c (Purchase Consider-		
Land & Building	60,000	1,90,000	ation)		2,10,000
Capital A/c (Profit)					
Suresh	62,000				
Vinod	62,000	1,24,000			
		3,14,000			3,14,000

Partner's Capital A/c

	Suresh Rs.	Vinod Rs.		Suresh Rs.	Vinod Rs.
To Shares A/c	1,05,000	1,05,000	By Bal. b/d	40,000	40,000
			By General Reserve	3,000	3,000
			By Realisation A/c	62,000	62,000
	1,05,000	1,05,000		1,05,000	1,05,000

Purchasing Company A/c

	Rs.		Rs.
To Realisation A/c (P.C)	2,10,000	By Shares A/c	2,10,000
	2,10,000		2,10,000

Shares Account

Purchasing Co. A/c	2,10,000	By Suresh Capital A/c	1,05,000
		By Vinod Capital A/c	1,05,000
	2,10,000		2,10,000

Note :

(i) Since the company is issuing Rs.210000 in Equity Shares, that means purchase consideration is fixed at Rs.210000.

(ii) No need of calculation of goodwill because purchase consideration is given in the problem.

(iii) Loan creditor accepted 7.5% redeemable preference shares the entry of which will be passed in the books of company.

Illustration 7 :

A, B and C carried on business partnership sharing profits and losses the ratio of Rs.2:1:1.

They decided to convert their business into a private limited company. A new company, Prospective Pvt. Ltd. was duly formed with an Authorised capital of Rs.6,00,000, divided into 45,000 equity shares of Rs.10 each and 15,000 cumulative pref. shares of Rs.10 each.

The company took over the firm's business as on 31st March 2013 on which date the firm's balance sheet as under.

Balance Sheet as on 31-3-2013

Liabilities		Rs.	Assets	Rs.
Capital Accounts		3,10,000	Machinery	65,000
A	1,50,000		Motor Car	18,000
B	1,00,000		Furniture & Fitting	6,000
C	60,000		Stock in Trade	1,80,000
Current Accounts		50,000	Debtors	52,000
A	29,250		Bank	86,000
B	20,750		B's Current A/c	21,000
A's Loan		40,000		
Creditors		28,000		
		4,28,000		4,28,000

The debtor's are all good and taken over by A who also agreed to pay the creditors.

The company took over machinery at its book value, stock at an agreed value of Rs.1,66,000. Furniture at Rs.4,500, Motor Car at Rs.16,000 and bank balance. The value of goodwill of the firm was agreed at Rs.40,000. The company also agreed to discharge A's loan by the issue to him at par of Rs.3,000 6% cumulative preference shares of Rs.10 each and cash payment of Rs.10,000.

The purchase consideration was discharged by the company by the issue at per of 30,000 equity shares of Rs.10 each and the balance in cash.

You are required to prepare the necessary accounts to close the books of the firm.

Solution :

In the Books of the Firm
(Realisation A/c)

Liabilities		Rs.	Assets		Rs.
To Sundry Assets		4,07,000	By Liabilities		28,000
Machinery	65,000		Creditors	28,000	
Motor Car	18,000		By A's Current A/c		
Furniture &			(Debtors)		52,000
Fittings	6,000		By Prospective Ltd. A/c		
Stock	1,80,000		(p.c.)		3,77,500
Debtors	52,000				
Bank	86,000				
To A's Current					
A/c (Creditors)		28,000			
To Current A/c					
(Profit)		22,500			
A -	11,200				
B -	5,625				
C -	5,625				
		4,57,500			4,57,500

Purchasing Co. A/c (Prospective Ltd. A/c)

To Realisation A/c	3,77,500	By Equity Shares A/c	3,00,000
		By 6% Cumulative Pref.	
		Shares A/c	30,000
		By Cash A/c	47,500
	3,77,500		3,77,500

Cash A/c

To Prospective Ltd. A/c	47,500	By A's Loan A/c		10,000
		By Capital A/c		
		A -	18,500	37,500
		B-	9,405	
		C -	9,595	
	47,500			47,500

Equity Shares A/c

To Prospective Ltd. A/c	3,00,000	By A's Capital A/c	1,48,000
		By B's Capital A/c	75,220
		By C's Capital A/c	76,780
	3,00,000		3,00,000

A's Loan A/c

To 6% Cumulative Pref.		By Balance b/d	40,000
Shares	30,000		
To Cash A/c	10,000		
	40,000		40,000

Partner's Current A/c

Particulars	A	B	C	Particulars	A	B	C
	Rs.	Rs.	Rs.		Rs.	Rs.	Rs.
To Current A/c	-	15,375	-	By Balance b/d	1,50,000	1,00,000	60,000
(Transfer)				By Current A/c	16,500		26,375
To Shares A/c	1,48,000	75,220	76,780				
To Cash A/c	18,500	9,405	9,595				
	1,66,500	1,00,000	86,375		1,66,500	1,00,000	86,375

Conversion of a Partnership Firm into a Limited Company / 145

6% Cumulative Pref. Shares A/c

To Prospective Ltd. A/c	30,000	By A's Loan A/c	30,000
	30,000		30,000

Working Note :

(1) The shares have been divided among the partners in the proportion of the amount finally due to them which is calculated as follows.

Capitals	A	B	C
Add Current A/c	1,50,000	1,00,000	60,000
	+29,250	(-)21,000	+20,750
		(Dr.)	
	1,79,250	79,000	80,750
Add Profit on	11,250	5,625	5,625
Realisation	1,90,500	84,625	86,375
	1,332	677	691

A will get equity shares of Rs. 1,48,000

$$\left(\frac{300,000}{1} \times \frac{1332}{2700} \right)$$

B will get equity shares of Rs. 75,220

$$\left(\frac{300,000}{1} \times \frac{677}{2700} \right)$$

C will get equity shares of Rs. 76,780

$$\left(\frac{300,000}{1} \times \frac{691}{2700} \right)$$

(2) Calculation of Purchase Consideration

Assets taken over (Agreed value)		Satisfaction	
Machinery	65,000	In Shares	
Stock	1,66,000	30,000 equity	
Furniture	4,500	shares of	
Motor Car	16,000	Rs. 10 each	3,00,000
Bank	86,000	In Cumulative Pref. Shares	
Goodwill	40,000	3,000 6%	
	3,77,500	Cum Pref.	
Less Liabilities		Shares of	
taken over	–	Rs.10 each	30,000
		Cash	47,500
Purchase		(10,000 + 37,500)	
Consideration Rs.	3,77,500		3,77,500

Illustration 8 :

Mayur and Virendra were partner's sharing profits and losses in the ratio of 3:2 respectively. Their balance sheet as on 31st December 2012 was as follows :

Balance Sheet as on 31-12-2012

Liabilities	Rs.	Assets	Rs.
Sundry Creditors	12,000	Plant & Machinery	22,000
Bills Payable	4,000	Motor Car	4,000
Mayur's Loan	5,000	Investment	4,000
Outstanding Salary	2,000	Bills Receivables	3,000
Reserve Funds	4,000	Stock	8,000
Capital A/c's		Debtors	5,000
Mayur	13,000	Cash	7,000
Virendra	13,000	**Current A/c**	
Current A/c		Virendra	2,000
Mayur	2,000		
	55,000		55,000

The partnership firm was converted into a limited company on the above date subject to the following adjustments :

(i) The company agreed to take over the following assets and liabilities and goodwill of the values stated below :

Plant and Machinery Rs.32,000 Stock Rs.7,000

Debtors Rs.5,000, Creditors at 10% Discount and Bills payable at 20% discount.

(ii) Goodwill was valued at three year's purchase of the average profits of the last three years.

Profits being as under :

2012	Profit	Rs.7,000
2011	Profit	Rs.5,000
2010	Loss	Rs.3,000

(iii) Motor car was sold at Rs.5,000.

(iv) Bills receivables were taken over by Mayur at Rs.2,500 and Virendra took over investment at Rs.1,000.

(v) Mayur's loan and outstanding salary were paid in full.

(vi) Realisation expenses amounted to Rs.1,000.

(vii) Purchase consideration was charged by issuing 3,000 shares of Rs.10 each at Rs.8 per share and balance in cash.

(viii) Shares received from the limited company are to be shared by partner's in their profit sharing ratio.

Prepare : (i) Realisation account

(ii) Cash account

(iii) Partner's capital account

(iv) Limited company account.

Solution :

Realisation A/c

Liabilities		Rs.	Assets		Rs.
To Sundry Assets		46,000	**By Liabilities**		18,000
Plant & Mach.	22,000		Creditors	12,000	
Motor Car	4,000		Bills Payable	4,000	
Investment	4,000		Outstanding		
Bills Receivables	3,000		Salary	2,000	
Stock	8,000		By Purchasing		
Debtors	5,000		Co. A/c (p.c.)		39,000
To Cash A/c			By Cash A/c.		
(Out. Salary)		2,000	(Motor Car)		5,000
To Cash A/c (Exp.)		1,000	By Mayur		
To Capital A/c (Profit)		16,500	Current A/c		2,500
Mayur	9,900		(Bills Receivable)		
Virendra	6,600		By Virendra Current A/c		1,000
			(Investment)		
		65,500			65,500

Cash A/c

	Rs.		Rs.
To Balance b/d	7,000	By Mayur's Loan A/c	5,000
To Purchasing Co A/c	15,000	By Realisation A/c	2,000
To Realisation	5,000	(out. Salary)	
(Motor Car)		By Realisation (Exp.)	1,000
		By Mayur Capital A/c	10,400
		By Virendra Capital A/c	8,600
	27,000		27,000

Purchasing Co. A/c

	Rs.		Rs.
To Realisation A/c	39,000	By Cash A/c	15,00
		By Shares A/c	24,000
	39,000		39,000

Capital Accounts

	Mayur Rs.	Virendra Rs.	Particulars	Mayur Rs.	Virendra Rs.
To Shares A/c	14,400	9,600	By Balance b/d	13,000	13,000
To Cash A/c	10,400	8,600	By Current A/c	11,800	5,200
			(balance transfer)		
	24,800	18,200		24,800	18,200

Current Accounts

	Mayur Rs.	Virendra Rs.	Particulars	Mayur Rs.	Virendra Rs.
To Balance b/d	-	2,000	By Balance b/d	2,000	-
To Realisation (B.R.)	2,500	-	By Reserve Funds	2,400	1,600
To Realisation (Inv.)	-	1,000	By Realisation A/c	9,900	6,600
To Capital A/c	11,800	5,200			
(Bal. transfer)					
	14,300	8,200		14,300	8,200

Mayur's Loan Account

To Cash A/c	5,000	By Balance b/d	5,000
	5,000		5,000

Share's Account

To Purchasing Co. A/c	30,000	By Mayur Capital A/c	18,000
		By Virendra Capital A/c	12,000
	30,000		30,000

Working Notes :
(i) Calculations of Purchase Consideration

Particulars	Rs.	Satisfaction of p.c.	Rs.
Assets taken over (Agreed Value)		In shares	
Plant & Mach.	32,000	3,000 equity shares of Rs.	
Stock	7,000	10 each	30,000
Debtors	5,000	in cash	9,000
Goodwill	9,000		
	53,000		
Less Liabilities taken over (Average Value)			
Creditors 10,800	14,000		
Bills Payable 3,200			
	39,000		39,000

(ii) Calculation of Goodwill

1990 Profit	Rs.	7,000
1989 Profit	Rs.	5,000
		12,000
Less 1988 Loss	Rs.	3,000
		9,000
Average Profit	Rs.	3,000

Goodwill = 3 years purchase of Average Profit
$$= 3 \times 3,000$$
$$= Rs. 9,000$$

(iii) Shares are distributed among the partners according to their profit sharing ratio as it is clearly stated in the problem.

Illustration 9 :

Ajay and Vijay sharing profits and losses equally wanted to convert their partnership into a Limited Co. Their Balance Sheet as on 31st December 2012 was as under :

Balance Sheet as on 31-12-2012

Liabilities		Rs.	Assets	Rs.
Sundry Creditors		27,000	Sundry Debtors	50,000
Loan Creditors		25,000	Bills Receivables	7,000
Bank Overdraft		10,000	Stock	20,000
Reserve Fund		15,000	Patents	5,000
To Capital A/c		50,000	Plant & Machinery	10,000
Ajay	25,000		Land & Building	35,000
Vijay	25,000			
		1,27,000		1,27,000

(i) The Goodwill of the firm was to be valued on the basis of two years purchase of average profits calculated on the previous three years profits which were 2010 Rs.20,000, 2011, Rs.23,000 and in 2012 Rs.26,000 after setting aside Rs.5,000 to Reserve fund each year and charge Rs.1500, Rs.1800 and Rs.2100 respectively in resepct of income Tax.

(ii) The Land and Buildings and Plant and Machinery were taken over at on revaluation of Rs.75,000 and Rs.15,000 respectively.

(iii) 5% Debentures of Rs.100,000 were issued at a discount of 5%.

(iv) Partners were issued Rs.15,000 ordinary shares of Rs.10 cash towards the purchase consideration and the balance in cash.

(v) The purchasing company immediately pays off sundry creditors and Bank overdraft and issue 6% Pref. shares of Rs.100 each to loan creditors for Rs.25,000.

You are required to give :

(i) Statement showing purchase consideration.

(ii) Realisation Account and Partners Capital Account.

(iii) Opening Balance Sheet of the company assuming that all transactions are duly completed.

Solution
In the Books of the Firm (Realisation Account)

Liabilities		Rs.	Assets		Rs.
To Sundry Assets		1,27,000	**By Liabilities**		62,000
Debtors	50,000		Creditors	27,000	
Bills Receivable	7,000		Loan Creditor	25,000	
Stock	20,000		Bank Overdraft	10,000	
Patents	5,000				
Plant & Mach.	10,000		By Purchasing (p.c.)		1,66,000
Land & Building	35,000				
To Capital A/c Profit		1,01,000			
Ajay	50,500				
Vijay	50,500				
		2,28,000			2,28,000

Capital Accounts

	Ajay Rs.	Vijay Rs.	Particulars	Ajay Rs.	Vijay Rs.
To Shares A/c	75,000	75,000	By Balance b/d	25,000	25,000
To Bank A/c	8,000	8,000	By Reserve Fund	7,500	7,500
			By Realisation A/c	50,500	50,500
	83,000	83,000	(Profit)	83,000	83,000

Statement Showing Purchase Consideration

Particulars		Satisfaction	
Assets taken over (Average value)		In Shares	
Goodwill	56,000	15,000 ord. shares	1,50,000
Land & Building	75,000	of Rs.10 each	
Plant & Machinery	15,000	In Cash	16,000
Stock	20,000		
Bills Receivable	7,000		
Patents	5,000		
Debtors	50,000		
	2,28,000		
Less Liabilities taken over (A.V.)			
Creditors 27,000			
Loan Creditors 25,000			
Bank Overdraf 10,000	62,000		
	1,66,000		1,66,000

Working Note :
(i) Valuation of Goodwill
  Profit for 3 Years

2006	Rs.	20,000
2007	Rs.	23,000
2008	Rs.	26,000
Total Profit		69,000
Add transferred to Reserve		15,000
Total Divisible Profit		84,000
Average Profit	Rs.	28,000

$$84,000 \times \frac{1}{3}$$

Goodwill = Average Profit x 2
    = 28,000 x 2
    = Rs. 56,000

(Hint : Payment of Income tax should be ignored because for calculation of goodwill, divisible profit must be considered)

In the Books of Company
Balance Sheet as on 1st Jan.2013

Liabilities	Rs.	Assets	Rs.
Share Capital		Fixed Assets	
Authorised Capital	-	Goodwill	56,000
	----------	Land & Building	75,000
Issued & Subscribed	-	Plant & Machinery	15,000
called & paidup capital		Patents	5,000
15,000 ordinary shares of	1,50,000	Current Assets	
Rs.10 each		Stock	20,000
250 6% Pref shares	25,000	Debtors	50,000
of Rs. 100 each		Bills Receivable	7,000
Secured Loan	1,00,000	Bank	42,000
5% Debentures		**Miscellaneous**	
		Discount on issue	
		of Debentures	5,000
	2,75,000		2,75,000

Working Note :

Calculation of Bank Balance

Cash received on issue of 1

Rs.1,00,000 @ 5% Deb. @ 5% Discounts		95,000
Less Cash paid to	Rs.	
Creditors	27,000	
Bank Overdraft	10,000	
Partnership firm	16,000	
	---------	53,000
Shown in B/s		--------
		42,000

3.6 Exercises (Objective)

A) State whether the following statements are True or False

1) Assets and liabilities taken over by the purchasing company will not form the part of purchase consideration.

2) Conversion of partnership into a limited Co. is referred to sale of partnership business to a company.

3) Purchase consideration means the amount at which the company agreed to purchase the partnership business.

4) Purchase consideration is the price paid by the limited co. to the firm.

5) In convention the business of the firm is sold to the company.

6) Under net assets method of purchase consideration goodwill is nil.

7) On receipt of purchase consideration purchasing co. A/c should be debited.

8) Unless otherwise stated, shares received from company should be distributed among the partners in profit sharing ratio.

Ans : 1) False 2) True 3) True 4) True 5) True 6) True 7) False 8) False.

B. Fill in the Blanks :

1) Assets and liabilities not taken over nor sold can be transferred to ------------- account.

2) Conversion of partnership into a limited co in referred to as of business to a company.

3) Goodwill = Purchase considering -----------

4) Capital Reserve = Net Assets -------------

5) Purchase consideration = cash + -------- + Debentures received from the company.

6) Only assets and liabilities ---------- over is considered while determing purchase consideration.

7) When partnership firm converts its business into a Ltd co. it is known as -----------

8) When there is conversion ----------- is required to be fixed in the first instance.

9) P.C. = ----------- minus agreed value of liabilities taken over.

10) Generally the shares and Debentures received from the company are distributed to the partners in their -------------- ratio.

Ans : 1) Partner's Capital 2) Sale 3) Net Assets 4) Purchase consideration 5) Shares 6) taken 7) Conversion 8) Purchase consideration 9) Agreed values of Assets taken over 10) Final claim.

Exercise

1) A and B are Partners. They share profits and losses in the ratio of 3:2. Their Balance Sheet as on 31-12-2012 was as follows:

Liabilities	Rs.	Assets	Rs.
A's Capital	30,000	Goodwill	5,000
B's Capital	20,000	Other Fixed Assets	30,000
Reserve	15,000	Joint Life Policy	20,000
Current Liabilities	30,000	Other Assets	40,000
	95,000		95,000

On 30-6-2013 AB Ltd was formed to take over the Partnership Business. Up to that date a net profit of Rs.10,000 was made after charging depreciation of fixed assets @ 10% p.a. For the purpose of transfer, Goodwill was valued at Rs.30,000. The joint life policy was surrendered for Rs,15,000 and nothing was withdrawn by partners.

Purchase consideration was paid by shares of Rs.10 each. The company also issued 15,000 shares of Rs.10 each to the public as fully paid. All shares were sold.

Close the books of the firm by showing only Realisation Account and Capital Account. Prepare Opening Balance Sheet of ABC Ltd.

(**Ans.** Purchase consideration Rs.95,000/ Profit Rs.25,000)

2) The Balance Sheet of Ram, Rahim and Karim stood as follows. On 31st December 2012.

Balance Sheet as on 31-12-12

Liabilities		Rs.	Assets		Rs.
Sundry Creditors		17,000	Cash at Bank		6,200
Bills Payable		1,200	Sundry Debtors	20,000	
Capital Accounts		50,000	- R.D.D.	1,000	19,000
Ram	20,000		Stock		22,000
Rahim	20,000		Plant & Machinery		15,000
Karim	10,000		Fixtures		1,500
			Goodwill		4,500
		68,200			68,200

It was decided that to sell their business to a newly formed company named Jayhind Co. Ltd.

The company agreed to allot 6000 fully paid shares of Rs.10 each in all the assets except bank balance.

The partners shared profits and losses in proporion of 1/2, 1/3 and 1/6 respectively.

Close the books of the firm, assuming that shares were duly alloted to partners according to original capital ratio.

[**Ans.** Profit Rs.15,000 Shares to Ram Rs.24,000
Rahim Rs.24,000,
Karim Rs.12,000]

3) X, Y and Z are in partnership sharing profits and losses in the ratio of 3:2:1. On 31st March 2013 their balance sheet stood as follows:

Balance Sheet as on 31-3-2013

On the above date the business is sold to a company.

The valuation placed for various assets and liabilities is as follows :

Liabilities		Rs.	Assets	Rs.
Capital Accounts		1,20,000	Buildings	60,000
X	50,000		Plant & Machinery	70,000
Y	40,000		Patents	30,000
Z	30,000		Stock	20,000
Reserve Fund		30,000	Debtors	15,000
Bills Payable		30,000	Cash at Bank	5,000
Sundry Creditors		20,000		
		2,00,000		2,00,000

Buildings Rs.50,000, Plant and Machinery Rs.95,000 Stock Rs. 30,000 Debtors Rs.14,500 Bills payable Rs.30,000.

Patents not taken over by the company were sold Rs.36,000 and creditors were paid off. Cost of winding up amounted to Rs.500.

The company paid 13,500 shares of Rs.10 each fully paid and the balance in cash.

Prepare necessary ledger accounts to close the books of the firm.

[**Ans.:** Realisation profit Rs.30,000
Final claim ratio X,Y,Z is 4:3:2]

4) Manik and Rohit carrying on business in partnership sharing profits and losses in the ratio of 3:2 wish to dissolve the firm and sell the business to a limited company on 31st December 2012.

Balance Sheet as on 31-12-2012

Liabilities	Rs.	Assets	Rs.
Capital Accounts		Furniture	8,000
Manik	70,000	Motor Car	12,000
Rohit	50,000	Stock	81,000
Reserve	20,000	Debtors	60,000
Sundry Creditors	25,000	Cash	4,000
	1,65,000		1,65,000

A limited company with an authorised capital of Rs.3,00,000 in equity shares of Rs.10 each is registered to purchase the above business on the following terms :

(i) Goodwill is valued at Rs.30,000

(ii) Furniture and stock are revalued at Rs.6,000 and Rs.85,000 respectively.

(iii) Debtors are subject to 5% provision.

The motor car is not required by the company and Manik takes over the same at an agreed valuation of Rs.3,000.

The purchase consideration is satisfied by issue of equity shares of Rs.10 each at par.

Prepare necessary ledger accounts to close the books of the firm.

[**Ans. :** Profit on realisation Rs.25,000]

5) Lion and Tiger were in partnership sharing profits and losses in the ratio of 3:1. The following is the balance sheet of the partnership as at 31st March 2013.

Balance Sheet

Liabilities		Rs.	Assets	Rs.
Capital Accounts		32,000	Fixed Assets	21,000
Lion	24,000		Stock	11,200
Tiger	8,000		Debtors	19,600
Current Accounts		6,200	Cash at Bank	3,720
Lion	4,200			
Tiger	2,000			
Tiger's Loan		3,000		
Creditors		14,320		
		55,520		55,520

Elephant Ltd. agreed to take over stock and fixed assets excluding the value of motor car Rs. 4100 for a consideration of Rs.48,000 which is to be satisfied by payment of cash Rs.16,000, allotment of 160 Pref. shares of Rs.100 each valued at Rs.75 per share and the balance by allotment of 1600 equity shares of the face value of Rs.10 each.

The debtors realised Rs.19,200 and creditors were settled for Rs.14,000.

The Following was agreed between the partners.

(i) Equity shares should be allotted in the ratio of the partners capital accounts as per balance sheet.

(ii) Lion to take over the Motor Car at an agreed value of Rs.4,200.

(iii) The Pref. shares to be alloted to Tiger to the value of his loan and the remainder to be alloted equally between the partners.

(iv) Balance remaining to be settled in cash.

You are required to show :

(i) Realisation Account (ii) Partner's Capital Account

(iii) Bank Account   (iv) Working of Shares Allotment.

[Ans. Realisation Profit Rs.19,920]

6) Anil and Sunil were partners sharing profits in the ratio of 3:1 respectively. Their balance sheet as on 31-12-2012 was as follows :

Liabilities	Rs.	Assets		Rs.
Creditors	40,000	Fixed Assets		1,00,000
Bills Payable	8,000	Loose Tools		8,000
Anil's Loan	12,000	Bills Receivable		16,000
Outstanding Exp.	8,000	Stock		30,000
General Reserve	16,000	Debtors	28,000	
Capital Account	98,000	- R.D.D.	4,000	2,4000
Anil 64,000		Cash		4,000
Sunil 34,000				
	1,82,000			1,82,000

The partnership was converted into limited company on that date, subject to the following adjustments :

(i) Fixed assets include a Motor Car of Rs.16,000.

(ii) The Company agreed to take over other Fixed Assets at Rs.1,04,000. Stock at Rs.28,000. Debtors at Rs.26,000. The company also agreed to pay creditors and bills payable at 10% discount.

(iii) Motor Car was sold by the firm for Rs.20,000.

(iv) Bills receivable were taken over by Anil for Rs.14,000 where as Sunil took loose tools for Rs.6,000.

(v) Anil's Loan and outstanding expenses were paid in full.

(vi) Realisation expenses amounted to Rs.4,800.

(vii) Goodwill was valued at 3 years purchase of the average profits of last 4 years.

The profit figures are as follows :

2009 profit Rs.8,000

2010 profit Rs.16,000,2011 Loss Rs.4,000 and 2012 Profit Rs.28,000.

(vii) The purchase consideration was discharged by issuing 15,000 equity shares of Rs.10 each at Rs.8 per share and the balance in cash.

Prepare necessary ledger accounts in the books of the firm.

[**Ans. :** Realisation Profit Rs.56,000]

7) Raj and Narayan were the partrners sharing profits and losses in the proportion of 5:3 respectively. They decided to convert their partnership into a limited co. Under the name of Rajnarayan Ltd. Their Balance Sheet as at 31st March 2013 was as follows :

Balance Sheet as on 31-3-2013

Liabilities	Rs.	Assets	Rs.
Raj's Capital A/c	2,20,000	Camera & Equipment	1,80,000
Narayan's Capital A/c	1,50,000	Shooting Vans	80,000
General Reserve	60,000	Copy Rights	20,000
Loan from Raj	40,000	Stock of Films	1,70,000
Bank Overdraft	80,000	Bills Receivable	1,20,000
Sundry Creditors	50,000	Sundry Debtors	30,000
	6,00,000		6,00,000

The terms and conditions of conversion of their business into a limited company were as follows :

(i) Goodwill of the firm to be valued on the basis of average profits of the previous three years, which were Rs.70,000, Rs.75,000 and Rs.71,000 after setting aside Rs.20,000 to general reserve each year.

(ii) Camera and equipments to be taken over at revaluation of Rs.2,00,000.

(iii) 5% debentures in Rajnarayan Ltd. to be issued to discharge loan from Raj.

(iv) Rajnarayan Ltd. to pay off Bank overdrafts and Creditors immediately for which the company should sell away stock of films at an estimated value of Rs.1,72,000.

(v) Partners to be issued 200 @ 6% preference shares of Rs.100 each fully paid add 9600 equity shares of Rs.400 each, Rs.50 per share paid up and the balance in cash.

(vi) Partners to distribute equity shares in Rajnarayan Ltd. in their profit sharing ratio.

You are required to show necessary accounts to close the books of the firm.

8) Shri Black, White and Red are equal partners of M/s. Colour Production and co. The balance sheet of the firm as at 31st December 2012 was as follows :

Balance Sheet as on 31-12-2012

Liabilities	Rs.	Assets	Rs.
Black Capital A/c	2,50,000	Land	2,50,000
White Capital A/c	5,00,000	Plant & Machinery	10,00,000
Loan from Bank	25,00,000	Buildings	3,50,000
Creditors	5,00,000	Stock	15,00,000
		Debtors	5,00,000
		Red's Account	1,50,000
	37,50,000		37,50,000

On that date it is decided to convert the partnership into a limited company on the following term :

(i) Land to be valued at Rs.7,50,000.

(ii) Plant and Machinery to be valued at Rs.12,50,000.

(iii) Depreciation amounting to Rs.1,00,000 to be written off buildings.

(iv) A provision of 10% of book value to be made for obsolete stocks.

(v) A reserve for doubtful debts to be made at 10% of the debtors.

(vi) A discount of 6% would be earned on creditors when paid out.

(vii) The new company will issue 6000 equity shares of Rs.100 each credited as fully paid up, such share capital being valued at Rs.7,50,000 and the balance payable is to be discharged by issue of 8%. Debentures of Rs.1000 each.

Show necessary ledger accounts to close the books of Colour production and Co and Opening Balance Sheet of the new company with assumption that :

(1) All partners are solvent and have sufficient cash resources as may be necessary for the purpose of settling accounts.

(2) Share's and cash are divided equally among the partners.

[**Ans.:** Profit 4,80,000. Purchase consideration Rs.10,80,000]

◻◻◻

Chapter 4

Computerised Accounting Environment

4.1	**Meaning and Introduction :**
4.1.2	**Importance of Computer in Modern World :**
4.2	**An Overview of Computerised Accounting System:-**
4.3	**Salient Features of Computerised Accounting**
4.4	**Accounting Packages and Consideration for their Selection:-**

4.1 Meaning and Introduction :

Accounting is a systematic but flexible exercise. It involves basic recording of the transactions. Out of the basic records, the profit has to be ascertained based on some accounting rules which are generally acceptable to the proffesion. When the basic records are kept manually, it is referred to as manual book-keeping and final process leading to generation of financial statements of business as manual accounting.

Nowadays, we are living in computerised age. The cost of computerisation is also coming down consistently. This has led to widespread usage of computers even in small businesses. When accounts are written with the help of computers, it is called computerised accounting. At present many computer programmes help in proper basic recording of business transactions. However, it requires human intervention, to correctly calculate profit because all possible situations cannot be inserted in computer programmes. Hence, what these programmes actually perform is computerised rather than computerised accounting. Thus, recording of business transactions which are repetitive in nature is best candidate for computerisation. The basic difference among various terms is summarised in the following diagram :

Working of accounting systems - Manual Vs Computerised.

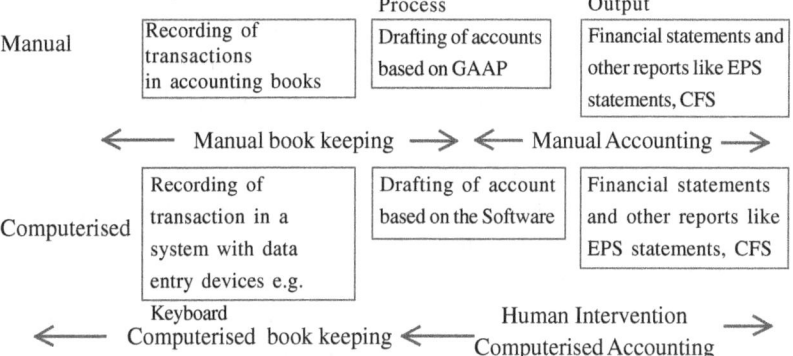

		Process	Output
Manual	Recording of transactions in accounting books	Drafting of accounts based on GAAP	Financial statements and other reports like EPS statements, CFS

⟵ Manual book keeping ⟶ ⟵ Manual Accounting ⟶

Computerised	Recording of transaction in a system with data entry devices e.g. Keyboard	Drafting of account based on the Software	Financial statements and other reports like EPS statements, CFS

⟵ Computerised book keeping ⟵ Human Intervention Computerised Accounting ⟶

It is important to note that the fundamentals of accounting do not change whether books of accounts are maintained manually or are computerised. The same principle of debit and credit is applied for recording business transactions. However, since the recording medium is something else compared to hard copy documents and considerable reliance have to be placed on the software for the input, in processing and output of the data certain precautions, methodologies and techniques are to be adopted while maintaining accounts in a computerised environment.

Computer Definitions : Generally, a computer is known as a machine which computes number i.e. performs arithmetic operations. But besides this a computer can be used to perform non-arithmetic operations also. Text manipulation, creation of graphical images, playing games etc. are all non-arithmetic operations. Almost in all organisations e.g. educational, industrial, financial or research and development invariably large amount of data is produced. Processing this data becomes a very tedious and time consuming task. Computer is most suitable for such repetitive monotonous tasks.

Computer can be defined in different ways -

1) "A Computer is a fast and accurate electronic data processing system that is designed to automatically accept and store data, process it and produce output results under the direction of a step-by-step instructions.

2) "A computer is an electronic device which stores data, processes it and then displays the output on a monitor."

3) "A computer is an electronic machine which works on the user's instructions and gives the desired output."

4) " A computer is an electronic machine that processes raw data under programme control to generate meaningful information with speed and accuracy."

Characteristics of Computer

The important characteristics of computer are speed, accuracy, efficiency, storage and versatility.

1) Speed : The speed of a computer is measured in terms of number of instructions performed in a second. Computers are very fast. They can process millions of instructions per second (MIPS). Small computers can perform hundreds or thousands of operations in a second, while large computer systems can execute over millions of instructions per second.

2) Accuracy : Besides being fast, computer work with greater accuracy also. They never make any mistake. It is the greatest advantage of computers. It can repeat the same job as many times as required in exactly the same way without any mistake. Computer marks mistake only if the data fed by the programmer are wrong. In fact, it is a mistake of programmer and not of computer. A computer is therefore, very useful in getting very accurate scientific calculations.

3) Efficiency : The efficiency of a human decreases with the age, whereas the efficiency of a computer does not decreases with the age. The speed of a computer remains the same over the years.

4) Storage : Computer has main memory for storing data and instruction required while processing. Computer systems may also have auxiliary storage devices of high capacity such as floppy disk, hark disk, magnetic tape etc. These devices are used to store huge amount of data for future use.

5) Versatility : Computer are very versalite. Besides mathematical problems, computer can handle problems which are not related to numbers such as railway reservation, database management system, graphic representation etc. Computer can perform wide range of operations based on the instructions fed to it and the available hardware capabilities.

6) Automatic : Once the process has started it would continue without requiring manual intervention till its completion. Thus, in a broad sense a computer is an automatic device.

4.1.1 Importance of Computer in Modern World :

We saw that computer is a machine which performs various mathematical and logical operations on symbols and other forms of information and produce results in a form readable by humans and machines. In present modern world, computer is very useful in almost all walks of life. Some of the major criteria for using computers are listed as under.

1) Quick Information : This is the most important point for using computer for processing raw data and converting it into meaningful information. An electronic computer works at high speed, therefore, it makes available the desired information to user quickly and promptly.

2) Accurate and Reliable Information : Data processed by utilising the services of properly programmed computer is highly accurate, reliable and dependable. It is so because computers perform their task as per the given programme.

3) Preparation of Various Reports : Computers facilitates the preparation of various type of financial and nonfinancial reports required by executives for planning, decision making and control in that period of time.

4) Reduction in Paper Work : The use of computer for data processing has helped the management of business organisations to cope with the increasing problem of paper handling by speeding up the process and eliminating some of the paper needs through the storage of data by properly constructed data beases and files, from where they can be taken out when needed.

5) Preparing Salary Slip and Tax Statement : Computer is most useful for preparing payroll and generating various other useful statements such as income tax statement etc.

6) Identification of Problems : Computer facilitates the identification of business problem by carrying out the analysis of available data. It also helps the management to take corrective action over the business problem.

4.2 An Overview of Computerised Accounting System:-

Computerised accounting system performs the same function as manual accounting system. The significance of computerisation of accounting system may be summarised as follows :-

1) Greater speed and efficiency where the transactions are entered into the system and all related accounts are instantly updated.

2) Less chance of errors as each transaction is recorded only once with all related accounts and reports being updated with the same amount.

3) Real time processing where a transaction can be recorded in the system as the transaction occurs with all related system, accounts and reports being updated simultaneously.

4) Instant access to timely and accurate reports.

As with manual system, input data is required in the form of business documents. Documentary information is entered into the computer usually by the keyboard. The accounting package acts as processing centre by recording the transaction in all accounts in all related systems allowing a host of reports to be extracted.

These input processing and output functions are illustrated in the following diagram.

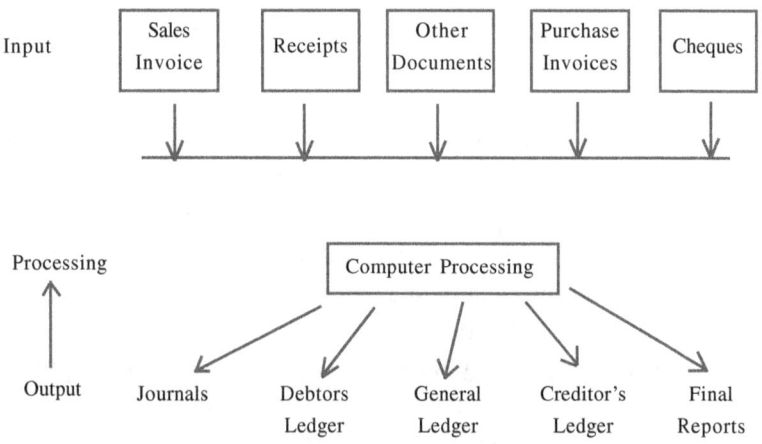

4.3 Salient Features of Computerised Accounting
1) Fast, Powerful, Simple and Integrated :

Computerised accounting is designed to automate and integrate all the business operations, such as sales, finance, purchase, inventory and manufacturing. With computerised accounting, accurate, upto date business information is literally at the fingertips. The computerised accounting combine with enhanced MIS, Multilingual and Data organization capabilities to help the company simplify all the business processes easily and cost-effectively.

2) Complete Visibility :

Computerised accountings giving the company sufficient time to plan, increase the customer base, and enhance customer satisfaction. With Computerised accounting the company will have greater visibility into the day-to-day business operations and access to vital information.

3) Enhanced User Experience :

Computerised accounting allows the company to enter data in a variety of ways which makes work a pleasure. Adapting to the specific business needs is possible.

4) Accuracy, Speed :

Computerised accounting has User-definable templates which provides fast, accurate data entry of the transactions; thereafter all documents and reports can be generated automatically, at the press of a button.

5) Scalability :

Computerised accounting adapts to the current and future needs of the business, irrespective of its size or style.

6) Power :

Computerised accounting has the ability to handle huge volumes of transactions without compromising on speed or efficiency.

7) Improved Business Performance :

Computerised accounting is a highly integrated application that transforms the business processes with its performance enhancing features which encompass accounting, inventory, reporting and statuatory processes. This helps the company access information faster and takes quicker decision. Computerized accounting also guarantees real time optimization or operations and enhanced communication.

8) Quick Decision Making :

Generates real time, comprehensive MIS reports and ensures access to complete and critical information instantly.

9) Complete Reliability :

Computerized accounting makes sure that the critical financial information is accurate, controlled and safe from data corruption.

Concept of grouping and codification of accounts :-

Under manual accounting system accounts codes are rarely used. However, under a computerised accounting system coding system is frequently used. A coded accounting system is more convenient where there are various account heads. By using this system is reduces the posibility of the some account existing in several names due to spelling mistakes or abbreviations used.

A proper codification requires a systematic grouping of accounts. The major groups or heads could be Assets, Liabilities, Revenue Receipts, Capital Receipts, Reserve Expenditure, Capital Expenditure. The sub-groups or minor heads could be "Cash" or "Receivables" or " Payables" and so on. The grouping and codification is depended upon the type of organisation and the extent of sub-division required for reporting on the basis of profit centres or product lines. There could a classification based on geographical location as well.

An example of our account code classification could be the following :

Assets	(0-499)
Cash	(51-99)
51	Petty Cash
60	Main Cash
65	Cash at Bank
70	Cheques in Hand
Receivables -	(100 to 149)
100	Debtors - Secured
105	Debtors - Unsecured
110	Others
Inventories -	(150-199)
150	Insurance
160	Others
Fixed Assets	(200-299)
220	Buildings
250	Plant & Machinery

270	Furniture & Fixture
280	Vehicles
Other Assets -	(300-349)
330	Employee Advances
Liabilities & Shareholder Fund - (500 to 9999)	
Payables	(500-529)
520	Sundry Creditors
524	Commission Payable
526	Rates & Taxes Payable
529	Sundry Deposits
Pay roll payables	(530-559)
531	Salaries & Wages Payable
535	Leave Encashment Payable
552	TDS Salaries
553	Profession Tax Payable
554	Gratuity Payable
555	P.F. Payable
Accrued Expenses	(560-579)
561	Rent
563	Electricity
565	Telephone
579	Other
Other Liabilities	(700-799)
701	Bank Loan
Provision	(800-899)
801	Income Tax
810	F.B.T.
820	Depreciation
830	Proposed Dividend
835	Tax on Proposed Dividend
Shareholder Fund	(900-999)
901	Paid up Share - Capital
920	General Reserve
930	Capital Reserve
950	Contingency Reserve
Net Profits	(1000-9999)

Revenue	(1000-1999)
1100	Domestic
1200	Export
1500	Other
Expenses	(2000-9999)
Cost of Sales	(2000-2999)
2100	Raw Material Consumed
2200	Labour
2500	Other
Manufacturing Expense	(3000-3999)
3210	Salaries/ Wages and Bonus
3220	Contribution to P.F. and other funds.
3230	Power & Fuel
3240	Consumption of Stores and Spare Parts
3300	Outward Freight and Handling Charges
Selling Expenses	(500-6999)
5250	Advertisement/Sales Promotion
5251	Commissions
5295	Market Research
5350	Brokerage and Discount
Administrative Expense	(7000-7999)
7250	Postage Telephone etc.
7260	Repairs to Building
7265	Repairs to Machinery
7266	Other Repairs
7270	Legal Expenses
7280	Audit Expenses
7600	Travel & Conveyance
7610	Other Expense
7701	Depreciation
7730	Insurance
7740	Rates & Taxes
7750	Rent
7760	Donation & Contributions
Other Expenses	(8000-8999)
8100	(Interest on Loan)

8900	Other
Other Tax	(9000-9999)
9800	Income Tax
9900	VAT

The above chart of accounts is only an example. The actual account classification may contain fewer, more or different accounts depending upon the industry and complexity of the business. Here account codes were 3 digits for assets & Liabilities and uniformity 4 digits for revenue & expenditure. However, many organisations prefer to have unifarmity 4 digits. Where 4 digits account codes are used, the first digit in the code will indicate whether it is revenue receipt or a capital receipt or a revenue expenditure or a capital expenditure or loan & advances or shareholder fund. Thus, if the first digit is "O" or "1" the Head of account will represent Revenue Receipt "2' or "3" will represent Revenue Expenditure "4" or "5" capital Expenditure "6" or "7" Loans & Advances Head, and "8" will represent shareholders Fund.

Adding 2 to the first digit of the Revenue Receipt will give the code number alloted to corresponding Revenue Expenditure head, adding another 2 - the capital expenditure head and another 2 - the loans and advances head of Accounts; e.g.

0401	represents the receipt head for T.V. manufacture.
2401	represents the Revenue Expenditure head for T.V. manufacture.
4401	represents capital outlay on T.V. manufacture.
6401	represents loans for T.V. manufacture.

Such a pattern may not be relevant for these departments which do not operate capital/loan head of accounts. Where receipt/expenditure is not heavy, certain major heads may be combined under a single number, the major heads themselves forming sub-major heads under that number.

The range of code numbers allotted under the scheme of codification is shown below :-

	Major Head Code Nos.
Receipt Heads (Revenue Account)	0020-1999
Expenditure Heads (Revenue Account)	2011-3999
Receipt Heads (Capital Account)	4000

Expenditure Heads (Capital Account)	4046-5999
Loans & Advances	6001-7999
Shareholders Fund	8001-8995

Thus,

a) The main unit of classification of accounts should be the major head which should be divided into minor heads, each of which should have a number of subordinate heads, generally shown as sub-heads. The sub-heads are further divided into their further division into minor heads.

The major heads, minor heads, sub-heads and detailed heads together may constitute a four tier arrangement of the classification structure of accounts.

b) Major heads of account falling within the receipt heads (Revenue Account) may correspond to different activities or line of business of the company which as T.V. manufacture, servicing of T.V., repairs & maintenance of T.V.s, while minor heads subordinate to them shall identify the specific manufacturing activity like manufacture of T.V. kits, components & spare parts etc. A manufacture of T.V. may consist of a number of activities like the manufacture of the kits, picture tube, screen, cabinet etc. These will then correspond to 'subheads' below the minor head represented by the main activity- T.V. manufacture.

c) A 'detailed head' is often termed as an object classification. In the expenditure account being considered in the above example the main purpose of the detailed head is to control expenditure on an item basis and at the same time group the objects according to the nature. Example if such detailed head could be salaries, office expenses, salesman expenses, showroom expenses etc.

d) The detailed classification of account heads and the order in which the major and minor heads shall appear in all account records, should be approved by the top management of the organisation and should be received by the auditor before they are introduced in the computerised accounting environment.

4.4 Accounting Packages and Consideration for their Selection :- A business organisation performs various activities e.g. financial accounting activities, inventory control, payroll etc. Previously these activities were carried out manually. But it was a laboures and time consuming work. Computers manufacturers have come to the rescue of business organisation. They have developed packages program for carrying out the activities like payroll- prepared inventory control and financial account. These packages are useful for any organisation.

There are many accounting packages available in the market. It may be summarised as follows :

Spreadsheets : Accounts can be maintained in a computerised environment by using a spreadsheet package. To do so the user will have to use his knowledge and skills of spread sheet software to keep control of the figures. Special spreadsheet controls including physical spreadsheet controls like spreadsheets locked on a protected shared drive with restricted access and read/write access control and password-protected cells and formulas with password should be used. Spreadsheet softwared allow grouping of accounts, replication of cell contents, formulas and macros, pivot tables, calculation and functions which help in the maintenance of the accounts. Probably the most common use of spreadsheets is in business. Business large and small need to track income and expenses, forecast profit or losses, and analyse sales trends. The following list describes a few ways in which typical business departments use spreadsheets.

i) Sales departments use spreadsheets to calculate sales commission for their sales people.

ii) Purchasing departments can create invoice that are built around spreadsheets, then use the information to create running totals of their costs.

iii) Manufactring departments use spreadsheets to keep records of maintenance performed on equipment and to record transfers of finished goods to warehouses.

iv) Personnel department use spreadsheet to track wages & salaries paid to employees as well as the costs of employee benefits.

v) Marketing departments often use spreadsheets to explore the costs of new products.

A data file created with a spreadsheets is called a worksheet. The process of creating a worksheet can involve organizing the data, designing the worksheet, entering data, creating formulas editing, formatting, adding charts, analysing data and printing the worksheet.

Advantages :

1) It is simple to use and easy to understand.

2) Common functions like calculation, setting formulas, macros, replication of cell contents etc, can be easily done in a spreadsheet.

3) Grouping & regrouping of accounts is possible.

4) Presentation can be made in various forms including graphical presentations.

5) Basic protection like restricted access and password protection of cell can be used to give security to the spreadsheet dates.

Disadvantages :-

1) It has data limitations.

2) Simultaneous access as a network may not be possible. As in modern software, while updating the data, locking of the table is not possible in a spreadsheet.

3) Double entry is not automatically completed. Some formulas or other means have to be adopted to complete the double entry.

4) Reports are not automatically formatted and generated.

Database Management : To make large collection of data useful, companies use computers as an efficient database management system. The goal of database management software is to gather large volumes of data and process them into useful information.

Like a warehouse a database is a repository for collections of related data or facts. A database management system (DBMS) is a software tool that allows multiple users to access store and process the data or facts into useful information.

Functions of a DBMS :

DBMS Functions	Computer system function
1) Collect the relevant data	Input
2) Preserve the data for later use	Storage
3) Organise the data into logical & meaningful sets (information)	Processing
4) Create meaningful subsets of the data (information) for specific purposes	Processing
5) Obtain meaningful subsets of the data (information) in printed form.	Output

Working with Database : The DBMS provides the vehicle that presents the rate to the user and the tools required to work with the data. This is what is meant by the DBMS's interface. The interface is the visual tool that is used to perform the important DBMS functions that manage data productively, e.g.

i) Creating tables.

ii) Entering & editing data.

iii) Viewing data using filters and forms.

iv) Sorting the records

v) Querying the database to obtain specific information.

vi) Generating reports to print processed information.

Prepackaged Accounting Software : There are several pepackaged accounting software which are available in the market and are used extensively for small and medium sized organisation. There software are easy to use, relatively less expensive and readily available. The installation of these software are very simple. An installation diskette or Cd is provided with the software which can be used to install the software on a personal computers. A network version of this software is also generally available which needs to be installed on the server and work can be performed from the various workstations or modes connected to the server. Along with the software an user manual is provided which guides the user how to use the software. After installation of the software, the user should check the version of the software to ensure that they have been provided with the latest. The vendor normally provides regular updates to take care of the changes of law as well as add features to the existing software. These software normally have a section which provides for the creating of a company. The name, address, phone no. and other details of the company like VAT registration No. PAN and TAN numbers are fed into the system. The accounting period has to set by inserting the first and last day of the financial year. The next step in the use a this software could be the creation of accounts. This is done by adding the accounts along with their codes into the master files. Each account is classified into Asset a Liability or an Income & Expenditure account. Whether the account has other subsidiary ledgers under it needs to be indicated to the system. The opening balance are to be entered with the master files. The company parameturs need to be set at this point of time so that the accounts which are the cash, bank, sundry debtors, sundry creditors etc. are know to the system. The customers name, address and other basic details are also entered in the customers master file. Similarly, the creditors details are entered with the creditor master file. Product details are entered through and product matter file. Here the unit of measurement and the opening stock quantities including the values are provided. The system of valuation of stock like the FLFO, LIFU weighted average etc. are defined in the product master file. Once the basic parameters are set and the master files are updated the system is ready for use.

Any prepackaged software will have the following matter file screens: company monthly file, Accounts master file, sub-ledger master file, customer master file, vendor master file, product master file, Division master file.

The entry screens differ in look and feel from software to software and from vendor to vendor. However, the basic entry screens are the following.

Cash Receipts & Payment Entry, Book Receipts & Payment Entry, Petty Cash Voucher Entry, Journal Entry, Purchase order, GRN, Bill Purchase Return Entry, Sales Order, Challan, Invoice, Sales Return Entry, Debit Note & Credit Notes Entry, Cash Sales & Purchases Memos, Stock Transfer etc.

Each of these screens are provided with the add, modify or delete options, special option like the date modification and voucher number modification are provided in some of the softwares.

The next reactions that the software provides is the reports section where the following reports are common to most of the softwares :

Cash Book, Bank Book, Petty cash book, Purchase Book, Sales Books. Cash Sales Book, Cash Purchase Book, Purchase Return & Sales Return Register, Journal Book, General ledger, Subsidiary ledger, Debtors and Creditors Ledger, Debit note & Credit note Register, Stock ledger,Stock movement register. production & Consumption register, Document printing option like printing of purchase order challans & bills, Sales order, challans & invoices declaration forms & return forms.

Trial Balance, Profit & Loss Account and Balance Sheet

Some of the software provide Bank Reconciliation Statement

options. There are special reports also provided by some software like the cards, bank maintenance report which shows any date on which the cash or bank by mistake had credit balance. There are also MIS reports like aging of debtors, slow moving & non-moving stock etc.

The last section also called the housekeeping section of these softwares provide the system maintenance features. Backup can be taken and restored under the housekeeping section. Clean-up, fine tuning and re-indexing of the software is part of this section of the software.

Advantages of Pre-packaged Accounting Software :-

1) It is easy to install.
2) It is relatively less expensive.
3) It is easy to use.
4) Backup procedure is simple.
5) It is flexible in case of some software.
6) It is quite useful for small & medium size businesses.

Disadvantages :-

1) It does not cover peculiarities of specific business
2) It does not cover all functional area.
3) It is not possible customisation in most such software.
4) It does not serve the purpose or reports generated is not sufficient.
5) It does not provide security.
6) It may provide bugs in the software which takes long to be rectified by the vender.

Customised Accounting Software :-

This software is developed on the basis of requirement specifications provided by the organisation. The choice of customised accounting software could be because of the typical nature of the business or else the functionality desired to be computerised is not available in any of the prepackaged accounting software. An organisation desiring to leave an integrated software package covering most of the functional area may have the financial module as part of the entire customised system. Before developing customised software a feasibility should be made. The life cycle of a customised accounting software begins with the organisation providing the user requirements. After this system analyst prepares a requirement specification which is given for approval by the user management. Once the requirement specification is approved, the designing process begins. Development, testing and implementation are the other components of the system development life cycle.

Advantages of a Customised Accounting Package :-

1) The financial areas get computerised.

2) The input screens can be tailor made to match the input documents for ease of data entry.

3) The reports can be as per the specification of the organisation. Many additional MIS reports can be included in the list of reports.

4) Bar-code scanners can be used as input devices suitable for the specific needs of an individual organisation.

Disadvantages :-

1) Requirement Specification are incomplete or ambiguous resulting in a defensive system.

2) Inadequate testing results in bugs remaining in the software.

3) Documentation is not complete.

4) Frequent changes made to the system.

5) Vender unwilling to give support of the software due to other commitments.

6) Vender is not willing to part with the source code or enter into an agreement.

7) Control measures are inadequate.

The choice of customised accounting packages is made on the basis of the vendor proposals.

ERP (Enterprise Resource Planning) Accounting Software :-

Big organisations generally use ERP Package where finance comes as a module. An ERP is an integrated software package that manages the business process across the entire enterprise.

Aims :-

i) To reduce invoice inputting time.

ii) To reduce invoice processing costs.

iii) To reduce paper archive volume.

iv) To reduce the errors resulting from manual inputting.

v) To have permanent access to all invoices.

Features :-

i) Many integration possibilities - ODBC Access, DIL Access, API Access, Command Line.

ii) Automatic Content Analysis and recognition of key information.

iii) Automatic recognition of the supplier.

iv) Upto six user define Free Form Fields.

v) Colour, bitonal and dual stream support.

vi) Direct support of most twain scanners.

vii) Display invoices from any external application.

viii) Very easy addition of new suppliers.

ix) User-friendly validation with drag-and-drop OCR.

x) Encoding of line item by drag-and-drop OCR.

xi) Recognition of foreign invoices.

Steps :-

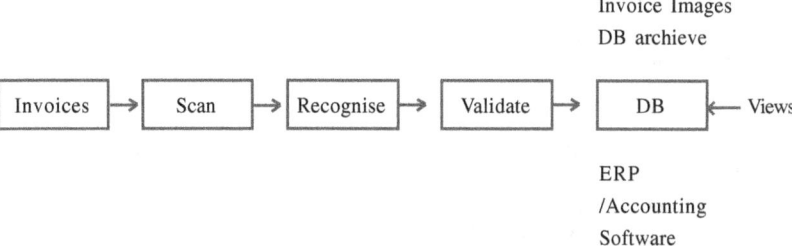

Advantages :-

1) An ERP is a generalised package which covers most of the common functionalities of any specific module.

2) Standardised reports are available.

3) Duplication of data is avoided.

4) Greater information is available.

Disadvantages :-

1) It is not so flexible.

2) There may be implementation hurdles.

3) It is very expensive.

4) It is not so easy to understand.

Attachement 3 : The statement of expenditure

Measure	Rs.	
0	1	2
Current Expenditure		
Cumulated Current Expenditure		
Personal		
Cumulated Personal		
Materials & Services		
Cumulated Materials & Services		
Subventious		
Cumulated subventious		
Transfers		

Attachment -4
When & Where are reported the final's statements

No.	The financial Statement 1	The period covered by the statements 2	The final term for reporting 3	Where reported 4
1.	Balancesheet	Year		DIBA
2.	The financial statement	Jan. to March April to June July to Sept. Oct. to Dec.		DIBA
3.	The notes on the accounts	Jan to March April to June July to Sept. Oct to Dec.		DIBA
4.	The executed payments statement of each	Jan to Dec.		DIBA NF
5.	The statement of Expenditure	Jan. to June		NAO NF

◻◻◻

Chapter 5

Introduction and Relevance of Accounting Standards

5.1 Overview of Accounting Standards in India - Concept.
5.2 Scope of Accounting Standards
5.3 Study of AS-1, AS-2, AS-4 and AS-9.

5.1 Overview of Accounting Standards in India - Concept

Accounting Standards are written documents, policy documents issued by expert accounting body or by Government or other regulatory body covering the aspects of recognition, measurement, treatment, presentation and disclosure of accounting transactions in the financial statements. Accounting Standards in India are issued by the Institute of Chartered Accountants of India (ICAI).

Objective of Accounting Standards

Objective of Accounting Standards is to standardize the diverse accounting policies and practices with a view to eliminate to the extent possible the non-comparability of financial statements and add reliability to the financial statements.The Institute of Chartered Accountants of India, recognizing the need to harmonize the diverse accounting policies and practices, constituted an Accounting Standard Board (ASB) on 21st April, 1977.

Compliance with the Accounting Standards

The accounting Standards will be mandatory from the respective date(s) mentioned in the Accounting Standard(s). The mandatory status of an Accounting Standard implies that while discharging their attest functions, it will be the duty of the members of the Institute to examine whether the Accounting Standard is complied with in the presentation of financial statements covered by their audit. In the event of any deviation from the Accounting Standard, it will be their duty to make adequate disclosures in their audit reports so that the users of financial statements may be aware of such deviation.

Ensuring compliance with the Accounting Standards while preparing the financial statements is the responsibility of the management of the enterprise. Statutes governing certain enterprises requires the enterprises that the financial statements should comply with the Accounting Standards, e.g., the Companies Act, 1956 (Section 211), and the Insurance Regulatory and Development Authority (Preparation of Financial Statements and Auditor's Report of Insurance Companies) Regulations, 2000.

Financial Statements cannot be described as complying with the Accounting Standards unless they comply with all the requirements of each applicable Standard.

Advantages and Disadvantages of Accounting Standards –

The setting of Accounting Standards has the following advantages:-

1) Standards reduce to a reasonable extent variation in the accounting treatments used to prepare the financial statements.

2) There are certain areas where important information is not required by law to be disclosed, standards may require such disclosure.

3) It facilitates comparison of financial statements of different companies situated at different places.

The disadvantages of setting Accounting Standards are :-

1) There are may be a trend towards rigidity in applying accounting standards.

2) Differences in accounting standards are bound to be because of differences in the traditions and legal system from one country to another.

3) Accounting Standards cannot override the law. The standards are required to be framed within the ambit of prevailing statute even though it is not an acceptable standard.

4) The choice between better alternative Accounting treatment in a particular situation is eliminated.

Accounting Standard and The Auditors

Auditors are duty bound while discharging their attest function to ensure that the Accounting Standards issued and made mandatory by the ICAI are implemented. Section 227(3) of Companies Act, 1965 requires the auditors to report whether in their opinion the Profit & Loss Account and Balance Sheet comply with the Accounting Standards referred in Section 211 (3C) of Companies Act, 1956.

5.2 Scope of Accounting Standards

Efforts will be made to issue Accounting Standards which are in conformity with the provisions of the applicable laws, customs, usages and business environment in India. However, if a particular Accounting Standard is found to be not in conformity with law, the provisions of the said law will prevail and the financial statements should be prepared in conformity with such law. The accounting Standards by their very nature cannot and do not override the local regulations which govern the preparation and presentation of financial statements in the country. However, the ICAI will determine the extent of disclosure to be made in the financial statements and the auditor's report. Such disclosure may be by way of appropriate notes explaining the treatment of particular items. The Accounting Standards are intended to apply only to items which are material. Any limitations with regard to the applicability of a specific Accounting Standard will be made clear by the ICAI from time to time. The date from which a particular Standard will come into effect, as well as the class of enterprises to which it will apply, will also be specified by the ICAI. In formulation of Accounting Standards, the emphasis would be on laying down accounting principles and not detailed rules.

An individual standard should be read in the context of the objective stated in that standard.

List of Accounting Standards issued by the Institute of Chartered Accountants of India

AS 1   Disclosure of Accounting Policies
AS 2   Valuation of Inventories
AS 3   Cash Flow Statement
AS 4   Contingencies and Events Occurring after the Balance Sheet Date
AS 5   Net Profit or Loss for the Period, Prior period Items, Changes in Accounting policies
AS 6   Depreciation Accounting
AS 7   Accounting for construction contacts
AS 8   Withdrawn and included in AS-26
AS 9   Revenue Recognition

AS 10   Accounting for Fixed Assets

AS 11   The Effects of Changes in Foreign Exchange Rates

AS 12   Accounting for Government Grants

AS 13   Accounting for Investments

AS 14   Accounting for Amalgamations

AS 15   Employee Benefits

AS 16   Borrowing Costs

AS 17   Segment Reporting

AS 18   Related Party Disclosure

AS 19   Leases

AS 20   Earning Per Share

AS 21   Consolidated Financial Statements & Accounting for Investments in Subsidiaries in Separate Financial Statements

AS 22   Accounting for Taxes on Income

AS 23   Accounting for Investment in Associates

AS 24   Discontinuing Operations

AS 25   Interim Financial Reporting

AS 26   Intangible Assets

AS 27   Financial Reporting of Interests In Joint Ventures

AS 28   Impairment of Assets

AS 29   Provisions, Contingent liabilities and Contingent Assets

AS 30   Financial Instruments- Recognition and Measurement

AS 31   Financial Instruments-Presentation

AS 32   Financial Instruments- Disclosures

5.3 Study of AS-1, AS-2, AS-4 and AS-9
AS -1 DISCLOSURE OF ACCOUNTING POLICIES
What are Accounting Policies

Accounting policies refer to specific accounting principles and the method of applying those principles adopted by the enterprise in the preparation and presentation of the financial statements. At the time of preparation of financial statements (i.e. Balance Sheet, Profit and Loss Account), there are many areas, which have more than one method of accounting treatment, e.g. : **Methods of Depreciation :** Straight Line Method, WDV Method**, Valuation of Inventories :** FIFO,

Weighted Average, Standard Cost, Retail Method.

There are many areas other than above, where more than one method can be followed for accounting. Methods which have been followed in preparation of Balance Sheet, Profit and Loss Account is disclosed as accounting policies. Hence accounting policies contains the information about the method adopted for the preparation of financial statement.

Need for disclosure of Accounting Policies

For proper and better understanding of financial statement, it is required that all significant accounting policies followed in preparation of financial statement should be disclosed. Because assets and liabilities in Balance Sheet and Profit and Loss Account are significantly affected by accounting policies followed. All significant accounting policies should be disclosed at one place because it would be helpful to the reader of financial statements.

Fundamental Accounting Assumptions

It is generally assumed that financial statements are prepared on the basis of fundamental accounting assumptions.

Fundamental Accounting assumptions are :

1) Going Concern – It means that enterprise had intention for continuing the operation in foreseeable future.

Foreseeable means coming one or two years.In other words, neither there is intention of discontinuance of business, nor necessity of liquidation of organization or discontinuance of major operations of the business.

2) Consistency – It means that same accounting policies are followed from one period to another.

3) Accrual – It means that financial statements are prepared on mercantile system only. Under this system, the effects of transaction and other events are recognised when they occur (and not as cash or its equivalent is received or paid) and they are recorded in the accounting records and reported in the financial statements of the period to which they relate.

Financial statements prepared on accrual basis inform users not only of past transactions involving the payment and receipt of cash but also of obligations to pay cash in the futures and of resources that represent cash to be received in the future.

Other accounting assumption like business entity, money measurement, matching are not fundamental accounting assumptions as per this accounting standard.

Assumption as regards fundamental accounting assumptions

If nothing has been written about the fundamental accounting assumption in the financial statements, it is assumed that fundamental accounting assumptions have been followed in preparation of financial statements. If any fundamental accounting assumption has not been followed, then this fact must be disclosed in financial statements.

Selection of Accounting Policies

Basic objective of selection of accounting policies is that the financial statements should be prepared on the basis of such

accounting policies, which exhibit true and fair view of state of affairs of balance sheet and the profit and loss account.

Major points which are considered for the purpose of selection and application of accounting policies

1) Prudence – Generally maker of financial statements has to face uncertainties at the time of preparation of financial statements. These uncertainties may be regarding collection from debtors, number of warranty claims that may occur. Prudence means making of estimates, which is required under conditions of uncertainty.

2) Substance over form – It means that transactions should be accounted for in accordance with actual happening and economic reality of the transactions not by its legal form.

3) Materiality – Financial Statement should disclose all the items and facts which are sufficient enough to influence the decisions of reader or user of financial statements.

Changes in Accounting Policies

A change in accounting policies should be made in the following conditions :

1) Adoption of different accounting policies is required by statute or for compliance with an Accounting Standard.

2) It is considered that change would result in more appropriate presentation of financial statements.

3) If there is any change in accounting policies in preparation of

financial statement from one period to subsequent period, and such change affects the state of affairs of Balance Sheet and Profit and Loss Account of the current period or such change affects the financial statements of a later period, then such change must be disclosed in financial statements. The amount, by which the financial statements are affected should be disclosed to the extent ascertainable.

Exercise

1) What are the main provisions of AS-1 ?
2) What are Accounting Policies ? Why should Accounting Policies be disclosed ?
3) Which are the points that should be considered in selection and application of Accounting policies ?

AS-2 VALUATION OF INVENTORIES

The objective of this standard is to formulate the method of computation of cost of inventories/stock, determine the value of closing stock/inventory at which, the inventory is to be shown in balance sheet till it is not sold and recognized as revenue.

Definition : Inventories consist of the following :

1) Held for sale in the ordinary course of business (finished goods)

2) In the process of production of such sale (raw material and work-in-progress)

3) In the form of materials or supplies to be consumed in production process or in the rendering of services (stores, spares, raw material, consumables). Inventories do not include machinery.

Accounting for machinery spares

- Machinery spares, which are not specific to a particular item of fixed asset but can be used generally for various items of fixed assets, should be treated as inventories for the purpose of AS-2. Such machinery spares should be charged to the statement of profit and loss as and when issued for consumption in the ordinary course of operations.
- Whether to capitalise machinery spare under AS-10 or not will depend on the facts and circumstances of each case. However, the machinery spares of the following types should be capitalised

being of the nature of capital spares / insurance spares.

1) Machinery spares which are specific to a particular item of fixed asset, i.e., they can be used only in connection with a particular item of the fixed asset, and

2)Their use is expected to be irregular.

- Machinery spares of the nature of capital spares/insurance spares should be capitalised separately at the time of their purchase whether procured at the time of purchase of the fixed asset concerned or subsequently. The total cost of such capital spares/ insurance spares should be allocated on a systematic basis over a period not exceeding the useful life of the principal item, i.e., the fixed asset to which they relate.
- When the related fixed asset is either discarded or sold, the written down value less disposal value, if any, of the capital spares/ insurance spares should be written off.
- The stand-by equipment is a separate fixed asset in its own right and should be depreciated like any other fixed asset.

Applicability

Accounting Standard-2 is not applicable in the following cases :

1)Work-in-progress arising under construction contract including directly related to service contract.

2) Work-in-progress arising in ordinary course of business for service providers (Incomplete consultancy services,

Incomplete merchant bank activities, Medical services in progress)

3) Financial Instrument held as stock-in-trade (Shares, Debentures, Bonds etc.)

4)Producer's inventories like livestock, agricultural and forest products, mineral oils, ores and gases. Such inventories are valued at net realisable value.

Valuation of Inventories

Inventories should be valued at lower of cost and net realisable value.

Major points for valuation of Inventories :

- 1) Determination of cost of inventories.
- 2) Determination of net realisable value of inventories.
- 3) Comparison between the cost and net realisable value.

Cost of inventory includes –

1)Cost of purchase

2)Cost of conversion and

3) Other costs (incurred in bringing the inventories to their present location and condition)

1) Cost of Purchase – Cost of purchase includes-

- Purchase price
- Duties and Taxes
- Freight Inward
l Other expenditures directly attributable to the acquisition.

Less :

- Duties and taxes recoverable by enterprises from taxing authorities
- Trade discount
- Rebate
- Duty drawback
- Other similar items.

2) *Cost of Conversion* : It consists of the cost directly related to the units (i.e. Direct Labour, Direct Material, Direct Expenses) Systematic Allocation of fixed and variable production overheads that are incurred in converting material into finished goods.

- **Fixed production overheads :** Indirect cost of production that remains relatively constant regardless of volume of production (i.e. Depreciation and Maintenance of factory building, cost of factory management).
- **Variable Production Overheads :** Indirect cost of production that varies directly or nearly directly with the volume of production (i.e. indirect material, indirect labour).
- **Allocation of fixed production overhead :** On normal capacity. In periods of abnormally high production, the amount of fixed production overheads allocated to each unit of production is decreased so that inventories are not measured above cost.
- **Allocation of variable production overhead :** On actual production.
- **In case of joint-products :** When the cost of conversion of each product is not separately identifiable, total cost of conversion is allocated between the products on the rational and consistent basis

(i.e. allocation on the basis of relative sale value of product).

- **In case of by-product :** If by-products, scrap or waste materials are not of material value, they are measured at net realisable value, then net realisable value is deducted from cost of conversion.Net cost of conversion (i.e. cost of conversion – net realisable value)is distributed among the main products.

3)Other Costs : Cost incurred in bringing the inventories to their present location and condition. Inclusion of excise duty in valuation of finished goods – Excise duty contributes directly to bringing inventory to its present location and condition and is a direct cost, which should be included in the valuation of inventories. Excise duty is required to be included in the valuation of finished goods as per AS-2, though excise duty is paid only when goods are removed from the factory. In estimation of the provision required for the purpose, factors such as whether the finished goods lying in stock in the current year would form part of the exempted goods next year and whether excise duty exemptions will continue in the next year should be considered. For example, on stock meant for exports no excise duty would be included since excise is not leviable on goods meant for exports.Since on the one hand, a provision for excise duty will be made and on the other hand, such provision will also be included as cost of inventory, the impact on profit and loss account will be Nil.

Exclusions from cost of Inventories : Following costs are excluded from the cost of Inventories :

Abnormal amount of wasted materials, labour, other production costs

- Storage cost
- Administrative overhead
- Selling and distribution cost
- Interest and borrowing cost. However, if AS-16 allows such cost to be included it, can form part of the cost.

Cost Formula

(I) Specific identification method for determining cost of inventories

Specific identification method means directly linking the cost with specific item of inventories. This method has application in the following conditions :

a) In case of purchase of item specifically segregated for specific project and is not ordinarily inter-changeable.
b) In case of goods or services produced and segregated for specific project.

(II) *Where specific identification method is not applicable* –

Where specific identification method is not applicable, the cost of inventories is valued by the following methods :

a) FIFO (First In First Out)
b) Weighted Average cost.

Cost of inventories in certain conditions -

When it is impractical to calculate the cost, the following methods may be followed to ascertain cost:

1) Standard Cost
2) Retail Method

These methods may be used for convenience if the results approximate actual cost.

1) Standard Cost – It takes into account normal level of consumption of material and supplies, labour, efficiency and capacity utilization. It must be regularly reviewed and revised taking into consideration the current condition.

2) Retail Method – It is generally used in retail business, when it is difficult to ascertain cost of individual item. It is applicable when items of inventories are rapidly changing items and have similar margins and for which it is impracticable to use other costing method.

Under this method, the cost of inventory is determined by reducing from the sale value of inventories the approximate percentage of gross margin. The percentage used takes into consideration the inventory that has been marked down to below its original selling price.

Net Realisable Value

Net Realisable value means the estimated selling price in ordinary course of business, less estimated cost of completion and estimated cost necessary to make the sale. Net realisable value is estimated on the basis of most reliable evidence at the time of valuation. Estimation of net realisable value also takes into account the purpose for which the inventory is held. Estimation of net realisable value is made as at each balance sheet date.

Estimation of net realisable value

The net realisable value of the materials and other supplies held for use in production of finished goods is estimated as under:

- If finished product in which raw material and supplies used is sold at cost or above cost, or above cost, then the estimated realisable value of raw material and supplies is considered more than its cost.
- If finished product in which raw material and supplies used is sold below cost. Then the estimated realisable value of raw material or supplies is equal to replacement price of raw material or supplies.

Comparison between cost and net realisable value

The comparison between cost and net realisable value should be made item or by group of items.

Disclosure in the financial statement

The financial statement should disclose the following:

- Accounting policy adopted in measuring inventories.
- Cost formula used.
- Classification of inventories- like finished goods, WIP, raw materials, spare parts and its carrying amount.

Amendments in AS-2

When an enterprise purchases the inventories on deferred payment system, the difference between the purchase price for normal credit terms and amount paid is to be treated as interest expense over the period of financing as the arrangement effectively contains the financial element.

This limited revision comes into effect in respect of accounting periods commencing on or after the date on which accounting standard (AS) 30, "Financial Instruments : Recognition and Measurement" comes into effect.

Examples -

Q.1. Raw material was purchased at Rs.100 per Kg. Price of raw material is on the decline. The finished goods in which the raw material is incorporated are expected to be sold at below cost. 5,000 Kgs. of raw material is in stock at the year-end. Replacement cost is Rs.60 per Kg. How will you value the inventory?

Solution : As per AS-2 on valuation of inventories, material and other supplies held for use in the production of inventories are not written down below cost if the finished products in which they will be incorporated are expected to be sold at or above cost. However, when there has been a decline in the price of materials and it is estimated that the cost of the finished products will exceed net realisable value, the materials are written down to net realisable value. In such circumstances, the replacement cost of the material may be the best available measure of their net realisable value.

Hence in this case, the stock of 5,000 Kgs. Of raw material will be valued at Rs.60 per Kg. The finished goods, if on stock, should be valued at cost or net realisable value, whichever is lower.

Q. 2. How will you value the inventory per Kg. of finished goods consisted of :

Material Cost	Rs.110 per Kg.
Direct Labour Cost	Rs.20 per Kg.
Direct variable production overhead	Rs.10 per Kg.

Fixed production charges for the year on normal capacity of one Lakh Kgs. Is Rs.10 Lakhs. 500 Kgs. of finished goods are on stock at the year-end.

Solution : As per AS-2, the costs of conversion include a systematic allocation of fixed and variable production overheads that are incurred in converting materials into finished goods. The allocation of fixed production overheads for the purpose of their inclusion in the cost of conversion is based on the normal capacity of the production facilities.

Thus, cost per Kg. of finished goods can be computed as follows:

	Rs.
Material Cost	110
Direct Labour Cost	20
Direct variable production overhead	10
Fixed production overhead (Rs.10,00,000/100000	10
	150

Thus, The value of 500 Kgs. of finished goods on stock at the year-end will be Rs 70,000 (500 kgs x Rs 140)

Exercise -
    1. Explain the following:-
    (a) Cost of purchase   (b) Cost of Conversion
    (c) Standard Method   (d) Retail Method
    (e) Specific Cost Method   (f) Net Realisable Value
    2. A Ltd. Produces chemical, X which has following production cost per unit
    Raw Material = Rs 6
    Direct Labour = Rs 2
    Direct Expenses = Rs 4
    Normal capacity = 3,000 units per annum
    Actual production = 1,000 units
    Fixed Production Overhead = Rs 18,000 per annum
    The company has 600 units of unsold stock lyig with it at the end of year. You are required to value the closing stock.

AS-4 CONTINGENCIES AND EVENTS OCCURING AFTER THE BALANCE SHEET DATE (AS-4)

In preparing financial statements of a particular enterprise, accounting is done by following accrual basis of accounting and prudent accounting policies to calculate the profit or loss for the year and to recognize assets and liabilities in Balance Sheet.

While following prudent accounting policies, the provision is made for all known liabilities and losses even for those liabilities/events, which are probable.

Objective of this standard is to prescribe the accounting of contingencies and the event, which takes place after the balance sheet date but before approval of balance sheet by Board of Directors. The Accounting Standard deals with:
- Contingencies
- Events occurring after the Balance Sheet date.

Applicability of Accounting Standard

Accounting Standard does not apply in following cases :

- Liabilities of life assurance and general insurance.
- Obligations under retirement benefit plans.
- Commitments arising from long-term lease contracts.

Contingency refers to –
- Existing conditions or situation.
- Result of which (contingency) is not known on the balance sheet date.
- Result of which (contingencies) would be known only on happening or non-happening of certain events in future.
- Result may be either a gain or loss.

Example -

A company has files a legal suit against the debtor from whom Rs.20 lakh is recoverable as on 31-3-2013.

The chances of recovery by way of legal suit are less as per legal opinion . How the company should disclose this debtors in the

Balance Sheet as on 31-3-2013.

As per AS-4, company should make the provision for bad and doubtful debts, as situation of non-recovery from the debtors is existing on balance sheet date result of which will be known in future. The amount of provision for bad and doubtful debts should be shown as deduction from total debtors in Balance Sheet.

Following are some examples of Loss Contingency
- Collectability of recoverable/debtors.
- Litigation, claims and assessments for recovery of assets.

Estimation of outcome of contingency is determined by management.

The estimates of outcome and financial effects of contingencies are determined by the management. The management takes decision on the basis of information available upto the date of approval of accounts.

Methods to be followed for estimation of contingent loss -

Contingency loss can be estimated by following flow chart :-

Contingencies (other than covered by AS-29)

Provision for loss is estimated on the basis of information available upto the date of approval of accounts by competent authority. But the contingency must exist on the date of Balance Sheet. If contingency does not exist on Balance Sheet date no provision nor notes to accounts is required.

Provisions covered by AS-4

In view of non-applicability of AS-29 to provision for bad and doubtful debts and other similar provisions which are shown in the Balance Sheet as adjustment to the carrying amount of assets, the Institute of Chartered Accountants of India has made announcement that till Accounting Standards (AS-30) on Financial instruments becomes applicable the provision for bad and doubtful debts would continue to be covered by AS-4.

Events occurring after the Balance Sheet date are as under :-

- Events, which occur between the Balance Sheet date and date on which financial statements are approved by
- competent authority.
- These events are significant events and they may be favourable and unfavourable.

For example : Balance Sheet date is 31st March, 2013 and Board of Directors approved the accounts on 30th August, 2013. Any event that occurs between 31st March, 2013 and 30th August, 2013 is termed as event occurring after the Balance Sheet date.

Suppose there was fire in the factory on 27th July, 2013, destroyed plant worth Rs.15 crores.

For the purpose of accounting treatment the events are classified in two categories.

1) Adjusting Events : These events relate to circumstances existing on the balancesheet date. In this case, loss should be accounted in the accounts and assets & liabilities to be adjusted

2) Non –Adjusting Events : These events are not related to circumstances existing on the balancesheet date.In this case, disclosure by way of notes to accounts should only be made. Adjustments in accounts is not required.

Examples :

Insolvency of a customer (Adjusting event) – Insolvency of a customer, which occurs after the Balance Sheet date usually, provides additional information on the condition that existed at the Balance Sheet date. Therefore, the carrying amount receivables should be adjusted for the event; assumptions are made as follows.

- The condition of insolvency existed at the Balance Sheet date
- The entity could not collect the completed information about the collectability of the receivable because of the unreasonable effort and cost required to collect information.
- Therefore, it could not estimate the insolvency of the customer

However, insolvency caused by a major casualty occurring after the Balance Sheet date is not an adjusting event.

For example, insolvency caused by a major fire in the factory and the warehouse is an unadjusting event. Accordingly, the carrying amount of the receivables should not be adjusted for the event.

Decline in the market value of investment (Non-adjusting event)- Decline in the market value of investments between the Balance Sheet date and the date of approval of financial statements by the appropriate authority does not normally relate to conditions that existed at the Balance Sheet date. Therefore, the event does not result in adjustment of the carrying amount of the investment. Similarly, the entity does not update the amount of the investment. Similarly, the entity does not update the amount disclosed for the investments in the Balance Sheet. The assumption is that the conditions, which resulted in decline in the market value of investment, occurred after the Balance Sheet date.

Events effecting going concern

Events occurring after the Balance Sheet date may indicate that the enterprise ceases to be going concern (e.g., destruction of a major production plant by a fire after the Balance Sheet date) may indicate a need to consider whether it is proper to use the fundamental accounting assumption of going concern in the preparation of the financial statements.

Proposed Dividend

Dividend in respect of the period covered by the financial statements, which are proposed or declared after the Balance Sheet date but before approval of the financial statements, should be adjusted in accounts.

Event occurring after approval of accounts : Event occurring after the balance sheet date and also after approval of accounts by board of directors of a company such event should be disclosed in the director's report if material.

Disclosure

If material contigent loss is not provided for, its nature and an estimate of financial effect should be disclosed by way of note.If estimate of financial effect cannot be made, the fact should be disclosed.

Note : From the date the Accounting Standard (AS-30), Financial Instruments: Recognition and Measurement becoming mandatory, the Paragraph dealing with contingencies of Accounting Standard (AS-4) would stand withdrawn. The mandatory application of AS-30 has been postponed from 01.04.2011 till further announcement.

Examples -

Q.1. A company entered into an agreement to sell its land included in the Balance Sheet at Rs 60 lakhs to another company for Rs. 90 lakhs. The agreement to sell was concluded on 31-1-2013 and the sale deed was registered on 30-4-2013. How this will be treated in Balance Sheet as on 31-3-2013.

Solution : As per AS-4 Assets and liabilities should be adjusted for events occurring after the balance sheet date that provide additional evidence to assist the estimation of amounts relating to conditions existing at the balance sheet date. In this case sale of land was concluded before approval by the Board. This is clearly an event occurring after the balance sheet date.

Agreement to sell was entered into before the balance sheet date. Registration of the sale deed simply provides additional information relating to the conditions existing at the balance sheet date. In this case sale of land was concluded before approval by the Board. This is clearly an event occurring after the balance sheet date. Agreement to sell was entered into before the balance sheet date. Registration of the sale deed simply provides additional information relating to the conditions existing at the balance sheet date. So adjustments to assets are necessary and Asset will be derecognized in the balance Sheet as on 31-3-2013.

Q.2. Advise B Ltd. about the treatment of the following in the final statement of accounts for the year ended 31st March, 2013.

On 20th April, 2013, due to destruction of the factory by fire (fire took place on 12th March, 2013), one of the company's debtors, declared himself insolvent. He owed Rs. 5,20,000 to B Co.Ltd.

Solution : As per AS-4 Adjustment of assets and liabilities is to be made if event relates to the condition existing on the balance sheet date and provides additional evidence to assist the estimation of amounts relating to conditions existing at the balance sheet date. In this case the fire took place on 12th March, 2013 before the date of balance sheet and debtors are declared insolvent on 20th April, 2013, the event of 20th April, 2013 only provides the additional evidence to estimate the amount of loss.

Accordingly, adequate provision for bad debts should be created to cover the loss arising out of insolvency for the year ended 31st March, 2013.

Exercise -

1. A major fire has damaged the assets in factory of a company on 10nd April 2013. Accounts were closed on 31st March,2013. The loss is estimated at Rs.10 crores out of which Rs 6crores will be recoverable from the insurers. Explain briefly how the loss should be treated in the final account for the previous year.

2. One of the manufacturing units of A Ltd. Wherein equal to 60% of the total assets was destroyed in fire for which there was no insurance cover. The chief accountant of company contests that the destruction of unit took place only after the date of the Balance Sheet and therefore there was no need to make a disclosure of loss in the annual account as at Balance Sheet date. Whether contention of chief accountant was correct.

3. Board of Directors approved the financial account of year 2012-13 on 31st July, 2013. The following events occurred before the approval of financial accounts by Board of Directors. Sate how would you deal with these situations:

a) The Board of Directors at their meeting on June 20, 2013 has recommended a dividend of 10% to be paid to the shareholders after it is approved at the annual general meeting.

b) A fire occurred in the godown on April 9, 2013 damaging a huge quantity of stock of value Rs 15 lakhs.

4. What are the disclosure requirements pertaining to

(i) Contingencies

(ii) Events occurring after the balance sheet date under the accounting standards.

AS-9 REVENUE RECOGNITION

The standard explains when the revenue should be recognized in profit and loss account and also states the circumstances in which revenue recognition can be postponed. Revenue means gross inflow of cash, receivable or other consideration arising in the course of ordinary activities of an enterprise such as sale of goods, rendering services and use of the enterprises resources by others yielding interest, dividend and royalties.

In other words, revenue is charge made to customers / clients for goods supplied and services rendered.

Timing of Revenue Recognition -

Revenue from sale of rendering services should be recognized at the time of the sale or rendering of services. However, if at the time of rendering of services or sale there is significant uncertainty in ultimate collection of the revenue, then the revenue recognition is postponed and in such cases revenue should be recognized only when it becomes reasonably certain that ultimate collection will be made. It also applies to the revenue arising out of escalation of price; export incentives, interest, etc.

Applicability - This Accounting Standard is not applicable to the following revenue or gain –

1)Revenue arising from construction contracts

2)Revenue arising from hire purchase, lease agreements

3)Revenue arising from Govt. grants and subsidies

4)Revenue of Insurance companies arising from insurance contracts

5)Gain – realized or unrealized gain. Example: Profit on sale of fixed asset.

Revenue from sale of goods - It is recognized when all the following conditions are fulfilled :-

Seller has transferred the ownership of goods to the buyer for a price. **Or**

All significant risks and rewards of ownership have been transferred to buyer

Seller does not retain any effective control of ownership of the transferred goods

There is no significant uncertainty in collection of the amount of consideration (i.e. cash, receivables etc.)

Revenue Recognition when the delivery of goods is delayed at buyers request – Delivery of goods is delayed at buyer's

request and the buyer takes title and accepts billing. Revenue should be recognized immediately but goods must be in hand of

seller, identified and ready for delivery at the time of recognition of Revenue.

Revenue Recognition when delivery of goods sold subject to conditions –

Installation and inspection : Revenue should be recognized when

- Goods are installed at the buyers's place to his satisfaction
- Goods are inspected and accepted by the buyer.

Sale on approval -

Revenue should be recognized when buyer confirms his desire to buy such goods by communication.

Guaranteed sales -

Revenue should be recognized as per the substance of the agreement of sale or after the reasonable period has expired.

Warranty Sales -

Sales should be recognized immediately but the provision should be made to cover unexpired warranty.

Consignment Sales -

Revenue should be recognized only when the goods are sold to third party.

Special order and shipments -

Revenue from such sales should be recognized when the goods are identified and ready for delivery.

Subscriptions for Publication -
- Items delivered vary in value from period to period
  Revenue should be recognized on the basis of sales value of items delivered.
- Items delivered do not vary in value from period to period
  Revenue should be recognized on straight-line basis over time.

● **Installment Sales**

Revenue of sale price excluding interest should be recognized on the date of sale. Interest should be recognized proportionately to the unpaid balance.

Revenue from rendering of the services -

Revenue from service is generally recognized as the service is performed. The performance of service is measured by two methods as under :-

1 *Completed service contract method* – Revenue is recognized when service is about to be completed and no significant uncertainties exist about the collection of amount of service charges.

2 *Proportionate Completion Method* – Revenue is recognized by reference to the performance of each Act. The revenue recognized under this method would be determined on the basis of contract value, associated costs, number of Acts or other suitable basis. Further, no significant uncertainty exists about the collection of amount of service charges of performed Acts.

Examples of Revenue Recognition of Service -

● **1) Installation Fees**

It is recognized when the installation has been completed and accepted by the clients.

● **2) Advertising and Insurance Agency Commission**
- Advertising commission is recognized when the advertisement appears before public
- Insurance Commission is recognized on the effective commencement/renewal date of the policies.

3) Financial Service Commission -

Recognition of revenue depends upon :-

- Whether the service has been provided "once and for all" or is on a continuing basis

- The incidence of costs relating to the service
- When the payment for the service will be received.

Generally, commission charged for arranging or granting loan and other facilities should be recognized when a loan is sanctioned and accepted by borrower. Commitment facility or loan management fees which related to continuing obligations or services should normally be recognized over the life of the loan.

4) Admission Fee- Revenue from artistic performance, banquets and other special events should be recognized when event takes place.

5) Tuition Fees -Revenue should be recognized over the period of instruction.

6) Entrance and Membership Fees -Recognition depends upon the nature of service being provided against entrance and membership fees, however entrance fees are generally capitalized and membership fees should be recognized on systematic and rational basis having regard to timing and nature of service provided.

7) Revenue From Interest -Revenue from interest should be recognized on time proportion basis.

8) Revenue From Royalties- On accrual basis as per terms of agreement.

9) Revenue From Dividend- When the declaring company declares dividend.

10) Subsequent uncertainty in collection - When uncertainty of collection of revenue arises subsequently after the revenue recognition, it is better to make provision for the uncertainty in collection rather than adjustment in already recognized revenue.

Disclosure -When revenue recognition is postponed, the disclosure of the circumstances necessitating the postponement should be made.

Disclosure of Revenue from Sales Transactions -

The amount of turnover should be disclosed in the following manner on the face of the statement of profit and loss :

Turnover (Gross)	xx
Less : Excise Duty	xx
Turnover (Net)	xx

The amount of excise duty to be deducted from turnover should be the total excise duty for the year except the excise duty related to the difference between the closing stock and opening stock. The excise duty related to the difference between the closing stock and opening stock should be recognized separately in the statement of profit and loss, with an explanatory note in the notes to accounts to explain the nature of the two amounts of excise duty

Examples -

Q.1 The board of directors of A Ltd decided on 31-3-2013 to increase the sale price of certain items retrospectively from 10th January, 2013. In view of this price revision, the company has to receive Rs.40 Lakhs from its customers in respect of sales made from 10th January, 2013to 31st March, 2013 and the accountant cannot decide whether to include Rs.40 lakhs in the sales for 2012-13. Suggest.

Solution : Price revision effected during the current accounting period 2012-13. As a result, the company stands to receive Rs. 40 lakhs from its customers in respect of sales made from 1st January, 2013 to 31st March 2013. If the company is able to assess the ultimate collection with reasonable certainty, then additional revenue arising out of the said price revision may be recognized in 2012-13 as per AS-9 .

Q.2. A Ltd. used certain resources of B Ltd. In return B Ltd. received Rs 15 lakhs and Rs 35 lakhs as interest and royalties respectively from A Ltd. during the year 2012-13. Explain whether and on what basis these revenues can be recognized by B Ltd.

Solution: As per AS-9 on Revenue Recognition, revenue arising from the use by others of enterprise resources yielding interest and royalties should only be recognized when no significant uncertainty as to its measurabilityor collectability exists.

These revenues are recognized on following bases:

(i) **Interest:** On a time proportion basis taking into account the amount outstanding and the rate applicable.

(ii) **Royalties:** On an accrual basis in accordance with the terms of the relevant agreement.

Here in this case interest should be recognized in the year to which it pertains, not in the year in which it is received. It is not clear from the question whether interest of Rs 15 lakhs pertains to 2012-13 or it pertains to earlier year and received in 2012-13. Same is the case with royalty. If both the interest and royalty accrue in 2012-13, it should be recognized in this year only.

Exercise -

1) When do you recognize revenue in the following cases as per AS-9
   Sale of goods
   Rendering of Services

2) How would you recognize the revenue in respect of the following transactions ?
   Sale subject to installation, inspection etc
   Entrance and membership fees of clubs
   Commission receivable by advertising agencies

Chapter 6

Royalty Accounts (Excluding Sub Lease)

6.1	**Meaning of Royalty**
6.2	**Important Terms**
6.2.1	**Minimum Rent**
6.2.2	**Shortworkings & Lapse of Shortworkings**
6.3	**Journal Entries and Ledger Accounts in the books of Landlord and Lessee**
6.4	**Illustrations**
6.5	**Questions :- Objective Types Questions and Problems.**

6.1 Meaning of Royalty :

Royalty means a periodical payment made by the user to the owner. There are some parties, who have exclusive right or ownership over certain things. For example, A landlord has exclusive right over a mine. An author has exclusive right over his writing. A patent holder has exclusive right over his patent and so on. The owner does not sell his product or patent but he allows another person to use the product and receives some amount for the exchange of his product.

This amount is called royalty. The royalty is usually payable in the following cases.

(i) For the extraction of coal, oil, minerals from the mines.

(ii) To the author for sale of his book i.e. writing.

(iii) To the patentholder for the use of his patent. In short royalty is payable by the user to the owner. In other words royalty is payable by tenant to the landlord.

Definitions of Royalty :

1) "The remuneration payable to a person in respect of the use of an asset, whether hired or purchased from such person, calculated by reference to and varying with quantities produced or sold as a result of such asset. "   **By William Pickle.**

2) "When a person having an exclusive right of some sort transfers it to another in exchange for a certain amount calculated with reference to quantity produced or sold, such amount is known as royalty.

However, rent is different than royalty. Rent is fixed in advance and it is paid by tenant to landlord on monthly basis. Royalty is generally payable on yearly basis. Royalty is payable for the use of a certain right. So it may differ from year to year.

In short, the royalty is paid by lessee of mine to the owner of mine, or by the publisher to author or by licensee (the user of patent) to the patentee (owner of patent) by music recording company to singer and so on. Thus, the amount payable by one person to another for using the right is called a Royalty.

Royalty is payable either on the basis of production / output or sales. It is calculated on the basis of ton of coal extracted from mine or per copy of the book sold etc.

The amount of Royalty is an expense to the lessee and the amount of royalty received is an income to the lessor or landlord.

Royalty payable on production is treated as a manufacturing expense and debited to Manufacturing or Trading Account. But royalty based on sales is treated as selling expenses and charged to profit and loss Account.

In short royalty is a payment for using rights. It is not a payment of goods or services. It is also not a rent payable by tanent to landlord. It is a payment for acquiring the right to use certain assets.

6.2 Important Terms or Words

In order to understand the topic of royalty, the reader must be familiar with the following important terms.

1) Landlord or Lessor : -

A person, who is the owner of fixed asset or mine is called landlord. He donot use his asset but he allows to use the asset to some other person and in exchange, receives the payment. i.e. royalty. The landlord is also called as lessor or owner.

2) Lessee or Tenant : -

A person who is not the owner of the asset but uses the asset for earning profit is called lessee or tenant. He is only using the asset. He is making payment to landlord in the form of royalty.

3) Royalty agreement or lease agreement.

The agreement between landlord (lessor) and tenant (lessee) is called lease agreement. It is a mutual agreement and binding on both parties. It includes the terms and conditions of utilisation of the asset and the payment as (i) Rate of Royalty (ii) Minimum Rent (iii) Period of Lease (iv) Right to recoup shortworking and other conditions which may be mutually decided by landlord and tenant.

4) Period of Lease :-

Period of lease specifices the period for which the lessee has right to use the asset of lessor. It is period for which the lessee has to pay the royalty.

5) Rate of Royalty : -

It is the rate of which the lessee is required to pay royalty to the lessor. The rate is determined by lessor and lessee and it is generally per unit of production i.e. per ton or per copy etc.

6.2.1 Minimum Rent :

Minimum Rent is also know as Dead Rent, Fixed Rent, Rock Rent, Head Rent or Sleeping Rent. This is a minimum amount which is to be paid by the tenant to the landlord irrespective of the production. In the beginning or initial stage, there may not be adequate production, hence the landlord may not get sufficient amount of royalty, Therefore, there is a provision of minimum rent in the agreement of royalty.

In the initial stage, it takes a lot of time to dig a mine. There is no output during this period. As there is no output, there would be no royalty which may be payable to the landlord. The landlord will have to suffer hardships. Similarly, it takes a lot of time to setup a factory to produce a patented articles. There is no production in the initial period, hence the patentee may not be entitled to any royalty. Similarly, the author may not get any royalty in the initial stages as there is no sale or low sales of books.

Sometimes, there may be other contingencies like accident, strikes, lockout, earthquake, resulting into no or inadequate royalty due to no or low production or sales. Therefore, in order to assure the owner of the right of definite income, there is a stipulation that a fixed amount or minimum amount must be paid by the lessee. Such minimum amount payable to the lessor or landlord as per agreement is called as Minimum Rent.

Further, question generally arises which amount is to be paid to the landlord or lessor, the amount of actual royalty or minimum Rent ? While settling this problem following rule should always be borne in mind.

RULE : - "Minimum Rent on Actual Rent whichever is higher is payable to the landlord "

For example : - Mr. 'X' has taken a mine on a lease at a minimum rent of Rs.10,000 per year. The rate of royalty is Rs.2 per ton. Suppose in the first year the output is 3,000 tons, in the second year, it is 4,000 tons and in the third year output is 6000 tons.

In above example, royalty for the first year is Rs.6,000 (3000 x 2), for the second year it is Rs.8,000 (4000 x 2) and for the third year, it is Rs. 12,000.

As the royalty of first and second year is less than minimum rent, minimum Rent i.e. Rs.10,000 is to be paid to landlord. But in the third year Actual Royalty i.e. Rs.12,000 is more than minimum Rent. Hence, Actual royalty is to be paid to landlord.

6.2.2. Short Workings :

The difference between Minimum Rent and Actual Royalty is known as short workings. It is the excess of minimum rent over royalties. It means royalty is less then minimum rent or minimum rent is more than royalty. The shortworkings is also termed as Redeemable minimum Rent. In simple words, shortworkings is ascertained as under.

Shortworkings = Minimum Rent - Actual Royalty.

For example : - Suppose, the minimum rent is, Rs.15,000 and the actual royalty is 10,000. Then the shortworkings will be calculated as under.

Minimum Rent	- Actual royalties	= Short workings
Rs 15,000	- Rs.10,000	= Rs. 5,000.

Thus, Rs.5000 will be the amount of shortworkings.

6.2.3 Recoupment of Shortworkings :
(Recovery of Short working) and Lapse of Shortworking -

Short workings means excess payment to landlord. Short workings is usually recoverable. Recoupment means recovery of excess payment. The agreement generally provides for recoupment of short workings. In other words, it means that the excess payment to landlord is recoverable.

As the lessee (tenant) is required to pay the lessor the minimum rent, if Royalty is less, the excess payment made to lessor, represents a loss to a lessee. But the lessor generally allows the lessee to carry forward such loss for certain period and during this period he is allowed to recover the loss. i.e. short workings from the surplus.

Thus, the lessor promises to return the amount of short workings, out of the excess Royalties earned from subsequent years. This process is known as Recoupment of shortworkings or recovery of shortworkings. The recovery is possible only when the amount of royalty is more than Minimum Rent. However, the right of recoupment is limited to certain number of years, which may be fixed by landlord and tenant.

The recoupment period may be : -

(a) Fixed Period

(b) Floating Period

(c) Recoupment within the life of lease.

(a) Fixed Period : -

The amount of shortworkings can be recovered or recouped during the "first few years only". for example during the first three/four of five years. Once the period of recoupment is over, the right of recoupment of shortworking is also lost and the balance of short workings is transferred to profit and loss account as a loss. Thus, in case of fixed period, the right of recoupment is available only during a fixed number of years from the date of shortworkings.

The balance of shortworkings account is carried forward to next years till it is recovered, according to the agreement of lessor and lessee. The balance of shortworkings account will appear on the asset side of the balance sheet of lessee and it will appear on the liability side of the lessor, till the right of recoupment is lost. After the expiry period, if there is a balance of shortworkings it is transferred to profit and loss account. The lessee will transfer the balance of shortworking account on the debit side of profit and loss account and the lessor will transfer the balance of shortworkings account to the credit side of profit and loss account.

(b) Floating Period :

When the amount of shortworkings is recovered in the next/ subsequent years, it is said to be a floating recoupment period. In case of floating period, the right of recoupment is available for a fixed number of year from the date of shortworkings. For example, suppose a lease provide that each year's excess of minimum rent over actual royalties (i.e. shortworkings) is to be recouped during the next three years and if there is a shortworkings of Rs. 5,000 in the year 2004, then the short workings will be recouped during the next three years i.e. 2005,2006 and 2007.

(c) Recoupment within the life of a lease :

In this case the amount of shortworkings can be recouped from years excess royalties. Therefore, the problem of irrecoverable Shortworkings will not arise till the end of last but one year of the lease. This is because, if in the last year of the lease there is any shortworkings, the same will have to be written off against profit and loss account.

Thus, in general the period of recovery of shortworkings may be certain number of years, say 4 or 5 years, from the year of commencement or certain number of years from the year of each shortworkings.

Unrecouped amount of shortworkings on the expiry of the time limit should be treated as loss and written off against profit and loss account.

Strikes, Accidents, lockouts and stoppage of work.

Sometimes, it happens that there is a stoppage of work due to strike, accident, lockout or death of lessee. In such a case, it is provided for in the agreement that the "Minimum Rent Account" is to be reduced proportionately" having regard to the length of stoppage.

For example, suppose that the Minimum Rent is fixed at Rs.18,000 p.a. and strike in a particular year, lasted for 3 months. In such a case the minimum rent for that year is to be calculated for the remaining period of the year.

As there is a stoppage of work for 3 months, the minimum rent for remaining period i.e. for 9 months will be calculated as under :

$$\text{Minimum Rent} = \frac{\text{Minimum Rent Remaining Period.}}{12}$$

$$= \text{Rs. } \frac{18000}{12} \times \frac{9}{1}$$

$$= \text{Rs. } 13,500.$$

6.3 Accounting Treatment of Journal Entries in the books of Landlord and Lessee.

Journal Entries in the books of Lessee.

(A) When Royalty is less than Minimum Rent (i.e. where there is a short workings)

(i) For Minimum Rent Payable

Royalty A/c	Dr.	(Actual Royalty)
Short workings A/c	Dr.	(Short workings)
To Landlords A/c		(Minimum Rent)

(Being minimum rent payable)

(ii) For Payment to landlord

Landlord A/c	Dr.	(Minimum Rent)
To Cash/Bank A/c		(Minimum Rent)

(Being Minimum Rent Paid to Landlord)

(iii) For Closing Royalty Account.

Profit and Loss A/c	Dr.	(Actual Royalty)
To Royalty A/c		(Actual Royalty)

(Being royalty transferred to Profit & Loss Account)

Above three journal entries will be passed till the Royalty is less than minimum rent. Short workings Account is closed by carrying forward the balance till the period of recovery continues. Therefore, shortworkings Account shows a debit balance every year in the books of lessee and it will appear on the Asset side of Balance Sheet.

(B) When Royalty is more than Minimum Rent.

(i.e. Where shortworkings are to be recoverd out of the excess of Royalty over Minimum Rent)

(i) For Royalty Payable

Royalty A/c	Dr.	(Actual Royalty)
To Landlord A/c		(Actual Royalty)
(Being Royalty Payable)		

(ii) Landlord A/c   **Dr.**   (Actual Royalty)

To Shortworkings A/c	(S.W. Recovered)
To Cash/Bank A/c	(Amount paid)

(Being shortworkings recovered and royalty paid to landlord)

OR

Instead of showing recovery of shortworkings on landlord A/c, some authors show it on the Royalties A/c and in that case the entries will be under.

(i) Royalties A/c   **Dr.**   (Actual Royalty)

To Short workings A/c	(S.W.Recoverd)
To Landlord A/c	(Amount Payable)

(Being shortworkings recovered and royalties payable)

(ii) Landlords A/c   **Dr.**   (Amt Payable)

To Bank A/c	(Amt Payable)
(Being royalty paid)	

But since I consider the first method as most appropriate, I follow the first method in all solutions.

(iii) For Closing Royalty Account

Profit and loss A/c   Dr.

To Royalty A/c

(Being royalty transferred to P & L A/c)

Above three journal entries will be passed as long as Royalty is more than Minimum Rent and recoupment takes place in the year in which royalty is more than minimum Rent.

(C) When the Right of Recoupment is lost or when the unrecoverable balance of short workings A/c is transferred to P & L A/c.

Profit and Loss A/c   **Dr.**

    To Shortworkings A/c

(Being irrecoverable balance of S.W.

transferred to Profit & Loss A/c)

This entry will be passed in the particular year in which the right of recoupment is lost due to the expiry of time limit and the balance if any being irrecoverable.

(D) When Minimum Rent Account is Opened.

Sometimes an examination problem requires you to open Minimum Rent Account. Minimum Rent Account will be opened as long as Royalty is less than Minimum Rent. Minimum Rent Account will not be opened or recorded in those years in which royalty is more than Minimum Rent. When Minimum Rent Account is to be opened, the following journal entries will be passed in the books of lessee.

(1) For Minimum Rent Payable

    Minimum Rent A/c   Dr.

        To Landlord's A/c

    (Being Minimum Rent Payable)

(ii) For Actual Royalty and Short workings

    Royalty A/c   Dr.

    Shortworkings A/c   Dr.

        To Minimum Rent A/c

    (Being actual Royalties and Shortworkings)

(iii) For Payment of Minimum Rent

    Landlord A/c   Dr.

        To Cash or Bank A/c

    (Being Minimum Rent Paid)

(iv) For transfer of Royalty to P & L A/c

Profit and Loss A/c   Dr.

To Royalty A/c

(Being Royalty transferred to P & L A/c)

Above four journal entries are to be passed for those years in which Minimum Rent is more than Royalty (i.e. Royalty is less than minimum Rent and where there is a shortworkings) and only when Minimum Rent Account is asked for in the problem. Minimum Rent Account will not be opened in those years in which royalty is more than minimum rent.

From the above journal entries lessee is required to open the following ledger Accounts in his books under simple method.

(a) Royalty Account

(b) Shortworkings Account

(c) Landlord's Account

Under Minimum Rent Account method Lessee is required to open following Accounts.

(a) Minimum Rent Account

(b) Royalty Account

(c) Shortworkings Account.

(d) Landlord's Account.

(E) When Royalty is equal to Minimum Rent following Journal entries are to be maintained in the books of lessee.

(i) Royalty Payable

Royalty A/c   Dr.

To Landlord's A/c   (Actual Royalty)

(Being Royalty Payable)

(ii) For Payment to landlord

Landlord's A/c   Dr.   (Actual Royalty)

To Cash/Bank A/c

(Being Royalty Paid)

(iii) For Closing of Royalty A/c

Profit and Loss A/c   Dr.   (Actual Royalty)

To Royalty A/c

(Being Royalty transferred to P & L A/c)

Journal Entries in the Books of Landlord or Lessor.

(A) When the Royalty is less than Minimum Rent

(i) For Royalty Receivable

Lessee's A/c   Dr.   (Minimum Rent)

To Shortworkings Allowable A/c(S.W.Allowed)

To Royalties Receivable A/c (Actual Royalty)

(Being shortworking allowed and royalty receivable)

Note : Some authors use Royalties suspense A/c instead of shortworkings Allowable A/c.

(ii) For Royalty Received

Cash A/c   Dr.

To Lessee's A/c

(Being Royalty Received)

(iii) For Closing Royalty Receivable A/c

Royalties Receivable A/c Dr.   (Actual Royalty)

To Profit and Loss A/c

(Being Royalty transferred to P & L A/c)

(B) When Royalty is more than Minimum Rent
(i) For Royalty Receivable

Lessee's A/c   Dr.

To Royalties Receivable A/c

(Being Royalties Receivable)

(ii) For Cash Received

Cash / Bank A/c   Dr.   (Amount Received)

Shortworking allowable A/c   Dr.   (Amount Recovered)

To Lessee's A/c

(Being cash received and S.W. allowed)

(ii) For Closing Royalty Receivable A/c

Royalties A/c   Dr.

To Profit & Loss A/c

(Being Royalties transferred to P & L A/c)

(IV) If there is any balance of Shortworkings Allowable Account and is no longer recoverable, it is transferred to Profit and Loss Account as under.

Shortworkings Allowable A/c   Dr.
    To Profit and Loss A/c
(Being the balance of S.W. Allowable
A/c transferred to P & L A/c)

From the above journal entries landlord is required to open the following accounts in his ledger.
(a) Royalties Receivable Account.
(b) Shortworkings Allowable Account.
(c) Lessee's or Tenant's A/c

6.4 Illustrations

Illustration 1

The Raniganj Coal Co.Ltd. took from Bharat a lease of coal field for the period of 10 years from 1st January 2000 on a Royalty of Rs.2 Per ton of Coal raised, with a minimum Rent of Rs.15,000 per year and power to recoup Shortworkings during the first 3 years of the lease. The annual output was as follows:

Year	Output (tons)
2004	2,000
2005	7,000
2006	10,000
2007	12,000

You are required to pass the journal entries in the books of Raniganj Coal Co.Ltd. and Bharat and also open necessary accounts in the books of both parties.

Solution

Working

1) Lessee : - The Raniganj Coal Co.Ltd.
2) Lessor : Mr. Bharat
3) Royalty : Rs.2 per ton of Coal taken out.
4) Minimum Rent Rs.18,000 per year.
5) Right of recoupment of shortworkings : First 3 Years.

Table Showing the workings of Royalty, Shortworkings S.W. Recovered & S.W. Unrecovered.

Year	Output (tons)	Minimum Rent Rs.	Royalty Rs.	Shortworking (Rs.)	S.W. Recoverd	S.W. Unrecovered	Payment to Landlord Rs.
2000	2,000	15,000	4,000	11,000	Rs.	-	15,000
2001	7,000	15,000	14,000	1,000	-	-	15,000
2002	10,000	15,000	20,000	-	-	7,000	15,000
2003	12,000	15,000	24,000	-	5,000	-	24,000

Journal Entries in the books of
Raniganj Coal Co. Ltd. (lessee)

Date	Particulars	L/F	Debit Rs	Credit Rs.
31-12-04	Royalties A/c Dr.		4,000	
	Shortworkings A/c Dr.		11,000	
	To Bharat's A/c			15,000
	(Being Royalties Payable at Rs. 2 per ton subject to minimum Rent Rs.15,000)			
31-12-04	Bharat's A/c Dr.		15,000	
	To Bank A/c			15,000
	(Being minimum Rent paid to landlord)			
31-12-04	Profit and Loss A/c Dr.		4,000	
	To Royalties A/c			4,000
	(Being the balance of Royalties transferred to P & L A/c)			
31-12-05	Royalties A/c Dr.		14,000	
	Shortworkings A/c Dr.		1,000	
	To Bharat's A/c			15,000
	(Being Royalties payable at Rs.2 per ton subject to minimum Rent Rs.15,000)			
31-12-05	Bharat's A/c Dr.		15,000	
	To bank A/c			15,000
	(Being Minimum Rent paid to landlord)			
31-12-05	Profit & Loss A/c Dr.		14,000	
	To Royalties A/c			14,000
	(Being the balance of Royalties transferred to P & L Account)			

(Journal Entries Contd.)

Date	Particulars	L/F	Debit Rs	Credit Rs.
31-12-06	Royalties A/c Dr.		20,000	
	To Bharat's A/c			20,000
	(Being Royalty Payable to Landlord)			
31-12-06	Bharat's A/c Dr.		20,000	
	To Bank A/c			15,000
	To Shortworkings A/c			5,000
	(Being minimum Rent paid to Landlord and Shortworking recovered)			
31-12-06	Profit and loss A/c Dr.		20,000	
	To Royalties A/c			20,000
	(Being the balance of royalties transferred to P & L A/c)			
31-12-06	Profit & Loss A/c Dr.		7,000	
	To Shortworking A/c			7,000
	(Being Shortworking not recovered transferred to Profit & Loss A/c)			
31-12-07	Royalties A/c Dr.		24,000	
	To Bharat's A/c			24,000
	(Being Royalties Payable to Landlord)			
31-12-07	Bharat's A/c Dr.		24,000	
	To Bank A/c			24,000
	(Being Royalties paid to Landlord)			
31-12-07	Profit and loss A/c Dr.		24,000	
	To Royalties A/c			24,000
	(Being the balance of royalties transferred to Profit and Loss A/c)			

Ledger Accounts in the books of Raniganj Coal Co.Ltd.

Dr.   **Royalties Account**   **Cr.**

Date	Particulars	LF	Rs.	Date	Particulars	LF	Rs.
31-12-04	To Bharat's A/c		4,000	31-12-04	By P & L A/c		4,000
			4,000				4,000
31-12-05	To Bharat's A/c		14,000	31-12-05	By P & L A/c		14,000
			14,000				14,000
31-12-06	To Bharat's A/c		20,000	31-12-06	By P & L A/c		20,000
			20,000				20,000
31-12-07	To Bharat's A/c		24,000	31-12-07	By P & L A/c		24,000
			24,000				24,000

Dr.   **Bharat's Account**   **Cr.**

Date	Particulars	LF	Rs.	Date	Particulars	LF	Rs.
31-12-04	To Bank A/c		15,000	31-12-04	By Royalties A/c		4,000
					By Shortworkings A/c		11,000
			15,000				15,000
31-12-05	To Bank A/c		15,000	31-12-05	By Royalties A/c		14,000
					By Shortworkings A/c		1,000
			15,000				15,000
31-12-06	To Bank A/c		15,000	31-12-06	By Royalties A/c		20,000
	To Shortworkings A/c		5,000				
			20,000				20,000
31-12-07	To Bank A/c		24,000	31-12-07	By Royalties A/c		24,000
			24,000				24,000

Dr.   **Shortworkings A/c**   **Cr.**

Date	Particulars	LF	Rs.	Date	Particulars	LF	Rs.
31-12-04	To Bharati's A/c		11,000	31-12-04	By bal.b/d		11,000
			11,000				11,000
31-12-05	To Bal. b/d		11,000	31-12-05	By bal. b/d		12,000
31-12-05	To Bharat's A/c		1,000	31-12-05			
			12,000				12,000
31-12-07	To Bal b/d		12,000	31-12-07	By Bharat's A/c		5,000
					By P & L A/c		7,000
			12,000				12,000

Journal Entries in the Books of Bharat

Date	Particulars	L/F	Debit Rs	Credit Rs.
31-12-04	Raniganj Coal Co.'s A/c Dr.		15,000	
	To Royalties Receivable A/c			4,000
	To Shortworkings Allowable A/c			11,000
	To Royalties Suspense A/c			
	(Being Royalties receivable and shortworkings allowable)			
31-12-04	Bank A/c Dr.		15,000	
	To Raniganj Coal Co.'s A/c			15,000
	(Being Minimum Rent received)			
31-12-04	Royalties Receivable A/c Dr.		4,000	
	To Profit & Loss A/c			4,000
	(Being Royalties receivable transferred to P & L A/c)			
31-12-05	Raniganj Coal Co.'s A/c Dr.		15,000	
	To Royalties Receivable			14,000
	To Shortworkings Allowable A/c			1,000
	To Royalties Suspense A/c			
	(Being Royalties receivable and short workings allowable)			
31-12-05	Bank A/c Dr.		15,000	
	To Raniganj Coal Co.'s A/c			15,000
	(Being minimum rent received)			
31-12-05	Royalties Receivable A/c Dr.		14,000	
	To Profit & Loss A/c			14,000
	(Being Royalties receivable transferred to P & L A/c)			
31-12-06	Raniganj Coal Co.'s A/c Dr.		20,000	
	To Royalties Receivable			20,000
	(Being Royalties receivable)			

(Journal Entries Contd.)

Date	Particulars	L/F	Debit Rs	Credit Rs.
31-12-06	Bank A/c Dr. Shortworkings Allowable A/c Dr. To Raniganj Coal Co.'s A/c (Being Minimum Rent received and allowed shortworkings to be recovered by Raniganj Coal Company)		15,000 15,000	 20,000
31-12-06	Royalties Receivable A/c Dr. To Profit & Loss A/c (Being Royalties receivable transferred to P & L A/c)		20,000	 20,000
31-12-06	Shortworkings Allowable A/c Dr. To Profit & Loss A/c (Being Shortworkings transferred to P & L A/c)		7,000	 7,000
31-12-07	Raniganj Coal Co's A/c Dr. To Royalties Receivable A/c (Being Royalties Receivable)		24,000	 24,000
31-12-07	Bank A/c Dr. To Raniganj Coal Co's A/c (Being Royalties received)		24,000	 24,000
31-12-07	Royalties Receivable A/c Dr. To Profit and Loss A/c (Being Royalties receivable transferred to Profit and Loss A/c)		24,000	 24,000

Ledger Accounts in the Books of Bharat
Raniganj Coal Company

Dr.   **Cr.**

Date	Particulars	LF	Rs.	Date	Particulars	LF	Rs.
31-12-04	To Royalties Receivable A/c		4,000	31-12-04	By Bank A/c		15,000
	To S.W. Allowable A/c		11,000				
			15,000				15,000
31-12-05	To Royalties Receivable A/c		14,000	31-12-05	By Bank A/c		15,000
31-12-05	To S.W. Allowable A/c		1,000				
			15,000				15,000
31-12-06	To Royalties Receivable A/c		20,000	31-12-06	By Bank A/c		15,000
				31-12-06	By S.W. Allowable A/c		5,000
			20,000				20,000
31-12-07	To Royalties Receivable A/c		24,000	31-12-07	By Bank A/c		24,000
			24,000				24,000

Dr.   **Shortworkings Allowable A/c**   **Cr.**

Date	Particulars	LF	Rs.	Date	Particulars	LF	Rs.
31-12-04	To Bal c/d		11,000	31-12-04	By Raniganj Coal Co. A/c		11,000
			11,000				11,000
31-12-05	To Bal. c/d		12,000	31-12-05	By Bal b/d		11,000
				31-12-05	By Raniganj Coal Co. A/c		1,000
			12,000				12,000
31-12-06	To Raniganj Coal Co. A/c		5,000	31-12-06	By Bal b/d		12,000
31-12-06	To Profit & Loss A/c		7,000				
			12,000				12,000

Royalty Accounts (Excluding Sub Lease) / 225

Dr.   **Royalties Receivable A/c**   **Cr.**

Date	Particulars	LF	Rs.	Date	Particulars	LF	Rs.
31-12-04	To P & L A/c		4,000	31-12-04	By Raniganj Coal Co.A/c		4,000
			4,000				4,000
31-12-05	To P & L A/c		14,000	31-12-05	By Raniganj Coal Co.A/c		14,000
			14,000				14,000
31-12-06	To P & L A/c		20,000	31-12-06	By Raniganj Coal Co.A/c		20,000
			20,000				20,000
31-12-07	To P & L A/c		24,000	31-12-07	By Raniganj Coal Co.A/c		24,000
			24,000				24,000

Illustration 2

Bihar Coal Company Ltd. leased a piece of land from a landlord Mr. Ram for 10 years from 1st January 1995 on the following terms.

Bihar Coal company Ltd. shall pay a minimum rent of Rs.20,000 for the first year with annual increase of Rs.1,000 per year in every subsequent year. The Royalty is Rs.3 per ton of Coal with a power to recover the shortworking in the first three years only. The output of the first 4 years was as follows.

Year	Production (in tons)
2004	3,000
2005	6,000
2006	11,500
2007	10,000

Pass the Journal Entries in the books of Bihar Coal Company Limited and Mr. Ram.

Solution :

Working

1) Lessee : Bihar Coal Company Ltd.
2) Landlord : Mr. Ram
3) Royalty : Rs. 3 per ton
4) Minimum Rent : Rs.20000+annual increase of Rs.1000 p.a.
5) Right of Recoupment of shortworkings : First 3 years.

Table Showing calculation of Rayalties Shortworkings, Shortworking recovered and Shorworking Unrecovered.

Year	Output (tons)	Minimum Rent Rs.	Royalty Rs.	Shortworking (Rs.)	S.W. Recoverd Rs.	S.W. Unrecovered	Payment to Landlord Rs.
2004	3,000	20,000	9,000	11,000		-	20,000
2005	6,000	21,000	18,000	3,000	-	-	21,000
2006	11,500	22,000	34,500	-	-	1500	22,000
2007	10,000	23,000	30,000	-	12,500	-	30,000

Journal Entries in the books of Bihar Coal Company Ltd.

Date	Particulars	L/F	Debit Rs	Credit Rs.
31-12-04	Royalties A/c Dr.		9,000	
	Shortworkings A/c Dr.		11,000	
	To Ram's A/c			20,000
	(Being Royalties Payable)			
31-1204	Ram's A/c Dr.		20,000	
	To Bank A/c			20,000
	(Being Minimum rent paid to landlord)			
31-12-04	Profit & Loss A/c Dr.		9,000	
	To Royalties A/c			9,000
	(Being Royalties transferred to P & L A/c)			
31-12-05	Royalties A/c Dr.		18,000	
	Shortworkings A/c Dr.		3,000	
	To Ram's A/c			21,000
	(Being Royalties Payable)			
31-12-05	Ram's A/c Dr.		21,000	
	To Bank A/c			21,000
	(Being Minimum rent paid to landlord)			
31-12-05	Profit & Loss A/c Dr.		18,000	
	To Royalties A/c			18,000
	(Being royalties transferred to P & L A/c.)			

Date	Particulars	L/F	Debit Rs	Credit Rs.
31-12-04	Bank A/c Dr. To Bihar Coal Co's A/c (Being Minimum rent received)		20,000	20,000
31-12-04	Royalties Receivable A/c Dr. To Profit & Loss A/c (Being the transfer of Royalties receivable to P & L A/c)		9,000	9,000
31-12-05	Bihar Coal Co's A/c Dr. To Royalties Receivable A/c To Shortworking Allowable A/c / Royalties Suspense A/c (Being Royalties at Rs.3 per ton on 6000 tons subject to Minimum rent Rs.21000 Received)		21,000	18,000 3,000
31-12-05	Bank A/c Dr. To Bihar Coal Co's A/c (Being Minimum rent received)		21,000	21,000
31-12-05	Royalties A/c Dr. To Profit and Loss A/c (Being the transfer of royalties receivable to profit & Loss Account)		18,000	18,000
31-12-06	Bihar Coal Co's A/c Dr. To Royalties Receivable a/c (Being the Royalties at Rs.3 per ton on 11500 tons received)		34,500	34,500
31-12-06	Bank A/c Dr. Shortworkings Allowable/ Royalties Suspense A/c Dr. To Bihar Coal Co's A/c (Being Royalties received and Shortworkings Allowed.)		22,000 12,500	34,500

Date	Particulars	L/F	Debit Rs	Credit Rs.
31-12-06	Royalties Receivable A/c Dr.		34,500	
	To Profit & Loss A/c			34,500
	(Being transfer of Royalties receivable to profit & loss Account)			
31-12-06	Shortworking Allowable/ Royalties Suspense A/c Dr.		1500	
	To Profit & Loss A/c			1500
	(Being Shortworkings Allowable transferred to P & L A/c)			
31-12-07	Bihar Coal Co's A/c Dr.		30,000	
	To Royalties Receivable A/c			30,000
	(Being Royalties Receivable)			
31-12-07	Bank A/c Dr.		30,000	
	To Bihar Coal Co's A/c			30,000
	(Being Royalties Received)			
31-12-07	Royalties Receivable A/c Dr.		30,000	
	To Profit & Loss A/c			30,000
	(Being the transfer of royalties receivable to P & L A/c.)			

Illustration 3

The Bengal Coal Company Ltd. leased a piece of land from Eastwala for 10 years on 1st Jan. 2003 on the following terms.

1) Royalties to be paid at 50 paise per tonne of Coal.

2) Minimum Rent at Rs.18,000 p.a.

3) Each Year's excess of minimum rent over actual royalties was to be recouped during the next three years.

4) If in any year the normal rent was not attained due to strike or accident the minimum rent was to be reduced proportionately according to the length of stoppage.

Following was the output.

2003 - 6000 tonnes   2004 - 28000 tonnes

2005 - 36000 tonnes   2006 - 48000 tonnes

2007 - 30000 tonnes

During the year 2007 there was a strike for four months.

Write up necessary accounts in the books of lessee and landlord.

(Pune University March 1998)

Solution : -

Working

Lessee : Bengal Coal Company Limited.

Lessor/Landlord : Eastwala.

Royalty : Re 0.50 per ton

Minimum Rent : Rs. 18000

Period of Recoupment : Next three years from shortworkings.

Table showing the calculation of Royalties, shortworkings, shortworkings recovered and Unrecovered.

Year	Ouput (tons)	Minimum Rent Rs.	Royalty Rs.	Shortworking (Rs.)	S.W. Recoverd Rs.	S.W. Uncovered	Payment to Landlord Rs.
2003	6,000	18,000	3,000	15,000	-	-	18,000
2004	28,000	18,000	14,000	4,000	-	-	18,000
2005	36,000	18,000	18,000	-	-	-	18,000
2006	48,000	18,000	24,000	-	6,000	9,000	18,000
2007	30,000	12,000	15,000	-	3,000	1,000	12,000

Notes :

(1) Shortworkings of 2003 are recoverable upto 2006. In the year 2006 only Rs.6,000 could be recovered and remaining balance of Rs.9000 could not be recovered.

(2) In the year 2007 there was a strike for 4 months. Therefore, minimum rent of 8 months will be taken into consideration and it is Rs.12,000.

Ledger Accounts in the books of Bengal Coal Co. Ltd.

Dr. Royalties A/c Cr.

Date	Particulars	LF	Rs.	Date	Particulars	LF	Rs.
31-12-03	To Eastwala's A./c		3,000	31-12-03	By P. & L. A/c		3,000
			3,000				3,000
31-12-04	To Eastwala's A./c		14,000	31-12-04	By P. & L. A/c		14,000
			14,000				14,000
31-12-05	To Eastwala's A./c		18,000	31-12-05	By P. & L. A/c		18,000
			18,000				18,000
31-12-06	To Eastwala's A./c		24,000	31-12-06	By P. & L. A/c		24,000
			24,000				24,000
31-12-07	To Eastwala's A./c		15,000	31-12-07	By P. & L. A/c		15,000
			15,000				15,000

Dr. Eastwala's (Landlords A/c) Cr.

Date	Particulars	LF	Rs.	Date	Particulars	LF	Rs.
31-12-03	To Bank A/c		18,000	31-12-03	By Royalties A/c		3,000
					By Shortworkings A/c		15,000
			18,000				18,000
31-12-04	To Bank A/c		18,000	31-12-04	By Roytalites A/c		4,000
					To Shortworkings A/c		14,000
			18,000				18,000
31-12-05	To Bank A/c		18,000	31-12-05	BY Royalties A/c		18,000
			18,000				18,000
31-12-06	To Bank A/c		18,000	31-12-06	By Royalties A/c		24,000
	To Shortworkigns A/c		6,000				
			24,000				24,000
31-12-07	To Bank A/c		12,000	31-12-07	By Royalties A/c		15,000
	To Shortworkigns A/c		3,000				
			15,000				15,000

Dr. Shortworkings A/c Cr.

Date	Particulars	LF	Rs.	Date	Particulars	LF	Rs.
31-12-03	To Eastwala's A./c		15,000	31-12-03	By Balance c/d		15,000
			15,000				15,000
31-12-04	To Balance b/d		15,000	31-12-04	By Balance c/d		19,000
	To Eastwala's A/c		4,000				
			19,000				19,000
31-12-05	To Balance b/d		19,000	31-12-05	By Balance c/d		19,000
31-12-06	To Balance b/d		19,000	31-12-06	By Eastwala's A/c		6,000
					By P & L A/c		9,000
					By Balance c/d		4,000
			19,000				19,000
31-12-07	To Balance b/d		4,000	31-12-07	By Eastwala's A/c		3,000
					By P & L A/c		1,000
			4,000				4,000

In the Books of Eastwala (Landlord)

Dr.   **Royalties Receivable Account**   **Cr.**

Date	Particulars	LF	Rs.	Date	Particulars	LF	Rs.
31-12-03	To P. & L.A/c		3,000	31-12-03	By Bengal Coal Co's A/c		3,000
			3,000				3,000
31-12-04	To P. & L.A/c		14,000	31-12-04	By Bengal Coal Co's A/c		14,000
			14,000				14,000
31-12-05	To P. & L.A/c		18,000	31-12-05	By Bengal Coal Co's A/c		18,000
			18,000				18,000
31-12-06	To P. & L.A/c		24,000	31-12-06	By Bengal Coal Co's A/c		24,000
			24,000				24,000
31-12-07	To P. & L.A/c		15,000	31-12-07	By Bengal Coal Co's A/c		15,000
			15,000				15,000

Dr.   **Bengal Coal Company's A/c**   **Cr.**

Date	Particulars	LF	Rs.	Date	Particulars	LF	Rs.
31-12-03	To Royalties Receivable		3,000	31-12-03	By Bank A/c		18,000
	To Shotworkigs A/c		15,000				
	/ Allowable A/c						
			18,000				18,000
31-12-04	To Royalties Receivable		14,000	31-12-04	By Bank A/c		18,000
	To Shotworkigs A/c		4,000				
	/ Allowable A/c						
			18,000				18,000
31-12-05	To Royalties Receivable A/c		18,000	31-12-05	By Bank A/c		18,000
			18,000				18,000
31-12-06	To Royalties Receivable A/c		24,000	31-12-06	By Bank A/c		18,000
					By Shortworkings A/c		6,000
					/ Allowable A/c		
			24,000				24,000
31-12-07	To Royalties Receivables A/c		15,000	31-12-07	By Bank A/c		12,000
					By Shortworkigs A/c		3,000
					/ Allowable A/c		
			15,000				15,000

Dr.   S/W Allowable A/c / Royalties Suspense A/c   Cr.

Date	Particulars	LF	Rs.	Date	Particulars	LF	Rs.
31-12-03	To Balance c/d		15,000	31-12-03	By Bengal Coal's Co.A/c		15,000
			15,000				15,000
31-12-04	To Balance c/d		19,000	31-12-04	By Balance b/d		15,000
					By Bengal Coal's Co's A/c		4,000
			19,000				19,000
31-12-05	To Balance c/d		19,000	31-12-05	By Balance b/d		19,000
			19,000				19,000
31-12-06	To Bengal Coal Co's A/c		6,000	31-12-06	By Balance b/d		19,000
	To P & L A/c		9,000				
	To Balance c/d		4,000				
			19,000				19,000
31-12-07	To Bengal Coal Co's A/c		3,000	31-12-07	By Balance b/d		4,000
	To P & L A/c		1,000				
			4,000				4,000

Illustration 4

Prof. R.K.Jain wrote a book on Advanced Accountancy and got it published with Sahitya Prakashan Ltd. on the terms that royalties will be paid at Rs.10 per copy sold subject to a minimum rent of Rs.20,000. Each year's excess of minimum rent over the actual royalties is recoverable out of the royalties of the next year only. Following are the details of number of copies printed and closing stock.

Year	Number of copies printed	Closing Stock
2000	1700	200
2001	2000	300
2002	2500	400
2003	3000	500

Write up necessary ledger accounts in the books of sahitya Prakashan.

Solution :

Workings

1) Lessee : Sahitya Prakashan
2) Lessor : Prof. R.K. Jain
3) Royalty : Rs. 10 per copy sold.
4) Minimum Rent : Rs.20,000 per year.
5) Right of Recoupment of shortworkings : one year.

In this problem royalty is to paid on number of copies sold, hence we have to calculate number of copies sold. The number of copies sold is calculated as under.

Year	Copies Printed	Opening Stock	Closing Number of Stock	Copies sold
2000	1700	+ Nil	-200	1500
2001	2000	+ 200	-300	1900
2002	2500	+300	-400	2400
2003	3000	+400	-500	2900

Copies printed + Opening stock - Closing stock = Number of copies sold.

Note : Closing stock of present year will be the opening stock of next year. Table showing the calculations of Royalties, Shortworkings, Shortworkings Recovered and S.W.Unrecovered.

In the Books of Sahitya Prakashan

Dr.   **Mr. R.K. Jain's A/c**   **Cr.**

Year	Output (tons)	Minimum Rent Rs.	Royalty Rs.	Shortworking (Rs.)	S.W. Recoverd Rs.	S.W. Uncovered	Payment to Landlord Rs.
2000	1500	20,000	15,000	5,000	-	-	20,000
2001	1900	20,000	19,000	1,000	-	5,000	20,000
2002	2400	20,000	24,000	-	1,000	-	23,000
2003	2900	20,000	29,000	-	-	-	29,000

Dr.   **Shortworkings A/c**   **Cr.**

Date	Particulars	LF	Rs.	Date	Particulars	LF	Rs.
31-12-00	To Bank A/c		20,000	31-12-00	By Royalties A/c		15,000
					By Shortworkings A/c		5,000
			20,000				20,000
31-12-01	To Bank A/c		20,000	31-12-01	BY Royalties A/c		19,000
					By Shortworkings A/c		1,000
			20,000				20,000
31-12-02	To Bank A/c		23,000	31-12-02	By Royalties A/c		24,000
			1,000				
			24,000				24,000
31-12-03	To Bank A/c		29,000	31-12-03	By Royalties A/c		29,000
			29,000				29,000

Dr.   **Royalties A/c**   **Cr.**

Date	Particulars	LF	Rs.	Date	Particulars	LF	Rs.
31-12-00	To R.K. Jain's A/c		5,000	31-12-00	By Balance c/d		5,000
			5,000				5,000
31-12-01	To Balance b/d		5,000	31-12-01	By Profit & Loss A/c		5,000
	To R.K. Jain's A/c		1,000		By Balance c/d		1,000
			6,000				6,000

(Shortworkings A/c contd.)

Date	Particulars	LF	Rs.	Date	Particulars	LF	Rs.
01-01-02	To Balance b/d		1,000	01-01-02	By R.K. Jain's A/c		1,000
			1,000				1,000

Dr.   **Royalties A/c**   **Cr.**

Date	Particulars	LF	Rs.	Date	Particulars	LF	Rs.
31-12-00	To R.K. Jain's A/c		15,000	31-12-00	By P & L A/c		15,000
			15,000				15,000
31-12-01	To R.K. Jain's A/c		19,000	31-12-01	By P & L A/c		19,000
			19,000				19,000
31-12-02	To R.K. Jain's A/c		24,000	31-12-02	By P & L A/c		24,000
			24,000				24,000
31-12-03	To R.K. Jain's A/c		29,000	31-12-03	By P & L A/c		29,000
			29,000				29,000

Illustration 5

Bihar Mining Co.Ltd. took a mine on a Lease at a Royalty of Rupee one per ton. The minimum rent was fixed at Rs.4000 for the first year, Rs.6000 for the second year and Rs.8000 per year thereafter. Shortworkings of any year could be recouped out of the royalties of the next two years only. The production during the first five years was as follows.

Years	Output in tonnes
1	2000
2	4500
3	6000
4	9000
5	12000

Pass the necessary Journal Entries in the books of the company.

(P.U.April 1995)

Solution

Working

Lessee :- Bihar Mining Co.Ltd.

Lessor : Name not given

Royalty : One Rupee per ton.

Minimum Rent : Rs.4,000 Rs.6,000 for Ist and IInd year and thereafter Rs.8,000 per year.

Period of Recoupment of shortworkings : Next two years.

Table showing the calculation of Royalties, Shortworkings, Shortworking Recovered and Shortworkings Unrecovered.

Year	Output (tons)	Minimum Rent Rs.	Royalty Rs.	Shortworking (Rs.)	S.W. Recoverd Rs	S.W. Unrecovered	Payment to Landlord Rs.
2001	2,000	4,000	2,000	2,000	-	-	4,000
2002	4,500	6,000	4,500	1,500	-	-	6,000
2003	6,000	8,000	6,000	2,000	-	2,000	8,000
2004	9,000	8,000	9,000	-	1,000	-	8,000
2005	12,000	8,000	12,000	-	2,000	-	10,000

Journal Entries in the Books of Bihar Mining Co.Ltd.

Date	Particulars	L/F	Debit Rs.	Credit Rs.
First year	Royalties A/c Dr.		2,000	
	Shortworkings Dr.		2,000	
	To Landlords A/c			4,000
	(Being Royalties payable at Rs. one per ton subject to Minimum Rent Rs.4000)			
	Landlords A/c Dr.		4,000	
	To Bank A/c			4,000
	(Being Minimum rent paid to Landlord)			
	Profit and Loss A/c Dr,		4,000	
	To Royalties A/c			4,000
	(Being transfer of Royalties to Profit & Loss Account.)			

Date	Particulars	L/F	Debit Rs.	Credit Rs.
Second year	Royalties A/c Dr. Shortworkings Dr. 　　To Landlords A/c (Being Royalties payable at Rs. one per ton subject to Minimum Rent Rs.4000)		4,500 1,500	 6,000
	Landlords A/c Dr. 　　To Bank A/c (Being Minimum rent paid to Landlord)		6,000	 6,000
	Profit and Loss A/c Dr. 　　To Royalties A/c (Being transfer of royalties to Profit & Loss Account.)		4,500	 4,500
Third year	Roytalties A/c Dr. Shortworkings A/c Dr. 　　To Landlords A/c (Being Royalty payable at Rs.one per ton subject to minimum rent Rs.6000)		6,000 2,000	 8,000
	Landlords A/c Dr. 　　To Bank A/c (Being minimum rent paid to landlord)		8,000	 8,000
	Profit and Loss A/c Dr. 　　To Royalties A/c 　　To Shortworkings A/c (Balance on royalties account and un-covered amount of shortworkings are transferred to P & L A/c)		8,000	 6,000 2,000
Fourth year	Royalties A/c Dr. 　　To Landlords A/c (Being Royalties payable		9,000	 9,000
	Landlord A/c Dr. 　　To Bank A/c 　　To Shortworking A/c (Being minimum rent paid to landlord & shortworking recovered)		9,000	 8,000 1,000

Date	Particulars	L/F	Debit Rs.	Credit Rs.
	Profit & Loss A/c　　　　　　Dr.		9,500	
	To Royalties A/c			9,000
	To Shortworkings A/c			500
	(Balance on Royalties account and un- covered amount of shortworkings are transferred to profit & loss account)			
Fifth year	Royalties A/c　　　　　　　Dr.		12,000	
	To landlords A/c			12,000
	(Being royalties payable)			
	Landlords A/c　　　　　　　Dr.		12,000	
	To Bank A/c			10,000
	To Shortworkings A/c			2,000
	(Being minimum rent paid to landlord and shortworking recovered)			
	Profit and Loss A/c　　　　　Dr.			
	To Royalties A/c			
	(Balances on Royalties A/c are transferred to profit & Loss A/c)			

Illustration 6

Ajay Ltd leased a colliery on 1st January 1990 from M/s Sathe at a minimum Rent of Rs.40,000/- p.a., at a royalty of Rs.3 per ton with a right to recover shortworking over the first three years of the lease.

The output for the first four years of the lease was as follows.

Years	Output (tons)
2004	10,000
2005	12,000
2006	14,000
2007	20,000

Give necessary Journal Entires with minimum rent in the books of Ajay for the above four years.

Solution

Working

Lessee : Mr. Ajay

Lessor : Mr. Sathe

Royalty : Rs. 3 per ton.

Minimum Rent : Rs. 40,000

Period of Recoupment of Shortworkings :First three years.

Table showing the calculation of Royalties, shortworkings, shortworking Recovered and shortworking unrecovered.

Year	Output (tons)	Minimum Rent Rs.	Royalty Rs.	Shortworking (Rs.)	S.W. Recoverd Rs.	S.W. Uncovered	Payment to Landlord Rs.
2004	10,000	40,000	30,000	10,000	-	-	40,000
2005	12,000	40,000	36,000	4,000	-	-	40,000
2006	14,000	40,000	42,000		2,000	12,000	43,000
2007	20,000	40,000	60,000		-	-	60,000

Note : Entries through minimum rent are opened only when the amount of Royalties are less than minimum rent.

Journal Entries in the books of

Ajay (Lessee)

Date	Particulars	L/F	Debit Rs.	Credit Rs.
31-12-04	Royalties A/c Dr.		30,000	
	Shortworkings A/c Dr.		10,000	
	To Minimum Rent A/c			40,000
	(Being royalites & shortworkings charged to minimum rent A/c)			
31-12-04	Minimum Rent A/c Dr.		40,000	
	To M/s Sathe A/c			40,000
	(Being Minimum rent payable to M/s sathe)			

Royalty Accounts (Excluding Sub Lease) / 239

Date	Particulars	L/F	Debit Rs.	Credit Rs.
31-12-04	M/s Sathe's A/c Dr. To Bank A/c (Being minimum rent paid to landlord)		40,000	40,000
31-12-04	Profit & Loss Account Dr. To Royalties A/c (Being transfer of Royalties to P & L A/c)		30,000	30,000
31-12-05	Royalties A/c Dr. Shortworking A/c Dr. To Minimum Rent A/c (Being Royalties and shortworkings charged to minimum Rent A/c)		36,000 4,000	40,000
31-12-05	Minimum Rent A/c Dr. To M/s Sathe's A/c (Being minimum Rent payable to M/s Sathe)		40,000	40,000
31-12-05	M/s Sathe's A/c Dr. To Bank A/c (Being minimum rent paid to landlord)		40,000	40,000
31-12-05	Profit and Loss A/c Dr. To Royalties A/c (Being transfer of Royalties to P & L A/c)		36,000	36,000
31-12-06	Royalties A/c Dr. To M/s Sathe's A/c (Being royalties Payable)		42,000	42,000
31-12-06	M/s Sathe's A/c Dr. To Bank A/c To Shortworkings A/c (Being minimum rent paid and shortworkings recovered)		42,000	40,000 2,000

Date	Particulars	L/F	Debit Rs.	Credit Rs.
31-12-06	Profit and Loss A/c Dr. To Royalties A/c To Shortworking A/c (Being Royalties and shortworkings transferred to profit and loss account)		54,000	42,000 12,000
31-12-07	Royalties A/c Dr. To M/s Sathe's A/c (Being royalties payable)		60,000	60,000
31-12-07	M/s Sathe's A/c Dr. To Bank A/c (Being royalties paid to landlord)		60,000	60,000
31-12-07	Profit & Loss A/c Dr. To Royalties A/c (Being transfer of Royalties to Profit & loss account)		60,000	60,000

Illustration 7

B Company Ltd leased a property from Star mining Company Ltd at a royalty of Rs.1.50 per ton with a minimum rent of Rs.20,000 p.a. Each year's excess of minimum rent over royalties is recoverable out of the royalties of the next five years. In the event of strike and the minimum rent not being reached, the lease provided that the minimum rent would stand reduced proportionately to time actually worked. The result of the working were as follows :

Year	Actual Royalties (Rs.)
2001	Nil
2002	6,500
2003	18,500
2004	22,500
2005	35,000
2006	12,000
2007	30,000

Write up Minimum Rent Account, Royalties Account, Shortworkings Account and landlords accounts in the books of B. Company Ltd. for all years.

Solution

Workings

1) Lessee : B Company Limited
2) Lessor : Star Mining Company Ltd.
3) Royalty : Rs. 1.50 per ton.
4) Minimum Rent : - Rs. 20,000.
5) Period of Recoupment of shortworking : Next 5 years from shortworkings.

Table showing the calculation of Royalties shortworkings, shortworking Recovered and shortworking uncovered.

Year	Minimum Rent(tons)	Royalty Rs.	Shortworking (Rs.)	S.W. Recoverd Rs.	S.W. Uncovered	Payment to Landlord Rs.
2001	20,000	Nil	20,000	-	-	20,000
2002	20,000	6,500	13,500	-	-	20,000
2003	20,000	18,500	1,500	-	-	20,000
2004	20,000	22,500	-	2,500	-	20,000
2005	20,000	35,000	-	15,000	-	20,000
2006	15,000	12,000	3,000	-	2,500	15,000
2007	20,000	30,000	-	10,000	3,500	20,000

Note :

In the year 1999, there was a strike for 3 months hence the minimum rent is reduced proportionately.

Dr.   **Minimum Rent Account**   **Cr.**

Date	Particulars	LF	Rs.	Date	Particulars	LF	Rs.
31-12-01	To Star Mining Co' A/c		20,000	31-12-01	By Shortworkings A/c		20,000
			20,000				20,000
31-12-02	To Star Mining Co' A/c		20,000	31-12-02	By Royalties A/c		6,500
					By Shortworkings A/c		13,500
			20,000				20,000
31-12-03	To Star Mining Co' A/c		20,000	31-12-03	By Royalties A/c		18,500
					By Shortworkings A/c		1,500
			20,000				20,000
31-12-06	To Star Mining Co' A/c		15,000	31-12-06	By Royalties A/c		12,000
					By Shortworkings A/c		3,000
			15,000				15,000

Dr.   **Royalties Account**   **Cr.**

Date	Particulars	LF	Rs.	Date	Particulars	LF	Rs.
31-12-01	To Minimum Rent A/c		6,500	31-12-01	By Profit & Loss A/c		6,500
			6,500				6,500
31-12-02	To Minimum Rent A/c		18,500	31-12-02	By Profit & Loss A/c		18,500
			18,500				18,500
	To Star Mining Co' A/c		22,500		By Profit & Loss A/c		22,500
31-12-03			22,500	31-12-03			22,500
	To Star Mining Co' A/c		35,000		By Profit & Loss A/c		35,000
			35,000				35,000
31-12-04	To Minimum Rent A/c		12,000	31-12-04	By Profit & Loss A/c		12,000
			12,000				12,000
	To Star Mining Co' A/c		30,000		By Profit & Loss A/c		30,000
			30,000				30,000

Dr.   **Shortworkings Account**   **Cr.**

Date	Particulars	LF	Rs.	Date	Particulars	LF	Rs.
31-12-01	To Minimum Rent A/c		20,000	31-12-01	By Balance c/d		20,000
			20,000				20,000
31-12-02	To Balance b/d		20,000	31-12-02	By Balance c/d		33,500
31-12-02	To Minimum Rent A/c		13,500	31-12-02			
			33,500				33,500
01-01-03	To Balance b/d		33,500	01-01-03	By Balance c/d		35,000
31-12-03	To Minimum Rent A/c		15,000	31-12-03			
			35,000				35,000
01-01-04	To Balance c/d		35,000	01-01-04	By Star Mining Co's A/c		2500
					By Balance c/d		32,500
			35,000				35,000
01-01-05	To Balance c/d		32,500	01-01-05	By Star Mining Co's A/c		15,000
					By Balance c/d		17,500
			32,500				32,500
01-01-06	To Balance b/d		17,500	01-01-06	By P & L A/c		2,500
	To Minimum Rent A/c		3,000		By Balance c/d		18,000
			20,500				20,500
01-01-07	To Balance b/d		18,000	01-01-07	By Star Mining Co's A/c		10,000
					By Profit & Loss A/c		3,500
					By Balance c/d		4,500
			18,000				18,000
01-01-08	To Balance b/d		4,500				

Illustration 8

'A' Colliery Co. holds a Coal field on a lease for the period of 15 years beginning from 1st January 2004. The terms of the lease are as follows.

(a) To pay a minimum rent of Rs. 32000 p.a.

(b) Each year's excess of minimum rent over actual royalties i.e. shortworkings can be recovered during the subsequent two years.

(c) If any year due to accident or strike the actual royalty is less than minimum rent it is to be reduced by 25% for that year.

(d) Royalty is to be calculated at 75 paise per ton. The output was as follows :

Year	Output
2004	24,000 tons.
2005	32,000 tons.
2006	56,000 tons.
2007	40,000 tons.

2007 is the year of strike.

Pass the Journal Entries in the books of 'A' Colliery Co.

Solution

Working

1) Lessee - 'A' Colliery Company.

2) Lessor - Not given.

3) Royalty - Re 0.75 per ton.

4) Minimum Rent : Rs. 32,000.

5) Period of Recoupment of shortworkings : subsequent two years.

Table Showing Calculation of Royalties and Shortworkings

Year	Output (tons)	Minimum Rent Rs.	Royalty Rs.	Shortworking (Rs.)	S.W. Recoverd Rs.	S.W. Unrecovered	Payment to Landlord Rs.
2004	24,000	32,000	18,000	14,000	-	-	32,000
2005	32,000	32,000	24,000	8,000	-	-	32,000
2006	56,000	32,000	42,000	-	10,000	4,000	32,000
2007	40,000	24,000	30,000	-	6,000	2,000	24,000

Note : In the year 2007, there was a strike and therefore minimum rent is reduced by 25%; so it is Rs.24,000.

Journal Entries in the books of 'A' Colliery Co.

Date	Particulars	L/F	Debit Rs.	Credit Rs.
31-12-04	Royalties A/c Dr.		18,000	
	Shortworkings A/c Dr.		14,000	
	To Landlords A/c			32,000
	(Being Royalties Payable)			
31-12-04	Landlords A/c Dr.		32,000	
	To Bank A/c			32,000
	(Being minimum rent paid to landlord)			
31-12-04	Profit & Loss A/c Dr.		18,000	
	To Royalties A/c			18,000
	(Being transfer of royalties to P & L A/c)			
31-12-05	Royalties A/c Dr.		24,000	
	Shortworking A/c Dr.		8,000	
	To Landlord's A/c			32,000
	(Being royalties payable)			
31-12-05	Landlord's A/c Dr.		32,000	
	To Bank A/c			32,000
	(Being minimum rent paid to landlord)			
31-12-05	Profit & Loss A/c Dr.		24,000	
	To Royalties A/c			24,000
	(Being transfer of royalties to P & L A/c)			
31-12-06	Royalties A/c Dr.		42,000	
	To Landlord A/c			42,000
	(Being Royalties payable)			
31-12-06	Landlords A/c Dr.		42,000	
	To Bank A/c			32,000
	To Shortworkings A/c			10,000
	(Being minimum rent paid and shortworkings recovered)			

(Journal Entries in the books of 'A' Colliery Co. contd.)

Date	Particulars	L/F	Debit Rs.	Credit Rs.
31-12-06	Profit & loss A/c Dr.		46,000	
	To Royalties A/c			42,000
	To Shortworkings A/c			4,000
	(Being transfer of royalties and shortworkings to profit & loss A/c)			
31-12-07	Royalties A/c Dr.		30,000	
	To Landlords A/c			30,000
	(Being royalties payable)			
31-12-07	Landlord's A/c Dr.		30,000	
	To Bank A/c			24,000
	To Shortworkings A/c			6,000
	(Being Minimum rent paid and shortworkings recovered)			
31-12-07	Profit & Loss A/c Dr.		32,000	
	To Royalties A/c			30,000
	To Shortworkings A/c			2,000
	(Being the transfer of royalties and shortworkings to Profit & Loss A/c)			

Illustration 9 :

X Ltd. took from Y Ltd. a lease of Coal field for the period of 10 years from 1st Jan. 2003. The said lease provided for the payment of Royalties to Y Ltd. at Re. 00.50 per tonne with a minimum rent of Rs.8000 per annum.

Each year excess of minimum rent over the actual royalties were recoverable during the subsequent two years. The lease, however, stipulated that if in any year the normal rent was not attained due to accident, the minimum rent was to be regarded having been reduced proportionately having regards to the length of stoppage. The output was as follows :

2003 - 7000 tonnes   2005 - 20000 tonnes
2004 - 14000 tonnes   2006 - 12000 tonnes

During the year 2006 there was a stoppage of work due to accident lasting for three months.

Pass the Journal Entries in the books of X Ltd. for four years.

Solution

Workings

1) Lessee : 'X' Ltd.

2) Lessor : 'Y' Ltd.

3) Royalty : 50 N.P. per ton.

4) Minimum Rent Rs.8000 per year.

5) Period of Recoupment of Shortworkings : - Subsequent two years.

Table Showing Calculation of Royalties and Shortworkings

Year	Output (tons)	Minimum Rent Rs.	Royalty Rs.	Shortworking (Rs.)	S.W. Recoverd Rs.	S.W. Unre-covered	Payment to Landlord Rs.
2003	7,000	8,000	3,500	4,500	-	-	8,000
2004	14,000	8,000	7,000	1,000	-	-	8,000
2005	20,000	8,000	10,000	-	2,000	3,500	8,000
2006	12,000	6,000	6,000	-	-	-	6,000

Journal Entries in the books of X Ltd.

Date	Particulars	L/F	Debit Rs.	Credit Rs.
31-12-03	Royalties A/c Dr.		3,500	
	Shortworkings A/c Dr.		4,500	
	To Y Ltd. A/c			8,000
	(Being royalty payable)			
31-12-03	Y Ltd A/c Dr.		8,000	
	To Bank A/c			8,000
	(Being minimum rent paid)			
31-12-03	Profit & Loss A/c Dr.		3,500	
	To Royalties A/c			3,500
	(Being transfer of royalties to Profit & Loss A/c)			
31-12-04	Royalties A/c Dr.		7,000	
	Shortworkings A/c Dr.		1,000	
	To Y Ltd.A/c			8,000
	(Being royalties Payable)			
31-12-04	Y Ltd A/c Dr.		8,000	
	To Bank A/c			8,000
	(Being minimum rent paid)			
31-12-04	Profit & loss A/c Dr.		7,000	
	To Royalties A/c			7,000
	(Being transfer of royalties to Profit & Loss A/c)			
31-12-05	Royalties A/c Dr.		10,000	
	To Y Ltd A/c			10,000
	(Being royalties payable)			
31-12-05	Y Ltd A/c Dr.		10,000	
	To Bank A/c			10,000
	To Shortworkings A/c			
	(Being minimum rent paid and shortworkings recovered)			

Date	Particulars	L/F	Debit Rs.	Credit Rs.
31-12-05	Y's Ltd A/c Dr.		10,000	
	To Royalties A/c			8,000
	(Being transfer of royalties to Profit &			2,000
	Loss A/c)			
31-12-05	Profit and Loss A/c Dr.		10,000	
	To Royalties A/c			10,000
	(Being transfer of royalties to profit &			
	Loss A/c)			
31-12-05	Profit and loss A/c Dr.		3,500	
	To Shortworkings A/c			3,500
	(Being shortworkings transferred to P			
	& L A/c)			
31-12-06	Royalties A/c Dr.		6,000	
	To Y Ltd A/c			6,000
	(Being royalties payable)			
31-12-06	Y Ltd A/c Dr.		6,000	
	To Bank A/c			6,000
	(Being royalties paid to landlord)			
31-12-06	Profit and Loss A/c Dr.		6,000	
	To Royalties A/c			6,000
	(Being royalties transferred to profit &			
	loss Accounts)			

Illustration 10

The Kapil mines company obtained a mine on lease on 1st Jan.2004 on the following terms form Mr.Gulab.

(a) Royalty was payable at Re 0.75 per ton.

(b) Minimum rent was fixed at Rs.36,000 p.a.

(c) Each years excess of minimum rent over actual royalties can be recovered during the subsequent two years.

(d) Due to strike or accident, minimum rent is to be reduced by 25% for that year.

Production was as follows :

Years	Production in tons.
2004	42,000
2005	44,000
2006	70,000
2007	60,000 (strike for 3 months)

Give the journal entries in the books of kapil mines company for above four years.

Solution :

Working

1) Lessee : Kapil Mines Company.

2) Lessor : Mr. Gulab

3) Royalty : 75 N.P. per ton.

4) Minimum Rent : Rs. 36,000 p.a.

5) Period of recoupment of short workings - subsequent two years.

Table Showing Calculation of Royalties and Shortworkings

Year	Output (tons)	Minimum Rent Rs.	Royalty Rs.	Shortworking (Rs.)	S.W. Recoverd Rs.	S.W. Uncovered	Payment to Landlord Rs.
2004	42,000	36,000	31,500	4,500	-	-	36,000
2005	44,000	36,000	33,000	3,000	-	-	36,000
2006	70,000	36,000	52,500	-	7,500	-	45000
2007	60,000	27,000	45,000	-	-	-	45,000

Journal Entries in the books of Kapil Mines Co.

Date	Particulars	L/F	Debit Rs.	Credit Rs.
31-12-04	Royalties A/c Dr.		31,500	
	Shortworkings A/c Dr.		4,500	
	To Gulab's A/c			36,000
	(Being royalties payable)			
31-12-04	Gulab's A/c Dr.		36,000	
	To Bank A/c			36,000
	(Being minimum rent paid to landlord)			
31-12-04	Profit & Loss A/c Dr.		31,500	
	To Royalties A/c			31,500
	(Being the transfer royalties to profit and Loss Account)			

Date	Particulars	L/F	Debit Rs.	Credit Rs.
31-12-05	Royalties A/c Dr. Shortworkings A/c Dr. To Gulab's A/c (Being royalties at Re.75 per ton payable)		33,000 3,000	36,000
31-12-05	Gulab's A/c Dr. To Bank A/c (Being minimum rent paid to landlord)		36,000	36,000
31-12-05	Profit and loss A/c Dr. To royalties A/c (Being the transfer of royalties to Profit & Loss A/c)		33,000	33,000
31-12-06	Royalties A/c Dr. To Gulab's A/c (Being Royalties payable)		52,500	52,500
31-12-06	Gulab's A/c Dr. To Bank A/c To Shortworkings A/c (Being royalties paid and shortworkings recoverd)		52,500	45,000 7,500
31-12-06	Profit & Loss A/c Dr. To royalties A/c (Being transfer of royalties to profit and loss Account)		52,500	52,500
31-12-07	Royalties A/c Dr. To Gulab's A/c (Being royalties payable)		45,000	45,000
31-12-07	Gulab's A/c Dr. To Bank A/c (Being royalties paid to landlord)		45,000	45,000
31-12-07	Profit & Loss A/c Dr. To Royalties a/c (Being transfer of royalties to P & L A/c)		45,000	45,000

Illustration 11

Archana Coal Company Limited leased a land from Suchitra at a royalty of 25 paise per ton of coal raised. Minimum rent was Rs. 24,000. Shortworkings was to recouped during the first four years.

The Coal raised in the first four years are as follows :

Years	Tons
2003	80,000
2004	90,000
2005	60,000 Strike for 3 months.
2006	1,20,000

There was a provision for proportionate reduction in minimum rent in case of a stoppage of work by strike, lockouts, accident etc.

Pass the necessary Journal Entries in the books of Archana Coal Co. Ltd. for four years. Accounting year ends on 31st Dec.every year.

Solution

Working

1) Lessee : Archana Coal Company.

2) Lessor : Suchitra

3) Royalty : 25 paise per ton.

4) Minimum Rent : Rs. 24000 p.a.

5) Period of recoupment of shortworking : First 4 years.

Table Showing Calculation of Royalties and Shortworkings

Year	Output (tons)	Minimum Rent Rs.	Royalty Rs.	Shortworking (Rs.)	S.W. Recoverd Rs.	S.W. Uncov- ered -	Payment to Landlord Rs.
2003	80,000	24,000	20,000	4,000	-	-	24,000
2004	90,000	24,000	22,500	1,500	-	-	24,000
2005	60,000	18,000	15,000	3,000	6,000	2,500	18,000
2006	1,20,000	24,000	30,000	-			24,000

Note : As there is a strike in the year 2005 for 3 months. Minimum rent is reduced proprotionately. So the proportionate Rent for 9 months will be Rs.18,000.

Journal Entries in the books of Archana Coal Co. Ltd.

Date	Particulars	L/F	Debit Rs.	Credit Rs.
31-12-03	Royalties A/c Dr. Shortworkings A/c Dr. To Archana's A/c (Being royalties payable at paise 25 per ton subject to minimum rent)		20,000 4,000	 24,000
31-12-03	Archana's A/c Dr. To Bank A/c (Being minimum rent paid)		24,000	 24,000
31-12-03	Profit & Loss A/c Dr. To Royalties A/c (Being transfer of royalties to profit & Loss Account)		20,000	 20,000
31-12-04	Royalties A/c Dr. Shortworking A/c Dr. To Archanas A/c (Being royalties payable)		22,500 1,500	 24,000
31-12-04	Archana's A/c Dr. To Bank A/c (Being minimum rent paid to landlord)		24,000	 24,000
31-12-04	Profit & Loss A/c Dr. To Royalties A/c (Being transfer of royalties to profit & Loss A/c)		22,500	 22,500
31-12-05	Royalties A/c Dr. Shortworkings A/c Dr. To Archana's A/c (Being Royalties Payable)		15,000 3,000	 18,000
31-12-05	Archana's A/c Dr. To Bank A/c (Being minimum rent paid)		18,000	 18,000

Date	Particulars	L/F	Debit Rs.	Credit Rs.
31-12-05	Profit & Loss A/c Dr. 　　To Royalties A/c (Being transfer of Royalties to Profit & Loss A/c)		15,000	15,000
31-12-06	Royalties A/c Dr. 　　To Archana's A/c (Being royalties Payable)		30,000	30,000
31-12-06	Archana's A/c Dr. 　　To Bank A/c 　　To Shortworking A/c (Being minimum rent paid and shortworkings recovered)		30,000	24,000 6,00
31-12-06	Profit & Loss A/c Dr. 　　To Royalties A/c 　　To Shortworkings A/c (Being the transfer of royalties and shortworkings to profit and loss A/c)		36,000	30,000 6,000

6.5 Questions :- Objective Type Questions & Problems
Objective Type Questions :
(i) True or False

(a) Royalty means the sum payable by one person called lessee to another person called lessor for using the right by former vested in the latter.

(b) The lessee is not required to pay minimum rent to the lessor if he do not get any benefit out of the right rented out to him.

(c) Shortworking is the excess of minimum rent over actual royalties.

(d) The shortworking account shows a credit balance in the books of lessor.

(e) The object of dead rent is that the landlord should not get more than certain amount per year.

(f) Royalty means amount paid by lessor to lessee.

(g) Shortworkings = Actual Royalty - Minimum Rent

(h) The minimum rent or Royalty whichever is more, is to be paid to the landlord.

(i) Mining and Patent royalties are based on sales.

(j) Copyright royalties are payable on sales.

Answers:- a-True, b-False, c-True, d-True, e- True f-False, g-False, h-True, i-False, j-True.

(ii) Select the most appropriate answer.

1) Royalty account is of the nature:

(a) Nominal account (b) Personal account (c) Real account.

2) Royalty payable is debited by lessee to :

(a) Royalty account (b) landlord account (c) P & L account

3) In case the right to recoup shortworking has expired, the balance of shortworkings account is transferred to:

(a) landlords account (b) P & L account (c) Royalty Account

4) Royalty earned by the lessor is credited to :

(a) Trading account (b) Profit & Loss account (c) Royalty receivable account

5) The lessee's right to recoup shortworking is related to:

(a) First three years (b) terms of agreement (c) subsequent two years

Answers: 1-a, 2-a, 3-b, 4-c, 5-b

(iii) Fill in the blanks from the brackets

1) Landlord is also known as-----

(a) Lessee, (b) Lessor, (c) Tenant

2) In case of copyrights royalties are based on------

(a) Production (b) Sales (c) None of these

3) Minimum Rent is also known as-------

(a) Annual (b) Rock (c) Short

4) The balance of shortworkings account is transferred to -----

(a) Royalty account (b) Trading account (c) P & L account

5) Mining and Patents royalties are based on
(a) Sales (b) Production (c) Purchased
Answers:- 1-b, 2-b, 3-b, 4-c, 5-b.

1. What do you mean by Royalty ? How shortworking is recouped?
2. Define shortworkings and shortworkings allowable. Explain right of recoupment.
3. Write short notes on:
(1) Dead Rent (2) Recoupment of shortworkings (3) Royalty (4) Royalty agreement (5) Shortworkings (6) Shortworkings Allowable or Royalties suspense account.
1. The Maharashtra Coal Company took a coalfield on lease from Bengal Coal from 1st Jan 2001. Royalty was at Rs.2 per ton of coal taken out. Minimum Rent was Rs.40000 per year. Shortworkings were to be recovered within the first four years of the contract. The coal taken out during the first four years was as follows :

Year	Tons
2004	8,000
2005	14,000
2006	22,000
2007	34,000

Pass the Journal Entries in the books of Maharashtra Coal Company.
Answers : Shortworking 2004 Rs.14000, 2005 Rs.12000.

2. The Bombay Coal Company acquired on lease a mine owned by Mr. Gandhi. The minimum rent was Rs.25000 p.a. Royalty was fixed at Rs.2.50 per ton of coal raised. Shortworkings were to be recouped during the first five years of lease. The output for the first five years was as follows :

Years	Tons of coal raised
2002	2,000
2003	5,000
2004	10,000
2005	14,000
2006	16,000

Record the above transactions in the books of Bombay Coal Company by means of Journal entries and also write up Royalty A/c, shortworkings A/c and Mr. Gandhi's A/c.

Answers : Shortworkings 2002-Rs.20,000, 2003-Rs.12,500.

3. The Coal India took a lease of a mine from Mehta for a period of 30 years from 1st Jan 2004. The royalty was fixed at Re.1 per ton with a minimum rent of Rs.10,000 per year. Shortworkings of a year could be recovered within next two years. The output for the first four years was as follows:

Year	Output in tons
2004	5,000
2005	7,000
2006	11,000
2007	12,000

You are requested to show Royalty A/c, shortworkings A/c and Mehta's A/c in the books of Coal India Ltd.

Answers :- Shortworking 2004-Rs.5000, 2005-Rs.3000.

4. Coal Co. Ltd. leased land from Sushil Kumar at a Royalty of 25 paise per ton of coal raised. Minimum rent was Rs.24,000. Shortworkings was to be recouped during the first four years. The coal raised in the first four years was as follows :

Year	Output (Tons)
2004	80,000
2005	90,000
2006	60,000 (strike for 3 months)
2007	1,20,000

There was a provision for proportionate reduction in the minimum rent in case of stoppage of work by strike, lockout or accidents etc.

Show the necessary ledger accounts in the books of Coal Co. Ltd.

Answers :- Shortworking 2004-Rs.4000, 2005-Rs.1500, 2006-Rs.3000.

5. A Colliery Co. worked for Coal under a lease which provided for the payment of royalties at 50 paise per ton with a minimum rent of Rs.12000 per annum. The power to recoup shortworkings is given during the subsequent two years.

If in any year rent was not attained due to strike or accident the minimum rent was to be reduced proportionately according to the length of stoppage.

The output in tonnes was as follows :

Year	Tonnes
2003	4,000
2004	20,000
2005	38,000
2006	50,000
2007	20,000

During the year 2007, there was a strike lasting for 3 months.
Pass the Journal entries in the books of the Colliery Coal

Answers :- Shortworking 2003-Rs.10,000, 2004-Rs.2,000.

6. A Colliery worked under a lease which provided for payment of Royalties at 50 paise per ton with a minimum rent of Rs.12,000 p.a. with the condition that each year excess of minimum rent over the actual royalties was recoverable during the subsequent 3 years. The lease, however, stipulated that if in any year the normal rent was not attained due to strike or accident, the minimum rent will be reduced proportionately having regard to the length of stoppage. The output was as follows :

Year	Output (Tons)
2001	Nil
2002	4,000
2003	20,000
2004	38,000
2005	50,000
2006	16,000
2007	60,000

During the year 2006, there was a strike lasting for 3 months. Give the royalties account, shortworkings account and landlords account in the books of Colliery.

Answers :- Shortworkings
2001-Rs.12,000
2002-Rs.10,000
2003-Rs. 2,000
2006-Rs. 1,000

7. The Bengal Coal Co. Ltd. leased a piece of land from Eastwala for 10 years on 1st Jan.2003 on the following terms :

1. Royalty to be paid at 50 paise per tonne of Coal
2. Minimum Rent at Rs.18,000 p.a.
3. Each year excess of minimum rent over actual royalties was to be recouped during the next three years.
4. If in any year the normal rent was not allowed due to strike or accident the minimum rent was to be reduced proportionately according to the length of stoppage.

Following was the output
2003- 6,000 tonnes
2004- 28,000 tones
2005- 36,000 tonnes
2006- 48,000 tones
2007- 30,000 tonnes

During the year 2007 there was a strike for 4 months

Pass the necessary Journal Entries in the books of Bengal Coal Co. Ltd. for five years.

Answers :- S.W. 2003- Rs.15000, 2004-Rs.4000

8. The Kanpur Colliery Co. Ltd leased a property of Hasan at a Royalty of Re.0.75 per ton with a minimum rent of Rs.20,000 p.a. Each years excess of minimum rent over royalties was recoupable out of the royalties for the next two years. In the event of strike the minimum rent not being reached, the lease provided that the actual royalties earned for the year discharged all rental obligations for the year.

Year	Tons of coal raised
First year	No coal raised
Second year	8,800
Third year	24,000
Fourth year	30,000
Fifth year 36,000	
Sixth year 48,000	
Seventh year	20,000
Eighth year	40,000

Write up minimum rent A/c, Royalties a/c and shortworkings account in the books of Kanpur Collilery Co. Ltd. and also prepare Kanpur Colliery Co.'s A/c, Royalties Receivable A/c, Shortworkings Allowable A/c in the books of the Landlord, Shri Hasan.

Answers :- S.W.- I year-Rs.20,000, II year-Rs.13,400, III year-Rs.1,400.

9. The B Colliery company Ltd. leased a property from A at a royalty of Rs.1.50 per tonne with a minimum rent of Rs.8000 p.a. Each year's excess of minimum rent over actual royalties is recoverable out of the royalties of next two years. In the event of strike and the minimum rent not being reached. The lease provided that shortworking would stand reduced proportionately to time actually worked.

The results of the workings were as follows.

Year	Actual Royalties
2002	2,600
2003	7,400
2004	9,000
2005	14,000
2006	4,800 (Strike for 3 months)
2007	12,000

Prepare Royalty A/c. Shortworking A/c and Landlord A/c in the books of B Colliery Co. Ltd.

Answers : S.W. 2002 Rs.5400, 2003 Rs. 600, 2006 Rs.1200.

10. On 1-1-2003 'A' obtained from 'B' a lease of coal mine. The lease provided that a royalty of Re 1 per tonne of Coal raised is payable subject to a minimum rent of Rs.5000 p.a. with a right to recoup shortworkings over the first 4 years of the lease.

From the following details show (a) Royalties Account (b) Shortworkings Account and 'B' Account in the books of A.

Year	Sales (tonnes)	Closing Stock (tonnes)
2003	3,300	450
2004	5,250	750
2005	6,900	600
2006	8,700	900
2007	10,500	1,200

Answers : S.W. 2003 Rs. 2150, 2004 Rs. 50.

❑❑❑

Chapter 7

Hire Purchase & Instalment System.
(Excluding H. P. Trading)

7.1   Basic Concepts.
7.1.1   Hire Purchase Agreement and its Content.
7.1.2   Rights of Hirer.
71.3   Termination of Hire Purchase Agreement
7.2   Accounting Records.
7.2.1   Journal Entries in the Books of Hire Purchaser.
7.2.2   Journal Entries in the Books of Hire Seller.
7.3   Calculation of Interest and Cash Price with various
        Illustrations.
7.4   Default & Repossession
7.5   Instalment System
7.6   Distinction between Hire Purchase System and
        Instalment System.
7.7   Accounting Entries in respect of Instalment System.
7.8   Illustrations
7.9   Questions :- Objective Type Questions and Problems.

9.1 Basic Concepts

Generally the goods can be sold to the purchaser either for cash or on credit. In case of cash sales, the purchaser pays the cash price which is also known as cash down price and gets the possession and ownership of the goods. There are many persons who intend to purchase the costly articles, but cannot purchase due to higher prices. They purchase costly articles on credit basis. In credit sales they are allowed to pay the price of goods in convenient instalments.

Hire purchase system is the midway between cash and credit sales. In this method a purchaser is not required to pay the price in lump sum but in different convenient instalments. Therefore this system is beneficial to purchaser and seller. The purchaser can easily purchase the costly items like computer, T.V., washing machine, refrigerator, motor cycle even though his financial position is weak and a seller can increase sales as the goods are sold on credit basis.

In India the hire purchase transactions are governed by Hire Purchase Act 1972. This act came into force with effect from 1st September 1973. The Act applies to whole of the India except the state of Jammu and Kashmir. According to the agreement of this act, the important features of this Hire Purchase are as under-

Features of Hire Purchases -

1) Hire Purchase transactions originates from an agreement.

2) The agreement is made between Hire Purchaser and Hire Seller.

3) The agreement is made for supply of goods.

4) Possession of goods is transferred to purchaser on signing the contract or agreement.

5) The ownership in the goods is not passed on to the purchaser till the last instalment is paid by him.

6) The purchaser pays the price of goods in agreed instalments. The instalment may be weekly, monthly, quarterly, half yearly or yearly as per term of agreement.

7) Each instalment is treated as a hire charge.

8) If the purchaser fails to pay any instalment or instalments, the hire seller has a right of repossession of goods.

9) The hire purchaser must keep the goods in good condition.

10) The hire purchaser cannot pledge or sell the asset till the last instalment is paid.

11) The seller charges interest at a certain rate on the outstanding balance of cash price. The excess of total payment over cash price is taken as interest.

In short, under hire purchase system, the purchaser gets the possession of the goods immediately and agrees to pay the total hire purchase price in instalments. The purchaser can use the goods after the payment of last instalment. In case the purchaser makes any default in payment of any instalments, the seller will have right to repossess the goods and forfeit the amount received from purchaser treating as hire charge.

Terms used in Hire Purchase Agreement -

1) Hirer : A person who gets the possession of goods from the owner under the Hire purchase agreement. He is the buyer of goods on Hire purchase basis.

2) Hire : It is the sum payable periodically by the hirer under the agreement. It is a rent paid by the buyer to the hire-vendor.

3) Cash Price : Cash Price means price at which the goods may be purchased today by the hirer for cash.

4) Down Payment : It is the initial payment made by buyer to the Hire seller at the time of signing the agreement. It is the amount paid to seller at the time of taking delivery of goods.

5) Hire-Purchase Price : It is the total amount payable by the purchaser as per blive purchase agreement to complete the transaction. It is equal to cash price plus interest. Hire purchase price may be shown in the form of equation as under.

Hire purchase price = cash price or cash portion + Interest
on outstanding balances.

6) Hire Purchase Charges : Hire purchase charges means the difference between Hire purchase price and cash price. Hire purchase charges are popularly known as interest. In other words Hire purchase charges means Hire purchase price minus cash price=interest.

7) Instalment : It is the amount inclusive of principal and interest paid at the end of certain period. It is divided as per function of agreement.

8) Hire Purchaser : A person who takes the possession of goods after signing the contract, is called Hire purchaser. He is the purchaser of goods.

9) Hire Seller : Hire seller means a person who delivers or has delivered the possession of goods to the hire purchaser under the hire purchase agreement.

Depreciation of Asset

Under Hire purchase system, the ownership of asset is not transferred to purchaser till he pays the last instalment. Hence there is a dispute about charging of depreciation on asset. Under this system the purchaser gets the possession of asset after signing the agreement and he can use the asset. Therefore, from the practical point of view, depreciation should be charged at certain rate on cash price of the asset acquired. Moreover, the purchaser is going to be the owner of asset after the payment of last instalment. Hence it will be prudent policy to charge depreciation on asset acquired under Hire purchase system.

If the depreciation is not charged by the hire purchaser till he becomes the owner of asset, he will have to charge depreciation for all previous years, in one year only, in which the purchaser pays last instalment. This will inflate the profits of previous years, where as the profit of that year in which depreciation is charged is adversely affected. Hence depreciation must be charged every year. Depreciation is always charged on **cash price** of the asset. It should not be charged on Hire purchase price.

7.1.1 Hire Purchase Agreement and its Contents

Hire Purchase Agreement :- According section 2(c), Hire purchase agreement means an agreement under which the hirer has an option to purchase them in accordance with the terms of agreement and includes the agreement under which : (a) Possession of goods is delivered by the owner thereof to a person on condition that such person pays the agreed amount in periodical instalments.

(b) the property in goods is to pass to such a person on the payment of the last instalment. and,

(c) Such a person has right to terminate the agreement at any time before the property so passes.

Contents of Hire Purchase Agreement (section 3 & 4) :

Every Hire Purchase Agreement has to be in writing and should be signed by all parties thereof. It should state the following:

(i) The Hire Purchase Price of the goods to which the agreement relates.

(ii) Cash Price of Such goods.

(iii) The date on which the agreement shall be deemed to have commenced.

(iv) The number of instalments in which the hire purchase price is to be paid and the amount of each of those instalments and the date or mode of determining the date upon which it is payable and the person to whom and place where it is payable.

(v) The goods to which the agreement relates in a manner sufficient to identify them.

7 :1 : 2 Rights of the Hirer : -

The following rights are given in the Act in addition to usual right i.e. returning the goods to the vendor.

(i) The seller is required to give a notice in writing to terminate the hire purchase agreement if there is a default in payment of hire or breach of expressed conditions.

(ii) The right to repossess the goods will not exist unless sanction by the court in certain cases.

(iii) The hirer has right of receiving statement from vendor.

(iv) If the hirer has paid excess amount them hire purchase price, the excess payment should be returned back by the vendor.

7:1:3 Termination of Hire Purchase Agreement : -

The Hire purchase may at any time terminate the hire purchase agreement after giving the owner at least 14 days notice in writing. He has to redeliver the goods to the owner any pay any instalment of hire which might have become due before the termination. In order to protect the hire purchaser from require to pay unreasonable amount, which may be named by the higher vendor in the hire purchase agreement in case of termination of the hire purchase agreement, the following provisions have been made in Hire purchase Act.

(a) Where the sum total of the amounts paid and the amount due in respect of the hire purchase price immediately before the termination exceed one-half of the Hire purchase price, the hirer shall not be Liable to pay the sum so named.

(b) Where the sum total of the amounts paid and the amounts due in respect of the hire purchase price immediately before termination does not exceed one half of the hire purchase price, the hirer shall be Liable to pay the difference between the said sum total and said one-half or the sum named in the agreement whichever is less.

7:2 Accounting Records

There are two parties in the hire purchase agreement i.e. buyer and seller. The according entries for recording of hire purchase transactions in the books of both parties are being explained as below.

7:2:1 Entries in the books of Hire Purchaser

There are two methods for making accounting entries of the hire purchase transactions in the books of hire purchaser transactions in the books of hire purchaser. These are under.

(a) When the asset is recorded at the cash price actually paid.

(b) When the asset is recorded at full cash price.

(c) When the asset is recorded at the cash price actually paid (Treading the goods not becoming the property of the hirer at the time of signing contract)

Under this method hire purchaser does not become the owner of goods till he makes payment of final instalment. Hence no entry is passed when agreement for hire purchases is signed Entries are passed at the time of payment of each instalment. under this method following journal entries are passed in the books of Hire purchaser.

1) When the asset is purchased on hire purchase system.

No Entry

2) On signing of an agreement and payment of cash (cash down payment)

(1) On signing the agreement

Asset A/c ----　　　　　Dr

　　To Vendor's A/c

(Being amount payable to seller

on signing the agreement)

(2) For payment of Cash on the day of signing of agreement.

Vendor's A/c ---- Dr

　　To Bank / Cash A/c

(For Payment of Cash to Seller)

Instead of above two entries, following entry can be passed.

Asset A/c --- Dr (with cash down payment)

　　To Bank A/c

Note : - The first instalment is generally paid at the time of signing the agreement hence if donot include any interest. The whole amount of that instalment is for the part payment of the value of the asset.

3) When the Subsequent instalments become due.

Asset A/c ---- Dr (Payment towards cash price)

Interest A/c ---- Dr (For Interest)

To Hire Vendor's A/c (Amount of Instalment)

(Being instalment payable including interest to Vendor)

4) On Making Payment of Instalments

Hire Vendor A/c ---- Dr

To Cash/ Bank A/c

(Being the amounts of Instalment Paid)

At the end of year.

5) When Depreciation is charged

Depreciation A/c ---- Dr

To Asset A/c

(Being depreciation charged on Asset)

(**Note :** Depreciation is always charged on total cash price of asset)

6) When the interest and Depreciation accounts are closed by transfer to Profit & Loss Account.

Profit & Loss A/c ---- Dr

To Depreciation A/c

To Interest A/c

(Being the balances of Interest and Depreciation are transferred to P & L A/c)

Notes

(1) Entries No 3 & 4 are to be repeated every year till the last year.

(2) Asset will be shown in the Balance sheet at purchase cost minus the depreciation.

(b) When the asset is recorded at full cash price (Trating the goods as out right property of purchaser)

Some accountants are of the opinion that the goods purchased on hire purchase system should be treated as the outright property of the business on the assumption that the asset has been purchased with the intention of paying all instalments on the due date to acquire the asset for the business. Under this method following entries are to be passed in the books of Hire purchaser.

(1) **For Purchase of Asset**

  Asset A/c ---- Dr   With full cash

   To Hire Vendor's A/c } price of Asset

  (Being asset purchased)

(2) **For Making cash down payment.**

  Vendor's A/c ---- Dr   With actual

   To Cash / Bank A/c } down payment

  (For making cash down payment)

(3) **For Interest due at the end of year**

  Interest A/c ---- Dr

   To Hire vendor's A/c

  (Being Interest Payable)

(4) **For Payment of Instalment**

  Hire Vendors A/c ---- Dr

   To Cash/ Bank A/c

  (Being instalment Paid)

(5) **For Depreciation Charged**

  Depreciation A/c ---- Dr

   To Asset A./c

  (Being depreciation Charged)

(6) **For Transfer of Interest and Depreciation to Profit and Loss Account.**

  Profit and Loss A/c ---- Dr

   To Depreciation A/c

   To Interest A/c

(Being the balances of depreciation and interest are transferred to P. & L. A/c)

Note : (1) Entries No.3 to 6 will be repeated in subsequent years.

2) Asset in this case will be shown in the Balance sheet after deducting depreciation and balance due to Vendor from the asset's beginning balance.

(3) Generally first method is preferred to the second method it is most logical.

7:2:2 Entries in the books of Hire Vendor (Seller)

The hire vendor taken the sale of goods on hire purchase as ordinary sale. He therefore debits the account of hire purchases and credits the sales account with the full cash price as soon as the agreement is signed. Following journal entries are to be passed in the books of hire vendor.

1) When the goods are sold on hire purchase.

Hire Purchase Account ---- Dr } with full
To Sales A/c } cash price
(Being good sold on hire purchase)

2) Cash down payment received on signing the contract

Cash / Bank A/c ---- Dr
To Hire purchaser A/c
(Being down payment received)

3) For Interest Due on instalment at the end of year.

Hire purchaser A/c ---- Dr
To Interest A/c
(Being interest due on outstanding
balance with hire purchaser.)

4) For Receipt of the amount of Instalment

Cash A/c ---- Dr
To Hire Purchaser
(Being the amount of Instalment received)

5) For transferring the balance of interest to profit and loss Account.

Interest A/c ---- Dr
To Profit & Loss A/c
(Being the balance of interest transferred to P & L A/c)

Note : Entries no 3 & 4 will be repeated in subsequent years.

7 :3 Calculation of Interest and Cash Price

Different techniques can be used for the calculation of Interest depending upon the information given in the problem. on the basis of type of information given the problems can be classified as follows.

(a) When cash price, Hire purchase price and Rate of Interest are given.

When Cash price, Hire purchase price, Rate of Interest and number of Instalments etc are given in the problem. The calculation of Interest is very simple. The interest is to be calculated on the outstanding balance of the cash price at the stipulated rate. The interest on final instalment is not calculated. It is the difference between final instalment and cash price outstanding. This will be clear with the following illustrations.

Illustration 1

M/s Ahmednagar Roadways purchased on 1st Jan 2004 a TATA Truck on Hire purchase system from TATA Motors Ltd. The cash price of which was Rs.1,12,000 According to Hire purchase agreement. They paid Rs.30000 on signing the agreement and agreed to pay Rs.30000 each in three equal annual instalments. According to Hire Purchase Agreement interest was charged annually at 5% per annum.

M/s Ahmednagar Roadways follow the written down value method of depreciation for providing the depreciation into their books of account. Their practice is to provide the depreciation on truck at 20% p.a.

Draft Journal entries in the books of both the parties and also prepare necessary ledger accounts.

Solution : Asset is recorded at the cash price

Information given in the problem.

1) Hire Purchase Price	Rs.1,20,000
2) Cash Price	Rs.1,12,000
3) Total Interest	Rs. 8,000
4) Cash Down Payment	Rs. 30,000

5) Rate of Interest at 5% per year.

6) Rate of Depreciation at 20% per annum.

Calculation of Interest & Cash Portion

Particulars	Cash Price Rs.	Due date of Inst.	Instalment Rs.	Instalment Rs.	Cash Price Portion Rs
On 1-1-2004	1,12,000	1-1-2004	30,000	-	30,000
Paid on 1-1-04	30,000				
Outstanding bal on 1-1-2004	82,000				
Paid on 31-12-2004	25,900	31-12-04	30,000	4100	25,900
Outstanding bal on 1-1-05	56,100			$\left(\dfrac{82000 \times 5}{100}\right)$	
Paid on 31-12-2005	27,195		30,000	2805	27195
Outstanding bal on 1-1-2006	28905	31-12-06	30,000	$\left(\dfrac{56000 \times 5}{100}\right)$ 1095	
Paid on 31-12-2006	28905			(3000-28905)	28905
Total	-		1,20,000	8,000	1,12,000

Calculation of Depreciation

Total Cash Price	1,12,000
- Dep. at 20% =	22,400
on 31-12-2004	89600
Balance on 1-1-2005	
- Dep.at 20%	
on 31-12-2005	17,920
Balance on 1-1-2006	71,680
Dep. on 31-12-2006	14,336
Balance on 1-1-2007	57,344

Journal Entries
In the books of Ahmednagar Roadways

Date	Particulars	Debit (Rs.)	Credit (Rs.)
1-1-04	Motor Truck A/c ---- Dr To Tata Motors Ltd. A/c (Being amount payable to Tata Motors Ltd. at the time of singing agreement)	30,000	30,000
1-1-04	Tata Motors Ltd. A/c ---- Dr To Cash/Bank A/c (Being cash down payment to Vendor)	30,000	30,000
31-12-04	Motor Truck A/c ---- Dr Interest A/c ---- Dr To Tata Motors Ltd. A/c (Being Instalment including interest payable to vendor)	25,900 4,100	30,000
31-12-04	Tata Motors Ltd. A/c ---- Dr To Cash/Bank A/c (Being annual instalment paid to seller)	30,000	30,000
31-12-04	Depreciation A/c ---- Dr To Motor Truck A/c (Being depreciation on charged at 20% on original price of Truck)	22,400	22,400
31-12-04	Profit & Loss A/c ---- Dr To Depreciation A/c To Interest A/c (Being Interest and Depreciation transferred to Profit & Loss A/c)	26,500	26,500
31-12-04	Motor Truck A/c ---- Dr Interest A/c ---- Dr To Tata Motors Ltd. A/c (Being instalment including interest payable to seller)	27,195 2,805	30,000

Date	Particulars	Debit (Rs.)	Credit (Rs.)
31-12-05	Tata Motors Ltd A/c ---- Dr To Bank / Cash A/c (Being annual instalment paid to seller)	30,000	30,000
31-12-05	Depreciation A/c ---- Dr To Motor Truck A/c (Being depreciation charged at 20% on Truck)	17,920	17,920
31-12-05	Profit & Loss A/c ----- Dr To Depreciation A/c To Interest A/c (Being depreciation & interest transferred to P & L A/c)	20,725	20,725
31-12-05	Motor Truck A/c ----- Dr Interest A/c ---- Dr To Tata Motors Ltd. A/c (Being instalment including interest payable to Vendor)	28,905 1,095	30,000
31-12-05	Tata Motor's Ltd. A/c ---- Dr To Cash / Bank A/c (Being annual instalment paid)	30,000	30,000
31-12-05	Depreciation A/c ---- Dr To Motor Truck A/c (Being depreciation charged at 20% on Motor Truck)	14,336	14,336
31-12-05	Profit & Loss A/c ---- Dr To Depreciation A/c To Interest A/c (Being depreciation and interest transferred to P & L A/c)	15,431	15,431

Ledger
Tata Truck A/c

Dr   **Cr**

Date	Particulars	Rs.	Date	Particulars	Rs.
1-1-04	To Tata Motor's Ltd A/c	30,000	1-1-04	By Dep. A/c	22,400
				By Balance c/d	33,500
31-12-04	To Tata Motor's Ltd A/c	25,900	31-12-04		
		55,900			55,900
1-1-05	To Balance b/d	33,500	1-1-05	By Dep. A/c	17920
31-12-05	To Tata Motor's Ltd. A/c	27,195	31-12-05	By Balance c/d	42775
		60,695			60,695
1-1-06	To Balance b/d	42,775	1-1-06	By Dep. A/c	14336
31-12-06	To Tata Motor's Ltd. A/c	28,905	31-12-06	By Balance c/d	57,344
		71,680			71,680
1-1-07	To Balance b/d	57,344			

Tata Motor's A/c

Dr   **Cr**

Date	Particulars	Rs.	Date	Particulars	Rs.
1-1-04	To Cash A/c	30,000	1-1-04	By Tata Track A/c	30,000
31-12-04	To Cash A/c	30,000	31-12-04	By Tata Truck A/c	25,900
		60,000			60,000
31-12-05	To Cash A/c	30,000	31-12-05	By Tata Truck A/c	27,135
				By Interest A/c	2805
		30,000			30,000
31-12-05	To Cash A/c	30,000	31-12-06	By Tata Truck A/c	28,905
			31-12-06	By Interest A/c	1095
		30,000			30,000

Depreciation A/c

Dr					Cr
Date	Particulars	Rs.	Date	Particulars	Rs.
31-12-04	To Tata Truck A/c	22,400	31-12-04	By P & L A/c	22,400
31-12-04	To Tata Truck A/c	17920	31-12-04	By P & L A/c	17920
31-12-05	To Tata Truck A/c	14336	31-12-05	By P & L A/c	14336

Interest A/c

Dr					Cr
Date	Particulars	Rs.	Date	Particulars	Rs.
31-12-04	To Tata Motors Ltd A/c	4100	31-12-04	By P & L A/c	4,100
31-12-04	To Tata Motors Ltd A/c	2805	31-12-04	By P & L A/c	2805
31-12-05	To Tata Motors Ltd A/c	1095	31-12-05	By P & L A/c	1095

Journal Entries in the Books
of Tata Motors Ltd (Hire Vendor)

Date	Particulars	Debit (Rs.)	Credit (Rs.)
1-1-04	Ahmednagar Roadway's A/c---- Dr	1,12,000	
	To Sales A/c		1,12,000
	(Being truck sold to Ahmednagar Roadways on hire purchase system)		
1-1-04	Bank / Cash A/c ---- Dr	30,000	
	To Ahmednagar Roadways A/c		30,000
	(Being cash received from Ahmednagar Roadways on signing the contract)		

Date	Particulars	Debit (Rs.)	Credit (Rs.)
31-12-04	Ahmednagar Roadway's A/c---- Dr To Interest A/c (Being interest due from Ahmednagar Roadways)	4,100	4,100
31-12-04	Bank / Cash A/c ---- Dr To Ahmednagar Roadways A/c (Being annual instalment Received)	30,000	30,000
31-12-04	Interest A/c ---- Dr To Profit & Loss A/c (Being interest transferred to Profit & Loss A/c)	4,100	4,100
31-12-05	Ahmednagar Roadway's A/c Dr To Interest A/c (Being interest due from Ahmednagar Roadways)	2,805	2,805
31-12-05	Cash/Bank A/c ---- Dr To Ahmednagar Roadway's A/c (Being annual instalment received)	30,000	30,000
31-12-05	Interest A/c ---- Dr To P & L A/c (Being a interest transferred to profit & Loss A/c)	2,805	2,805
31-12-06	Ahmednagar Roadway's A/c ---- Dr To Interest A/c (Being interest due from Ahmednagar Roadways)	1,095	1,095
31-12-06	Bank/Cash A/c ---- Dr To Ahmednagar Roadway's A/c (Being annual instalments received)	30,000	30,000
31-12-2006	Interest A/c ---- Dr To P & L A/c (Being interest Transferred to P & L A/c)	1,095	1,095

Illustration : 2 (Where cash price and Rate of Interest is given)

On 1st January 2001, the India Ltd. Purchased the machine from H.M.T.Ltd. on Hire purchase system. The cash price of the machine was Rs.25000. India Ltd paid Rs.10,000 on signing of the agreement and agreed to pay balance in 5 instalments of Rs.15000 each payable annually on 31st December. The H.M.T. Ltd Charged 5% interest p.a. on yearly balances.

India Ltd decided to provide depreciation at 10% p.a. on Reducing Balance Method. Open necessary ledger A/cs in the books of both parties.

Solution (Asset is recorded at full cash price)

Information given in problem.

	Rs.
1) Cash Price	75,000
2) Cash Down Payment	10,000
3) Hire Purchase Price	85,000 (Rs.75000+10000)
4) Total Interest	10,000 (Rs.85000+75000)

5) Rate of Interest 5% Per annum

6) Rate of Depreciation 10% per annum. (Reducing Balance System)

Illustration : 3

(Cash Price, H.P.Price, Rate of Interest etc are given)

A Ltd purchased Auto Rickshaw from Bajaj Ltd. on 1st Jan

Calculation of Interest & Depreciation

Particulars	Cash Price	Due Date	Instalment Rs	Interest Rs.	Cash portion Rs.	Depreciation Rs.
On 1-1-01	75,000	1-1-2001	10000	-	10,000	75000
paid on 1-1-01	10000					
on 1-1-01	65000					
Paid on 31-12-02	11750	31-12-2001	15000	3250 (65000x5)/100	11750	-7500
on 1-1-02	53250					67500
paid on 31-12-02	-12337	31-12-2002	15000	2663 (53250 x 5)/100	12337	-6750
on 1-1-03	40913					60750
paid on 31-12-03	12954	31-12-2003	15000	2046 (40913 x 5)/100	12954	6075
on 1-1-04	27959					54675
paid on 31-12-04	13602	31-12-2004	15000	1398 (27959 x 5)/100	13602	-5468
on 1-1-05	14357					49207
paid on 31-12-05	14357	13-12-2005	15000	643 (15000-14357)	14357	4921
Total Balance	-		85000	10,000	75,000	44286

Ledger
Ahmednagar Roadway's A/c

Dr   **Cr**

Date	Particulars	Rs.	Date	Particulars	Rs.
1-1-04	To Sales A/c	1,12,000	1-1-04	By Cash A/c	30,000
31-12-04	To Interest A/c	4100	31-12-04	By Cash A/c	30,000
			31-12-04	By Balance c/d	56,100
		1,16,100			1,16,100
1-1-05	To Balance b/d	56,100	31-12-05	By Cash A/c	30,000
31-12-05	To Interest A/c	2805	31-12-05	By Balance c/d	28,905
		58,905			58,905
1-1-06	To Balance b/d	28905	31-12-05	By Cash A/c	30,000
31-12-06	To Interest A/c	1,095			
		30,000			30,000

Interest A/c

Dr   **Cr**

Date	Particulars	Rs.	Date	Particulars	Rs.
31-12-04	To P & L A/c	4100	31-12-04	By Ahmednagar Roadways A/c	4100
31-12-05	To P & L A/c	2805	31-12-05	By Ahmednagar Roadways A/c	2805
31-12-06	To P & L A/c	1095	31-12-06	By Ahmednagar Roadways A/c	1095

In the books of India Ltd. (Hire Purchaser)
Machine A/c

Dr   **Cr**

Date	Particulars	Rs.	Date	Particulars	Rs.
31-12-04	India Ltd A/c	75,000	31-12-01	By Depreciation A/c	7500
			31-12-05	By Balance c/d	67500
		75,000			75,000

Date	Particulars	Rs.	Date	Particulars	Rs.
1-1-02	To Bal b/d	67500	31-12-02	By Depreciation A/c	6750
			31-12-02	By Balance c/d	60750
		67500			67500
1-1-2003	To Bal. b/d	60750	31-12-03	By Dep. A/c	6075
			31-12-03	By Bal. c/d	54675
		60750			60750
1-1-2004	To Bal. b/d	54675	31-12-04	By Dep. A/c	5468
			31-12-04	By Bal c/d	49207
		54675			54675
1-1-2005	To Bal. b/d	49207	31-12-05	By Dep. A/c	4921
			31-12-05	By Bal. c/d	44286
		49207			49207
1-1-2006	To Bal b/d	44286			

H.M.T. Ltd A/c

Dr   **Cr**

Date	Particulars	Rs.	Date	Particulars	Rs.
1-1-2001	To Bank A/c	10,000	1-1-2001	By Machine A/c	75,000
31-12-01	To Bank A/c	15,000	31-12-2001	By Interest A/c	3,250
31-12-01	To Bal. c/d	53,250			78250
		78,250			
31-12-02	To Bank A/c	15,000	1-1-2002	By Bal. b/d	53,250
31-12-01	To Bal.c/d	40,913	31-12-02	By Interest A/c	2663
		55,913			55913
31-12-03	To Bank A/c	15,000	1-1-2003	By Bal. b/d	40,913
31-12-03	To Bal. c/d	27959	31-12-2003	By Interest A/c	2046
		42,959			42959
31-12-04	To Bank A/c	15,000	1-1-2004	By Bal b/d	27959
31-12-04	To Bal c/d	14,357	31-12-2004	By Interest A/c	1398
		29,357			29357
31-12-05	To Bank A/c	15,000	1-1-2005	By Bal. b/d	14357
			31-12-2005	By Interest A/c	643
		15,000			15000

Depreciation A/c

Dr   **Cr**

Date	Particulars	Rs.	Date	Particulars	Rs.
31-12-01	To Machine A/c	7,500	31-12-01	By P & L A/c	7,500
31-12-02	To Machine A/c	6750	31-12-02	By P & L A/c	6750
31-12-03	To Machine A/c	6075	31-12-03	By P & L A/c	6075
31-12-04	To Machine A/c	5468	31-12-04	By P & L A/c	5468
31-12-05	To Machine A/c	4921	31-12-05	By P & L A/c	4921

Interest A/c

Dr   **Cr**

Date	Particulars	Rs.	Date	Particulars	Rs.
31-12-01	To H.M.T. Ltd. A/c	3250	31-12-01	By P & L A/c	3250
31-12-02	To H.M.T. Ltd. A/c	2663	31-12-02	By P & L A/c	2663
31-12-03	To H.M.T. Ltd. A/c	2046	31-12-03	By P & L A/c	2046
31-12-04	To H.M.T. Ltd. A/c	1398	31-12-04	By P & L A/c	1398
31-12-05	To H.M.T. Ltd. A/c	643	31-12-05	By P & L A/c	643

2004 on hire purchase price. The cash price of the rickshaw is Rs.29800. The terms of payment were Rs.8000 half yearly instalment over two years. The first instalment is to be paid on 30th june 2004. The rate of interest payable is 6% p.a. A Ltd closed its books on 30th June every year and decided to written of depreciation on Rickshaw at the rate of 10% on streight Line Method.

Prepare necessary ledger A/c in the books of a Ltd.

Solution :

Information given in problem.

1) Cash Price Rs.29800
2) Total Interest Rs.2200
3) Hire Purchase Price Rs.32000
4) Cash Down Price Rs.8000
5) Rate of Interest at 6% p.a.
6) Rate of Depreciation at 10% p.a.
7) Instalment is payable on 30th June and 31st Dec. every year.
8) Year ends on 30th June every year.

In the Books of H.M.T. Ltd. (Hire Sellers)
India Ltd. A/c

Dr.   Cr

Date	Particulars	Rs.	Date	Particulars	Rs.
1-1-2001	To Sales A/c	75,000	1-1-2001	By Bank A/c	10,000
31-12-01	To Interest A/c	3,250	31-12-01	By Bank A/c	15,000
			31-12-01	By Bal. c/d	53,250
		78,250			78,250
1-1-2002	To Bal. b/d	53,250	31-12-02	By Bank A/c	15,000
31-12-02	To Interest A/c	2,663	31-12-02	By Bal c/d	40913
		55,913			55913
1-1-2003	To Bal b/d	40,913	31-12-03	By Bank A/c	15,000
31-12-03	To Interest A/c	2,046	31-12-03	By Bal. c/d	27959
		42,959			42959
1-1-2004	To Bal b/d	27,959	31-12-03	By Bank A/c	15000
31-12-04	To Interest A/c	1,398	31-12-03	By Bal. c/d	14357
		29,357			29357
1-1-2005	To Bal b/d	14,357	31-12-03	By Bank A/c	15,000
31-12-05	To Interest A/c	6,43			
		15,000			15,000

Interest A/c

Dr.   Cr

Date	Particulars	Rs.	Date	Particulars	Rs.
31-12-01	To P. & L. A/c	3250	31-12-01	By India Ltd. A/c	3250
31-12-02	To P. & L. A/c	2663	31-12-02	By India Ltd. A/c	2663
31-12-03	To P. & L. A/c	2046	31-12-03	By India Ltd. A/c	2046
31-12-04	To P. & L. A/c	1398	31-12-04	By India Ltd. A/c	1398
31-12-05	To P. & L. A/c	643	31-12-05	By India Ltd. A/c	643

Calculation of Interest & Depreciation

Particulars	Cash Price Rs	Due Date	Instalment Rs	Interest Rs.	Cash portion Rs.	Depreciations Rs.
Balance on 1-1-04	29800	-	-	-		29800
Paid on 30-6-04	7106	30-6-2004	8000	894 $\left(\dfrac{29800 \times 6}{100} \times \dfrac{1}{2}\right)$	7106	1490 (For 6 months)
Balance on 1-7-04	22694	-	-		-	28310
Paid on 31-12-04	7319	31-12-2004	8000	681 $\left(\dfrac{22694 \times 6}{100} \times \dfrac{1}{2}\right)$	7319	
Balance on 1-1-2005	15375	-	-	461	-	-
Paid on 30-6-2005	7539	30-6-2005	8000	$\left(\dfrac{15375 \times 6}{100} \times \dfrac{1}{2}\right)$	7539	2980
Balance on 1-7-05	7836	-	-	161	-	25330
Paid on 31-12-05	7836	31-12-2005	8000	8000 -2836	2836	
Total	-		32000	2200	29800	
Depreciation on 30-6-2006						2980
Balance						22350

In the Books of A Ltd
Auto Rickshaw's A/c

Date	Particulars	Rs.	Date	Particulars	Rs.
31-12-01	To Bajaj Ltd. A/c	7106	31-12-01	By Depreciation A/c	1490
					5616
		7106	31-12-02	By Balance c/d	7106
	To Bal b/d	5616	31-12-03	By Depreciation	
	To Bajaj Ltd. A/c	7319		A/c	2980
	To Bajaj Ltd. A/c	7539	31-12-04	By Balance c/d	17494
			31-12-05		
		20474			20474
	To Bal b/d	17494		By Depreciation	
	To Bajaj Ltd A/c	7836		A/c	2980
				By Balance c/d	22350
		25330			25330

Depreciation A/c

Date	Particulars	Rs.	Date	Particulars	Rs.
30-6-04	To Rickshaw A/c	1490	31-12-01	By P & L A/c	1490
30-6-05	To Rickshaw A/c	2980	31-12-02	By P & L A/c	2980
30-6-06	To Rickshaw A/c	2980	31-12-03	By P & L A/c	2980

Bajaj Ltd A/c

Dr.   **Cr**

Date	Particulars	Rs.	Date	Particulars	Rs.
30-6-04	To Cash A/c	8000	31-06-04	By Auto Rickshaw's A/c	7106
			31-06-04	By Interest A/c	894
		8000			8000
30-12-06	To Cash A/c	8000	31-12-04	By Auto	
	To Cash A/c	8000		Rickshaw's A/c	7319

Date	Particulars	Rs.	Date	Particulars	Rs.
30-6-05	To Cash A/c	8000	31-12-04	By Interest A/c	681
			30-6-05	By Auto Rickshaw's A/c	7539
			30-6-05	By Interest A/c	461
		16000			16000
31-12-05	To Cash A/c	8000	31-12-05	By Auto Rickshaw's A/c	7836
			31-12-04	By Interest A/c	164
		8000			8000

Interest A/c

Dr.   **Cr**

Date	Particulars	Rs.	Date	Particulars	Rs.
30-06-04	To Bajaj Ltd A/c	894	30-06-04	By P & L A/c	894
31-12-04	To Bajaj Ltd A/c	681	31-06-04	By P & L A/c	1142
30-06-05	To Bajaj Ltd A/c	461			
		1142			1142
31-12-05	To Bajaj Ltd A/c	164	30-06-06	By P & L A/c	164

Notes : -

1) The First instalment is paid six month after the delivery of goods, hence it includes interest for 6 months.

2) As the instalments are half yearly interest at each stage is calculated for 6 months.

3) As the financial year close on 30th June, Depreciation is charged for 6 months for first 6 months.

from 1-1-2004 to 30-6-2004 for first year. Thereafter depreciation is charged for full year.

II When Cash Price is not given but Hire purchase Instalments and Rate of Interest are given.

Interest is generally calculated on the outstanding balances of cash portion. But in some problem, cash price is not given. In such cases interest in instalment can be calculated as below.

Step I :

The Rate of Interest in added to 100 suppose the rate of interest is 10%. Then 100+10 = 110. This means that if the instalment is 110, it included the interest of Rs.10.

Step II :

Interest in the instalment is calculated first, on the above ------- and the cash price in the last instalment is traced out. Suppose the last instalment is Rs.1100 and Rate of Interest is 10%. Then cash price is calculated as under.

Instalment	Instalment	Rate of Interest	
110	1100	10	$= \dfrac{100 \times 1100}{110} = 100$

Hence Cash Price = $\dfrac{\text{Instalment} - \text{Interest} = \text{Cash Price}}{1100 \quad - \quad 100 \ = \ 1000}$

Step III :

The cash price is to be added to proecding instalment and interest in that instalment is calculated by applying above procedure.

Step IV :

The above procedure is to be continued till the first instalment in which interest is included. Interest in not included in the payment which is made at the time of signing the agreement.

Illustration 4 :

'X' Purchased a Motor cycle on Hire purchase system from Hero Honda Ltd on 1st Jan. 2002 on paying Rs.12000 down. The remaining amount was to be paid at the end of each year as under.

Date	Amt (Rs.)
31-12-2002	25600
31-12-2003	19600
31-12-2004	14000
31-12-2005	8800

The Rate of Interest is at 10% p.a. Depreciation was charged at 10% under fixed instalment system.

Open necessary account in the books of both and show the calculations of interest and cash price.

Solution : -

Information given in the problem.

Hire purchase price	Rs.80000
Rate of Interest	10% p.a.
Rate of Depreciation	10% p.a.(Fixed instalment system)

Inter Books of 'X'
Motor Cycle A/c

Dr.   **Cr**

Date	Particulars	Rs.	Date	Particulars	Rs.
1-1-02	To Hero Honda Ltd. A/c	12,000	31-12-02	By Depreciation A/c	6800
31-12-02	To Hero Honda A/c	20,000		By Bal c/d	25,200
		32,000			32,000
1-1-03	To Bal b/d	25,200	31-12-03	By Depreciation A/c	6800
31-12-03	To Honda Ltd A/c	41200		By Bal. C/d	34,400
					41200
1-1-04	To Bal. b/d	34,400	31-12-04	By Depreciation A/c	6800
31-12-04	To Hero Honda Ltd A/c	12,000		By Bal c/d	39600
		46,400			46,400
1-1-05	To Bal. b/d	39600	31-12-05	By Depreciation	
31-12-05	To Hero Honda Ltd A/c	8000	31-12-05	A/c	6,800
				To Bal. c/d	40,800
		47,600			47,600
1-1-06	To Bal. b/d	40,800			

Hero Honda Ltd.A/c

Dr.   **Cr**

Date	Particulars	Rs.	Date	Particulars	Rs.
1-1-02	To Bank A/c	12,000	1-1-2002	By Motor Cycle A/c	12,000
31-12-02	To Bank A/c	25600	31-12-02	By Motor Cycle A/c	20,000
			31-12-02	By Interest A/c	5600
		37,600			37,600
31-12-03	To Bank A/c	19,600	31-12-03	By Motor Cycle A/c	16,000
			31-12-03	By Interest A/c	3600

Date	Particulars	Rs.	Date	Particulars	Rs.
		19600			19600
31-12-04	To Bank A/c	14000	31-12-04	By Motor Cycle A/c	12,000
			31-12-04	By Interest A/c	2000
		14000			14000
31-12-05	To Bank A/c	8800	31-12-05	By Motor Cycle A/c	8000
			31-12-05	By Interest A/c	800
		8800			8800

Depreciation A/c

Dr.   **Cr**

Date	Particulars	Rs.	Date	Particulars	Rs.
31-12-02	To Motor Cycle A/c	6800	31-12-02	By P & L A/c	6800
31-12-03	To Motor Cycle A/c	6800	31-12-03	By P & L A/c	6800
31-12-04	To Motor Cycle A/c	6800	31-12-04	By P & L A/c	6800
31-12-05	To Motor Cycle A/c	6800	31-12-05	By P & L A/c	6800

Interest A/c

Dr.   **Cr**

Date	Particulars	Rs.	Date	Particulars	Rs.
31-12-02	To Hero Honda Ltd A/c	5600	31-12-02	By P & L A/c	5600
31-12-03	To Hero Honda Ltd A/c	3600	31-12-03	By P & L A/c	3600
31-12-04	To Hero Honda Ltd A/c	2000	31-12-04	By P & L A/c	2000
31-12-05	To Hero Honda Ltd A/c	800	31-12-05	By P & L A/c	800

Dr.   **Cr**

Date	Particulars	Rs.	Date	Particulars	Rs.
1-1-02	To Sales A/c	68,000	1-1-02	By Bank A/c	12,000
31-12-02	To Interest A/c	5600	31-12-02	By Bank A/c	25,600
			31-12-02	By Bal c/d	36,000
		73,600			73,600
1-1-03	To Balance b/d	36,000	31-12-03	By Bank A/c	19,600
31-12-03	To Interest A/c	3600	31-12-03	By Balance c/d	20,000
		39,600			39,600
1-1-04	To Balance b/d	20,000	31-12-04	By Bank A/c	14,000
31-12-04	To Interest A/c	2000	31-12-02	By Balance c/d	8,000
		22,000			22,000
1-1-05	To Balance b/d	8000	31-12-05	By Bank A/c	8800
31-12-05	To Interest A/c	800			
		8800			8800

Interest A/c

Dr.   **Cr**

Date	Particulars	Rs.	Date	Particulars	Rs.
31-12-02	To P & L A/c	5600	31-12-02	By X Ltd A/c	5600
31-12-03	To P & L A/c	3600	31-12-03	By X Ltd A/c	3600
31-12-04	To P & L A/c	2000	31-12-04	By X Ltd A/c	2000
31-12-05	To P & L A/c	800	31-12-05	By X Ltd A/c	800

III Where plus Interest Instalment are given
Illustration 5

On 1st Jan 2004, A Purchased a computer from Microsoft Ltd on hire purchase system. The particulars are as follows.

(a) Cash Price Rs.20,000 (b) Amount to be paid on signing contract Rs.5000 (c) Balance to be paid in three (yearly) instalments of Rs.5000 each plus interests. (d) Interest charged on outstanding balance at 10% p.a. (e) Depreciation at 10% p.a. on written down value method. You are required to show necessary accounts in the books of 'A'

Solution : Information given in the problem.

1) Cash Price Rs.20000 2) Interest Rate at 10% p.a. 3) Rate of Depreciation at 10% p.a.

Calculation of Interest Cash Price and Depreciation

Particulars	Cash Price Rs	Due Date	Cash Price	Interest Rs.	Instalment	Depreciation 10% W.D.M.
on 1-1-04	20000	1-1-2004	5000	-	5000	29800
Paid on 1-1-2004	5000					1490
Balance on 1-1-04	15000					(For 6 months)
Paid on 31-12-04	5000	31-12-2004	5000	$1500\ \left(\dfrac{15000 \times 10}{100}\right)$	6500	28310
Balance on 1-1-2005	5000					
Paid on 31-12-05		31-12-2006	5000	$1000\ \left(\dfrac{10000 \times 6}{100}\right)$	6000	-
Balance on 1-1-06						2980
Paid on 31-12-06	5000	31-12-2006	5000	$500\ \left(\dfrac{5000 \times 10}{100}\right)$	5500	25330
		-				
Total	-		20,000	3000	23000	2980
Balance	-					22350

Note:-

Rs. 5000 is paid at the time of signing the contract, hence it does not include interest.

In the Books of 'A'

Dr.   Cr

Date	Particulars	Rs.	Date	Particulars	Rs.
1-1-2004	To Microsoft A/c	5000	31-12-04	By Depreciation A/c	2000
1-1-2005	To Microsoft A/c	5000	31-12-04	By Balance c/d	8,000
		10,000			10,000
1-1-2005	To Balance b/d	8000	31-12-05	By Depreciation A/c	1800
31-12-05	To Microsoft A/c	5000	31-12-05	By Balance c/d	11200
		13,000			13000
1-1-2006	To Balance b/d	11200	31-12-06	By Depreciation A/c	1620
31-12-06	To Microsoft A/c	5000	31-12-06	By Balance c/d	14580
		16200			16200
1-1-2007	To Balance b/d	14580			14580

Microsoft Ltd A/c

Dr.   Cr

Date	Particulars	Rs.	Date	Particulars	Rs.
1-1-2004	To Bank A/c	5000	1-1-2004	By Computer A/c	5000
31-12-04	To Bank A/c	6500	31-12-04	By Computer A/c	5000
			31-12-04	By Interest A/c	1500
		11500			11500
31-12-05	To Bank A/c	6000	31-12-05	By Computer A/c	5000
			31-12-05	By Interest A/c	1000
		6000			6000
31-12-06	To Bank A/c	5500	31-12-06	By Computer A/c	5000
			31-12-06	By Interest A/c	500
		5500			5500

Depreciation A/c

Dr.   **Cr**

Date	Particulars	Rs.	Date	Particulars	Rs.
31-12-04	To Computer A/c	2000	31-12-04	By P & L A/c	2000
31-12-05	To Computer A/c	1800	31-12-05	By P & L A/c	1800
31-12-06	To Computer A/c	1620	31-12-05	By P & L A/c	1620

Interest A/c

Dr.   **Cr**

Date	Particulars	Rs.	Date	Particulars	Rs.
31-12-04	To Microsoft Ltd A/c	1500	31-12-04	By P & L A/c	1500
31-12-05	To Microsoft Ltd A/c	1000	31-12-05	By P & L A/c	1000
31-12-06	To Microsoft Ltd A/c	500	31-12-05	By P & L A/c	500

(iv) Cash Price and Hire Purchase Price are given but Rate of Interest is not given.

In this case the information about rate of interest is not given in the problem, the interest included in each instalment will be calculated on the ------- of hire purchase price outstanding in the beginning of each year.

Illustration 6

Shri. Arvind purchased a Television set from sony world on 1-1-2006 under hire purchase system. The cash price of T.V. was Rs.8400. The instalment were to be paid as under.

Rs.1000 on delivered i.e. on 1-1-2006

Rs.4000 on 30-4-2006

Rs.3000 on 31-8-2006

Rs.2000 on 31-12-2006

Show T.V. Account and Interest A/c in the books of Arvind whose books are closed on 31-12-2006 every year. Depreciation is to be charged 20% p.a.

Solution :

Information given in the problem.

a) Hire purchase price Rs.10000

b) Cash Price Rs.8400

c) Total Interst (10000-8400) Rs.1600

d) Rate of depreciation 20% per year.

Step I : Hire purchse price = Down Payment + Instalment Rs.10,000 = Rs. 1000 + 9000

Step II : Total Interest = H.P. Price - Cash Price Rs.1600 = Rs.10000 - Rs.8400.

Step III : Calculation of Outstanding Balances.

Hire Purchase Price Rs.10000

Less paid on signing the	1000	
Contract (1-1-2006)	9000	Outstanding bal.1-1-06
Less Paid on 30-04-2006	4000	
	5000	Outstanding bal.1-5-06
Less Paid on 31-08-2006	3000	
	2000	Outstanding bal.1-9-09
Less Paid on 31-12-2006	2000	
	-	

Outstanding Balance at the beginning = 9000 : 5000 : 2000

Ratio of Outstanding Balance   9   :   5   :   2

The total interest Rs.1600 is, Therefore divided in the ratio of 9 : 5 : 2. Thereafter the interest and cash price will be as under.

Date	Instalment Rs.	Interest Rs.	Cash Price Rs.	Calculation of Interest
1-1-2006	1000	-	1000	
30-4-2006	4000	900	3100	16:1600:9 = 900
31-8-2006	3000	500	2500	16:1600:5 = 500
31-12-2006	2000	200	1800	16:1600:2 = 200
Total	10000	1600	8400	

Television A/c

Dr.					Cr.
Date	Particulars	Rs.	Date	Particulars	Rs.
1-1-06	To Sony World A/c	1000	31-12-06	By Depreciation A/c	1680
30-4-06	To Sony World A/c	3100	31-12-06	By Balance c/d	6720
30-8-06	To Sony World A/c	2500			
31-12-06	To Sony World A/c	1800			
		8400			8400

Interest A/c

Dr.					Cr.
Date	Particulars	Rs.	Date	Particulars	Rs.
31-4-06	To Sony World A/c	900	31-12-06	By Profit & Loss	1600
31-8-06	To Sony World A/c	500		A/c	
31-12-06	To Sony World A/c	200			
		1600			1600

Depreciation A/c

Dr.					Cr.
Date	Particulars	Rs.	Date	Particulars	Rs.
31-12-06	To Television A/c	1680	31-12-06	By Profit & Loss A/c	1680

Soni World A/c

Dr.					Cr.
Date	Particulars	Rs.	Date	Particulars	Rs.
1-1-06	To Bank A/c	1000	1-1-06	By T.V. A/c	1000
30-4-06	To Bank A/c	4000	30-4-06	By T.V. A/c	3100
			30-4-06	By Interest A/c	900
		5000			5000
31-6-06	To Bank A/c	3000	31-8-06	By T.V. A/c	2500
			30-4-06	By Interest A/c	500
					3000
31-12-06	To Bank A/c	2000	31-12-06	By T.V. A/c	1800
			31-4-06	By Interest A/c	200
		2000			2000

(v) When based on Annuity (When Hire Purchase Price and Rate of Interest are given in the problem)

In some problem the present value of annuity for certain number of years at certain rate of interest is given according to annuity of years at certain rate of interest is given according to annuity table. Total cash price is not given it is to be trace out. Once it is traced out, interest can be calculated according to first Method.

Illustration : 7

On 1st Jan.2002, Mr. P. Purchased a computer on Hire Purchase system over the period of 5 years payable by annual instalments of Rs.8000 at the end of each year. The vendor charges interest at the rate of 5% p.a. on yearly balances. Find out cash prices of computer and interest included in each instalment.

The present value of annuity of one rupee for 5 years at 5% is Rs.4.329477.

Solution : -

Information given in the problem.

1) Annual Instalment Rs.8000.

2) Total Hire Purchase Price 8000 x 5 = Rs.40,000

3) Rate of Interest at 5% p.a.

4) Annuity Table showing annuity value on under Rs.4.329477.

Calculation of Total Cash Price

$$\text{Total Cash Price} = \frac{\text{Present Value of an annuity of Rs.one} \times \text{Total Instalments (amount)}}{\text{Rate of Interest} \times 1}$$

$$= \frac{4.329477 \times 40000}{5}$$

= Rs.34635.81 or Rs.34636 (to nearest Rupee)

= Rs. 34636

Table Showing Calculation of Interest & Cash Price

Particulars	Cash Price Rs	Due Date	Instalment	Interest Rs.	Instalment
Total Cash Price	34636				
- Cash Paid	6268	31-12-02	8000	$\dfrac{34636 \times 5}{100}$ = 1732	6268
Balance at the Beginning	28368				
- Cash paid	6582	31-12-03	8000	$\dfrac{28368 \times 5}{100}$ = 1418	6582
Balance after beginning	21786				
- Cash paid	6911	31-12-04	8000	$\dfrac{21786 \times 5}{100}$ = 1089	6911
Balance at the beginning	14875				
Cash paid	7256	31-1205	8000	$\dfrac{14875 \times 5}{100}$ = 744	7256
Balance at the beginning	7619				
Cash Paid	7619	31-12-06	8000	(8000-7619) = 381	7619
Total	-		40,000	5364	34636

(Calculations are made to the nearest Rupees)

Annuity Based Method/When Rate of Interest and Cash Price is given Hire Purchase Price is not given.

Illustration : - 8

Mr 'X' Purchased Washing Machine from Mr 'Y' on 1-1-2004. The Cash Price of washing Machine is Rs.20000 payable in 3 equal annual instalments commencing from 31st Dec. 2004. The seller charged interest outstanding cash price at 10% p.a. The annuity Table shows that the present value of Re.1 for 3 year at 10% p.a. is 2.49960.

You are required to show the Hire purchase price and interest paid every year.

Solution : -

1) Total Cash Price Rs.20000

2) Rate of Interest at 10% p.a.

3) Annuity Value as per Annuity Table 2.49960

In this problem, instalment is not given, it is calculated as under.

Annual Instalment $= \dfrac{\text{Total Cash Price}}{\text{Annuity Value}}$

$\qquad\qquad\qquad = \dfrac{\text{Rs.20000}}{2.49960}$

$\qquad\qquad\qquad =$ 8000-64

$\qquad\qquad\qquad$ i.e. Rs.8000(.64 N.P. ignored)

Table Showing Interest and Instalments Paid

Particulars	Cash Price Rs	Due Date	Instalment	Interest Rs.		Instal ment
On 1-1-04 Cash Paid Balance at the	20,000 6000	31-03-04	8000	$\dfrac{20000 \times 10}{100}$	= 2000	6000
beginning Cash Paid Balance at the	14000 6600	31-03-04	8000	$\dfrac{14000 \times 10}{100}$	= 1400	6600
beginning Cash Paid	7400 7400	31-03-04	8000	$(8000-7400)$	= 600	7400
Total	-		24000		4000	

When only Hire Purchase Price is given neither cash nor the Rate of interest is given.

In this case, it is assumed that the balance of cash price (i.e.Total cash price less immediate payment) is devided equally over all instalments and as such the difference in instalment is due to amount of interest included in respective instalment.

Illustration : 9

Mr.Ram purchased computer on Hire purchase system. He paid Rs.10000 at the Hire of signing the agreement and Rs.10400 Rs.9600 and Rs.8800 at the end of every year - inclusive of interest.

Calculate the interest and cash price included in each instalment.

Solution : -

Information given in the problem.

1) Total Hire Purchase Price.

= Rs.10000 + 10400 + 9600 + 8800 = 3880

As earlier stated, it is assumed that the portion of cash value included in the instalment is equal. (for example 10400 - 9600 = amount of interest included in each instalment may be unequal as the total amount of each instalment is different.

Here the word 'C' denotes cash price and the word I denotes Interest. The equation will be C+I = 8800, C+2I = 9600 and C+3I - 10400 equation 2 ----------- equation 1'

$$= C + \quad 2I \quad = 9600$$
$$\text{Less} - C - I \quad = 8800$$
$$I \quad = 800$$

The interest included in each instalment is.

	Instalment	Interest Cash Price	
1)	10000	-	10,000
2)	10400 (3I = 800 x 3) =	2400	8000
3)	9600 (2I = (800 x 2) =	1600	8000
4)	8800 (I = (800 x 1) =	800	8000
Total	38,800	4800	34000

Illustration : - 10 (When maintenance charges are given)

The Madras Electronic company purchased a machinery from 'X' on Hire Purchase basis on 1st Jan.2007. The vendor agreed to carry out maintenance of machinery at a fixed charge. Payment was made in four quarterly instalment as under.

1) The first instalment of Rs.10000 was paid 31st March 2007. Interest at 12% p.a. and maintenance charges at Rs.2000 per annum were paid extra.

2) Each subsequent quarterly instalment exceeded its preceding instalment by Rs.5000. The Madras Electronic Company charged depreciation at 20% per annum on original cost.

Prepare necessary accounts in the books of Madras Electronic Company.

Solution :

Information given in the problem.

1) Total Cash Price   =   Rs.70,000
(10000+150000+20000+25000)

2) Rate of interest at 12% p.a.
3) Rate of Depreciation at 20% p.a.
4) Each subsequent instalment exceed by Rs.5000.

Calculation of Interest and Hire Purchase Price

Particulars	Cash Price Rs	Due Date	Instalment Rs.	Cash Portion in Instalment Rs.	Maintenance	Instalment
Opening Bal.	70000	-	-	-	-	-
Paid Cash	10000	31-03-07	$70000 \times \dfrac{12}{100} \times \dfrac{1}{4} = 2100$	10,000	500	12600
Balance	60000	30-06-07	$60000 \times \dfrac{12}{100} \times \dfrac{1}{4} = 1800$	15,000	500	17300
Cash paid	15000	30-09-07	$45000 \times \dfrac{12}{100} \times \dfrac{1}{4} = 1350$	20,000	500	21850
Balance	45000	31-12-07	$25000 \times \dfrac{12}{100} \times \dfrac{1}{4} = 750$	25,000	500	26250
Cash Paid	20000					
Balance	25000					
Cash Paid	25000					
Total	-			6000	70000	2000	28000

Note : - 1) Maintenance charges are equally divided over all instalments.

2) Interest for every quarter i.e. for 3 months is calculated.

In the Books of Madras Electronic Company

Dr   Cr

Date	Particulars	Rs.	Date	Particulars	Rs.
Mar 31	To 'X' Ltd A/c	10,000	2007		
June30	To 'X' Ltd A/c	15,000	Dec 31	By Depreciation A/c	14,000
Sept30	To 'X' Ltd A/c	20,000		By Balance c/d	56,000
Dec.31	To 'X' Ltd A/c	25,000			
2007		70,000			70,000
1-1-08	To Bal. b/d	56,000			

'X' Ltd A/c

Dr   Cr

Date	Particulars	Rs.	Date	Particulars	Rs.
2007			2007		
Mar 31	To Cash A/c	12600	Mar 31	By Machinery A/c	10,000
June 30	To Cash A/c	17300	Mar 31	By Interest A/c	2100
Sept 30	To Cash A/c	21850	Mar 31	By Repairs A/c	500
Dec 31	To Cash A/c	26250	June 30	Pry Machinery A/c	15,000
			June 30	By Interest A/c	1,800
			June 30	By Repairs A/c	500
			Sept.30	By Machinery A/c	20,000
			Sept.30	By Interest A/c	1,350
			Sept.30	By Repairs A/c	500
			Dec.31	By Machinery A/c	25,000
			Dec.31	By Interest A/c	750
			Dec.31	By Repairs A/c	500
		78,000			78,000

Interest A/c

Dr   **Cr**

Date	Particulars	Rs.	Date	Particulars	Rs.
2007			2007		
March 31	To 'X' Ltd A/c	2100	Dec 31	By P & L. A/c	6000
June 30	To 'X' Ltd A/c	1800			
Sept 30	To 'X' Ltd A/c	1350			
Dec 31	To 'X' Ltd A/c	750			
		6000			6000

Repairs A/c (Maintenance)

Dr   **Cr**

Date	Particulars	Rs.	Date	Particulars	Rs.
2007			2005		
March 31	To 'X' Ltd A/c	500	Dec 31	By P & L. A/c	2000
June 30	To 'X' Ltd A/c	500			
Sept 30	To 'X' Ltd A/c	500			
Dec 31	To 'X' Ltd A/c	500			
		2000			2000

Depreciation A/c

Dr   **Cr**

Date	Particulars	Rs.	Date	Particulars	Rs.
2007			2007		
Dec 31	To Machinery A/c	14000	Dec 31	By P & L. A/c	14000
		14000			14000

7.4 Default and Repossession

When the buyer makes default in payment of any instalment, the vendor her right to repossess the goods sold on hire purchase and forfeit whatever the amount he has already received treating it as hire charge. There are two possibilities of repossession of goods. Repossession of goods may be partial or full depending on the circumstances and agreement between the parties.

I. When the vendor takes repossession of a part of total asset sold on hire purchase basis.

In Case of partial repossession only a part of the amount paid by the hire purchaser will be forfeited by hire vendor. The hire vendor may, after repossessing the goods, spend some money on goods for getting them repaired or reconditioned and letter on sell them.

II. When the Vendor takes back the complete repossession of goods.

In this case, entries for interest and depreciation will be passed in the books of buyer and vendor except the entry for payment upto the date of default.

Buyer will close the account of vendor by transferring its balance to Asset A/c and by debiting the vendor's Account and crediting the asset account. Any balance remains on asset account is transferred to profit and loss account. The vendor also closes the account of purchaser by transferring the balance to Repossessing stock Account. It is debited by expenses incurred and credited by sales. If there remains balance, it is transferred to profit and loss account.

Accounting Entries

1) In the books of Buyer or Purchaser

Usual entries for interest and depreciation till the due date of instalment should be passed as explained earlier.

2) In case of full repossession : -

(a) For Closing Hire Vendor's A/c

      Hire Vendor's A/c

         To Asset A/c

Note : - This entry is passed with the amount due to the hire Vendor.

(b) For closing Asset Account.

(i) If there is a profit on repossession (when the amount due to Hire Vendor exceed the books value office asset)

Asset A/c ---- Dr

To Profit & Loss A/c

(ii) If there is a loss on repossession (when the books value of asset exceed the amount due to Hire Vendor.

Profit & Loss A/c ---- Dr

To Asset A/c

Alternatively any balance to the debit of the asset account may be transferred to vandor's Account. Any balance to the hire vendor's Account will be transferred to profit and loss Account. Normally an account having a smaller balance is transferred to an account having a bigger balance.

(3) The hire vendor may not be so harsh to take possession of the full asset. He may leave a portion of the asset with the hire purchaser. In such a case an agreement is made regarding the value at which the repossed asset will be taken back by the hire vendor. The value so agreed will be debited to the hire vendor and credited to asset account. Such value is generally lower than the value at which the asset is appearing in the books of hire purchaser. The difference between the book volume of the asset and the value at which it has been taken over by hire vendor is a loss which will be written off from the profit and Loss Account.

In the books of Hire Vendor / Seller

(i) The Hire vendor will pass usual entry for the interest due from hire purchaser till the date of instalment.

(ii) On Repossession of goods

Goods Repossessed A/c ---- Dr

To Hire Purchaser' A/c

Note : This entry is passed with the revalued amount of goods repossessed.

(iii) For amount spent on repairs and reconditioning of goods repossed.

Goods Repossessed A/c ---- Dr

To Cash/Bank A/c

(iv) For sale of goods repossessed

    Cash/ Debtors A/c ---- Dr

       To Goods Repossessed A/c

(v) For loss on sale of Goods Repossessed

    Profit & Loss A/c ---- Dr

       To Goods Repossessed A/c

(vi) For Profit on sale of goods Repossessed)

    Goods Repossessed A/c ---- Dr

       To Profit & Loss A/c

N.B. In case of Repossession, it is convenient to follow full cash price or sales Method.

Illustration : 11 (Complete Repossession)

'X' purchased a Motor Cycle on Hire Purchase system for Rs.56000. Payment to be made as below Rs.15000 down and 3 instalments of Rs.1500 each at the end of every year. Rate of interest is charged at 5% p.a. The purchaser is depreciating the asset at 10% p.a. on written down value method.

Because of financial difficulties, 'X' after having paid down payment and first instalment at the end of Ist year could not pay IInd instalment and the seller took possession of the Motor Cycle. Seller after expending Rs.350 on repairs of the asset sold it away for Rs.30110.

open ledger Accounts in the books of both parties to record the transactions

Solution : - (Full Cash Price Method)

(1) Total Cash Price of Motor Cycle Rs.56000

(2) Hire Purchased paid cash down payment and payment of first instalment (15000+15000)

(3) The Seller spend for Repairs of asset Rs.350

(4) The Seller sold the repossessed Asset for Rs.30110.

(5) Rate of Depreciation is at 10% p.a.

(6) Rate of Interest is at 5% p.a.

In the Books of 'X'
Motor Cycle A/c.

Dr   **Cr**

Date	Particulars	Rs.	Date	Particulars	Rs.
Year I Jan 1	To Hire Vendor's A/c	56000	Year I Dec.31	By Depreciation A/c (at 10%)	5600
				By Balance c/d	50400
		56000			56000
II Jan 1	To Balance b/d.	50400	II Dec 31	By Depreciation A/c	5040
				By Hire Vendor's A/c	29453
				By P & L A/c (Balancing figure)	15907
		50400			50400

Hire Vendor A/c

Dr   **Cr**

Date	Particulars	Rs.	Date	Particulars	Rs.
Year I Jan 1	To Bank A/c	15000	Jan 1	By Motor Cycle A/c	56000
Jan 1	To Bank A/c	15000	Dec 31	By Interest A/c	2050
Dec 31	To Balance c/d	28050	Year I		
		58050			58050
Year II	To Motor Cycle		Jan 1	By Balance b/d	28050
Dec 31	A/c	29453	Dec 31	By Interest A/c	1403
		29453	Year II		29453

Repossessed Stock A/c

Dr   **Cr**

Date	Particulars	Rs.	Date	Particulars	Rs.
Year II Dec 31	To X's A/c	29453	Year II Dec 31	By Sales A/c	30110
	To Cash/Bank (expenses)	350			
	To P & L A/c	307			
		30110			30110

P & L A/c

Dr						Cr
Date	Particulars	Rs.	Date	Particulars		Rs.
			Year II Dec 31	By Repossessed stock A/c		307

Illustration : 12 (Partial Repossession)

M/s Sandeep Radio acquired Five Radios on hire purchase system from philips Radio Company. The cash down price for each radio being Rs.5000. The price was payable in five instalment of Rs.1100 each. every year, the first being paid on signing the agreement and the instalments included interest charged at 5% per annum. The philips Radio Company decided to provide depreciation at 10% per annum calculated on the diminishing balance method. It paid the first instalment due at the end of Ist year but couldnot pay the next books.

Give the necessary Ledger Accounts in the books of both parties for two years if the philips Radio company agreed to leave three radios against the amount due. The radios were valued on the basis of 20% depreciation annually. The Hire vendor spend Rs.400 on getting radios throughly overvalued and sold them from Rs.8800.

Solution (Full Cash Price Method)

Information given in the problem.

1) Total cash price of 5 Radio's (5000 x 5) Rs. 25000.

2) Price of Radio is to be paid in Five instalment

3) Default after paying First Instalment.

4) Two radios are taken back.

5) Rate of Interest is at 5% p.a.

6) Rate of Depreciation is at 10% p.a.

Working Notes :

1) Value of two Radios taken up by Philips Radio Company

	Ist Year (Rs.)	IInd Year (Rs.)
Value of two Radios	10,000	8,000
-Depreciation for the year at 20%	2000	1600
Balance at the end of Ist Year and II Year	8000	6400
	Rs.	Rs.
Value of Three Radios	15000	13500
- Depreciation for the year at 10%	1500	1350
Balance at the end of Ist & II Year.	13500	12150

In the books of Sandeep Radio's
Radio A/c

Dr   Cr

Date	Particulars	Rs.	Date	Particulars	Rs.
Year I Jan 1	To Philips Radio Company's A/c	25000	Year I Dec.31 Dec.31	By Depreciation A/c By Balance c/d	2500 22500
		25000			25000
II Jan 1	To Balance b/d	22500	II Dec 31 Dec 31 Dec 31 Dec 31	By Dep. A/c By Philip Co.A/c (See working note) By P & L A/c By Balance c/d (W.N.2)	2250 6400 1700 12150
		22500			22500

Philips Radio Company's A/c

Dr | | | | | | Cr

Date	Particulars	Rs.	Date	Particulars	Rs.
YearI J.31	To Bank A/c	5500	Year I	By Radio's A/c	25000
Dec31	To Bank A/c	5500	Jan 1	By Interest A.c	975
Dec31	To Balance c/d	14975	Dec 31	(5/ on 19500)	
		25975	IInd		25975
II Dec31	To Radio's A/c	6400	Year	By Balance b/d	14975
Dec31	To Balance c/d	9324	Jan 1	By Interest A/c	
			Dec 31	(5% on 14975)	749
		15724			15724

In the Books of Philip Radio (Seller)

Dr | | | | | | Cr

Date	Particulars	Rs.	Date	Particulars	Rs.
Year I Jan.1	To Hire Sale A/c	25000	YearIJan.1	By Bank A/c	5500
Dec31	To Interest A/c	975	Dec 31	By Bank A/c	5500
			Dec 31	By Balance c/d	14975
		25975	IInd		25975
II Jan 1	To Balance b/d	14975	Dec 31	By Repossessed	
Dec 31	To Interest A/c	749		stock A/c	6400
			Dec 31	By Balance c/d	9324
		15724			15724

Repossessed Stock A/c

Dr | | | | | | Cr

Date	Particulars	Rs.	Date	Particulars	Rs.
Year II Jan.1	To Sandeep Radio's A/c	6400	Year II Dec 31	By Cash A/c	8800
Dec31	To Cash A/c (expenses)	400			
Dec31	To P & L. A/c	2000			
		8800			8800

7 :5 Instalment System

This system is also known as Deferred Instalment system. under instalment purchase system the possession as well as ownership passes from seller to the buyer immediately on entering the agreement but the buyer agrees to pay the total price in instalments. If the buyer makes any default in payment of any instalment. The seller has no right to repossess the goods. The seller can file a suit in the court of law for recovery of the price.

The following are the essential characteristics of this system.

1) It is a credit purchase.

2) The buyer gets immediate possession and ownership of the goods.

3) The payment of price has to be made by the buyer in agreed instalments.

4) In the event of default by the buyer in the payment of any instalment, the seller can bring a suit against the buyer for recovery of unpaid price and damages. In no case he can recover back the goods.

5) The buyer is free to sell or pledge or dispose off the goods even before full payment.

6) The relationship between buyer and seller is that of debtor and creditor.

7) The buyer may dispose off the goods and give good title to the bonafide purchaser.

7.6 Distinction between
Hire Purchase System and Instalment Purchase System.

Basis of Distinction	Hire Purchase system	Instalment purchase System
1) Act applied	It is governed by Hire Purchase Act 1972	It is governed by the sale of Goods Act 1930
2) Name of Parties	The Parties in Hire purchase system are called Hire Purchaser and Hire Seller	The Parties in Instalment system are called buyer and Seller.
3) Nature of agreement	It is an agreement of hiring	It is an agreement of Sale. Ownership passes from
4) Transfer of ownership	Ownership remains with the seller until the payment of last instalment	seller to buyer immediately on entering the agreement
5) Return of goods	The goods can be returned to seller if the buyer does not want to pay rest of the instalment	The goods cannot be return by the buyer to seller unless there is some default on the part of seller.
6) Right of disposal.	The hire purchaser cannot sell or dispose the goods as he is not a owner	The purchaser can sell the goods on he is the owner of the goods.
7) Right of Seller	The seller can repossess the goods in case of default in payment	The seller cannot repossess the goods even if there is any default made by purchaser in payment
8) Relationship between parties.	The relationship between hire purchaser and hire seller is that of Bailee and Bailor.	The relationship between buyer and seller is that of debtor & creditor till the payment of last instalment.
9) Forfeiture of Instalment	In case of default the seller can forfeit all instalment paid by buyer	In case of default the seller can adjust the amount paid against selling price and he can see only for the balance
10) Treatment of Instalment	Instalment is treated as hire charges.	Instalment is treated as the payment of interest and Principal.

7.7 Accounting Entries

Under Instalment purchase system following Journal Entries are to be passed in the books of buyer and seller.

Journal Entries in the books of Purchaser

1) On signing the agreement or purchase of Asset
   Asset A/c ---- Dr. (Full Cash Price)
   Interest Suspense A/c Dr (Total Interest)
       To Vendor's A/c
   (Being asset purchased on instalment-system)

2) For Down Payment
   Vendor's A/c ---- Dr
       To Bank/Cash A/c
   (Being Payment made at the time of agreement)

3) For Instalment falls due
   Interest A/c ---- Dr
       To Interest Suspense A/c
   (Being interest included in the instalment is transferred to Interest suspense A/c)

4) For Payment of Instalment
   Vendor's A/c ---- Dr
       To Bank/ Cash A/c
   (Being Payment of Instalment)

5) For Depreciation
   Depreciation A/c ---- Dr
       To Asset A/c
   (Being depreciation charged)

6) For transfer of Interest and Depreciation to Profit and Loss Account
   Profit & Loss A/c ---- Dr
       To Interest A/c
       To Depreciation A/c
   (Being transfer of Interest and Depreciation to Profit & Loss Account)

Note : - Entries No.3,4,5,6 are to be repeated every year till the payment of last instalment.

Journal Entries in the books of Vendor.

1) For Sale of asset on instalment basis on the date of agreement.

Purchaser's A/c ---- Dr   (With total Sales)

To Sales A/c   (With Cash price of Asset sold)

To Interest Suspense A/c   (Total Interest)

(Being asset sold on instalment system)

2) Down Payment Received

Cash/Bank A/c ---- Dr

To Purchase's A/c

(Being Down Payment received)

3) For transfer of Interest to Interest Suspense A/c

Interest Suspense A/c---- Dr

To Interest A/c

(Being transfer of interest to Interest Suspense Account)

4) For Receipt of Instalment

Cash/Bank A/c ---- Dr

To Purchaser A/c

(Being Instalment received)

5) For transfer of Interest to P & L A/c

Interest A/c ---- Dr

To Profit & Loss A/c

(Being transfer of interest to P & L. A/c)

Note : Entries No 3 to 5 will be repeated in subsequent years.

7.8 Illustration 13 (Cash Price is given)

The Madras Transport company purchased a lorry on instalment basis. on 1st Jan. 2004 paying Rs.20000 cash and agreeing to pay three further instalments of Rs.20000 each on 31st December each Year. The cash price of lorry was Rs.74500 and lorry company charges interest at 5% p.a. The Madras Transfer company charges depreciation at 10% p.a. on cash value of the lorry on diminishing balance method.

Pass the Journal entries and prepare necessary ledger account in the books of both.

Solution : -

Information Available

1) Total Cash Price Rs.74500
2) Rate of Interest at 5% p.a.
3) Rate of Depreciation at 10% p.a.(diminishing balance method)

Calculation of Interest and Depreciation.

Particulars	Cash Price Rs	Due Date	Payment of Instalment	Interest Rs.	Cash Price Rs	Depreciation Rs.
Opening Balance	74500	1-1-04	20,000	--	20000	74500
Paid Cash	20000					
Bal. 1-1-04	54500					
Paid Cash on 31-12-04	17275	31-12-04	20,000	$54500 \times \frac{5}{100} = 2725$	17275	7450
Bal.on 1-1-05	37225					67050
Paid Cash on 31-12-05	18139	31-12-05	20,000	$37225 \times \frac{5}{100} = 1861$	18139	6705
Bal.on 1-1-06	19086					60345
Paid Cash on 31-12-06	19086	31-12-06	20,000	$(20000-19086) = 914$	19086	6034
Total	-		80,000	5500	74500	54311
Balance on 1-1-07						

Journal Entries in the books of
Madras Transport Company

Date	Particulars	Debit (Rs.)	Credit (Rs.)
1-1-04	Lorry A/c ---- Dr	74,500	
	Interest Suspense A/c ---- Dr	5,500	
	To Vendors A/c		80,000
	(Being Lorry purchased on Instalment System)		
1-1-04	Vendor's A/c ---- Dr	20,000	
	To Bank / Cash A/c		20,000
	(Being Down Payment paid to seller)		
31-12-04	Interest A/c ---- Dr	2,725	
	To Interest Suspense A/c		2,725
	(Being interest is transferred to interest suspense A/c		
31-12-04	Vendor's A/c ---- Dr	20,000	
	To Bank or Cash A/c		20,000
	(Being first instalment paid)		
31-12-04	Depreciations A/c ---- Dr	7,450	
	To Lorry A/c		7,450
	(Being Depreciation charged)		
31-12-04	Profit & Loss A/c ---- Dr	10,175	
	To Depreciation A/c		10,175
	To Interest A/c		
	(Being Balances of Interest & Depreciation transferred to P & L A/c)		
31-12-05	Interest A/c ---- Dr	1,861	
	To Interest Suspense A/c		1,861
	(Being interest transferred to interest suspense A/c)		

Date	Particulars		Debit (Rs.)	Credit (Rs.)
31-12-05	Vendor's A/c ---- To Bank or Cash A/c (Being second instalment paid)	Dr	20,000	20,000
31-12-05	Depreciation A/c ---- To lorry A/c (Being Depreciation charged)	Dr	6,705	6,705
31-12-05	Profit & Loss A/c ---- To Depreciation A/c To Interest A/c (Being Depreciation & interest transferred to P & L A/c)	Dr	8,566 914	8,566 914
31-12-06	Vendor's A/c ---- To Bank/Cash A/c (Being final instalment paid)	Dr	20,000	20,000
31-12-06	Depreciation A/c ---- To lorry A/c (Being Depreciation charged)	Dr	6,034	6,034
31-12-06 31-12-06	Profit & Loss A/c ---- To Depreciation A/c To Interest A/c (Being depreciation and Interest transferred to profit and loss Account)	Dr	6,948	6,948

In the Books of Madras Transport Company
Lorry A/c

Date	Particulars	Rs.	Date	Particulars	Rs.
1-1-04	To Vendor's A/c	74500	31-12-04	By Depreciation A/c By Balance c/d	7450 67050
		74500			74500
1-1-05	By Balance b/d	67050	31-12-05	By Depreciation A/c By Balance c/d	6705 60345
		67050			67050

Date	Particulars	Rs.	Date	Particulars	Rs.
1-1-06	To Balance b/d	60345	31-12-06	By Depreciation A/c	6034
				By Balance c/d	54311
		60345			60345
1-1-07	To Balance b/d	54311			

Vendor's A/c

Dr   **Cr**

Date	Particulars	Rs.	Date	Particulars	Rs.
1-1-04	To Bank A/c	20000	1-1-04	By Lorry A/c	74500
31-12-04	To Bank A/c	20000	31-12-04	By Interest Suspense A/c	5500
31-12-04	To Balance c/d	40000			
		80000			80000
31-12-05	To Bank A/c	20,000	1-1-05	By Balance b/d	40,000
31-12-05	To Balance c/d	20,000			
		40,000			40,000
31-12-06	To Bank A/c	20,000	1-1-06	By Balance b/d	20,000
		20,000			20,000

Interest Suspense A/c

Dr   **Cr**

Date	Particulars	Rs.	Date	Particulars	Rs.
1-1-04	To Vendor's A/c	5500	31-12-04	By Interest A/c	2725
			31-12-04	By Balance c/d	2775
		5500			5500
1-1-05	To Balance b/d	2775	31-12-05	By Interest A/c	1861
			31-12-05	By Balance c/d	914
		2775			2775
1-1-06	To Balance b/d	914	31-12-06	By Interest A/c	914

Interest Suspense A/c

Dr   **Cr**

Date	Particulars	Rs.	Date	Particulars	Rs.
31-12-04	To Int.Sus.A/c	2775	31-12-04	By P & L A/c	2775
31-12-05	To Int.Sus A/c	1861	31-12-05	By P & L A/c	1861
31-12-06	To Int.Sus A/c	914	31-12-06	By P & L A/c	914

Journal Entries in the books of Vendor

Date	Particulars	Debit (Rs.)	Credit (Rs.)
1-1-04	Madras Transport Co's A/c ---- Dr	80,000	
	To Sales A/c		80,000
	To Interest Suspense A/c		
	(Being Lorry sold on Instalment Basis)		
1-1-04	Bank/Cash A/c ---- Dr	20,000	
	To Madras Transport Co's A/c		20,000
	(Being Down Payment Received)		
31-12-04	Interest Suspense A/c ---- Dr	2725	
	To Interest A/c		2725
	(Being transfer of Interest to Interest Suspense A/c)		
31-12-04	Bank / Cash A/c ---- Dr	20,000	
	To Madras Transport Co's A/c		20,000
	(Being first instalment received)		
31-12-04	Interest A/c ---- Dr	2725	
	To P & L A/c		2725
	(Being transfer of interest to P&L A/c)		
31-12-05	Interest Suspense A/c ---- Dr	1861	
	To Interest A/c		1861
	(Being transfer of interest to interest suspense A/c)		
31-12-05	Bank/Cash A/c ---- Dr	20,000	
	To Madras Transport Co's A/c		20,000
	(Being second instalment received)		
31-12-05	Interest A/c ---- Dr	1861	
	To Profit & Loss A/c		1861
	(Being interest transferred to profit & Loss Account)		

Date	Particulars		Debit (Rs.)	Credit (Rs.)
31-12-06	Interest Suspense A/c ----	Dr	914	
	To Interest A/c			914
	(Being interest transferred to interest suspense A/c)			
31-12-06	Bank / Cash A/c ----	Dr	20,000	
	To Madras Transport Co's A/c			20,000
	(Being final instalment received)			
31-12-06	Interest A/c ----	Dr	914	
	To P & L A/c			914
	(Being interest transferred to P & L A/c)			

In the books of Vender
Madras Transport Company's A/c

Dr   Cr

Date	Particulars	Rs.	Date	Particulars	Rs.
1-1-04	To Sales A/c	74,500	1-1-04	By Bank A/c	20,000
	To Interest Sus.		31-12-04	By Bank A/c	20,000
	A/c	5,500	31-12-04	By Balance c/d	40,000
		80,000			80,000
1-1-05	To Balance c/d	40,000	31-12-05	By Bank A/c	20,000
			31-12-05	By Balance c/d	20,000
		40,000			40,000
1-1-06	To Balance b/d	20,000	31-12-06	By Bank A/c	20,000
		20,000			20,000

Interest Suspense A/c

Dr   Cr

Date	Particulars	Rs.	Date	Particulars	Rs.
1-1-04	To Interest A/c	2725	1-1-04	By Madras Trans	
	To Balance c/d	2775		Co.A/c	5500
		5500			5500

Date	Particulars	Rs.	Date	Particulars	Rs.
31-12-05	To Interest A/c	1861	1-1-05	By Balance b/d	2775
31-12-05	To Blance c/d	914			
		2775			2775
31-12-06	To Interest A/c	914	1-1-05	By Balance b/d	917

Interest A/c

Dr   **Cr**

Date	Particulars	Rs.	Date	Particulars	Rs.
31-12-04	To P & L A/c	2725	31-12-04	By Int.Sus.A/c	2725
31-12-05	To P & L A/c	1861	31-12-04	By Int.Sus.A/c	1861
31-12-05	To P & L A/c	914	31-12-04	By Int.Sus.A/c	914

Sales A/c

Dr   **Cr**

Date	Particulars	Rs.	Date	Particulars	Rs.
31-12-04	To Trading A/c	74500	31-12-04	By Madras Transport Co.A/c	74520

Illustration : 14
(H.P. Price, Cash Price, Rate of Interest etc are given)

M/s. Dass Prvos Supplied Refrigerator to Durga Hotel on instalment system on 1st July 2002. The cash price of it was Rs.22350. Under instalment system it was agreed to pay Rs.6000 on that date Rs.6000 annually for three years. Interest was chargeable at 5% per annum and depreciation was to be written off the asset at 10% p.a.

show the ledger accounts in the books of Durga Hotel.

Solution

Information Available

1) Instalment Price Rs.24000

2) Cash Price Rs.22350

3) Total Interest Rs.1650

4) Rate of Interest at 5% p.a.

5) Rate of Depreciation at 10% p.a. (assuming diminishing balance method)

6) It is Presumed that year ends on 30th June every year.

Calculation of Interest & Depreciation

Particulars	Cash Price Rs	Due Date	Payment of Instalment	Interest Rs.	Cash Price Rs	Depreciation Rs.
Balance on 1-7-2002	22350	1-7-04	6000	–	6000	22350
Cash Paid on 1-7-2002	6000					
Balance on 1-7-2002	16350					2235
Paid on 30-6-2003	5182	30-6-03	6000	$16350 \times \dfrac{5}{100} = 818$	5182	20115
Balance on 1-7-2003	11168					2011
Paid on 30-6-2004	5442	30-6-04	6000	$11168 \times \dfrac{5}{100} = 558$	5442	18103
Balance on 1-7-2004	5726					1810
Paid on 30-6-2005	5726	30-6-05	6000	$(6000-5726) = 274$	5726	16293
Total Balance on 1-7-2005	–		24000	1650	22350	

In the books of Durga Hotel
Refrigerator's A/c

Dr   **Cr**

Date	Particulars	Rs.	Date	Particulars	Rs.
1-7-02	To M/s Dass Bros. A/c	22350	30-6-03	By Depreciation A/c	2215
			30-6-03	By Balance c/d	20115
		22350			22350
1-7-03	To Balance b/d	20115	30-6-04	By Depreciation A/c	2012
			30-6-04	By Balance c/d	18103
		20115			20115
1-7-04	To Balance b/d	18103	30-6-05	By Depreciation A/c	1810
			30-6-05	By Balance c/d	16293
		18103			18103
1-7-05	To Balance b/d	16293			

M/s Dass Bros A/c

Dr   **Cr**

Date	Particulars	Rs.	Date	Particulars	Rs.
1-7-02	To Bank A/c	6000	1-7-02	By Refrigerators A/c	22350
30-6-03	To Bank A/c	6000	1-7-02	By Interest Suspense A/c	1650
30-6-03	To Balance A/c	12000			
		24000			24000
30-6-04	To Bank A/c	6000	1-7-03	By Balance b/d	12000
30-6-04	To Balance c/d	6000			
		12000			12000
30-6-05	To Bank A/c	6000	1-7-04	By Balance b/d	6000
		6000			6000

Interest Suspense A/c

Dr   **Cr**

Date	Particulars	Rs.	Date	Particulars	Rs.
1-7-02	To M/s Dass A/c	1650	30-6-03	By Interest A/c	818
			30-6-03	By Balance c/d	832
		1650			1650
1-7-03	To Balance b/d	832	30-6-04	By Interest A/c	558
			30-6-04	By Balance c/d	274
		832			832
1-7-04	To Balance b/d	274	30-6-05	By Interest A/c	274
		274			274

Interest A/c

Dr   **Cr**

Date	Particulars	Rs.	Date	Particulars	Rs.
30-6-03	To Int.Sus.A/c	818	30-6-03	By P & L A/c	818
30-6-04	To Int.Sus.A/c	558	30-6-04	By P & L A/c	558
30-6-05	To Int.Sus.A/c	274	30-6-05	By P & L A/c	274

Illustration : 15

(H.P. Price, Rate of Interest, But Cash Price is not given)

M/s.Ranjit Transport Limited Purchased a Tempo from Sai Services Ltd on instalment system on 1st April will be payable in four annual instalments at the end of each accounting year on 31st March including interest at 10 % on Cash Price. The instalments paid were as follows.

	Rs.
31st March 2005	64000
31st March 2006	49000
31st March 2007	35000
31st March 2008	22000

Ranjit Transport Ltd charged Depreciation at 10% on Diminishing Balance Method. Prepare Tempo Account, Interest suspense Account, Sai services Ltd Account and Interest account in the books of Ranjit Transport Ltd.

Solution : - Information Available

1) Instalment Price Rs.200,000 2) Rate of Interest at 10% on Cash Price 3) Rate of Depreciation at 10% on diminishing balance system.

In this problem, Cash Price is not given, hence interest in the last instalment is calculated and thereafter in previous instalment. It is calculated as below.

Calculation Interest and Cash Price.

Date (1)	Instalment Amt (2)	Instalment Plus Sub-Sequent Portion of Cash Price (2+6)	Calculations of Interest at 10% p.a. (4)	Amount of Interest (5)	Portion of Cash Price (col2-col5) (6)
1-4-04	30000	-	-	-	30000
31-3-05	64000	(iv) 64000 + 40000 + 30000 +20000=154000	110:154000:10	= 14000	50000
31-3-06	49000	(iii) 49000 + 30000 + 20000 = 99000	110:99000:10	= 9000	40000
31-3-07	35000	(ii) 35000+20000 = 55000	1110: 55000 : 10	= 5000	30000
31-12-08	22000	(i) 22000+0=22000	110 : 22000 : 10	= 2000	20000
Total 2,00,000				30,000	1,70,000

Calculation of Depreciation

	Rs.
Balance of Tempo on 1-4-2004 = (Cash Price)	1,70,000
Depreciation on 31-3-2005 (Balance)	17000
	1,53,000
Depreciation on 31-3-2006	15300
Balance	1,37,700
Depreciation on 31-3-2007	13,770
Balance	1,23,930
Depreciation on 31-3-2008	12,393
Balance	1,11,537

In the Books of Ranjit Transport Ltd.
Tempo A/c

Dr   **Cr**

Date	Particulars	Rs.	Date	Particulars	Rs.
1-7-02	To Sai Services A/c	1,70,000	30-6-03	By Depreciation A/c	17000
			30-6-03	By Balance c/d	153000
		1,70,000			170000
1-7-03	To Balance b/d	1,53,000	30-6-04	By Depreciation A/c	153000
			30-6-04	By Balance c/d	137700
		1,53,000			153000
1-7-04	To Balance b/d	1,37,000	30-6-05	By Depreciation A/c	13770
			30-6-05	By Balance c/d	123930
		1,37,000			137700
1-7-05	To Balance b/d	1,23,930		By Depreciation A/c	123930
				By Balance c/d	111537
		1,23,930			123930

Sai Services A/c

Dr   **Cr**

Date	Particulars	Rs.	Date	Particulars	Rs.
11-4-04	To Bank A/c	30,000	01-04-04	By Tempo A/c	1,70,000
31-03-05	To Bank A/c	64,000	01-04-04	By Int.Suspense	
31-03-05	To Balance c/d	1,06,000		A/c	30,000
		2,00,000			2,00,000
31-03-06	To Bank A/c	49,000	1-4-05	By Balance b/d	1,06,000
31-12-06	To Balance c/d	57,000			
		1,06,000			1,06,000
31-03-07	To Bank A/c	35,000	1-4-06	By Balance b/d	57,000
31-03-07	To Balance c/d	22,000			
		57,000			57,000
31-12-08	To Bank A/c	22,000	1-4-07	By Balance b/d	22,000
		22,000			22,000

Interest Suspense A/c

Dr   **Cr**

Date	Particulars	Rs.	Date	Particulars	Rs.
01-04-04	To Sai Services		31-03-05	By Interest A/c	14,000
	A/c	30,000	31-03-05	By Balance c/d	16,000
		30,000			30,000
01-04-05	By Balance b/d	16,000	31-03-06	By Interest A/c	9,000
			31-03-06	By Balance c/d	7,000
		16,000			16,000
01-04-06	By Balance b/d	7000	31-03-07	By Interest A/c	5,000
			31-03-07	By Balance c/d	2,000
		7000			7,000
01-04-07	By Balance b/d	2000	31-03-08	By Interest A/c	2,000

Interest A/c

Dr   **Cr**

Date	Particulars	Rs.	Date	Particulars	Rs.
31-3-05	To Int.Sus.A/c	14000	31-3-05	By P & L A/c	14000
31-3-06	To Int.Sus.A/c	9000	31-3-06	By P & L A/c	9000
31-3-07	To Int.Sus.A/c	5000	31-3-07	By P & L A/c	5000
31-3-08	To Int.Sus.A/c	2000	31-3-08	By P & L A/c	2000

Illustration : 16

(Instalment Price and Cash Price are give but
Rate of Interest is not given.)

On 1-1-2005 Mr 'X' purchased Machinery from L & T Ltd. on Instalment system at cash price of Rs.77250 paying Rs.15000 on signing the contract. The annual instalment paid by them were as follows.

	Rs.
31-12-2005	37,500
31-12-2006	22500
31-12-2007	15000

Depreciation to be charged at 10% p.a. as per fixed Instalment Method.

You are required to show necessary ledger accounts in the books of Mr 'X' and L & T Ltd.

Solution :

Information Available

1) Instalment Price   Rs.90,000
2) Cash Price   Rs.77,250
3) Total Interest   Rs.12,750
4) Down Payment   Rs.15,000
5) Rate of Depreciation at 10 p.a. (D.B.M.)

Calculation of Interest

Total Instalment Price	Rs.90000
Less Cash Price	Rs.77250
Total Interest	Rs.12750

Instalment Purchase Price

	Rs.
On 1-1-2005	90,000
Less paid on 1-1-2005	15000
	75000 Outstanding Bal. on 1-1-05
Less Paid on 31-12-05	37500
	37500 Outstanding Bal.on 1-1-06
Less Paid on 31-12-06	22500
	15000 Outstanding Bal.on 1-1-07
Less Paid on 31-12-07	15000
	00000

Outstanding Balance at the beginning	75000	37500	15000
Ratio of Outstanding Balances	10 :	5 :	2

The total interest Rs.12750 will be apportioned in the radio at 10:5:2 as under.

Date	Instalment Rs.	Interest Rs.	Cash Portion Rs.	Calculation of Interest Rs.
1-1-05	15000	-	15,000	-
31-12-05	37500	7500	30,000	17 : 12750 : 10 = 7500 12750 x 10 17
31-12-06	22500	3750	18750	17 : 12750 : 5 = 3750 12750 x 5 17
31-12-07	15000	1500	13,500	17 : 12750 : 2 = 1500 12750 x 2 17
Total	90,000	12750	77,250	

Calculation of Depreciation	Rs.
Balance on 1-1-2005	77250
Depreciation at 10% on 31-12-05 =	7725
Balance on 1-1-2006	69525
Depreciation at 10% on 31-12-06 =	6953
Balance on 1-1-07	62572
Depreciation at 10% on 31-12-07	6257
Balance on 1-1-2008	56315

In the Books of Mr 'X'
Machinery A/c

Dr   Cr

Date	Particulars	Rs.	Date	Particulars	Rs.
1-1-05	To L & T Ltd. A/c	77250	31-3-05	By Depreciation A/c	7725
			31-3-06	By Balance c/d	69525
		77250			77250
1-1-06	To Balance b/d	69525	31-3-07	By Depreciation A/c	6953
			31-3-08	By Balance c/d	62572
		69525			69525
1-1-07	To Balance b/d	62572		By Depreciation A/c	6257
				By Balance c/d	56315
		62572			62572
1-1-08	To Balance b/d	56315			

L & T Ltd A/c

Dr   Cr

Date	Particulars	Rs.	Date	Particulars	Rs.
1-1-05	To Bank A/c	15000	1-1-05	By Machinery A/c	77250
31-12-05	To Bank A/c	37500	1-1-05	By Int.Sus.A/c	12750
31-12-05	To Balance c/d	37500			
		90000			90000

Date	Particulars	Rs.	Date	Particulars	Rs.
1-1-05	To Bank A/c	22,500	1-1-06	By Balance b/d	37,500
31-12-05	To Balance c/d	15,000			
31-12-05		37,500			37,500
31-12-07	To Bank A/c	15,000	1-1-07	By Balance b/d	15,000
		15,000			15,000

Interest Suspense A/c

Dr   **Cr**

Date	Particulars	Rs.	Date	Particulars	Rs.
01-01-05	To L & T Ltd.A/c	12750	31-12-05	By Interest A/c	7500
			31-12-05	BY Balance c/d	5250
		12750			12750
01-01-06	To Balance b/d	5250	31-12-06	By Interest A/c	3750
			31-12-06	By Balance c/d	1500
		5250			5250
01-01-07	To Balance b/d	1500	31-12-06	By Interest A/c	1500
		1500			1500

Interest A/c

Dr   **Cr**

Date	Particulars	Rs.	Date	Particulars	Rs.
01-01-05	To Interest Suspense A/c	7,500	31-12-05	By P. & L. A/c	7,500
01-01-06	To Interest Suspense A/c	3,750	31-12-06	By P. & L. A/c	3,750
01-01-07	To Interest Suspense A/c	1,500	31-12-07	By P. & L. A/c	1,500

Depreciation A/c

Dr						Cr
Date	Particulars	Rs.	Date	Particulars		Rs.
31-12-05	To Machinery A/c	7725	31-12-05	By P. & L. A/c		7725
31-12-06	To Machinery A/c	6953	31-12-06	By P. & L. A/c		6953
31-12-07	To Machinery A/c	6257	31-12-07	By P. & L. A/c		6257

In the Books of L & T Ltd.
Mr 'X' Account

Dr					Cr
Date	Particulars	Rs.	Date	Particulars	Rs.
01-01-05	To Sales A/c	77250	01-01-05	By Bank A/c	15,000
01-01-05	To Interest Sus.A/c	12,750	31-12-05	By Bank A/c	37,500
			31-12-05	By Bank A/c	37,500
		90,000			90,000
01-01-06	To Balance b/d	37,500	31-12-06	By Bank A/c	22,500
			31-12-06	By Balance c/d.	15,000
		37,500			37,500
01-01-07	To Balance b/d	15,000	31-12-07	By Bank A/c	15,000
		15,000			15,000

Interest Suspense A/c

Dr					Cr
Date	Particulars	Rs.	Date	Particulars	Rs.
31-12-05	To Interest A/c	7500	01-01-05	By 'X' A/c	12750
31-12-05	To Balance c/d	5250			
		12750			12750
31-12-06	To Interest A/c	3750	01-01-06	By Balance b/d	5250
31-12-06	To Balance c/d	1500			
		5250			5250
31-12-07	To Interest A/c	1500	01-01-07	By Balance b/d	1500
		1500			1500

Interest A/c

Dr   **Cr**

Date	Particulars	Rs.	Date	Particulars	Rs.
31-12-05	To P. & L. A/c	7500	31-12-05	By Int.Sus.A/c	7500
31-12-06	To P. & L. A/c	3750	31-12-06	By Int.Sus.A/c	3750
31-12-07	To P. & L. A/c	1500	31-12-07	By Int.Sus.A/c	1500

7.9 Objective Type Questions & Problems.

Objective Type Questions

State whether each of the following statement is true or false.

1) Under the Hire Purchase agreement, the ownership of good is transferred to buyer only when last instalment is paid.

2) Under Instalment system, the buyer becomes the owner of goods.

3) Under the Hire Purchase system, Asset will be debited with the cash price and interest.

4) The property in goods passes to hire purchaser as soon as the cash down payment is made.

5) Depreciation on asset is calculated on cash price of the asset.

6) Interest is calculated on the hire purchase price at the given rate of interest.

7) The buyer has option to return the goods in case of hire purchase.

8) In case the rate of interest is not given, interest is divided equally over the hire purchase instalment.

9) The seller can repossess the goods on failure of purchaser to pay the price in case of instalment system.

10) Under instalment system goods are sold to purchaser on credit.

Ans. 1) T 2) T 3) F 4) T 5) T 6) F 7)T 8) F 9) F 10)- F.

Select the most appropriate answers.

1) In case of Hire Purchase, asset account is debited with:

(a) Hire purchase price (b) cash price (c) cost price

2) The amount of interest is credited by the buyer to:

(a) Interest Account (b) Vendor's Account

(c) Asset Account

3) The Hire purchaser charges depreciation on :

(a) Hire purchase price (b) cash price (c) lower of the two

4) In case of instalment system total interest receivable by seller is credited to:

(a) Interest suspense Account (b) Interest Account

(c) Sales Account

5) The cost of goods sold on hire purchase is transferred to

(a) Sales Account (b) Purchase Account

(c) Trading Account

6) On Seizure of goods by hire vendor the balance in the asset account is transferred to :

(a) profit and loss account

(b) Hire Vendor's Account (c) Trading Account.

Answers : 1-b, 2-6, 3-b, 4-a, 5-b, 6-b.

Practical Problems (Hire Purchase System)

1) Ashok Bros. brought machinery from H.M.T. Ltd. on hire purchase basis on 1st Jan 2006. Rs.14000 were paid on signing the agreement and balance in three instalments of Rs.14000 each on 31st Dec. each year. The cash price of the machinery was Rs.49000. The seller charged interest at 10% p.a.

The buyer charged depreciation on machinery at 10% p.a. fixed instalment system.

Give necessary journal entries in the books of both parties.

Answers : Interest 2006-Rs.3500, 2007-Rs.2450, 2008-Rs.1050

2) X Ltd. purchased a Tempo on hire purchase system from Bajaj Auto Ltd., on 1st Jan 2005. Rs.15000 being paid annually for 3 years. The cash price of tempo was Rs.56000. Interest charged at 5%p.a., Depreciation was written off at the rate of 20% on reducing balance system. 'X' Ltd closed its books of accounts on 31st Dec each year.

Prepare necessary ledger accounts in the books of both parties.

Answers : Interest 2005-Rs.2050. 2006-Rs.1403, 2007-Rs.547.

3) Prof. S' Kumar purchased a car on hire purchase system from Maruti Udyog Ltd. on 1st Jan 2006. He paid Rs.10000 on signing the contract and thereafter four half yearly instalments of Rs.30000 each on 30th June and 31st Dec. every year. The Maruti Udyog Ltd charged insterest at 20% p.a. Depreciation is charged at 10% on diminishing balance system.

Prof. S' Kumar closed his books of accounts on 31st December every year.

Show the necessary ledger accounts in the books of Prof. S' Kumar and Maruti Udyog Ltd.

Answers : Interest June 2006-Rs.9500, Dec 2006- Rs.7450, June 2007 Rs.5195, Dec 2007-Rs. 2855.

4) Prakash purchased a computer on hire purchase system. The total cash price of computer is Rs.15980. payable Rs.4000 down and three instalments of Rs.6000, Rs.5000 and Rs.2000 payable at the end of first, second and third year respectively. Interest is charged at 5%p.a.

You are required to prepare ledger accounts in the books of Prakash. Rate of depreciation is 10% on straight line method. Calculations are to be made to the nearest rupee.

Answers : Interest I year-Rs.599, II year- Rs.329 and IIIrd year-Rs.92.

5) Patel Roadways purchased a truck from Telco Ltd. on hire purchase system on 1st January 2005. The cash price of truck was Rs.1,25000.

Payments were made as under-

	Rs.
1-1-2005	30000
31-12-2005	35000
31-12-2006	40000
31-12-2007	45000

Patel Roadways charged depreciation at 20% p.a. on original cost.

You are required to show necessary accounts in the books of Patel Roadways and Telco Ltd.

Answers : Interest Dec 2005-Rs.12000, Dec 2006- Rs.8500, Dec 2007-Rs.4500.

6) Dr Sharma purchased a machine on hire purchase system from HMT Ltd. on 2004 paying Rs.12000 down. The remaining amount (including interest) was paid as follows :

	Rs.
On 31-12-2004-	25600
On 31-12-2005	19600
On 31-12-2006	14000
On 31-12-2007	8800

The vendor charged interest at 10% p.a. on unpaid balance of cash price. The buyer decided to depreciate the machine at 10% on written down method.

Show the cash price of the machine and the necessary ledger accounts in the books of both parties.

Answers : Interest Dec 2004-Rs.5600, Dec 2005-Rs.3600, Dec 2006-Rs.2000, Dec 2007-Rs.800. Total cash price Rs.68000.

7) 'X' Ltd purchased heavy machinery from 'Y' Ltd. on hire purchase system and paid Rs.100000 against delivery on 1st January 2004. They paid the following instalments including interest at 10% p.a. on cash price.

	Rs.
31st December 2004	1,30000
31st December 2005	1,20000
31st December 2006	1,10000

'X' Ltd. charged depreciation on machinery at 20% p.a. under original cost method. Cash price of machinery amounted to Rs.400000

You are required to :-

1) Pass Journal entries for the first year.

2) Prepare machinery Account for first two years.

3) Prepare 'Y' Ltd. A/c for all three years in the books of 'X' Ltd.

Answers : Interest 31st Dec 2004-Rs.30000, 31st Dec 2005-Rs. 20000, 31st Dec 2005- Rs.10000.

8) 'A' Ltd. purchased a machinery on hire purchase system on 1-1-2005 from 'B'. The cash price of machinery was Rs.80000. A Ltd paid Rs.20000 on signing agreement and balance in three annual instalments of Rs.20000 together with interest at 12% p.a. on balance outstanding of cash price. Every year the books of accounts were closed on 31st December. Depreciation was to be written off at 15% p.a. on written down value method.

Prepare ledger accounts in the books of 'A' Ltd.

Answers : Interest Dec 2005-Rs.7200, Dec 2006-Rs.4800, Dec 2007-Rs.2400.

9) On 1st Jan 2005 'X' acquires on hire purchase system from 'Y' machinery valued at Rs.12000 payable in three yearly instalments was paid Y arranged immediately the second instalment had become due, to take back machinery, which cost Rs.8000 allowing Rs.4500

therefore providing that X paid all the interest due to that date on the full amount owing.

'X' had written off depreciation at 10% p.a. on diminishing balance. Show machinery account and Y account in the books of 'S',

Loss on Machinery Dec 2006- Rs.1980, Interest - Dec 2005- Rs.720, Dec 2006- Rs.480.

10) Jay Jawan Transport Ltd. purchased from Calcutta Motors 3 Auto Rickshaws costing Rs.50000 each on the hire purchase system. payment was to made Rs.20000 down and the reminder in 3 equal instalments together with interest at 9% p.a. Jay Jawan Transport Ltd. wrote off depreciation at 20% on diminishing balance. It paid the instalment due at the end of first year but could not pay the next. Calcutta Motors agreed to leave on Auto rickshaw with the purchaser, adjusting the value of other two rickshaws against the amount due. The rickshaws were valued on the basis of 30% depreciation annually. Show the necessary accounts in the books of Jay Jawan Transport Ltd for two years.

Draw up accounts in the books of vendor also assuming the rickshaws were repaired at the expenses of Rs.7500 and they were sold for Rs.60000 in the third year.

Answers : Loss on default Rs. 15000

Profit to vendors Rs.3500

Instalment system

1) Mr Shinde purchased a motor car from the Poona Motor Company Ltd. on instalment system on 1st January 2004 by paying Rs.3000 against delivery. He paid the balance in four instalments at the end of each year on 31st December including interest at 10% p.a. on cash price as follows.

Rs.6400, Rs.4900, Rs.3500 and Rs.2200 respectively. He charged depreciation on car at 10% on diminishing balance method.

Workout the figure of interest for each year and give the journal entries in the books of both parties.

Answers : Interest Dec 2004- Rs.1400. Dec 2005-Rs.900, Dec 2006-Rs.500, Dec 2007- Rs.200.

12) On 1st January 2006 the Rekha Colliery Co. bought wagons from Kirti Wagon Co. on instalment system. The cash price of wagon was Rs.5948 and the payment was to be made over the period of two years by half yearly instalments of Rs.1600. 6% interest was charged by Kirti Wagon Co. p.a. The Rekha Company had decided to write off 10% annually on diminishing balance of the value. Give the ledger accounts in the books of Rekha Colliery Co.

Answers : Interest June 2006 -Rs.178, Dec 2006- Rs.136, June 2007-Rs.92, Dec 2007-Rs.46.

13) Verma Bros. purchased machinery from Kirloskar Ltd. on instalment system on 1st January 2005. The cash price of the machinery was Rs.140000. Rs.20000 were to be paid on signing the agreement and the balance in annual instalments of 40000 plus interest at 12% p.a. Verma Bros. charged depreciation at 20% p.a. on written down value method. Show the necessary ledger accounts in the books of both parties.

Answers : Interest Dec 2005- Rs.14400, Dec 2006- Rs.9600, Dec 2007-Rs.4800.

14) Joker Brothers purchased a machinery from Circus Ltd.on instalment basis on 1st January 2005 paying Rs.10000 on signing the agreement, Rs.21000 on 31-12-2005, Rs.24500 on 31-12-2006 and Rs.27500 on 31-12-2007. The Circus Ltd. charged interest at 10% p.a. on unpaid balance of cash value. Joker Bros. charged depreciation at 15% p.a. on fixed instalment basis.

Show the necessary ledger accounts in the books of Joker Brothers and Circus Ltd.

Answers : Interest Dec 2005-Rs.6000, Dec 2006- Rs.4500, Dec 2007-Rs.2500. Cash price Rs.70000.

15) On 1st January 2005, Mr Ashok acquires a machine from Mr 'B' on instalment system. The rate of interest is 10% p.a. which is yearly chargeable. The buyer agrees to pay to the seller Rs.200000 on 1st January 2005, Rs.1,21000 on Dec 2005, Rs.1,33100 on 31st Dec 2006 and Rs.1,46410 on Dec 2007. Mr Ashok duly discharged all the sum.

Prepare machinery account, sellers account and interest suspense account in the books of Mr Ashok. Assume provide for depreciation at 20% p.a. on diminishing balance method.

Answers : Interest Dec 2005- Rs.33000, Dec 2006- Rs.24200, Dec 2007-Rs.13310.

Chapter 8

Departmental Account

8.1   Meaning and Introduction
8.2   Methods and Techniques
8.3   Allocation of Expenses
8.4   Inter Departmental Transfers
8.5   Provision for unrealized profits.

8.1 Meaning and Introduction :

Utility of Departmental Accounts

A business may have a number of departments each dealing in a different type of goods for example, one department may be dealing in medicines, another may be dealing in textiles, and yet another may be dealing in provisions, etc. In order to ascertain the profit or loss made by each department, it will advisable to prepare a Trading and Profit and Loss Account separately for each department at the end of the accounting year. Preparation of such Department Accounts is helpful to the business in following respects.

(i)   It enables the business to compare the performance of one department with that of another.

(ii)   It helps the business in formulating proper policies relating to the expansions of the business. New profitable lines of production or trading can be taken up while the existing lines of production or trading which are giving a loss can be closed down.

(iii) It helps in appropriate rewarding orpenalising the department employees on the basis of the result shown by them.

8.2 Maintenance of Columnar Subsidiary Books

The preparation of Department Trading and Profit and Loss Account require maintenacne of proper subsidiary books having appropriate columms for different departments for example if a business has three department A, B and C,the subsidiary books such as Purchases, Books, Purchases Returns Books, Sales Book, Sales Returns Books, etc.should have separate columns for each department. Cash Book may also have columns for recording cash sales of each departments separately in case the volume of cash sales in quite large. The specimen of a Purchases Book having columns for different departments is given below.

PURCHASES BOOK

Date	Particulars	LF.	Dept. A	Dept. B	Dept. C	Dept.D

The same pattern of rulings may be followed in case of other subsidiary books also.

8.3 (Allocation of Expenses) Departmentalisation of Expenses

In order to ascertain the profit or loss made by each department, it is necessary that each department is charged with a proper share of the various business expenses. The following basis may be adopted for departmentalisation of such expenses

(i) Expenses incurred specifically for a particular department should be directly charged to that department. For example, salaries payable to each of the departmental managers will be charged to the respective departments. Similarly, if there are separate electricity meters for each department, the electricity should be charged to them on the basis of the electricity bills received by each one of them.

(ii) Expenses which have been incurred for the business as a whole but capable of being apportioned over different departments on a suitable basis should be charged to the different department on such basis of course, there are no hard and fast rules as regards the basis to be applied for apportionment of such expenses. However, the following basis for apportionment may be adopted.

(a) *Departmental wages* Expenses which directly vary with

the departmental wages can be apportioned on this basis. For example, premium for workmen's compensation, insurance, E.S.I etc.

(b) *Capital value of the assets* Expenses such as depreciation of building, plants and machinery, fire insurance premiums in respect of these assets, etc, may be apportioned on this basis.

(c) *Floor area* such as lighting (unless metered separately) rent and taxes, wages of night watchman, etc. may be apportioned on this basis

(d) *Number of workers employed* Expenses of workers canteen welfare personnel, time keeping departments, etc, may be apportioned on this basis.

(e) *Production hours of direct labour* Works Manager's remuneration, general over-time expenses, and cost of interdepartmental transport should be charged to the various departments in the ratio which the Departmental Direct Labour Hours bear to the Total Factory Direct Labour Hours.

(f) *Technical estimate* Advice of the technical personnel may also be useful for the apportionment of certain expenses, eg. cost of steam consumed by a particular department may be worked out on the basis of the engineer's consumption estimate.

(iii) Expenses which cannot be allocated or apportioned over different departments in a reasonable manner should be charged to the total profit of all the departments taken together. For this purpose, the profit shown by different departments should be brought down in one account which will be terned as the General Profit and Loss Account. General Manager's salary Director's fees, Auditors remuneration, Interest on Debenture, etc. are some of the expenses which fall in this category.

Departmentalisation of Expenses

Illustration 1 M/s Wheels Auto Garage have three departments;

Viz (i) Cars and Trucks; (ii) Two wheelers, and (iii) Servicing. The first two sell spare parts and occupy a godown and a showroom. The servicing department uses a garage and the adjoining site.

The following particulars are extracted from the books of the business for the year ended 31st March 2013, from which you are required to prepare.

(a) A Departmental Trading and Profit and Loss Account,

(b) A General Profit and Loss Account, and

(c) A Balance Sheet.

	₹
Stock 1.4.2012	
Cars and Trucks	1,00,000
Two-wheelers	27,500
Purchases :	
Cars and Trucks	3,50,000
Two-wheelers	1,10,000
Sales :	
Cars and Trucks	6,00,000
Two-wheelers	3,00,000
Servicing	1,00,000
Wages of counter-salesmen.	
Cars and Trucks	30,000
Two-wheelers	12,000
Wages of garage labour	10,800
Office salaries and wages	12,000
Godown and showroom rent	24,000
Land and Garage Building	2,72,000
Office-Expenses	36,000
Garage Equipment	1,00,000
Showroom Furniture and Fittings	70,000
Office Van	24,000
Sundry Debtors	12,000
Sundry Creditors	60,000
Bank Overdraft	17,200

Power and Lighting	36,000
Bank Interest	1,000
Cash in Hand	900
Drawing Account	12,000
Proprietor's Capital Account	1,63,000

Following further information is available :

(i) Included in Land and Garage Building the cost of site used by the servicing department is ₹ 2,00,000

(ii) Charge fo 2009 at the departments; ₹

Cars and Trucks	90,000
Two-wheelers	32,500

(iii) 50% of power and lighting is to be charged to Servicing Department, the balance equally to the other departments.

(iv) Rates for depreciation are.

Building 5% Garage Equipments 15%,Showroom furniture etc. 10%,

Office van 20%,

(v) Outstanding expenses were interest 150; Office expenses 2,000

(vi) Interest and all expenses relating to the office are to be considered common and charged to the General Profit and Loss A/c.

(vii) The departments using the showroom share the space and furniture and fitting equally.

Solution :

M/S Wheels Auto Garage
DEPARTMENTAL TRADING AND PROFIT AND LOSS ACCOUNT
for the year ending March 31, 2013

Particulars	Cars & Trucks	Two Wheelers	Servicing	Particular	Cars & Trucks	Two Wheelers	Servicing
To Opening							
Stock	1,00,000	27,500	-	By Sales	6,00,000	3,00,000	1,00,000
To Purchases	3,50,000	1,10,000	-	By Closing			
				Stock	90,000	32,500	-
To Wages	30,000	12,000	10,800				
To Gross							
Profit c/d	2,10,000	1,83,000	89,200				
	6,90,000	3,32,000	1,00,000		6,90,000	3,32,000	1,00,000
To Godown &				By Gross			
Showroom Rent	12,000	12,000	-	Profit b/d	2,10,000	1,83,000	89,200
To Power &							
Lighting	9,000	9,000	18,000				
To Depreciation							
Building			3,600				
Garage							
Equipment			15,000				
Furniture	3,500	3,500	-				
To Net Profit c/d	1,85,500	1,58,500	52,600				
	2,10,000	1,83,000	89,200		2,10,000	1,83,000	89,200

GENERAL PROFIT AND LOSS ACCOUNT
for the year ending 31st March 2013

Particulars	Rs	Rs	Paticulars	Rs
To Office Salaries and Wages		12,000	By Profit b/d -	
To Office Expenses	36,000		Cars and Trucks Dept.	1,83,500
Add Outstanding	2,000	38,000	Two-wheelers Dept.	1,58,500
To Depreciation on Van		4,800	Servicing Dept.	52,600
To Bank Interest	1,000			
Add : Outstanding	150	1,150		
To Net Profit		3,40,650		
		3,96,600		3,96,600

BALANCE SHEET
as at 31st March 2013

Liabilities		₹	Assets		₹
Bank Overdraft		17,200	Current Assets -		
Outstanding Expenses -			Cash in Hand	900	
Interest	150		Sundry Debtors	12,000	
Office Expenses	2,000	2,150	Stock in Trade -		
Sundry Creditors		60,000	Cars and Trucks	90,000	
Capital	1,63,000		Two-wheelers	32,500	1,22,500
Add : Net Profit	3,40,650		Fixed Assets		
	5,03,650		Land		2,00,000
Less : Drawings	12,000	4,91,650	Garage Bldg.	72,000	
			Less Depreciation	3,600	68,400
			Garage Equipment	1,00,000	
			Less Depreciation	15,000	85,000
			Showroom Furniture		
			& Fittings	70,000	
			Less Depreciation	7,000	63,000
			Office Van	24,000	
			Less Depreciation	4,800	19,200
	5,71,000				5,71,000

Computation of Departmental Costs

Illustration 2 The following purchases were made by a business house having three departments :

Department	A	1,000 units	
Department	B	2,000 units	at a total cost of Rs. 1,00,000
Department	C	2,400 units	

Stock on 1st January were

Department A 120 units, Department B 80 units, Department C 152 units.

The sales were

Department	A	1,020 units @ Rs.20 each
Department	B	1,920 units @ Rs.22.50 each
Department	C	2,496 units @ Rs.25 each

The rate of gross profit is the same in each case. Prepare Departmental Trading Account

Solution :

In order to determine the rate of Gross Profit, it is assumed that all units purchased have been sold away.

		₹
Sales : Dept. A 1,000 units @ ₹ 20 each		20,000
Dept. B 2,000 units @ ₹ 22.50 each		45,000
Dept. C 2,400 units @ ₹ 25 each		60,000
Total Sales		1,25,000
Less : Cost of Purchases		1,00,000
Gross Profit		25,000

$$\text{Gross Profit as a percentage} = \frac{25,000}{1,25,000} \times 100 = 20\%$$

Cost price of units purchased for each department can now be ascertained as follows.

	Selling Price (₹)	Gross Profit	Cost (₹)
Dept. A	20.00	4.00	16
Dept. B	22.50	4.50	18
Dept. C	25.00	5.00	20

Units of Closing Stock	Opening Stock	+ Purchases	− Sales	
Dept.A	120	+ 1,000	− 1,020	= 100
Dept.B	80	+ 2,000	− 1,920	= 160
Dept.C	152	+ 2,400	− 2,496	= 56

Departmental Trading Account can now be prepared as follows.

DEPARTMENTAL TRADING ACCOUNT

Particulars	DeptA	DeptB	DeptC	Particular	DeptA	DeptB	DeptC
To Opening Stock	1,920	1,440	3,040	By Sales	20,400	43,200	62,400
To Purchases	16,000	36,000	48,000	By Closing Stock	1,600	2,880	1,120
To Gross Profit	4,080	8,640	12,480				
	22,000	46,080	63,520		22,000	46,080	63,520

Illustration 3 Mr. Manulal sells two products manufactured in his own factory. The good a made in two Departments *A* and *B* for which separate sets of accounts are maintained. Some of it manufactured goods of Department A are used as raw material by Department *B* and vice versa.

From the following particulars, you are required to ascertain the total cost of goods manufacture in Departments *A* and *B* :

Particulars	Dept. A	Dept.B
Total units manufactured	10,00,000	5,00,000
Total cost of manufacture (excluding interdepartmental transfers) (₹)	10,000	5,000

Department A transferred 2,50,000 units to Department B and the latter transferred 1,00,000 units to the former.

Solution :

Suppose a is the total cost of Department A and B the total cost of Department B

$$a = ₹ 10,000 + 1/5b$$
$$b = ₹ 5,000 + 1/4a$$

or

$$a = ₹ 10,000 + 1/5(5,000 + 1/4a)$$
$$a = ₹ 10,000 + 1,000 + 1/20a$$

$$
\begin{aligned}
& \text{a} &=& \ \text{₹ } 11,000 + 1/20a \\
\text{or} & \quad 20\,a &=& \ \text{₹ } 2,20,000 + a \\
\text{or} & \quad 19\,a &=& \ \text{₹ } 2,20,000 \text{ or } a = \text{₹ } 11,579 \\
\text{Now} & \quad b &=& \ \text{₹ } 5,000 + 1/4a = \text{₹ } 5,000 + 1/4 \times \text{₹ } 11.579 \\
& &=& \ \text{₹ } 5,000 + 2,895 \text{ or } \text{₹ } 7,895
\end{aligned}
$$

TOTAL COST OF GOODS MANUFACTURED

Particulars	Dept. A (₹)	Dept.B (₹)
Cost of determined above	11,597	7,895
Less Transfer to other department (1/3 and 1/5)	2,895	1,579
	8,684	6,316

8.4 Interdepartmental Transfers

Transfers of good or services may take from the one department to another. While preparing the Department Trading and Profit and Loss Account, the department receiving the goods or services shoud be debited with the value of the goods or services so supplied and department providing such goods or services should be credited with the same amount.

The transfer of goods from one department to another is usually at cost. However, if such transfer is at a profit, the profit or loss of each department should be ascertained on the basis of the transfer price itself. However, if the goods are transferred by one department to another at a profit, and still remain unsold with the transferee department, an appropriate reserve for unrealised profit will have to be created by means of the following journal entry.

General Profit and Loss Account   Dr.
   To Stock Reserve

In case the transferee Department also has some stock in the beginning of the accounting year. including some unrealised profit, against which stock reserve was created last year, such reserve will also be transferred to the General Profit and Loss Account by means of the following journal entry.

Stock Reserve Account   Dr.
   To General profit and Loss Account

Alternatively a single journal entry may be passed for the unrealised profit on the basis of the difference between unrealised profit included in the opening and closing stock. This will be clear with the help of the following illustration.

Illustration 4 From the following Trial Balance prepare Departmental 'Trading and Profit & Loss Account, for the year ending 31st March 2013 and the Balance Sheet as at that date.

₹ (in '000)

Stock 1st April 2012	A Department	1,700
	B Department	1,450
Purchases	A Department	3,540
	B Department	3,020
Sales	A Department	6,080
	B Department	5,125
Wages	A Department	820
	B Department	270
Rent, Rates, Taxes and Insurance		939
Sundry Expenses		360
Salaries		300
Lighting and Heating		210
Discount allowed		222
Discount received		65
Advertising		368
Carriage Inward		234
Furniture and Fittings		300
Machinery		2,100
Sundry Debtors		606
Sundry Creditors		1,860
Capital Account		4,766
Drawings		450
Cash at Bank		1,007

The following further information is available
(1) Internal transfer of goods from A to B Department Rs.42,000.
(2) The items Rent, Rates, Taxes and Insurance, Sundry Expenses, Lighting and Heating Salaries and Carriage are

to be apportioned 2/3rd to A Department and 1/3rd to B Department.

(3) Advertising is to be apportioned equally.

(4) Discount allowed and received are to be apportioned on the basis of Departmental Sales and Purchases (excluding Transfers)

(5) Depreciation at 10 per cent per annum on Furniture and Fitting and on Machinery is to be charged 3/4th to A Department and 1/4th to B Department.

(6) Services rendered by B Department to A Department are included in it wages Rs. 50,000

(7) Stock on 31st March 2013 in A Department was worth Rs. 16,74,000 and to B Department Rs. 12,05,000.

DEPARTMENTAL TRADING AND PROFIT & LOSS ACCOUNT
for the year ending 31st March 2013

Particulars	Dept.A	Dept.B	Particulars	Dept.A	Dept.B.
To Opening Stock	1,700	1,450	By Sales	6,080	5,125
To Purchases	3,540	3,020	By Transfer	42	50
To Wages	820	270	By Closing Stock	1,674	1,205
To Transfer	50	42			
To Carriage Inward	156	78			
To Gross Profit c/d	1,530	1,520			
	7,796	6,380		7,796	6,380
To Salaries	200	100	By Gross Profit b/d	1,530	1,520
To Rent, Rates,	625	313	By Discount	35	30
Taxes & Insurance			By Net Loss	126	–
To Sundry Expenses	240	120			
To Lighting &					
Heating	140	70			
To Advertising	184	184			
To Depreciation :					
Machinery	158	52			
Furniture	22	8			
To Discount	121	101			
To Net Profit	–	602			
	1,691	1,550		1,691	1,550

BALANCE SHEET
as on 31st March 2013

Liabilities		₹	Assets		₹
Capital	4,766		Machinery	2,100	
Add : Profit	476		Less : Depreciation	210	1,890
	5,242		Furniture and Fitting	300	
Less : Drawing	450	4,792	Less Depreciation	30	270
Sundry Creditors		1,860	Stock in Trade		2,879
			Sundry Debtors		606
			Cash in Bank		1,007
		6,652			6,652

Illustration 5 Hotel Taj Holidays prepares separate Department Profit and Loss Account. the nature of their operation required frequent supply of articles/services from one department to another. The Hotel consisted of three departments -Apartments, Boarding and Restaurant. It had been decided that the Apartments Department will charge for service supplied to other departments the cost thereof plus 10% thereon. Linkwise Boarding department was to charge the other department cost plus 20% thereof in respect of supplies made to them. The Restaurant Departments supplies to the other departments were charged at the prevailing rates applicable to outsiders. The accounts for the year ended on June 30, 2013 had been closed without taking into account the interdepartmental debits and credits. From the following figures, show the net variation in the departmental Profit and Loss Account as a result of such adjustments.

		₹
(1)	Cost of Apartments services extended to :	
	Boarding Staff	8,400
	Restaurant	4,500
(2)	Cost of supplies made by Boarding Department to :	
	Apartments Staff	29,800
	Restaurant Staff	5,400
(3)	Values of supplies made by the Restaurant to :	
	Apartments Staff	400
	Boarding Staff	5,600

In addition, the following are the charges to be made for interchange of staff from the department to another for temporary periods during the year.

Boarding staff lent to Apartments Dept.	4,400
Apartments staff lent to Boarding Dept.	1,100

Solution :

PROFIT AND LOSS (ADJUTMENT) ACCOUNT

Particulars	Apart ment A ₹	Board- ing B ₹	Restau- rant R ₹	Particulars		Apart ment A ₹	Board ing B ₹	Restau- rant R ₹
To Rent of Apartments	–	9,240	4,950	By Apartment rents from B	9,240	14,190	–	–
To Boarding Charges	35,760	–	6,480	R	4,950			
				By Boarding Charges				
To Restaurant Expenses	400	5,600	–	From A	35,760	–	42,240	–
To Charge in respect of staff borrowed	4,400	1,100	–	R	6,480			
				By Restaurant				
				sales A	400	–	–	6,000
				B	5,600			
To Increase in deptt. profit (or decrease in deptt.loss)	–	30,700	–	By Recoveries in respect of staff rent		1,100	4,400	–
				By Decrease in deptt. profit (or increase in deptt. loss		25,270	–	5,430
	40,560	46,640	11,430			40,560	46,640	11,430

Note : 10% has been added to costs of Apartments deptt. services to find out transfer price to Boarding and Restaurant. 20% has been added to costs of Boarding department to find out transfer price of Apartments and Restaurant.

Illustration 6 From the following balance extracted from the books of Royal Traders prepare Departmental Trading Account and General Profit and Loss Account for the year ended 31st December, 2012 and a Balance Sheet as on the date after adjusting the unrealised departmental profits if any;

Particulars	Dr. ₹	Cr. ₹
1. Capital		3,00,000
2. Land and Building		1,25,000
3. Furniture		25,000
4. Opening Stock Dept.A		30,000
Dept. B		40,000
5. Purchases Dept. A		10,00,000
Dept. B		15,00,000
6. Sales Dept. A		20,00,000
Dept. B		32,00,000
7. General Expenses		14,00,000
8. Sundry Debtors		2,00,000
9. Sundry Creditors	–	1,00,000
10. Drawing		2,80,000
11. Cash and Bank		10,00,000
	56,00,000	56,00,000

Additional Information :

(1) Closing stock Dept. A ₹ 1,30,000 including goods from Dept. B ₹ 40,000 at cost to Dept. A Dept. B ₹ 2,60,000 including goods form Dept. A ₹ 90,000 at cost to Dept.B

(2) Sales of Dept. A include transfer of goods to Dept.B of value ₹ 2,00,000 and sales of Dept. B include transfer of goods to Dept. A of value ₹ 30,000 both at market price to transfer Dept.

(3) Opening stock of Dept. A and Dept. B include goods of value ₹ 10,000 and ₹ 15,000 taken from Dept. B and Dept.A respectively at cost to transfer or Dept.

(4) Depreciate land and building by 5% and furniture by 10% p.a.

Royal Traders
DEPATMENTAL TRADING ACCOUNT AND GENERAL PROFIT AND LOSS.
for the year ended 31.12.2012

Particulars	Dept. A ₹	Dept. B ₹	Total ₹	Particular	Dept. A ₹	Dept. B ₹	Total ₹
To Opening Stock	30,000	40,000	70,000	By sales	18,00,000	29,00,000	47,00,000
To Purchases*	7,00,000	13,00,000	20,00,000	By Transfer	2,00,000	3,00,000	–
To Transfers	3,00,000	2,00,000	–	By Closing Stock	1,30,000	2,60,000	3,90,000
To Gross Profit c/d	11,00,000	19,20,000	30,20,000		21,30,000	34,60,000	50,90,000
	21,30,000	34,60,000	50,90,000		21,30,000	34,60,000	50,90,000
To General Expenses			14,00,000	By Gross			
To Depreciation				Profit b/d			
Land and Building		6,250		Dept A			11,00,000
Furniture		2,500	8,750	Dept. B			19,20,000
To Reserve on closing Stock :**							
Transfer from Dept. A		49,500					
Transfer from Dept.B		24,000	73,500				
To Net Profit transfer to capital Account			15,37,750				
			30,20,000				30,20,000

* Excluding inter department transfers.
** Since inter department transfers in stock are at costs. no stock reserve for opening stock has been created.

Royal Traders
BALANCE SHEET
as at 31st december, 2012

Liabilities		₹	Assets		₹
Capital : (Op.Bal)	3,00,000		Land & Building (Op.Bal) 1,25,000		
Add : Profit for	15,37,750		Less : Depreciation for		1,18,750
the year	18,37,750		the year	6,250	
Less : Drawings	2,80,000	15,57,750	Furniture (Op.Bal)	25,000	
			Less Depreciation for		
			the year	2,500	22,500
Sundry Creditors		1,00,000	Stock in trade	3,90,000	
			Less Stock Reserve	73,500	3,16,500
			Sundry Debtors		2,00,000
			Cash and Bank Balance		10,00,000
Total		16,57,750	Total		16,57,750

Note : The unrealised profit on interdepartment transfers is determined as under.

$$\text{Transfer included in Closing Stock} \times \frac{\text{Gross Profit}}{\text{Sales} + \text{Transfers}}$$

$$\text{Dept.A} = 40,000 \times \frac{19,20,000}{32,0,000} = ₹ \ 24,000$$

$$\text{Dept. B} = 90,000 \times \frac{11,00,000}{20,00,000} = ₹ \ 49,500$$

Illustration 7 ABC Ltd. has a factory which has two manufacturing departments X and Y. Part of the output of X Department is transferred to Y Department for further processing and the balance is directly transferred to the selling Department. The entire production of Y Department is transferred to the Selling Department. Interdepartmental stock transfers are made as follows.

X Department to Y Department of $33\frac{1}{3}$ % over departmental cost.

X Department to Selling Department of 50% over departmental cost

Y Department to Selling Department of 25% over departmental cost.

The following information is given for the year ending 31st March 2013.

Particulars	Department X		Department Y		Selling Dept.	
	MT	₹	MT	₹	MT	₹
Opening Stock	60	60,000	20	40,000	50	1,45,000
Raw Material Consumption	90	1,00,000	20	20,000		
Labour Charges	-	50,000	-	80,000	-	-
Sales	-	-	-	-	-	5,00,000
Closing Stock	30	-	50	-	60	-

Out of the total production in X Department, 30 MT were for transfer to selling department Apart from these stocks which were transferred during the year the balance output and the entire opening and closing stocks of X Department were for transfer to Y Department. The per tonne material and labour consumption in X Department on production to be transferred directly to the selling department is 300 percent of the labour and material consumption on production meant for Department.

(i) Prepare Departmental Profit and Loss Account and ii) General Profit and Loss Account. ignoring material wastages.

Solution :

DEPARTMENTAL TRADING AND PROFIT AND LOSS ACCOUNT

Particulars	Dept. X		Dept. Y		Selling Dept.		Particulars	Dept.X		Dept. Y		Selling Dept.	
	Qty	Amt.	Qty	Amt.	Qty	Amt.		Qty	Amt.	Qty	Amt.	Qty	Amt.
To opening							By Sales	-	-	-		-100	5,00,000
Stock	60	60,000	20	40,000	50	1,45,000	By Stock						
To Raw							Transfer	120	2,55,000	80	2,00,000		
Material													
Consumed	90	1,00,000	20	20,000	-	-	By Closing						
To Labour							Stock	30	30,000	50	1,00,000	60	1,80,000
Charges		50,000	-	80,000	-								
To Stock													
Transferred													
From X Dep.		-	90	1,20,000	30	1,35,000							
From Y Dep.		-	-	-	80	2,00,000							
To Gross													
Profit taken													
to profit &													
Loss A/c	-	75,000	-	40,000	-	2,00,00							
	150	2,85,000	130	3,00,000	160	6,80,000			150	2,85,000	30	3,00,000	160	6,80,000

* 90 tonnes ₹ 1,20,000
30 tonnes ₹ 1,35,000
120 tonnes ₹ 2,55,000

GENERAL PROFIT AND LOSS ACCOUNT

Particular	₹	Particular	₹
To Stock Reserve (increases required) :		By Gross Profit from	
Y Department	8,182	Deptt X	75,000
Selling Dept.	11,160	Deptt Y	40,000
To Net Profit	2,95,658	Selling Department	2,00,000
	3,15,000		3,15,000

Working Notes :

1. Value of Goods Transferred

	MT	Amount
(i) Department X		
Qty and Value of Production*	210	2,10,000
Transferred to Selling Dept.	90	90,000
Balance meant for transfer to Y Dept. 1	120	1,20,000
Closing Stock of Dept. X	30	30,000
Actual Transfer to Y Dept.	90	90,000
Add profit 33 $\frac{1}{3}$ %		30,000
Total Qty. and value of Goods transferred to Y Dept.	90	1,20,000
Cost of Goods transferred to Selling Dept.	30	90,000
Add profit 50%		45,000
Quantity and Value of Goods transferred to Selling Dept.	30	1,35,000

Total transfer 1,20,000 + 1,35,000 = 2,55,000 from Dept. x

(ii) Department Y		
Qty. and Value of Production	130	2,60,000
Less Closing Stock of Dept.Y	50	1,00,000
Cost of Goods transferred to selling Dept.	80	1,60,000
Add profit 35%		40,000
Quantity and Value of Goods transferred to selling Dept.	80	2,00,000

2(a) Stock Reserve for unrealised profit for y Dept.

Transfer from X Dept.	1,20,000
Own cost (Raw material and labour)	1,00,000
	2,20,000
Increase in closing stock (1,00,000 – 40,000)	60,000

Profit of X department = 60,000 $\times \dfrac{1,20,000}{2,20,000}$ 32,727

Unrealised profit (33 $\frac{1}{3}$ % on cost) or
25% on transfer price   8,182

2(b) Stock Reserve for Unrealised profit for selling Dept.

Transfer directly from Dept.X	1,35,000
Total Transfer from Dept.X and Y	3,35,000

Share in increase of unsold stock $\dfrac{1,35,000}{3,35,000} \times 35,000 = ₹\ 14,404$

Profit charged by Dept. X (50% on cost or $33\frac{1}{3}$ % on 14,104)

4,701 (a)

Transfer from Dept. Y to selling Dept.   2,00,000

Share of increase in unsold stock transferred from Dept. Y $= \dfrac{2,00,000}{3,35,000}$

$\times$ 35,000 = ₹ 20,896

Profit charged by Dept. Y (25% on cost or 20% on ₹ 20,896)

4,179 (b)

Cost of Dept. y of goods transferred to selling Dept. (₹ 20,896 – 4,179)   16,717

Share of goods transferred from Dept.X to Dept. Y in ₹ 16,717 =

$\dfrac{16,717 \times 1,20,000}{2,20,000} = ₹9.118$

Profit charged to Dept. Y on Goods transferred to Dept. Y

($33\frac{1}{3}$ % on cost or 1/2 of ₹ 9,118)   2,280 (c)

Total profit in closing stock with selling Dept. a + b + c

(4,701 + 4,179 + 2,280)   11,160

---

* The proportion of cost between output meant for Dept. Y and Selling Dept. is 1.3 Thus, the output of 30 units meant for selling Dept.is equivalent to 90 units of Dept. Y.

> **Key Terms :**
> - **Columnar Subsidiary Book :** A book containing separate information for each department regarding each item, e.g. sales book, purchase book etc.
> - **Department :** A division of an organization under the same roof.
> - **Stock Reserve:** If represent the unrealised profit included in the stock of a Department or Division.

Exercise

Objective type

1. State whether each of the following statements is True or False.

(i) If the rate of gross profit of the different department is the same, the cost price of these departments will be in the ratio of their respective sales prices.

(ii) The fire insurance on building is allocated on the basis of floor area occupied by each department.

(iii) Depreciation on plant is divided equally over the different departments.

(iv) Bad debts are charged to the General Profit and Loss Account since there is no proper basis for their apportionment.

(v) Management expenses are charged to the General Profit and Loss Account.

(vi) Stock Reserve for unrealised profit and interdepartmental transfer of goods is charged to General profit and loss account.

(vii) In Departmental Accounts, Workmen's Compensation Insurance should be apportioned on the basis of the number of workers in each department.

[**Ans.** (i) True, (ii) True, (iii) False, (iv) False, (v) True, (vi) True, (vii) False]

2. Select the most appropriate answer in each of the following cases;

(i) Non-departmental items of expenses are

(a) charged to departments on the basis of total sales.

(b) charged to the General Profit & Loss Account.

(c) charged to Departments according to the fixed assets employed.

(ii) Repair to machinery is apportioned over different departments according to the

(a) number of machines in each department.

Departmental Accounts/ 365

(b) value of machinery.

(c) floor area occupied by each machine.

(iii) In case goods are transferred from Department A to Department B at a price so as to include a profit or 25% on the cost, the amount of stock reserve on a closing stock of Rs. 6,000 in Department B will be

(a) ₹ 1,200   (b) ₹ 1,500   (c) ₹ 2,000

(iv) If the rate of gross profit for Department A is 25% of cost, the amount of gross profit on a turnover of Rs. 1 lakh will be

(a) ₹ 25,000   (b) ₹ 20,000   (c) ₹ 33,333

(v) The cost of electric power should be apportioned over different departments according to

(a) Horse Power of Motors.

(b) No. of Light Points

(c) Horse Power/Machine Hours.

[**Ans.** (i) b, (ii) b, (iii) a, (iv)b, (v) c]

Exercise (Theory)

1. Differentiate between a Branch and a Department. State the objectives of preparing separate Departments Account.

2. Differentiate between Direct and Indirect charges in Departmental Account. Discus in brief the allocation of such items at the time of preparation of Final Accounts.

Exercise (Practical)

Departmentalisation of Expenses

1. The Trading and Profit and Loss Account of Vijay Electronics for the year ending 31st March 2013 is as under.

Particular	₹	Particular	₹
Purchases :		Sales :	
Transistors (X)	1,60,000	Transistors (X)	1,75,000
Tape Recorder(Y)	1,25,000	Tape Recorders (Y)	1,40,000
Spare parts for servicing		Servicing and repair jobs(Z)	35,000
and repairs jobs (Z)	80,000	Stock on 31st March 2008	
Salaries and Wages	48,000	Transistors (X)	60,100
Rent	10,800	Tape Recorders (Y)	20,300
Sundry Expenses	11,000	Spare parts for servicing	
Profit	40,200	and repair jobs (Z)	44,600
	4,75,000		4,75,000

Prepare Departmental Account for each of the three Departments, X, Y, Z mentioned above, after taking into consideration the following.

(a) Transistors and Tape Recorders are sold at the showroom and repairs are carried out at the Workshop.

(b) Salaries and Wages comprise of the following.
    Showroom 3/4th   Workshop 1/4th
    It was decided to allocate the showroom salaries and wages in ratio 1 : 2 between Department X and Y.

(c) The Workshop rent is Rs. 500 per month. The rent of the showroom is to be divided equally between the Department X and Y.

(d) Sundry Expenses are to be allocated on the basis of the turnover of each Department.

[**Ans.** Net Profit Dept. X ₹ 55,200 Dept.Y ₹ 4,500 Net Loss Dept.Z ₹ 19,500)

2. Joshi Brothers are leading paper merchants and booksellers. Their wholesale business is in paper and their retail showroom conducts business in stationery, books and magazines. The following balance are extracted from their books as at the end of the financial year 31st March 2013.

	₹
Capital	3,00,000
Stock (1.4.2012)	
Paper	2,00,000
Stationery	50,000
Books	1,00,000
Magazines	25,000
Purchases	
Paper	8,00,000
Stationery	3,00,000
Books	3,50,000
Magazines	3,00,000
Sales	
Paper	10,00,000
Stationery	3,60,000
Books	4,20,000
Magazines	4,20,000
Rent	60,000
Lighting	24,000
Showroom maintenance	18,000
Showroom fittings	1,80,000
Sundry Debtors (for paper)	1,00,000
Sundry Creditors	1,50,000
Salaries :	
Showroom staff	36,000
Wholesale business staff	12,000
Showroom cashier	12,000
General office Salaries	11,000
General office Expenses	44,000
Cash and Bank balances	8,000

You are requested by the firm to prepare their Departmental Trading and Profit and Loss Account for the financial year under reference with the help of the following additional information.

(i) Closing stock at the end of the year in the various departments were.

Paper ₹ 1,80,000   Stationery ₹ 40,000
Books ₹ 1,20,000   Magazines ₹ 30,000

(ii) Rent and lighting are for premises taken on lease. General office accommodation is negligible. Wholesale department uses 1.500sq feet. The balance of 1.500sq feet is occupied by the showroom with equal division among stationery books and magazines.

(iii) Showroom fittings are to be depreciated by 10% p.a.

[**Ans.** Net profit paper ₹ 1,01,000, Stationery ₹ 600, Books ₹ 36,700, Magazines ₹ 71,700]

3. The following is the trial balance of Auto Motors on 31st March 2013

Particulars	₹	₹
Capital Account		76,250
Drawing	8,500	
Opening Stock		
Petrol and Oil	1,675	
Spare Parts and Tyres	5,500	
Tools	2,200	
Hire Cars	72,000	
Purchases :		
Tools	4,000	
Spare Parts and Tyres	32,000	
Petrol and Oil	41,250	
Advertising Expenses	4,500	
Rent, Rates and Taxes	12,000	
Insurance premia :		
On Hire Cars	4,000	
Fire, Theft and Burglary Cases	425	

Wages :		
Drivers	12,000	
Repairs Department	16,500	
Office	7,500	
Garage	1,000	
Sales :		
Petrol and Oil		23,000
Spare Parts and Tyres		37,000
Garage Receipts		4,000
Repairs Department		10,000
Hire Receipts		70,000
Licence fees permit fees for hire cars	3,000	
Office Expenses	4,000	
Sundry Debtors	400	
Sundry Creditors		1,200
Commission received on cars sold		5,000
Loan		4,000
Cash in Hand and at Bank	2,000	
	2,34,450	2,34,450

The following additional information is also given to you :

(a) The loan was taken on 1st January, 2013 on which interest at 12% is to be paid

(b) Stocks on hand on 31st March, 2013 were as under.

		₹
(i)	Tools	5,000
(ii)	Petrol and Oil	4,300
(iii)	Spare parts and tyres	10,000

(c) Petrol and Oil whose value was Rs. 15,600 and Rs. 1,800 were used by hire cars and repairs departments respectively. Besides, the owner of the garage drew petrol and oil worth Rs. 3,000 for his personal car.

(d) Repairs Department performed work during the year as under.

		₹
(i)	On owner's car	600
(ii)	On hire cars	7,500

(e) Spare parts used by the Repairs Department in the year cost ₹ 4,000 and by the hire cars ₹ 750.

(f) Depreciation on hire cars to be provided at 30% per annum.

(g) Licences and taxes amounting to ₹ 200 on owner's car have been paid and included in Rent,Rates, and Taxes.

(h) Rent, Rates, and Taxes to be distributed as under.

(i)	Repairs Department	1/2
(ii)	Spare parts	1/4
(iii)	Garage	1/8
(iv)	Office	1/8

You are required to prepare a departmental trading account, a profit and loss account for the year ended 31st March 2013 and a balance sheet as at that date.

[**Ans.** Profit Garage ₹ 1,525, Petrol & Oil ₹ 4,775, Spare parts ₹ 11,300, Hire cars ₹ 5,550; Loss, Repairs ₹ 7,300, Net Business Profit ₹ 2,830 B/S total ₹ 72,100]

4. Fair Traders Limited has three departments X Y and Z from the particulars given below,

compute

(a) the value of stock as on 31st December 2012 and

(b) the departmental trading results.

(i) Particulars	X ₹	y ₹	z ₹
Stock as on 1st Jan 2011	24,000	36,000	12,000
Purchases	1,46,000	1,24,000	48,000
Actual Sales	1,72,500	1,59,400	74,000
Gross Profit on normal Selling price	20%	25%	$33\frac{1}{3}\%$

During the year certain items were sold at discount and these discounts were reflected in the values of sales shown above. The items sold at discount were.

(i) Particulars	Dept. X ₹	Dept. Y ₹	Dept. Z ₹
Sales at normal prices	10,000	3,000	1,000
Sales at actual prices	7,500	2,400	600

[**Ans.** Gross Profit Dept. X ₹ 32,500, Dept.Y ₹ 39,400, Dept. Z ₹ 24,600]

Ascertainment of Departmental Costs

5. Babubhai purchased goods for his three departments as follows.
   Dept. A   2,000   pieces
   Dept. B   14,000   pieces   Total cost ₹ 51,000
   Dept. C   4,000   pieces
   Sales of three departments were as follows.
   Dept. A   1,800   pieces at ₹ 15 per piece
   Dept. B   15,000   pieces at ₹ 18 per piece
   Dept. C   4,500   pieces at ₹ 6 per piece.
   Other information about stock in the beginning was as follows.
   Dept. A   1,000   pieces
   Dept. B   4,000   pieces
   Dept. C   600   pieces
   Babubhai informs you that the rate of gross profit is the same in all departments.

   You are required to prepare trading account for the three departments.

   [**Ans.** Gross profit of Dept. A.₹ 22,500, Dept. B ₹ 2,25,000 Dept.C ₹ 22,500]

Inter Departmental Transfers

6. A firmhas two departments cloth and ready-made-clothes departments.The clothes are made by the firm itself out of cloth supplied by the cloth department at its usual selling price. From

the following figures, prepare Departmental Trading and profit and loss Account for the year 2012 :

Perticulars	Cloth Dept. ₹	Ready-made clothes Dept.₹
Opening Stock	2,40,000	48,000
Purchases	18,00,000	24,000
Sales	20,00,000	6,00,000
Transfer to Ready-made cloths Department	4,00,000	
Expenses on manufacturing	–	68,000
Expenses on selling	40,000	4,000
Closing Stock	3,00,000	60,000

The stock in the ready-made clothes department may be considered of 80% cloth and the rest as expenses.

The cloth department made a gross profit of 25% in 2006. General expenses of the business as a whole came to ₹ 1,80,000

[**Ans.** Cloth Dept.Gross profit ₹ 6,60,000 Net profit ₹ 4,72,400 Ready-made-clothes Gross profit ₹ 1,20,000 Net profit ₹ 80,000]

7. X Ltd. has two department A and B From the following particulars. Prepare Consolidated Trading Account and Department Trading Account for the year ending 31st December 2013

Particulars	A (₹)	B (₹)
Opening Stock (at cost)	20,000	12,000
Purchases	92,000	68,000
Sales	1,40,000	1,12,000
Wages	12,000	8,000
Carriage	2,000	2,000
Closing Stock		
(i) Purchased goods	4,500	6,500
(ii) Finished goods	24,000	14,000

Purchased goods			
transferred	by B to A	10,000	
	by A to B		800
Finished goods transferred	by A to B	35,000	
	by B to A		40,000
Return of Finished Goods	by A to B	10,000	
	by B to A		7,000

You are informed that purchased goods have been transferred mutually at their respective departments purchase cost and finished goods a departmental market price and that 20% of the finished stock (closing) at each department represented finished goods received from other department.

[**Ans.** Gross profit Dept.A ₹ 38,500 Dept. B ₹ 46,000 Cosolidated profit after adjusting for stock Reserve (Dept. A 1.555 + Dept. B 64) ₹ 82,384

8. Complex Ltd has three department A, B, C The following information is provided.

Particulars	A	B	C
Opening Stock	3,000	4,000	6,000
Consumption of direct materials	8,000	12,000	–
Wages	5,000	10,000	–
Closing Stock	4,000	14,000	8,000
Sales	–	–	34,000

Stocks of each department are valued at cost to the department concerned. Stocks of A department are transferred to B at margin of 50% above departmental cost. Stocks of B department are transferred to C department at a margin of 10% above departmental cost.

Other expenses were :

		₹
Salaries		2,000
Printing and Stationery		1,000
Rent		6,000
Interest paid		4,000
Depreciation		3,000

Allocate expenses in the ratio of departmental gross profits. Opening figures of reserves for unrealised profit on Departmental stocks were Department B ₹ 1,000 Department C ₹ 2,000 Prepare Departmental Trading and Profit and Loss Account

[**Ans.** Net loss Deptt A ₹ 2,000 Dept. B ₹ 1,000 Dept.C ₹ 1,000 after adjustment Total Net loss for stock Reserves ₹ 4,918]

9. M/s Dreams carried on business as Drapers and Tailors in Pune. The partners A. B and T. were incharge of the Department X, Y and Z respectively. The partners are entitled to a remuneration equal to 50% of the profit(without taking the partners remuneration into consideration)of the respective department of which they are incharge and the balance of the profits are to be divided among A.B and C. in the ratio of 5:3:2. The following are the balances of the revenue item in the books for the year 31st March 2013.

Particulars		₹	Particulars	₹
Opening Stock :			Salaries and Wages	96,000
Department X		75,780	Advertising	4,500
	Y	48,000	Rent	21,600
	Z	40,000	Discount Allowed	27,000
Purchases :			Discount Received	1,600
Department X		2,81,400	Sundry Expenses	24,300
	Y	1,61,200	Depreciation on	
			Furniture and Fitting	1,500
	Z	88,800		
Sales :				
Department X		3,60,000		
	Y	2,70,000		
	Z	1,80,000		

Closing Stock :		
Department X	90,160	
Y	34,920	
Z	43,180	

(i) Prepare the Departmental Account for each of the three Departments in a columnar, and

(ii) Show the distribution of profits amongst the partners after taking into account the following.

(a) Goods having a transfer price of Rs. 21,400 and Rs. 1,200 were transferred from Department X and Y respectively to Department Z. The interdepartmental transfers are made at 125% of the cost.

(b) The various items shall be apportioned among the three departments in the following proportion :

Particulars	Department X	Department Y	Department Z
1. Rent	2	2	5
2. Salaries	1	1	1
3. Depreciation	1	1	1
4. Discount received	8	5	3

5. All the other expenses on the basis of the sales (excluding interdepartmental transfers) of each department.

(c) The opening stock of Department Z does not include any goods transferred form other Departments, but the closing stock includes Rs. 17,100 valued at the interdepartmental transfer prices.

[**Ans.** Net profit Dept.X ₹ 63,880, Dept.Y ₹ 49,660, Dept. Z ₹ 20,580]

10. West Store Ltd. is a retail store operating two department. The company maintains a memorandum stock account and memorandum mark-up account for each of the department.

Suppliers issued to the departments are debited to the memorandum stock account of the department at cost plus the make-up and departmental sales are credited to this account. The make-up on supplier to the departments credited to the mark-up account for the department. When it is necessary to reduce the selling price below the normal selling price memorandum stock account and in the mark-up account Department has a mark-up cost and Department Z 50% on cost.

The following information has been extracted from the records of West Store Ltd. for the year ended 31st December 2012.

❑❑❑

www.ingramcontent.com/pod-product-compliance
Lightning Source LLC
Chambersburg PA
CBHW060926030726
47503CB00003B/495